ACCLAIM FOR *MISS MISERY*

"Much like its subject matter, *Miss Misery* is a novel of dichotomies: It's a romance that's also a mystery, it's an autobiography that isn't exactly true, and it's sad story that's pretty funny (and usually at the same time)."
—Chuck Klosterman, *New York Times* bestselling author of *Killing Yourself to Live*

"The atmosphere is distinctive and the emotions are real." —*Oregonian*

"*Miss Misery* is original, inspiring, and a frighteningly accurate portrayal of twenty-first-century New York culture. Andy Greenwald captures the rush of online courtship and confession in pleasantly surprising ways."
—Ned Vizzini, author of *Be More Chill*

"Andy Greenwald's keen-eyed debut novel depicts the world of modern romance and intimacy with great insight and affection. *Miss Misery* is a *Bright Lights, Big City* for a nightlife generation who increasingly make no distinction between staying in and going out."
—Marc Spitz, author of *Too Much Too Late*

"What's great about this book . . . is that Andy makes it interesting to both big-city dwellers in their late twenties who feel boring because they're not constantly sniffing things up their noses, and to small-town youngsters obsessed with emo and the Web." —*Jane* magazine

"Engaging. . . ." —*Entertainment Weekly*

"Full of witty one-liners and ultra-underground rock references, this book was designed for the aspiring hipster." —*ELLEgirl* magazine

"If you're not enraptured by *Miss Misery*'s climactic ending (complete with car chase) . . . just wait for the movie." —*Harp* magazine

"*Miss Misery* is a fast, entertaining read, comical and complicated without compromising the romantic elements with endless twists and turns."

—*Newcity Chicago*

"Greenwald evokes the wit of Noah Baumbach's classic *Kicking and Screaming* and the surreal sophistication of Haruki Murakami, but writes with warmth and yearning all his own. *Miss Misery* is an incredibly impressive debut."

—Ben Gibbard, Death Cab for Cutie and The Postal Service

ALSO BY ANDY GREENWALD

Nothing Feels Good: Punk Rock, Teenagers, and Emo

Miss Misery

A Novel by

ANDY GREENWALD

SSE

SIMON SPOTLIGHT ENTERTAINMENT

New York London Toronto Sydney

This book is a work of fiction. Any references to historical events, real people, or real locales are used fictitiously. Other names, characters, places, and incidents are the product of the author's imagination, and any resemblance to actual events or locales or persons, living or dead, is entirely coincidental.

SSE

SIMON SPOTLIGHT ENTERTAINMENT
An imprint of Simon & Schuster
1230 Avenue of the Americas, New York, New York 10020

Also available in a Simon Spotlight Entertainment hardcover edition.

Manufactured in the United States of America
First Edition 10 9 8 7 6 5 4 3 2 1
Library of Congress Cataloging-in-Publication Data
Greenwald, Andy.
Miss Misery : a novel / by Andy Greenwald.— 1st ed.
p. cm.
ISBN-13: 978-1-4169-0240-9 (hc)
ISBN-10: 1-4169-0240-6 (hc)
1. Authors—Fiction. 2. Young men—Fiction. 3. New York (N.Y.)—Fiction.
4. Electronic journals—Fiction. 5. Triangles (Interpersonal relations)—Fiction.
I. Title.
PS3607.R468M57 2006
813'.6—dc22
2005008729
ISBN-13: 978-1-4169-1835-6 (pbk)
ISBN-10: 1-4169-1835-3 (pbk)

To my father, MICHAEL GREENWALD,
and my grandfather, ARTHUR SILVERBLATT,
for telling me words and teaching me stories

CONTENTS

PROLOGUE: LATE APRIL 1

1: CITIES THAT BEGIN WITH "THE" 10

2: QUIZILLA CONQUERS BROOKLYN 24

3: MY AIM IS TRUE 37

4: MIXED MEDIA 50

5: AWFULLY CUTE, LIKE THE MARTIAN SKYLINE 80

6: BOOKS WITH MORE THAN ONE AUTHOR 90

7: HELLO? LUNCH? (OR: SURPRISE! YOURSELF.) 113

8: THE REAL ONE 126

9: DOESN'T THAT MEAN, LIKE, FLEXIBLE? 144

10: RING . . . RING . . . RING 180

11: INDEPENDENCE, DAZE 188

12: THE GRAND FINALE 206

13: ROLLER-COASTER SCREAMS 246

14: GREAT! SALT LAKE! 276

15: NEW ORDERS FROM MISSION CONTROL 330

16: (TRY AGAIN) 344

17: A WHOLE LOT MORE ACCURATE 353

ACKNOWLEDGMENTS 385

This is fact, not fiction, for the first time in years.

—DEATH CAB FOR CUTIE

PROLOGUE: LATE APRIL

MISS MISERY WAS ONLINE AGAIN. It was becoming more and more difficult to ignore her, waiting, crouched almost, feline—or was it supine?—in my buddy list. I knew where she was—online—but I still didn't know where she *was.* Other than in my head, of course, which was where she seemed to reside more and more often.

It was late April, and I was sitting at my desk, gray shirt, blue boxers. My laptop clock said it was 1:08 a.m., but it was running about ten minutes fast. On my headphones, a mix I had made for Amy's birthday skipped tracks; in the silence, I thought I heard her shift in her sleep. Or almost sleep. Another song started then, one by Rilo Kiley: "The Good That Won't Come Out." A jaunty number about creative constipation. Not bad, I thought. Appropriate, even. I wondered if the crescendo would be audible to Amy even through the headphones.

I caught a glimpse of my reflection in the window, framed in the halo of light from my computer screen. Familiar face, familiar situation. I looked tired, but that was the way I felt all the time these days. I was tired, but I didn't ever feel like sleeping.

Just then, Miss Misery switched on her away message. It was the usual one, a verse from the Cure's "To Wish Impossible Things." What was she doing at one in the morning? Who was she away with? Who was she away from?

Maybe it was all just a tease. A way of letting me and all of her other virtual admirers know that she was around—just not around for us. The lady in her chambers. The lady will see you now.

Except she won't. Behind me Amy coughed. I signed off, hushed the music. It was time for bed. Again.

[from **http://users.livejournal.com/~MzMisery**]

I remember those days

Time: 2:36 a.m.

Mood: Thoughtful

Music: Wheat, “Hope and Adams”

I’m smoking while I type this tonight - getting ash in between the pristine white keys, probably, and I don’t care. Benson & Hedges 100s, apparently. I think it’s what Mom used to smoke. Cody gave me three tonight before he dropped me off. I’m on number two now and won’t go to sleep until all three are gone.

When I went to the doctor back in January she asked me (like she does every year) if I smoked and blah blah blah and this year I just felt like fuck it basically and told her yes. She seemed kind of surprised at first, but then mostly just tired. She rattled off this long list of reasons why I shouldn’t smoke, but I could see it in her eyes that she had already given up on convincing me to quit. One of them was “your teeth will turn yellow” and I thought that (a) obviously this is the dumbest thing of all time to be worried about but also (b) I DON’T CARE. I mean, I LIKE the idea of old me with my yellow mouth - of my stupid too small teeth slowly picking up bits of tar and nicotine and whatever and changing color like leaves do in autumn. I’m looking at all this smoke that I’m taking into my body and then pushing out the open window here next to my desk and thinking - DON'T GO. I want to have evidence that I did it. Otherwise what's the point? I want it to change me. I want it to color me. Otherwise I wouldn't do it.

There were girls in my freshman year unit who were already obsessed with getting older. These girls were like 18 and they weren't afraid of leaving home and they weren't afraid of falling into wells - they were afraid of wrinkles. I think their priorities were entirely wrong, but none of them ever asked me. Sometimes when I walk around through the city in the early early morning (which is rare, I admit it - it's more likely to be the very very late night and I haven't gone to sleep yet) I think of myself being older and being actually old and I wish it could happen sooner. There are times when I don't like how unmarked and smooth my skin is, how utterly snappable my bones feel. I want density and debris; I want to live my life on the outside of my body for a change, not the inside. I want my life to be a suit I never have to take off. If I was old I wouldn't have to wonder all the time and I wouldn't have to blush. I could do things and people would trust me.

Right now (note: cigarette number three!) I feel pent up caught up choked up. I see middle-aged women with their pear bodies and raisin heads and I think - that's not what I'm going to become - that's what I already AM. That person IS me - it's not where I'm going, it's what's waiting inside to come out. This stupid skinny frame with the knotty elbows and knees is wound too tightly - I wish it would just give up, exhale, spread out. I wish - sometimes I wish it would just relax.

My father is still awake. He's playing more of that crazy Viennese modernist crickets dancing on vacuum cleaners in hell music. It's loud and there's no rhythm and I know he's in there, twirling his pen, keeping time to some beat only he can hear. He's such a sweetheart. I hope he can't smell this cigarette smoke tomorrow. I can't believe it's almost May.

ps I'm not drunk right now honest I'm not.

why the need to point out you're not drunk? This post reads like a real teen emo LJ post.

[from **http://users.livejournal.com/~thewronggirl87**]
Time: 3:01 a.m.
Mood: Dreaming
Music: The Weakerthans, "A New Name for Everything"

I should be asleep now because I have a trig exam tomorrow and I'm supposed to do super well on it but I can't sleep. I can't lie still. I'm still thinking about the concert. How amazing it was. How it made me feel. ::smiles:: My skin feels electric.

Maybe it's because I'm not allowed to go see many shows but I think it was more than that. This was special.

Krystal and I got there early (it was at the SaltAir - crappy, I know, but both bands are so BIG now). We got about halfway through the crowd and had a pretty good view of the stage when Krys gave me this LOOK and I knew what it meant - we just started laughing and DIVING through the crowd, like pinballs through a machine, bouncing off huge guys and their bitchy girlfriends. We got almost to the very front when this one gigantic guy in a Jazz jersey yells out, "Watch out for these two - they're SNEAKY." And for some reason this just made us crack up - like it was the funniest thing anyone had ever said. That's us. We're SNEAKY. ;-)

WHOO!!

But when Brand New came on I stopped worrying about what anyone else was thinking and just felt the music. It started in my ears but, like, MELTED into my sternum, into my waist, until I could feel every chorus in the bottom of my feet. Jesse Lacey has this way of singing onstage where you just KNOW he's feeling every single word like it's for the first time - the anger, the dreams, the tears, even the laughter - and it makes everyone in the audience feel the same way. I've listened to their albums approximately 1000 times in the last few months alone, but I felt like I was hearing every lyric, every note like it was - oh god bad pun - brand new. ::smiles::

omg yes!

And then Dashboard. Even from where we were standing Chris looked like a little boy - like a bird boy - but that VOICE. I wanted to punch all the teenyboppers around me who started screaming "chris yr so hottt" when he came onstage. He WAS hot but it was wilder than that. It felt like when I went to temple with my parents when I was too little to start hating it and I believed that whatever I heard there came directly from a higher power. That's what Chris singing those songs was like. I didn't even hesitate - I just started singing along with him at the top of my voice and Krys did the same and I didn't even mind it when the dudes who called us sneaky started singing along too. I felt connected to everyone then - the teeny-boppers, the jocks, the punks, the boys, the girls. All the crappy people of crappy Utah and they felt like family. When he sang "Swiss Army Romance" and the part about "searching just like everyone," I had tears in my eyes because I believed it. I felt for a second like I was bigger than my body and bigger than the entire arena. That I wasn't trapped. That I could escape.

I know it sounds stupid but I felt like these Russian wooden dolls that I've had on my desk since I was like 8 years old - you know they're different sizes but they each fit inside the bigger one? I felt like I've always been the smallest, most hidden doll, but the music and the crowd and the singing and the MOMENT made me feel like a hundred different dolls just ready to bust out.

I hope this is the greatest summer ever. And then next year at school goes in a heartbeat and then it'll all be over. It'll finally be time to escape.

::grins::`

Good night. I hope I get some sleep!

[DAVIDGOULD101's journal has been deleted. If you are DAVIDGOULD101 you have 30 days to reregister your journal.]

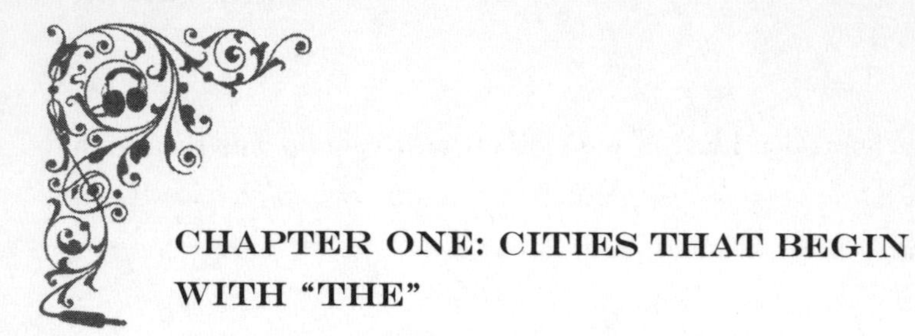

CHAPTER ONE: CITIES THAT BEGIN WITH "THE"

THE DAY AMY LEFT was the first nice day of the year – at least in terms of weather. She had told me not to bother going with her to the airport, so I didn't. When I woke up that morning, all the windows were open and she was gone.

It was early, still—well, early for me: ten a.m. I briefly considered spending the rest of the day in bed. It certainly was comfortable enough, and with Amy absent I could stretch out diagonally if I wanted. Her side was still warm; it smelled of herbal shampoo, and I burrowed into it. My mind began to dance at the possibilities of hibernation: I could spend the entire summer underneath the covers, master the art of controlled dreaming, and finally strip the excess layers of fat from my 135-pound frame. This was going to work; this was going to be an excellent solution. I turned onto my back and stretched, letting my eyes fall lazily toward the open window, where a small, mustachioed Mexican man was sitting—dangling, really—with a giant spackling tool in his left hand and a friendly wave in his right.

"Hola!" he said cheerily. "I paint the house today!"

"Hola," I said. And quickly scurried from the bed toward the bathroom.

• • •

The home that I had shared with my girlfriend up until that morning was somewhere between a railroad apartment and an incredible bargain. It was big enough to be a two-bedroom, but unless you enjoyed high-fiving your roommate on the way to the bathroom, it was ideally suited for a couple. It was a third-floor walk-up in a three-story brownstone in the Park Slope section of Brooklyn, a neighborhood with faux-French bistros and glowingly pregnant junior book editors in equal proportion. I liked living there because it was comfortable and not too hip—I liked the bars and I liked the trees and I liked not having electroclash bands vomiting PBR outside my window at three in the morning. Amy liked living there because I did.

The building was owned by Mrs. Armando, a tough-talking, Italian-born widow who still lived on the first floor. She kept her door open all day, occasionally made me soup, and seemed to have no idea what exactly I did for a living. I was fine with all three of these realities.

The apartment itself was a clash of Amy's sensibilities with my lack thereof. In the living room, she had contributed the coffee table (which she'd painted herself), the large Mucha print, and the stuffed bumblebee hanging from the closet door. My offerings included the futon-as-couch, the potato-chip crumbs currently nestled into the futon-as-couch, the pile of newspapers on the floor, and the Xbox. A fair trade-off, no doubt.

The strangest thing about the apartment—aside from it now being eerily empty and quiet save for the lusty Mexican painting songs emanating from the general direction of my bedroom—was that the bathroom was right off the kitchen. I'd spent hours thinking of it as a major health risk, but then again I didn't cook all that much, so why complain?

Just past the doorway to the bathroom, to the left of the kitchen sink, was a tall window blocked from the inside by a sliding security gate. Outside the window was a small fire escape upon which I'd set up a starter-kit herb garden that my friend Carrie had sent me for my birthday. The directions seemed simple enough: Fill with soil, sprinkle with seeds, set outside, water, repeat. Soon, Carrie promised, I'd be drowning in fresh basil, thyme, chives, and chervil. Innocent and excited, I'd asked, "Won't the pigeons eat all of the herbs?" She'd laughed at me, said of course not. Pigeons don't eat herbs. Carrie, it should be noted, lived in San Francisco. She didn't even know what a pigeon *was.*

I slid back the metal grating and stared at the mordantly obese, slate-gray pigeon that had taken up residence in the soil of my herb garden.

"Hey," I said.

The pigeon looked at me, no fear showing on its beaky visage.

"Get out of there," I said weakly, waving my arms. "Shoo."

The pigeon's beady eyes registered something between pity and disgust. A few days after the first green sprouts had appeared in the dirt, the neighborhood birds had ganged up and made their move. Carrie was right about one thing: Pigeons don't eat herbs. Pigeons do, however, rip baby herbs out of the dirt with their mouths, spit them onto the ground, and use the now empty planters as La-Z-Boys.

"She left today," I said. "She's gone for at least six months. To The Hague."

The pigeon rearranged its feathers to be more comfortable.

"What kind of city begins with 'the,' anyway?" I said. "It doesn't even make any sense."

The pigeon looked away.

"OK," I said, closing the gate. "Enjoy the chervil."

I went into the bathroom and took a shower.

Amy and I had been together for five years and living together for three of them. We had met senior year of college during a picture-perfect New England fall—we were introduced at a Concerned Democrats of America meeting and first made out at an Arab Strap show (though it could have been the other way around). She was the older of two girls, from St. Louis, tall and thin with hair that couldn't decide if it wanted to be brown or red. I was an only child from Providence, Rhode Island, not that tall and very thin. She was serious about lots of things: human-rights abuses, voter fraud, history as a construct, Albert Finney movies. I was serious about nothing, apart from my CD collection and her. It was a pretty good match.

The first few years in New York were pleasant ones: She was in law school, and I was always more than happy to adapt my freelance-writing schedule to her days and nights filled with homework and stress. In between the various exams, we had inside jokes and vacations with her family. We had rituals. We had matching sheets. I liked going to the movies and out to brunch and going to bed together by midnight. I liked not going anywhere in particular.

Except that then I started the project and she finished school, and it turned out she'd been going somewhere all along. I just wasn't necessarily along for the ride.

Usually I can spend all kinds of time in the shower—zoning out under the hot water, thinking about sports, thinking about nothing. But my shower had a big, barely curtained window that faced the backyard. I decided to wash quickly before the painter turned loofahing into a spectator sport.

When I emerged from the bathroom wrapped in a towel—dripping, red-faced, and nominally clean—my answering machine was blinking. My heart did a half skip because I thought that it had to be Amy calling from the airport: Her flight was canceled; her job was canceled; she had mistakenly booked her tickets to *A* Hague instead of *The* Hague. Anything that would get her back to me safely by lunchtime. But I pressed play and found out otherwise.

<YOU HAVE ONE NEW MESSAGE>

David? David, buddy! It's Thom calling. We haven't spoken in a while and you know I love to check in with my struggling authors! Not that you're struggling! Or not that I'd know! Ha, ha! Listen, David—call me! The manuscript is due in a month, and I'm *very* curious to hear the latest. You know my number. We should get drinks. Call me. Call me!

<MONDAY, 10:31 A.M.>

<END OF MESSAGES>

Thom Watkins, my editor at Pendant Publishing: the only man I knew who laughed like he was spelling the letters out, with exclamation points attached. Not that I really knew him; the only day Watkins and I had ever met face-to-face was back in March, when he took me to lunch, put a contract in front of me, and said, "You sure you don't want to get dessert? It's not like you're getting another one of these free meals! Ha, ha!" That was nearly three months ago. In the contract I was given four months to write a book. The funny bit—really "ha, ha!" funny—was that I still hadn't started the thing. Which is why I had yet to return any of Watkins's increasingly shrill phone messages.

Oh, did I somehow neglect to mention that part? That I was writing a book? And that I'd never written one before? That I was unable to get past the first paragraph, which led my girlfriend to leave both me and the country because I was paralyzed with indecision and she had a career to think about? Funny, that was usually the first thing I thought about in the morning.

Just then, a voice came from the living-room window.

"Señor, sorry to disturb, but you're dripping water on the wood floor!"

I turned to the painter, who was dangling in a different spot now but still smiling. "Gracias," I said, and walked back to the bedroom to get dressed.

Ha, ha!

The book was about diaries. Not itself a diary—who would want to read about a self-obsessed twentysomething with writer's block?—but a history of the medium written for a new, confessional generation: a handy, user-friendly tome that would trace the heretofore unseen connections between Samuel Pepys and the personal Web site of

Emolover48. The whole thing had started innocently enough: I was writing freelance stories about rock and roll, etc., for glossy magazines, making enough money to go out to dinner but not enough to take cooking lessons, when I received an assignment that interested me far more than the usual hand-jobby band profiles and navel-gazing record reviews. It was to be a quick, "newsy" piece on the explosion of teen-oriented online diary sites: the phenomenon that keeping a public, daily journal of life's mundanities was suddenly required behavior for the black-clad, occasionally pierced, under-eighteen set. Coming as it was after a run of five straight reviews of records that I'd only managed to listen to once, the assignment seemed promising. Plus, I had run out of adjectives.

So back in March I had logged on to LiveJournal.com and its bubbling competitors Diaryland, DeadJournal, iNotebook, and DailyCry. I "met" sad-eyed surfer girls in Orange County and furious hardcore boys in the Florida panhandle. I met Jaymie who cut herself and Margo who had a friend who did. I met crazy Theresa, drinking and fucking her way through freshman year at Ball State, and quiet, comic book–obsessed Edward, who listened to Cursive and Billie Holiday alone in his bedroom at night. I met Mike C., wry and funny, who was desperately in love with anyone in the tenth grade who would kiss him back if he made the first move during the third act of *Amelie.* And all four feet eleven inches of red-haired Emily, who took too many pills on Christmas Eve two years ago and will always regret it, even now as she applies to Yale.

I followed Lizzie through three boyfriends, two career goals, one major surgery, and more than 200 horrible, recklessly indulgent poems. I followed Gus on his first ever rock and roll tour—with his deathcore quintet Funereal Winch—which took him and his $150 bass (paid for by a miserable summer working at Quiznos) through suburban Ohio and northwestern Pennsylvania, and I followed him through all the exploded friendships and busted feelings that resulted from it. I followed Ronald and Chelsea from first date to first kiss, from awkward courtship to miserable, shrieking breakup, all without leaving my apartment.

Once I met these people and their friends I couldn't look away. I knew them, intimately—ridiculously intimately—but we'd never been in the same room. I knew their hopes, dreams, fears, crushes, likes, dislikes, and permanent scars, but I didn't know their last names. I started early on a Tuesday morning, tripping from one noisy shout of a life to another, and didn't stop until late the next day.

Because the thing was, it was possible to lose yourself in other people's online lives. Completely. Spend hours and days and weeks in other people's contexts, fill up your browser's bookmarks with pages like xBlueStarsx and WHITNEY'S JOURNAL, stop taking phone calls from your real friends, and forget what was new in your own existence. I certainly did.

It was all the voyeuristic thrills of eavesdropping, of reality TV, played out in front of me in real time, in real lives. It was messy, it was constant, it was happening. And more than anything else it gave me a feeling—a catch in the throat, a fuzziness in the stomach—that lay somewhere between nostalgia and hunger. It was the same feeling I got when I flipped through my high-school yearbook and read the strangely familiar things written in blue ink by people whose names I didn't remember; the same feeling I got when I Googled nursery-school playmates and summer-camp crushes. It was missed opportunity and lost youth and a fleeting memory of a time slightly before regret. Once I started, I couldn't stop. It felt like falling down the stairs.

And that was how I'd met her. Miss Misery, my online muse—or obsession. I hadn't actually *met* her, of course. That would be so twentieth century! Besides, she lived in Toronto, was five years younger than me, and had the sort of life that I'd never quite managed for myself, one that seemed fueled entirely by cigarettes, cheap vodka, and pasty-faced bands that aped the pasty-faced British bands of the eighties. Once I'd stumbled onto her diary, spied her oh-so-arty, oh-so-angled photo (hair: black, tousled; lips: pouting or bruised; background: rain-spattered car window; cumulative effect: heart-melting), I was in love or in lust, or in some as yet undetermined four-letter word beginning with *L* that referred to an intimate reaction only possible with a keyboard in front of you. She lived with her father and waited tables at a French-Asian-fusion bistro. She was allergic to peanuts and dogs, played softball and gin rummy, and reread Haruki Murakami's *Norwegian Wood* every year on her birthday. She drank and flirted like a professional. She was on a "leave of absence" from art school and didn't seem to have any intention of ever returning. She didn't know where she was going, but she went out every night anyway. Her name was Cath Kennedy and I thought about her constantly.

But I didn't e-mail her and I certainly didn't interview her for the story (which ran at 450 overly edited words in the February issue of *Transmission* magazine). No. Rather, I added her to my buddy list, watched her flickering presence sign on and off, and hit REFRESH on her diary at least five times a day.

And I didn't tell Amy about her. There was no good reason to. She knew about my adventures in Diaryland, of course—knew all too well after Thom Watkins called and offered me $7,500 to write a quickie paperback about the phenomenon for Pendant Publishing—but I think she thought it was cute or quirky, like my lifelong allegiance to certain pro sports teams or the assorted canned cookery of Chef Boyardee. I was already retreating by then and she knew it; if talk turned to her new job, I would change the subject or make passive-aggressive jokes about it. "You're a writer," she would say. "You can write anywhere." Which was technically true. But another truth was that I wasn't actually getting any writing done, and the sort of stalker-ish online loafing I was engaging in was only possible in the too-comfortable environs of our apartment. I didn't want to lose her, of course. But I felt lost myself. And so I ignored nearly everything until it was all too late.

When I signed the book contract (under the working title *True Fiction*—cute, eh?) I had tried to start my own diary, but it ended up being completely self-indulgent and useless, filled with lines like: "The day Amy left was the first nice day of the year—at least in terms of weather. She had told me not to bother going with her to the airport, so I didn't. When I woke up that morning, all the windows were open and she was gone." So I quickly deep-sixed the thing and got back to my real daily routine: hitting REFRESH on sports Web sites, eating two or three lunches, and, when I wasn't catching up with Gus or Lizzie or Jaymie, staring at the white wall in front of me.

I had never kept a diary, though my childhood bedroom was still filled with halfhearted attempts: spiral-bound notebooks and expensive leather journals and sketchbooks filled with two consecutive days' worth of dime-store-psychological scribbling about then girlfriends and other typical high-school woe-is-me-isms and the remainder of the pages left blank. I've never been particularly self-reflective; I have a bad habit of not noticing things until they've already happened. This can lead to good things, like getting paid to write a book at the age of twenty-seven, or bad things, like losing your girlfriend to the International Criminal Court. But at least I had those empty notebooks to prove I'd always been that way. Secret thoughts aren't only kept secret; in my muddy brain, they're positively buried. Other than: "My name is David Gould. Things seem to be going all right. I wake up in the morning and I go to bed at night." How much more does anyone need to know?

The kids I met online, though, seemed to be wired differently. When things happened to them, they felt compelled to unearth them, to share them, to dissect them in a virtual lecture hall in front of their friends, peers, and assorted sketchy cyberstalkers. Diaries didn't come with locks on them anymore—they came with stadium seating.

And the personalities displayed for the anonymous crowds were gargantuan—much larger than life. Operas could have been composed with the raw emotional ore that was mined from the lives of these kids before lunchtime. Breakups weren't mundane; they were earth-shattering. A fight with Mom registered on the Richter scale. The enthusiasm generated by a good rock and roll show could provide the U.S.A. with the alternative energy source it's long needed. And kisses—*closed-mouth* kisses—could change the orbit of the Earth around the sun.

So that's where the "fiction" part of the book title came from. These people weren't real to me; how could they be? And none of these feelings or events could truly be that huge—that life-changing. But the diaries—their adventures, their rogues' galleries, their quirks and habits—kept me company and kept me interested. They kept me from dealing with the lack of adventure, excitement, and romance in my own life. They kept me from dealing.

On my way out of the house, I ran into Mrs. Armando.

"David, where's Amy?" she said in her thick, still-not-adjusted-to-the-New-World accent.

"She left today, Mrs. Armando. Remember?"

"That's right, that's right."

I made a move for the door.

"You better not cat around on her! She's a good girl!"

"I know it, Mrs. Armando. I know it."

"No catting!"

I reached for the doorknob. "You know me! I would never."

"You a good boy, David—I know that. Oh!"

I froze.

"They paint the house today. I forget to tell you."

"I figured it out," I said. "Nice guy. Good singing voice."

Mrs. Armando chuckled to herself, and I made my hasty exit.

The day that greeted me just past the heavy wooden door was breathtakingly bright and blue. No clouds; the slightest whisper of wind. May had been unseasonably unsettled, with near constant rain. That day, the beginning of June, was finally the first without jackets. And girlfriends.

I wanted to call somebody then, anybody who would take me away from this house, this reality. Someone who would share the day with me, pull me deeper into it, mark it. Make it worth remembering instead of avoiding. But I couldn't call Amy—airplane phones were expensive and didn't have publicly listed numbers. I couldn't call my best friend, Bryce Jubilee, because he'd moved to Los Angeles in search of something or other two months before. The distance was too great. He was unpredictable at best—since he'd moved, we'd barely spoken. Rather, he'd taken to peppering my cell phone with text messages that were either world-weary and observant or maniacally childish; either "The sunlight is the same here everyday—I feel like I'm beginning to forget how to measure time" or "TITTIES!" He was that sort of friend. I thought about calling the pigeon and asking it to coffee, but I was still sore over what it had done to my poor defenseless basil.

So instead I trudged around the corner to the café, smiled extra at the woman who called me Small Skim, and then walked back home, back up the stairs, and back to the computer screen that had become my life.

Out my tiny office window, I could see a deep turquoise sky, perfect for losing a balloon in, for becoming untethered, for becoming lost and liking it. But when I had walked to coffee, past the dog-walking neighbors whose names I didn't know, past the Korean dry cleaner, the Chinese takeaway, and the Dominican supermarket with the animatronic dinosaur out front that played "Mary Had a Little Lamb" when children dropped in twenty-five cents for their thirty-second ride, I hadn't felt free. I had felt hunted. Trapped. Alone.

So I turned my eyes away from the window. I had work to do, though I was sure I wasn't going to finish much of it today. Amy was gone. This was just how it was now. It was time to get used to it.

I drank my coffee and watched the cursor blink.

CHAPTER TWO: QUIZILLA CONQUERS BROOKLYN

I remember doing a shit load of these back in the day. LOL

[from **http://users.livejournal.com/~davidgould101** as recovered from cache (journal has been deleted)]

---YOUR FULL NAME IS---

[x] David Rory Gould

---DESCRIBE---

[x] **The shoes you wore today**: brown Gola sneakers

[x] **Your eyes**: brown

[x] **Your fears**: dunno—falling?

---WHAT IS---

[x] **Your first thought waking up**: is it afternoon yet?

[x] **The first feature you notice in the opposite sex**: hair, laugh

[x] **Your best physical feature**: eyes

[x] **Your bedtime**: what's that?

[x] **Your most missed memory**: Amy's parents' beach house

---DO YOU---

[x] **Smoke**: no

[x] **Curse:** yeah

[x] **Take a shower everyday:** yes

[x] **Have any crushes:** not really

[x] **Who are they:** ???

[x] **Do you think you've been in love:** yes

[x] **Want to go to college:** been there, done that

[x] **Like high school:** I am the only person that did like it, yes

[x] **Want to get married:** yes

[x] **Type w/ your fingers on the right keys:** yes

[x] **Believe in yourself:** I used to

[x] **Like thunderstorms:** as long as I'm indoors

---IN THE PAST MONTH DID/HAVE YOU---

[x] **Gone to the mall:** no—I live in New York!

[x] **Eaten sushi:** vegetable sushi, yes

[x] **Been dumped:** depends who you ask

[x] **Dyed your hair:** no!

[x] **Stolen anything:** no

---HAVE YOU EVER---

[x] **Flown on a plane:** yes

[x] **Told a guy/girl that you liked them:** not for a long time

[x] **Cried during a movie:** never have

[x] **Had an imaginary friend:** no

[x] **Been in a fight:** never

[x] **Shoplifted:** a chapstick when I was 14 and I still regret it

---THE FUTURE---

[x] **Age you hope to be married:** . . .

[x] **Number of children:** one

[x] **How do you want to die:** I can't say I really want to

[x] **What do you want to be when you grow up:** ask me when I get there

---FAVORITES---

[x] **Fave color(s):** blue

[x] **Day/night:** evening

[x] **Summer/winter:** spring/fall

[x] **Fave food:** broccoli

[x] **Fave movies:** the third man

[x] **Fave sport:** baseball

---RIGHT NOW---

[x] **Right now wearing:** go-betweens t-shirt, jeans, socks.

[x] **Drinking:** Yuengling lager

[x] **Thinking about:** Amy

[x] **Listening to:** "Loss Leaders" —Spoon

---DO YOU BELIEVE IN---

[x] **Destiny/fate:** no

[x] **Angels:** no

[x] **Ghosts:** no

[x] **UFOs:** no

[x] **God:** no

of course he believes in nothing

---FRIENDS AND LIFE---

[x] **Do you ever wish you had another name:** no

[x] **Do you have a girlfriend/boyfriend:** depends who you ask

[x] **What's the best feeling in the world:** someone sleeping next to you

[x] **Worst feeling:** letting someone down

[x] **What time is it now:** 2am

---HAVE YOU/DO YOU---

[x] **Do drugs:** no

[x] **Pray:** only during the ninth inning. !yes!

[x] **Gotten drunk:** does now count?

[x] **Run away from home:** no

[x] **Made out with a stranger:** no

[x] **Three words that sum you up:** reliable, quick-witted . . . um, Jew?

---SOCIAL LIFE---

[x] **Boyfriend/girlfriend:** Amy

[x] **Attend church:** nope

[x] **Like being around people:** outlook hazy, ask again later

[from **http://users.livejournal.com/~MzMisery**]

---YOUR FULL NAME IS---

[x] Catherine Rose Kennedy (Miss)

---DESCRIBE---

[x] **The shoes you wore today**: brown cowboy boots

[x] **Your eyes**: green

[x] **Your fears**: spiders, knives, elevators, tequila, and whoever I stole these cowboy boots from

---WHAT IS---

[x] **Your first thought waking up**: that spider web wasn't there last night

[x] **The first feature you notice in the opposite sex**: eyes, ass

[x] **Your best physical feature**: shoulders? bile duct?

[x] **Your bedtime**: after 'golden girls'

[x] **Your most missed memory**: mom

---DO YOU---

[x] **Smoke**: I shouldn't but that wasn't the question, was it?

[x] **Curse**: fuck yeah

[x] **Take a shower everyday**: you know that's not actually good for your hair

[x] **Have any crushes**: what is the square root of one zillion?

[x] **Who are they**: the psychedelic furs circa 1982 and orlando cabrera

[x] **Do you think you've been in love:** of course not

[x] **Want to go to college:** still figuring that out

[x] **Like high school:** of course not

[x] **Want to get married:** I defy you, patriarchy

[x] **Type w/ your fingers on the right keys:** I defy you, patriarchy!

[x] **Believe in yourself:** of course not—I am a unicorn!

[x] **Like thunderstorms:** yessssssssssssssss

---IN THE PAST MONTH DID/HAVE YOU---

[x] **Gone to the mall:** I defy you . . . fuck it, yes I did to get tights.

[x] **Eaten sushi:** mmmmmmmyes

[x] **Been dumped:** always leave them wanting more

[x] **Dyed your hair:** I am no longer a teenager, thank you

[x] **Stolen anything:** I refuse to answer this on the advice of my attorney

---HAVE YOU EVER---

[x] **Flown on a plane:** as opposed to flying on a . . . ?

[x] **Told a guy/girl that you liked them:** only in esperanto

[x] **Cried during a movie:** I wear sunglasses during sad movies to prevent eye leakage

[x] **Had an imaginary friend:** yes but she came true

[x] **Been in a fight:** I was the featherweight champion of grade 7

[x] **Shoplifted:** have you met my attorney? he's really very persuasive.

---THE FUTURE---

[x] **Age you hope to be married:** 109

[x] **Number of children:** unsure, however I do believe the children are the future

[x] **How do you want to die:** in a tragic but inevitable hot-air balloon accident

[x] **What do you want to be when you grow up?** taller

---FAVORITES---

[x] **Fave color(s):** vermilion

[x] **Day/night:** night

[x] **Summer/winter:** summer

[x] **Fave food:** sashimi

[x] **Fave movies:** mmmmmTIE: rushmore, georgy girl, my beautiful laundrette, dirty dancing

[x] **Fave sport:** getting to third base

---RIGHT NOW---

[x] **Right now wearing:** tank top, pajama pants with monkey heads on them

[x] **Drinking:** ginger ale

[x] **Thinking about:** how many questions could possibly be left on this stupid thing

[x] **Listening to:** "You Can't Hide Your Love Forever" by Orange Juice

---DO YOU BELIEVE IN---

[x] **Destiny/fate:** not usually

[x] **Angels:** not the ones with wings

[x] **Ghosts:** sometimes

[x] **UFOs:** no

[x] **God:** that's so last century

---FRIENDS AND LIFE---

[x] **Do you ever wish you had another name:** yes. Catarina Amarynth Piccadilly. I have business cards that detail the name change in full.

[x] **Do you have a girlfriend/boyfriend:** not tonight

[x] **What's the best feeling in the world:** sex? eating japanese food? DOING BOTH AT THE SAME TIME?????!?!?!?

[x] **Worst Feeling:** xhangoversx

[x] **What time is it now:** after dark before morning

---HAVE YOU/DO YOU---

[x] **Do drugs:** only when they are available

[x] **Pray:** only during hangovers

[x] **Gotten drunk:** I am taking a night off tonight

[x] **Run away from home:** actually, I walked

[x] **Made out with a stranger:** too many times to count

[x] **Three words that sum you up:** tastes great, less-filling (sorry about the hyphen!)

---SOCIAL LIFE---

[x] **Boyfriend/girlfriend:** currently accepting applications

[x] **Attend church:** only when I need a place to hide from vampires

[x] **Like being around people:** everyone except vampires (j/k deb!)

[from **http://users.livejournal.com /~thewronggirl87**]

---YOUR FULL NAME IS---

[x] Ashleigh Courtney Bortch

---DESCRIBE---

[x] **The shoes you wore today**: black chucks

[x] **Your eyes**: blue

[x] **Your fears**: angry people, going deaf or blind, plane crashes

---WHAT IS---

[x] **Your first thought waking up**: don't wanna go 2 school

[x] **The first feature you notice in the opposite sex**: music taste?

[x] **Your best physical feature**: ha

[x] **Your bedtime**: midnight

[x] **Your most missed memory**: when I was happy

---DO YOU---

[x] **Smoke**: no

[x] **Curse**: try not to

[x] **Take a shower everyday**: absolutely

[x] **Have any crushes**: mmmmm . . . maybe!

[x] **Who are they**: not going to say HERE!

[x] **Do you think you've been in love**: once

[x] **Want to go to college**: hopefully

[x] **Like high school**: NO

[x] **Want to get married:** hopefully

[x] **Type w/ your fingers on the right keys:** dunno

[x] **Believe in yourself:** I used to

[x] **Like thunderstorms:** no! scary.

---IN THE PAST MONTH DID/HAVE YOU---

[x] **Gone to the mall:** yep

[x] **Eaten sushi:** no

[x] **Been dumped:** . . .

[x] **Dyed your hair:** yes

[x] **Stolen anything:** gum

---HAVE YOU EVER---

[x] **Flown on a plane:** not for a long time

[x] **Told a guy/girl that you liked them:** yes

[x] **Cried during a movie:** every movie

[x] **Had an imaginary friend:** yes, wish I still did

[x] **Been in a fight:** yes

[x] **Shoplifted:** just that gum

---THE FUTURE---

[x] **Age you hope to be married:** 23?

[x] **Number of children:** ONE

[x] **How do you want to die:** painlessly

[x] **What do you want to be when you grow up:** a writer

---FAVORITES---

[x] **Fave color(s):** black

[x] **Day/night:** night

[x] **Summer/winter:** both

[x] **Fave food:** sesame chicken, taco salad, pb+j

[x] **Fave movies:** saved!, donnie darko, the matrix, can't hardly wait

Yes! Yes! okay!

its alt.

[x] **Fave sport:** sports are stupid

LOL Hell no!

---RIGHT NOW---

[x] **Right now wearing:** drive-thru records PJs

HA!

[x] **Drinking:** vitamin water

[x] **Thinking about:** litmag

[x] **Listening to:** "Deja Entendu" —Brand New Yes!

---DO YOU BELIEVE IN---

[x] **Destiny/fate:** yes

[x] **Angels:** yes

[x] **Ghosts:** I try not to

[x] **UFOs:** no

[x] **God:** not like everyone else does

so because everyone else doesn't you don't either?!?

---FRIENDS AND LIFE---

[x] **Do you ever wish you had another name:** just another life

[x] **Do you have a girlfriend/boyfriend:** no. boys don't like me.

[x] **What's the best feeling in the world:** going to a concert

[x] **Worst feeling:** getting yelled at

[x] **What time is it now?:** 10:30 p.m.

---HAVE YOU/DO YOU---

[x] **Do drugs:** no drugs are gross

[x] **Pray:** not really, not anymore

haven't seen anyone type that in years!

[x] **Gotten drunk:** no way. sXe!

[x] **Run away from home:** it didn't work

[x] **Made out with a stranger:** no!

[x] **Three words that sum you up:** bruised. bitter. poetic.

---SOCIAL LIFE---

[x] **Boyfriend/girlfriend:** I wish you'd stop asking

[x] **Attend church:** when I am forced to

[x] **Like being around people:** no one I've met yet . . .

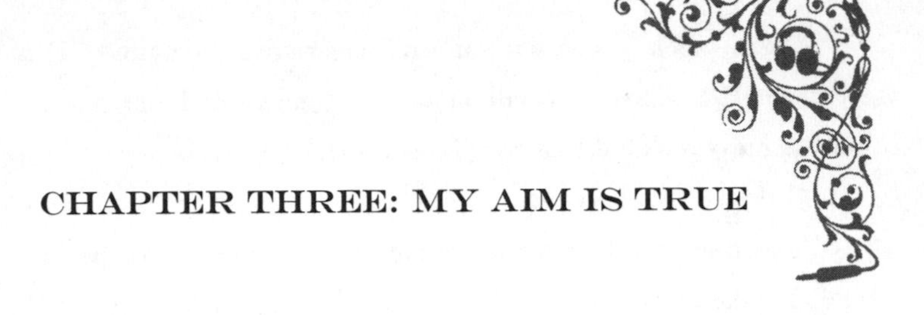

CHAPTER THREE: MY AIM IS TRUE

THE NIGHT AFTER AMY LEFT, I met Jack and Pedro for drinks at the Sparrow, the dank indie-rock bar a few blocks away from my house. Jack and Pedro were my "friends" in quotation marks—we saw one another socially, usually in the neighborhood, and talked shop: word rates, records, box scores. Jack was tall, aggressive, and quasi-bearded, with a shaggy mane of black hair that trailed to his shoulders; Pedro was painfully skinny, rocked a crew cut, and was fabulously gay. One was a journalist and one was a publicist, but sometimes it was hard to remember which was which.

"So, baby," Pedro said as he rattled the ice in his empty glass, "how's single life?"

"Not great," I said. And finished my third beer. In my own insulated and self-denying way, I was beginning to register the enormity of life without my girlfriend. It was, I imagined, the same sort of realization that dawns on someone who has been thrown out of a window: not so much that death is imminent, but that suddenly there is no longer a floor to hold the ground at bay.

"You should come out with us, man," Jack said, leaning dangerously far back in his chair. "We can show you a good time."

"Yeah?" I said.

"Yeah." Jack played with an unlit cigarette as he talked. "Diplo is playing a Brazilian dance hall set at APT tonight, and there's a record-release party for Oral B at the Gansevoort."

"I thought that was last night?"

"No, dummy," Pedro said. "That was his *prison* release party. This one's for the record."

"Oh," I said. And felt the ground getting closer.

"You should come with us." Jack sat up. "Pedro, when was the last time young David hung out with us?"

"Do you mean had two beers and went home to wifey? Or *hung out* hung out?"

"The latter."

Pedro chewed ice thoughtfully. "That would be never."

Jack stood up. "Exactly. I'm going to the john. Get me another?"

I watched him make a beeline for the back and wondered how he managed to have so much energy all the time. Just the thought of getting on the train to Manhattan at eleven p.m. paralyzed me with terror. Or apathy. I turned to Pedro.

"The Hague," I said drunkenly. "What *is* that? What kind of a city begins with 'the'? Seriously, I'm asking. Are there any others in the world?"

"Los Angeles," said Pedro with a smirk. "Las Vegas. Las Cruces."

"OK, OK," I said. "Fine. But that doesn't count. That's Spanish."

"So am I," said Pedro as he handed me his empty glass. "Do I count, David?"

"Touché," I said. And wandered up to the bar.

• • •

When I returned, drinks in hand, the two of them were looking at me strangely.

"We think you should come with us, David." Jack's eyes were bright.

"We will get you laid," added Pedro, enunciating each vowel.

I sat down. "Um," I said.

"Come to the bathroom with me," Jack said.

I gave him a funny look. "I thought *he* was the gay one," I said, pointing to Pedro.

Jack rolled his eyes. "Come to the bathroom with me and do a bump."

Suddenly I understood their relentless energy.

"You guys," I said. "It's Monday night."

Pedro tut-tutted me. "Technically it's almost Tuesday morning."

"No, you guys . . . I've never . . . no. Thanks, but no. I have work to do tomorrow."

"You had work to do today and you didn't do it. You've been complaining about it for almost two hours."

I felt suddenly small and predictable. "That's just not me, guys. Sorry."

Pedro rolled his eyes. "Why not? Because you're Mr. Responsible? With a job and a girlfriend waiting for you? Because correct me if I'm wrong, but it doesn't sound like you've got either of those things just now."

I watched their jittery, pirouetting eyes and could feel the anxious energy coming out of them, and for a second I wanted it—desperately. But instead I sipped my beer, resigned myself to routine.

"Maybe another time. Thanks."

"Your loss," said Pedro, and scooted off to the bathroom himself.

• • •

An hour later, once I had locked the door of my apartment behind me, thrown my bag to the floor, and managed to make the walls stop swimming, I pulled out my cell phone and texted Bryce:

```
Hey man things are no good here. She left.
She really did it. Feeling pretty empty.
Call if you can. Not sleeping soon.
```

I hit SEND and regretted it, but not enough to send a follow-up. Because the thing was, it was true. The only thing I was full of was Brooklyn Lager, and that hardly counted.

I sat down at my desk without turning any lights on and flipped open my computer. I signed onto IM and watched my buddy list fill up with the usual assortment of half-strangers, insomniacs, people who accidentally left their computers on at work, and . . . no one. She wasn't there. I wasn't sure if I was disappointed or relieved.

Just then, a window popped open.

```
TheWrongGirl87: hey
```

TheWrongGirl87 was seventeen-year-old Ashleigh Bortch from just outside Salt Lake City, Utah. I had interviewed her—or IMterviewed her, because we'd never spoken except on a computer screen—for the magazine story, and she had checked in with me almost daily ever since. Ashleigh was an emo kid, through and through, from the overly dramatic bands she obsessed about to the bleeding-heart poetry she scribbled in her livejournal, but she was something else too, behind all the clichés. She was smart, she was eager, and she was *trying*—something, anything. There was an ambition in her that I admired and recognized. Her parents certainly didn't; according to them, Ashleigh was headed straight toward premed at BYU. According to her, she planned to one day be a writer and live somewhere "different" like Boston or maybe even Berkeley.

davidgould101: Hey there, Ashleigh. What's new?

TheWrongGirl87: nmu?

davidgould101: Oh . . . ya know. Stuff.

TheWrongGirl87: yr up late

davidgould101: Yeah. I didn't get anything done today. So I thought I'd sit here a little longer.

TheWrongGirl87: longer? its like 1am.

davidgould101: OK, a lot longer.

davidgould101: I couldn't sleep.

TheWrongGirl87: wheres yr gf?

davidgould101: She left.

davidgould101: Today.

TheWrongGirl87: oooo. sorry, man.

davidgould101: Yeah. Me too.

davidgould101: It's ok.

TheWrongGirl87: dont worry i still think yr cool

davidgould101: Yeah? Thanks.

TheWrongGirl87: np

davidgould101: I think that just proves you don't know me very well.

I stood up then, stretched, and walked through my dark living room to the kitchen for another beer. I cracked it, drank deeply, and stared out the window for a moment. The light in my fridge—like many of the other bulbs around the house—had burned out, and I hadn't gotten around to replacing it. I think Amy and I were playing psychological chicken over who would actually act responsible first. As if there was ever any doubt about that.

Through the gated window to my left I could see into the backyards and bedrooms of all my neighbors. Unfortunately for the voyeur in me, everyone seemed to be asleep. One of the rare disadvantages of living in a neighborhood where strollers outnumber hipsters three to one.

I closed the refrigerator and padded barefoot back through my apartment. When I was settled in front of the glow of my laptop again, I noticed something: Miss Misery was online. I was worried about her then, to be honest. She was getting less sleep than I was. I put my headphones on and hit PLAY on iTunes. "On to You" by the Constantines started up. As good a song for an insomniac as I could hope for.

My IM window with Ashleigh was blinking angrily.

TheWrongGirl87: u still there?

TheWrongGirl87: hallooooo

TheWrongGirl87: my dad just asked why I was up and I told him homework. I don't think he remembered that classes are over.

davidgould101: Hey, sorry. I'm here. Was just getting a drink.

TheWrongGirl87: juicy juice?

davidgould101: Cute. No. Beery beer.

TheWrongGirl87: yick.

davidgould101: Don't knock it till you try it.

davidgould101: Wait, scratch that: Don't try it. You're 17.

TheWrongGirl87: and a half. But I'm not going to try it. It's gross.

davidgould101: Yeah. You don't need it.

TheWrongGirl87: I don't? do you?

davidgould101: Touche. But sadly, yes. The answer is yes.

TheWrongGirl87: :-(

TheWrongGirl87: people at school drink some but most of them just do pills.

davidgould101: Oh yeah? Like ephedrine, crap like that?

TheWrongGirl87: lol. no way dude that's like middle school. xanax, adderall. um. that diet pill that gave people heart attacks. ritalin.

davidgould101: Wow. When I was in middle school I did "Our Town."

TheWrongGirl87: well yr old.

davidgould101: Don't remind me.

davidgould101: :'-(

TheWrongGirl87: tell me about new york again

davidgould101: Ok. What else do you want to know?

TheWrongGirl87: Is it cold there now?

davidgould101: Cold? No way. It's June. It's warm. Kinda perfect.

TheWrongGirl87: When does it get cold again?

davidgould101: You like the cold that much you can have it! Not until like October. It has to get hot first!

TheWrongGirl87: how hot?

davidgould101: Really hot. Humid hot. Stupid hot. That starts in July.

TheWrongGirl87: . . .

TheWrongGirl87: I want to see it hot and cold. that's awesome.

davidgould101: That's the wrong attitude. You should see it when it's not-yet hot and not-yet cold, that's NYC at its best.

TheWrongGirl87: yeah

TheWrongGirl87: I guess

TheWrongGirl87: but things never stay lukewarm or in the middle like that

TheWrongGirl87: so whats the point?

I didn't have a good answer for that, so I told Ashleigh to be good and good night. But I didn't go to bed yet. I don't know if it was because I didn't want to face the covers alone or if I didn't want to face them drunk, but I logged onto Miss Misery's diary instead. There was a new entry:

[from **http://users.livejournal.com/~MzMisery**]
Time: 12:02 a.m.
Mood: Excited!
Music: Bloc Party, "Banquet"

So.

I did it.

I told my dad and it's official.

I. Am. Moving. (I'm typing it slowly, the way I'd want to say it if I could talk out loud without my dad thinking I'm either (a) insane or (b) insane enough to have snuck another guy into my bedroom after the Shane fiasco.)

So: I am FUCKING MOVING!

TO NEW YORK!!!

Wow. I just took 20 seconds to read that on the screen. I can't believe it's happening. But it is. At the end of the month. Tracee said she can hook me up with a waitressing job when I get there and I'm going to take art classes at CUNY. I'm moving in with Stevie. I am totally joining the VSC. It is so on.

!!!!!!!

Wake the fuck up NY! Get ready bitches! YOU ARE NOT READY FOR THIS!

Au revoir Toronto! Later Queen Street! Sayonara bubble tea in Kensington Street Market! Bye mean old cat lady who yells at me at the bus stop every morning!

Hello, life.

I pounded the rest of the beer and opened another. She was moving. *Here.*

Jesus.

One door opens . . .

(I looked at the empty bed behind me.)

Another slams shut.

Hello, life?

But suddenly, I had an idea.

The screen swam in front of me as I logged into my deleted and dormant Web diary and hit EDIT and DELETE ALL. The prompt asked me if I was sure. I took another swig of beer and clicked YES. I would have clicked HELL YES if it were an option, but my computer is polite like that. I thought of Amy walking through the predawn streets of the Netherlands, eyes alive and bright, taking in the sudden and beautiful reality of a career dream achieved. I thought of Bryce in Los Angeles, driving a beat-up convertible under palm trees, blasting his hip-hop mix tapes too loud, always between hot-spot destinations and the impossibly sexy women that frequented them. I thought of Jack and Pedro high-fiving over glasses of unmixed vodka, confident and totally zooted, refusing to give in to the realities of tomorrow. And I thought of Miss Misery, dreaming bigger than I ever could, zigging and zagging across a path that's meant to be walked in a straight line.

I clicked on NEW ENTRY.

I cracked another can of beer and closed my eyes. And then I started typing.

oh shit interpol
shit got real

[from **http://users.livejournal.com/~davidgould101**]
Time: 1:58 a.m.
Mood: Crazy
Music: Interpol, "Evil"

Went for it tonight with J and P - head still swimming. Started at Sparrow: 3 whiskeys, 4 keybumps in the bathroom. The night - hell the whole day - felt a lot better after that. What I realized - as we were screaming and smoking in the cab as it flew across the Manhattan Bridge, as J was charming the doorman and cutting the line for us at APT - was that any night can be a Saturday. It's just a question of how you treat it. I could have been sleeping or sulking but instead I was dancing and moving and flirting -

feeling my heart triple-timing in my chest, too many straight vodkas burning in my veins.

Pushed on to the second party - downtown, this time, no awning, no name. Every place we go it's just laughs and laughs and no waiting, and no problems, and no room to breathe. Someone said it was an afterparty and asked what band I played in. I just smiled and smiled. So many girls there; J and P seemed to know all of them. Introduced me to them, left me alone with drugs and drink money to talk to them. But the DJ was relentless - some screwed and chopped remix of an import white label that hasn't been released yet. Sounded like Chamillonaire fronting Gang of Four, or that might have just been my own voice, my own pulse in my ears. More lines, more drinks, more girls. Cornered one on the dance floor - dark hair that twirled like ski jumps just when it should have been touching her shoulders. She had a bull's-eye tattoo on the back of her calf, black tank top, red bra straps.

Her mouth tasted like spearmint and cigarettes when we kissed out on 2nd avenue, shielded by a pay-phone kiosk. I can still taste it. And I never even got her name.

This is me now. I have an appetite. I'm wired and my eyes are acrobats. I don't think I'll ever go to sleep again.

When I was finished I felt excited and guilty, and I read and reread what I had written at least four times. Then I hit POST and sent it out into the world. No one wanted to read about what was really happening to me—I didn't even want it to be happening. This way was better. This way felt . . . well, it felt more honest. For the first time in a while I felt . . . satisfied. Tomorrow I'd wake up and I'd do what I had to do. But with my new diary I could also do what I couldn't—or wouldn't—ever do. I liked my new phantom life. I liked it a whole heck of a lot better than the life of phantoms—Amy, Miss Misery, the impossible book contract weighing down my desk—that I had woken up to that morning.

It was almost three in the morning. I was decidedly drunk. And it was definitely time to go to bed. Again. I shut down the computer, changed quickly, and slipped between the sheets.

Just as I finally felt the heaviness behind my eyes relax and start to give a little—that wonderful warm ooze right before sleep—my cell phone let out a pitiful little chirp. I groaned and reached out a hand to my bedside table. It had to be Amy. She had made it safely across the ocean and wanted to let me know without waking me. She was sweet like that. Considerate. At least my nothing day would be bookended by her almost presence.

I flipped the lid of my phone and peeked one eye open.

```
1 New Text Message From: Bryce
3:56 a.m.
TITTIES!
```

I closed my eye and went to sleep.

CHAPTER FOUR: MIXED MEDIA

[from **http://users.livejournal.com/~MzMisery**]

Time: 3:37 a.m.

Mood: Tipsy

Music: Ulrich Schnauss, “Monday—Paracetamol”

We are so dramatic I could kiss myself. Wait - why do I say “could” like it’s some sort of impossibility? I can. I will. I shall.

KISS

There. I did it. On my knee which is raised up to my mouth (this is comfortable, honest; this is the way I always sit at my desk). I used to kiss my knee all the time, actually. Practicing, dontchaknow. It makes sense - why go into any fight unprepared? So prepared was I that I half expected to kiss Chris McKenzie on his hairy knee instead of his lips that day in grade 8 in the auditorium after school.

No tongue, tho.

Forgive me if I'm less than lucid. I copped two vicodins from Sarah (via her mom's prodigious medicine cabinet) and took them both with swigs of very very cheap pinot grigio at the end of my shift tonight. They don't make me feel drunk or messed up. They make me feel glowey. I like feeling glowey. Who wouldn't?

Tonight I was NOT feeling glowey at work. I was feeling slow and bad tips and blah blah blah. But then Sarah and Cody came and rescued me. Sarah was wearing a tiara that she found in the trunk of Cody's car and Cody was wearing . . . well, ordinary clothes, really, but he still looked cute. I was sitting in the kitchen counting my nothing money and wanting to cry but not in front of the busboys and well DROWNING basically. And they came and grabbed me up and swept me away from all of THAT like the way those naked baby angels picked up Venus in that Bottocelli (sp?) painting and boogie-boarded her on a seashell to a place where she was better appreciated.

Note: I am not the goddess of love nor am I irresistible (nor was I naked and nor - I LOVE TYPING "NOR"!!!! - is my hair long enough to cover my boobs). I was just lifted up by my own private-not-chubby angels.

So I popped some pills and hopped in Cody's car and away we went to Jiminy Chengs in Cabbagetown. Listened to

Head on the Door because my angels know its my favorite Cure album. Sarah and I both sat in the back and made Cody drive us - we didn't wear seatbelts and we danced like 11 year olds in the backseat, hopping up and down, making faces at other drivers. Before we went into the bar Cody pulled three yellow roses out of his glovebox and said that we were a team tonight and nothing could ever split us up. So he pinned the flowers on our shirts and kissed me and Sarah on the forehead.

Isn't that amazing the way any boring typical night can be transformed into extraordinary? That's alchemy. That's REAL alchemy - boredom into happiness, down into up, night into NIGHT. Life into gold. We should call Webster's and revise the definition of the word - my version is doable but no less astounding. So suddenly an evening that was all tattered and frayed around the edges started shining and looping in on itself until it never really had to end.

We went into the bar and ordered a bottle of wine - which they don't sell but they made an exception because Cody told the tender that Sarah and I were twins and it was our birthday. So we drank one bottle and then two and three more and embarrassed no one but ourselves. We played Felt and then the Arcade Fire on the jukebox and I distinctly remember lying on the floor of the bar while the songs crash-landed all around me, raising my hands up into the air and feeling like if I really, genuinely tried, I could reach forever.

Later a guy who said he was a student but was actually 54 years old (!) asked if he could dance with me and I said of course. He had a beard (!!) and smelled like garlic but was impossibly delicate - he held me the way I'd like to be held when I'm older and quieter and moved me just so. We slow-danced to this song called "Glorious" by this band called Adorable. The song is fast but we were slow. Good enough.

Now I'm home. Thank you angels. Thank you city and thank you springtime.

Happy birthday, Mom. I wish you were still alive. I know you would have danced with me, regardless.

<YOU HAVE TWO NEW MESSAGES>
David! Daaaavid! Guess who? Ha, ha! It's your humble editor, David. Not worried—no not me! Just . . . concerned! We're concerned, David! *Estamos nerviosos!* You and I have a deadline coming up and you have a manuscript for me . . . correct? *Correcto? Si? No?* Ha, ha! . . . No, seriously—David, call me right away. Seriously. Call.

<THURSDAY, 1:22 P.M.>

David? David? Are you there? Screening? No? Pick up if you are. This is expensive. . . . No? OK. I'm sorry I missed you. Again. It's me. I'm just back from work. The people here have been really wonderful—the city is great. You should . . . um . . . see it. Have you ever had Indonesian food? I think you'd like it. It's everywhere here and it's just your thing—endless courses, very little dishes . . . I miss you. I do. I hope you're working. I hope you're there. . . . You can . . . call me too, you know. I hope you know that. I lov—

<THURSDAY, 4:16 P.M.>

<END OF MESSAGES>

[from **http://users.livejournal.com/~davidgould101**]

Time: 12:02 a.m.

Mood: Deaf

Music: Echo & the Bunnymen, "Lips Like Sugar"

Was at the Bowery tonight for the Futureheads show - went with some of the Transmission mag crew which meant tons of pre-drinking, which occurred, of course, before the during-show drinking and the subsequent after-show drinking. Concert was good, spiky, loud. Found myself pogoing in the VIP area with two or three assistant fact-checkers who were totally cute and unhealthily into the band. They were all drinking Sparks which made them even more hyper, leading one of them to give me a ritalin since "she didn't need it." Felt full of energy after that. Fully focused.

Afterparty was at Rothko. Stuck with my new best friends and ended up at the roped-off table with the band. Drank their vodka, scored off of their roadies. Since all people in bands do is talk about being in bands, I went off with my fact-checkers to the claustrophobic miniature dance floor in the back room downstairs where a friend of theirs was DJing nothing but Prince and Rick James. Danced with them, made out with them, danced some more. Eventually - when I was seeing the bass lines in the air and felt like I could draw rainbows of strobe lights with my fingers when I caught the rhythm - someone pushed me behind the decks and so I ended up DJing until the place closed sometime after 5. I played hip-hop, mostly. Mid-'90s stuff that Bryce and I used to drive around listening to like Biggie, Raekwon, Jeru. When the fact-checkers would get bored, they'd come over to me and hotbox cigarette smoke in my mouth, run their hands through my hair, try to distract me. But they couldn't distract me. I liked playing the songs I wanted to play, being in control. Feeling a whole room full of people respond to my every whim. It felt like telepathy, beaming my thoughts, my music, straight into their brains. It made me feel golden. It made me feel alive.

TheWrongGirl87: hey mister

davidgould101: hey ashleigh

TheWrongGirl87: what'd you do today?

davidgould101: nothing. as usual.

TheWrongGirl87: ha. yeah right!

davidgould101: no, really. I didn't do anything at all.

[from **http://users.livejournal.com/~thewronggirl87**]
Time: 9:11 p.m.
Mood: Infinite
Music: The Postal Service, "We Will Become Silhouettes"

My dad always tells me to get my head out of the clouds and mom always tells me to stop living in the past - because I'm so obsessed with finding things in my closet like Strawberry Shortcake dolls or (gulp) Britney's first album. ::blushes:: Or how I'm always making her dig up the videos of our trip to Disneyland in 1994 or the photos from the time Dad's aunt Susan died and we had to go all the way to Boston for the funeral and we went to the aquarium and science museum there even though Jessie had the chickenpox. They all want me to live in the here and now and be here with them but they'll never get that that's the one place I don't want to be - even though it's the only place I CAN be. I want to live in the future. I don't want flying cars or picture phones or handsome screamo boys with studded belts to ask me out. I just want to be past here. *LOL yes. that used to be my type too*

I hate the present. And I'm always stuck in it. *aren't we all?*

[from **http://users.livejournal.com/~MzMisery**]

Time: 10:49 a.m.

Mood: Satisfied

Music: Lloyd Cole, "Perfect Skin"

Sarah told me that the reason I was stressed and freaking out had nothing to do with the move and everything to do with the fact that I haven't gotten laid since approximately Never (B.C.). I didn't agree with her, but after 3 margaritas in the afternoon I started to come around to her point of view.

So I got dolled up in that black dress (the one that I wear over the jeans and shut up if you hate that look I think it's cute), shaved my legs, bought a bottle of Popov, and cruised by the restaurant at closing time to pick up Shane. (Pause for jaws to hit the floor.)

OK defense: your witness. Ready? Ahem: I'M SORRY BUT HE'S REALLY FUCKING CUTE!!!

Also:

Exhibit A - excellent bestower of hickeys

Exhibit B - has own apartment near Kensington Market

Exhibit C - can see floor in said apartment and has sheets with high thread count

Exhibit D - will be omitted in case in some bizarro future my father ever finds this, but rest assured **it's worth it**

I know he's bad news, people. But bad news is better than no news, right?

(Oh, and you can't TELL he's 38 - especially in the dark!)

One empty bottle, one sleepless night, and one very red neck later, I am sore but not so stressed. Thank god for unshaven horndog bartenders.

Still no sleep though. I'm thinking of starting a business that rents sensitive emo boys out for the night - not for sex or anything, but just for sleeping/holding/etc. That's all they want and that's all I want out of THEM. All we'd need is a van (for delivery purposes), a closet full of clean pajamas, and easy access to a college town (for the boys). Seriously. We could make a fortune with this. Think about it.

It is weird, though, isn't it? That sleeping with someone and Sleeping With Someone are two completely different things?

My father laughed at me at breakfast this morning. Since I'm leaving him and moving away in two weeks, I must remember to behave.

<YOU HAVE THREE NEW MESSAGES>

Yo man, it's Bryce. It's awfully weird for it to be the middle of June and not be sweating to death, you know? Or swallowing air that's like ninety percent water? You feel me? Hello? You gotta start picking up this phone, dude. I know you're screening. I haven't heard from you in weeks and you should be in a work coma but God knows what you're really doing. Anyway, check it: Last night I was coming out of this dive bar in Echo Park called The Shortstop, and Sunset was completely deserted. The only person on the sidewalk was this dude—I shit you not, he had to have been like seven feet tall with enormous dreadlocks and a top hat. And he's beating on a drum like he's in the Cornhusker Marching Band screaming, 'WMDs! WMDs!' Thoughts? No? The women here are smokin' hot, by the way. Not that you'd care. Call a brother up! C'mon!

<WEDNESDAY, 6:16 p.m.>

Hey, it's Jack. You there? You're not picking up your cell, either, so I thought I'd try you at home. Look, man, we don't expect you to come into Manhattan—though that Futureheads show was fucking kick-ass, you should be sorry you missed it—but you can't even walk a few blocks to grab a beer? That's cold, man. That's cold.

<WEDNESDAY, 8:30 p.m.>

David, I'm beginning to think we should have signed your answering machine to a book contract—I bet it's got a lot of stories to tell. Ha, ha! Well, I'm sure you've guessed by now that it's your old editor friend Thom calling you. Again. We're just about at the deadline we agreed on. And still no word from you. I understand that you're a private sort of person, but this is my job too, you know! I'm sure it's going to be a good book, but you don't need to turn into a hermit crab like J.R. Salinger, right? Ha, ha!

<THURSDAY, 9:57 a.m.>

<END OF MESSAGES>

[from **http://users.livejournal.com/~thewronggirl87**]

Time: 6:21 p.m.

Mood: Mixed

Music: Taking Back Sunday, "Bonus Mosh, pt. II"

Today was the first day of summer and Krystal and I celebrated by treating ourselves to lunch at the mall.

I was planning on just getting a salad but the Panda Bear place was giving out free samples of sesame chicken ::yum:: so guess what I ended up eating? Afterwards we walked around and laughed at all the perfect blond prep lameos shopping for new boxer-briefs at Abercrombie or American Eagle or whatever until they started pointing back and called us freaks. Whatever. ::shrugs::

We went to Hot Topic so Krystal could get the first Taking Back Sunday album on CD (she wore out the copy I burned for her). She usually doesn't like the same music that I do - she mostly likes really metal stuff like Lamb of God and Atreyu ::gag:: - but maybe all the messed-up stuff she's been going through makes her relate to emotional stuff more. Is that possible? Can your taste change with your feelings? Like, if I was feeling 100% happy all the time would I want to listen to like, Britney? Or would I no longer like sesame chicken???? ::laughs:: I doubt it!

So we drove around in her car for a while after that and sang along and I finally got her to admit that "You're So Last Summer" is the best song. I know it sounds stupid but for a second just driving around with the AC on full blast and the volume up loud and all the windows open, and with my best friend and it's SUMMER you know, and we were both singing super loud - it was the best feeling in

totally agree!

the world. It felt like being in a movie, like it was something that wasn't just happening – it was something we were already REMEMBERING, you know? ::smiles::

But all movies end and instead of long boring credits I had to go home and find my dad sitting there waiting for me. He got some BYU crap in the mail and he wanted to go over it with me. I wanted to yell like YOU ALREADY WENT THERE YOU DON'T GET TO GO AGAIN! But it's like it's the most important thing in the world to him. He said that I'd better do extra studying this summer so I get my math boards up. If I don't he might take away my computer. It's like, doesn't he understand that's like saying he'd take away my ARMS!!

Well, gotta go. Dinner time. Can't wait to hear what he'll say to me NOW.

[from **http://users.livejournal.com/~MzMisery**]
Time: 1:13 a.m.
Mood: Disorganized
Music: Berlin, "Riding on the Metro"

They had a going away party tonight for me at the restaurant which was sweet because up until then I hadn't realized that I cared. But I did care – I can't help myself. Shane made everyone blue drinks with that stuff that I love to say but have no idea how to write (curacao?). Tommy said he told all of his tables that the crab special was named after me (such a sweetheart) and after closing everyone stuck around to get drunk - or at least as close to drunk as blue drinks can get you. Hector and Amilcar took turns trying to teach me how to salsa dance but I don't think I'm a natural.

Then I took the bus home and it took two strange looks from two different old ladies to make me realize I was crying. I swear - that's the first and last time I'm going to be anything but giddy about this. In two days I'll be in New York and that's all I've ever wanted.

But right now I'm sitting here and my life is in boxes all around me (very nice boxes that were once filled with very nice wine - Dad picked them up for me at his favorite snooty vino store). Nothing is packed though because how can it be? What can I bring? What can I leave behind? Instead I'm sitting here surrounded by a life that is quickly becoming my *old* life. I've been reading yearbooks and the track listings of old mix tapes and then putting them back on the shelf. Just to prove that I don't need them anymore.

When I was in middle school everyone had to do a sport after school and you know how athletic I am (I get great big purple bruises just from kneeling to tie my shoes) so you can imagine how that went. In the spring I took track and field because that's what all the slackers did - I remember Will Webster (the hot older elf-man who did plays and made grade 5 girls swoon) used to take people (only if they were cool enough) out behind the highjump mat and share a joint with them. Track and field wasn't serious, it was mostly waiting and wearing shorts and teaching other girls how to make grass kazoos. So that's what I did. But everyone had to do at least one event and the one Coach (Big) Bird had me do was the 400. Why? Because it wasn't a sprint and it wasn't distance. It was in the middle just like I was (which was just another way of saying not quite good enough at anything). It was just a lot of running.

So why am I talking about this (other than the fact that I just read what Coach wrote in my grade 8 yearbook: "Hope to see you trying harder next year." I mean: WTF?!? I was 14!)? Because the only thing I ever really liked about track and field was the moment just before the race started, when you'd have to dig into the red clay of the track and everyone else would just SHUT UP already. There was no more trashtalking or encouragement or people you barely knew shouting your name as if there's any real chance you're going to win. All that was just fucking OVER for a beautiful tangle of seconds. And the feeling, the anticipation of that gun going off, was so painful after a while it became delicious. It's actually kind of HOT, you know? The gun is going to go off. It's going to happen soon. You can't move anything in your body, no twitching, no itching, nothing. You just dance on the edge of your toes until you finally hear the gun saying MOVE GO NOW. But it wasn't the moment that you finally did get to fucking move that I got off on. It was the second just before that. Knowing it was going to happen, that there was nothing you could do to stop it. Knowing and not knowing. Being completely powerless, at the mercy of some random stranger(s). That was the best part.

And that's how I feel right now.

Good night, Toronto. Good-bye. Don't wait up for me.

[from **http://users.livejournal.com /~thewronggirl87**]
Time: 1:31 a.m.
Mood: Poetic
Music: Dashboard Confessional, "Carve Your Heart Out Yourself"

In blood red I
Saw you, watched you, waited for you

ANDY GREENWALD

Crossing the street
Crossing your heart
Hope to die?
Yes, I would in a (last)
heartbeat
if it only meant
That you could see again, without
veils, or vestments, or anything other
than your naked eyes
Push them into me,
break through my skin and
bones and fragile outsides of
paper, and books, and traditions
If your eyes were diamonds
Then they'd be sharp enough to cut
Through every ounce of me
Ribbon my flesh
And leave me there to be seen by
only you
In
Blood
Red.

[from **http://users.livejournal.com/~davidgould101**]
Time: 2:55 a.m.
Mood: Drunk
Music: The Stills, "Still in Love Song"

Really? you sure about that?

Sometimes - on nights like tonight when I'm so drunk/stoned/high/gone that I feel like I'm looking at the city from above like a game board and I know all my moves in advance - I like to think about the way I was before this summer, before I started going out, before I started living like this. And really, what I like to think is that I was pathetic - sitting at home, always pining for something or other, always complaining. Living like an old person in these last few years of youth that I have left.

Living here and ignoring the nighttime is like going to a movie with a blindfold on - what's the point? There are so many women, so many bars, so many songs, so many mistakes. What's the point of worrying about things before you've done them? Go, go, go. Hangovers are for tomorrows, and if you never stop, you never reach tomorrow.

Tonight I DJed again at a bar on the LES - one of those secret ones that doesn't have a name or a sign.

Free drinks and free phone numbers. Making out with girls in the bathroom whose names I never caught. Soundtracking my own descent.

I never could have had any of this before. It never could have happened. If I ran into the me I used to be on the subway - before any of this, before the drinking and the drugging and the DJing, before she left - I doubt I'd even recognize him. He'd be introverted, sad, pale, and disappearing. And if he stopped me to chat I know what I'd say to him: Everything is terrific. Everything is free. Everything is finally happening.

Is it possible to be having the time of your life and not remember any of it the next day?

The day after I wrote that I woke up late again, pushed aside the empty beer cans on my desk, and read what I had written. Ludicrous, as always. I hadn't DJed a party yesterday. I hadn't even left my apartment. There had been a part of yesterday when I was watching TV and another part when I had been shotgunning Rheingolds in front of my computer screen and that was about it. I sighed.

I was beginning to entertain the possibility that I was depressed, but the fact that the possibility entertained made me doubt it. It wasn't that I was screening calls; I was flat-out ignoring them. And it wasn't that I was sad or lonely. It went deeper than that—to a place where I could hear the little nags and groans and cries of sadness pinging against the roof of whatever emotional bunker I'd built for myself over the weeks since Amy had left, but I didn't feel particularly bothered to respond to them.

Even back when I was nominally happy, my friend Bryce actually went so far as to create a superhero alter ego for me: The Amazing Sublimated Man. A catchy name, but I was no doubt the only superhero in history to have both sides of his identity be equally mild-mannered. The gist of Bryce's argument was that if something was really bothering me, I'd always be the last to know it.

And so it was with this summer: I had barricaded myself rather handily in the days since Amy left. As an only child I was always more than capable of being alone, of entertaining myself, but this was something different. It was possible, I realized, to waste a season. You might not think so, but it's true. Days go by whether we want them to or not. You can ride them like an escalator: Stick your hands in your pockets and hope you see something worthwhile along the way. Or you can hop on that same escalator and give it an extra push, take the steps two at a time: Don't just give yourself over to the momentum; help it out. Get where you're going faster and with clean intent of purpose, even if where you're going happens to be another escalator, with another one waiting at the top of that.

I didn't need Bryce to tell me that something was wrong, but I had no idea in the world how to fix it.

Amy had been gone for nearly six weeks, and I had barely left my apartment and accomplished none of my work. The book seemed like a fever dream from a different life; so, in fact, did Amy. During the long mornings when I'd surfed blogs and sports Web sites and listened to Fleetwood Mac records and drunk my coffee in tiny sips to make the excitement of it last longer, I didn't necessarily feel like I was retreating from the world. I honestly couldn't think of anything else to do. The rhythm of life without Amy was hypnotic, easy, and lulling. I didn't notice the quiet in the apartment anymore, the spaces where her voice would have been. The more time I spent alone, the easier it was to be alone. And then the goal became finding a way to stay alone.

There was my fake diary, of course, which was becoming more and more out of control by the day. But the things that I found myself typing into it were fantasies—a useful vehicle to imagine myself out of my predicament. But the rock-star schmoozing and the anonymous hookups weren't the things I really wanted; I wasn't even capable of doing them. Writing the diary made me feel vibrant and mysterious, but it was nothing more than an artful bit of miscasting. In reality, I was the good guy. I was the guy with the girlfriend, the good credit rating. I was dependable. Trustworthy. Steadfast.

Safe.

There had been times—sure, many times—when I had been tempted to be otherwise: a fleeting kiss with a sophomore theater student during a drunken visit to Bryce's college; a few joints with Amy at the beach; an offer of an Ecstasy tablet at New Year's. But the problem with my brain was that it always clicked a few steps ahead: I saw the potential outcomes before I even did the deed. And so nothing illicit ever seemed quite worth it. Going out and clubbing and living that life was, at its root, hollow. I knew it, so I didn't do anything about it.

And now I just didn't do anything at all.

I sighed again. Went to the kitchen to pour myself a glass of orange juice. Came back and read through some diaries. Leslie was moving to Berlin in the fall for a semester abroad. Paige was outlining the six rules of a guilt-free hookup. Ashleigh was fighting with her parents again, with her sister, with her life. And Miss Misery? I didn't know; I always saved the best for last.

I knew from recent postings that she had made it to New York City safely, though the city that she described in her first few alcohol-fueled and exhaustion-drenched diary entries was nothing at all like the city I lived in. She was magical like that, transforming every scenario, every street corner, every bar stool into something distinctly her own, something vital, something alive. It was a world I tried to inhabit in my own diary entries but without success. If I was an interloper in her world, at least she was a vibrant tour guide.

Her diary filled my computer screen—a new entry at the top. I took a sip of juice and settled in to read it.

[from **http://users.livejournal.com/~MzMisery**]
Time: 1:55 p.m.
Mood: Exhausted
Music: Interpol, "NYC"

Oh yeah. THIS is why I moved here.

What a fucking night. Started innocently enough: Ben and Debra came over with bottles of wine and we ate leftover takeout Thai on the floor (Stevie sold his kitchen table - long story) and they toasted me and made me a provisional member of the VSC. Ben wasn't even being weird to me, which was nice for a change. Then Debra got cranky because it was hot in the apt (no AC yet - must change this immediately) so we went to Hi-Fi which is so totally the rock critic nerd bar on Avenue A but it also has a digital jukebox with like 3000 albums on it, so it's worth it.

So I was drinking beer because it was going to be a quiet night and I put 7 bucks in the jukebox and was taking forever to pick out songs (they have every New Order album on there - EVERY ONE) when I noticed this guy sitting in one of the booths, totally checking me out. Now this does not happen all the time but when you are a young lady in the big city it happens SOMETIMES right? But not like this. This was so brazen. He was not my usual type (kinda skinny) but had cool hair and big brown eyes and he was just boring holes into me with them. I kept trying to stare him down but he wouldn't even blink, so I ended up blushing and turning back to the jukebox. I was taking so long up there that Debra came up to me and was like "that dude is totally checking you out." But she didn't know who he was either. Finally when I ran out of credits I took a big drink and turned around and walked right over to him. He was just sitting there, staring at me as I walked over, with this totally cocky lazy smile - the kind you just want to smash either with your fist or your lips. I didn't know what to say so I was like "do we know each other?" And he just keeps smiling that lazy cat smile and says something like "I dunno but I'm pretty sure I know you." And I don't know what came over me but something about his confidence or his assholeishness (same diff) was so overwhelming I was just like "you are very cute." And he was like "you're not so bad yourself." I felt kinda queasy but kinda turned on and I felt - fuck it, right? This is NEW YORK CITY. This is where I live now. So I sat down with him just when my songs started on the jukebox.

The night took a different turn from there. The VSC wanted to leave and I didn't even notice them go because I was still talking to this guy - I'll call him "D." And the thing about him is that he's SMART but he's also older. He's a writer - about music and he's working on some kind of book - but not a dorky, trainspotting shut-in like most music writers. This guy was vibrating on some sort of crazy frequency and we just clicked but in a totally fun and confrontational way. We were arguing about movies and records and he got all my references and he laughed at all my jokes. We kept taking turns running outside for cigarettes because we didn't want to lose the booth. At midnight he ran out of money so I bought him two more drinks - he was drinking vodka on the rocks which seemed kinda cool and writerly - and then he asked me to go to the bathroom with him and I was kind of loaded at this point so I said sure.

We got some funny looks but the place was crowded and people were hammered so no one stopped us. He locked the door and broke out drugs and gave me bumps and then grabbed me just so and I let him kiss me for a while, pushed up against the flimsy wooden door, then we did some more and then I kissed him, harder this time, trapped him up against the sink. His tongue tasted like tobacco and I liked the way he held my head and hair while he made out with me - like it was a project for him, something he was working on. Like I was some sort of human canvas. And then I don't even remember the rest. We went back to the apartment and did more and drank more and listened to records until we woke Stevie up and took cell phone pictures of each other and made out more and . . .

I know you're not supposed to sleep with strangers in the big bad city and there was something about this guy that wasn't entirely . . . right. But I couldn't help it. He just left like 20 minutes ago - my whole futon smells like him now. I smell like him now. Crazy. Too crazy. But sometimes I like crazy. And I think I liked this guy.

```
Ten bucks (Canadian) says he'll never call me again.
I gotta get some sleep.
```

I read the entry three or four more times with my mouth open and my head shaking back and forth. She lives here for less than a week and hooks up with someone who could have been me. Perfect.

I sat back, took a breath. Really, I thought, as the photo of Amy tacked to the wall caught my eye, it's probably for the best. I never actually wanted to meet Cath Kennedy. I wanted to meet Miss Misery, lose myself in her daze and in her nights. But she was a fantasy—an online construct—that existed on the Internet and maybe in my head as well. No different from my own journal. Fake, fake, fake.

Still, though. I had a catch in my throat and a weird tinge of jealously. I knew where that bar was, what the jukebox was like. I'm a writer (supposedly). I have the same taste in books and music as her, not that guy. I could have been sitting there. I could have swept her off her feet. I could have, but I wouldn't have. Story of the year.

I leaned forward again and redirected my browser to my own diary. Time to check in on my exciting life. The truth is, I was running out of things to write about. How many times can you pretend to make out with anonymous younger girls, drink until you slosh when you walk, and vacuum up drugs that you've never really had any interest in trying? When does a fantasy life become mundane? Maybe today would be a quiet day for me online. Maybe I wouldn't have anything to say at all.

My diary loaded slowly on the screen in front of me. There was the entry about the Futureheads and there was that ridiculous one about "looking at the city from above." And then there was . . . something else.

[from **http://users.livejournal.com**
/~davidgould101]
Time: 2:08 p.m.
Mood: Satisfied
Music: none

I blinked. I hadn't written that. It was from today. From—I looked at my watch—minutes ago. My heart lurched and free-fell somewhere into my lap. I scrolled down, my eyes barely keeping up with the page. It felt like when a bathroom lock fails and someone walks in on you. It felt horrible.

[from **http://users.livejournal.com**
/~davidgould101]
Time: 2:08 p.m.
Mood: Satisfied
Music: none

Was sitting at Hi-Fi last night nursing a drink when I saw her - black hair, tall boots, long fingers, standing at the jukebox, looking tough, looking in control - and I couldn't look away. I knew she was the one I was looking for, and she knew it too, came over to me, liked the way I looked, the way I talked. She fell for it, like all of them do, but this one had something else - a spark, a light. And I knew there was no chance I was going to let it get away.

She was from Canada - just moved here - and loved to argue, so we tussled over the table for a while, over drinks, over movies. She liked most of the same records I do, even the same obscure Japanese books. Eventually I just couldn't wait anymore so I took her into the stall with me, got her high, got her to make out with me. She was a hell of a good kisser - twists her body into yours and grabs at your back so hard it leaves a mark. Like she was hungry for something, which is good because hungry is all I ever am these days.

She lived not far away - over by Avenue C - which was good because I had nowhere to go. She finally kicked me out half an hour ago (why does it ever have to be morning?). I am fired up and cooled off at the same time. She's a firecracker that just exploded into my summer.

Thanks, Cath. Now: What's next?

My mind was racing. No one read this thing—no one even knew about it. So who could have done this? Who could be fucking with me like this? I hit REFRESH again and again, hoping it was a glitch, a mistake, a dream. But it kept popping back up exactly the same. Who could have done this? Who would know to do this?

Who did Cath sleep with last night?

I glanced out the window in a panic, half expecting to see another pair of eyes looking back at me, but it was just my reflection as always. Calm down, I said to myself. There has to be an explanation. This has to be a coincidence.

But Cath called her new boyfriend "D." That was my initial. And whoever had updated my diary knew my taste in books. Knew me. Why would someone want to imitate me? My life was boring, unproductive, and stalled.

But it was still mine. I read and reread the entry until my eyes started to hurt from staring at the screen. It was creepy, invasive, bizarre. Impossible, even.

". . . because hungry is all I ever am these days."

In an instant, I made up my mind. I signed on to IM, scanned the buddy list, saw what I was looking for, took a deep breath, and did something I had thought I would never do.

davidgould101: hi, is this cath?

MzMisery: hey!

davidgould101: hi

MzMisery: how did you know how to find me on here?

davidgould101: well . . .

MzMisery: I totally didn't think you'd get in touch with me again

MzMisery: :-(

davidgould101: about that . . . listen, can we meet up? in person? something weird is going on and I think I need to talk to you about it.

MzMisery: mmmmmmm ok

MzMisery: I have a job interview tomorrow afternoon, but after that? like around 5:45? you're in the e village, right?

davidgould101: um, I can be.

MzMisery: ok, meet me at the Library bar—it's on Ave A and 1st street.

davidgould101: ok. I'll be there. tomorrow.

MzMisery: cool! I gotta run. get some sleep! I'm exhausted! xoxoxo

davidgould101: bye

"MzMisery signed off at 2:37 p.m."

I sat back and ran my hands through my hair. I could hear my heart pounding in my chest. She was a firecracker, all right. And it seemed like I had just lit the fuse.

wow! what is happening?
Is she real? Is he real?
Is she his sex? or his imagination?
What is going on.

CHAPTER FIVE: AWFULLY CUTE, LIKE THE MARTIAN SKYLINE

well you don't leave your apartment so yeah. you did

I WALKED UP AND OUT of the subway at First Avenue with my headphones on so not even the hipster panhandler at the top of the stairs could slow me down. All the F-train kids grab their cells and check their messages on the little half-block between Houston and First Street, so I cut across eastward to avoid them. The sun was still out—blazing, actually—and it seemed that capri pants were back in fashion this year. I must have missed the memo. As I walked past the taxi-driver curry stands and housing-project gardens of First Street, I tried to imagine what I was walking into. How to play the meeting? Pretend I know nothing? Leer like I know everything? I was wearing a non-ironic softball-team T-shirt, so leering was definitely out. Another thing: It was five thirty in the afternoon. Should I drink? Well, duh, yeah. But she was twenty-two years old. Would I get in trouble? Was I already in trouble? What if the Library didn't make Tom Collinses?

I paused in front of Nice Guy Eddie's and took my headphones off. Beenie Man was blaring out of at least six different car windows. A cocker spaniel wearing a beret had taken its owner out for a walk. Across the street in front of the Mercury Lounge another band wearing corduroy jeans that were far too tight was unloading gear and laughing. I was about to do something I'd always never wanted. Or something like that. I took a breath, smoothed out my T-shirt, turned the corner, and walked into the bar.

The air-conditioning was on, which was nice, but it wasn't working, which wasn't. The dark-haired bartender in the tattoos and tank top was on duty (as opposed to the blonde one with the tattoos and tank top), and she gave me her usual look, which roughly translated as "I would like to step on your brittle bones if only the satisfaction it would give me weren't so fleeting." There were some regulars at the bar bullshitting and reading the *New York Press.* Echo & the Bunnymen were on the jukebox. The tables at the back were empty.

"What do you need?" asked the killer without making eye contact.

"I'm meeting someone," I said for no conceivable good reason.

"Good for you," she said. And walked away.

"No, no," I called out. "I'll have a beer. Um. A Yuengling."

She poured the pint for me sloppily, letting the foam spill over and leach all over the sticky bar top. I paid her. She didn't give me a buyback ticket, which was fair enough for me being a dope. I glanced at the Centipede machine and took a seat in the back.

I drank half of my beer without noticing it. I wondered who was updating my journal. I tried to picture him: A lunatic? A friend? A vengeful editor? Whoever he was, my imagination seemed to feel strongly that he had a beard. Was he posting from his apartment? His penthouse? Kinko's? Maybe he was doing it right now, daydreaming about the VIP room at Lit, his greasy fingers flitting over the silver keyboard of a brand-new PowerBook on the first floor of the Apple Store on Prince, where all the homeless people, supermodels, and Italian tourists check their Hotmail accounts. It was a nice image, one that almost kept me from noticing (a) the people walking into the bar and (b) the fact that the clouds had shifted, leaving the blisteringly bright sunlight an unimpeded avenue straight from the front window to my eyes. I couldn't wear sunglasses inside—that would be pretentious or sketchy—and I couldn't move because that would be lame. Instead I squinted, thought about what songs I'd put on the jukebox if I weren't too nervous to stand up ("Some Girls Are Bigger Than Others," "Dream Police," and "Not That Funny" off of *Tusk*), and waited.

She was now five minutes late, which is a hell of a lot cooler than ten minutes early. Fifteen minutes is also a ridiculously ambitious amount of time to nurse the first beer of the day, but I was giving it the college try. (Literally, of course, the college try would be to chug it through a beer bong within ten seconds of arriving, but I don't like to quibble with myself.) Her diary profile photo was definitely angled, so it was plausible that she could be heavy. I knew that going in. But I also knew that she was someone who loved to laugh, who loved *Norwegian Wood* and the first Orange Juice album. Someone who had hired a naked Samoan belly dancer as a surprise for her own twenty-first-birthday party. Someone who seemed to get what she wanted most of the time. Someone who was standing right in front of me.

"Hey," she said in a voice pitched somewhere between dubious and flirty.

"Hi," I said, and squinted. I couldn't see her at all. The sun was too bright. I could see a tuft of black hair and shoulders like ice picks. Whoever she was, she was wearing a tight white pocket T and a pleated black skirt. She also leaned into my booth to give me a half hug, half kiss on the cheek. She smelled of sweat, Right Guard, and cinnamon. I couldn't decide if she was shorter or taller than I had imagined.

"You look different," she said. "Did you cut your hair?"

"Maybe," I said. "It could just be the light." I hadn't expected her to recognize me. What was that about?

"I'm gonna get a drink," she said sprightly. "Why don't you move to the table in the shade?"

Such a simple solution! I slid across the room to the opposite booth. She didn't sound Canadian, I thought. At least not yet.

When she came back to the table, holding something mixed in a highball glass (was a Tom Collins yellow? I couldn't remember) and another pint for me, I finally managed a decent look at her. Her cheekbones were what I expected; her left arm was ensnared in what looked like a dozen fluorescent club wristbands, there was an ADMIT ONE stamp fading on her right hand, and her eyes were dancing. But she looked young. High-school young, and breakable, too—there was a purplish bruise on her left knee and a tic-tac-toe board of red scrapes on her right. Her mouth was twisted into something like a grin, and I realized she was as nervous as I was.

"No," she said, putting the drinks down. "You look *really* different. Maybe it's the daylight. Maybe you're like Batman!" She giggled and squeezed a lemon wedge into her drink. "I've never known a superhero before."

She fumbled in her bag for a moment and came up with a bruised pack of Parliaments. "Elsie lets me smoke in here before six as long as I'm quick about it." She exhaled right in my face. "Do you want one?"

"I don't smoke," I said before I could catch myself.

There was a pause as she scanned my eyes for the joke, and then she burst out laughing. "Okaaaaay!"

She smoked well—too well, probably, for someone so young. But she had a real flair about it, letting her wrist flounce about just so as she inhaled, flicking the ash without ever looking to see where it was falling. Still, it wasn't what I expected. Miss Misery was slick, in control, alluring, and impossible. Cath Kennedy had a nervous laugh and a tendency to play with her hair. She was just a kid, and I was about to confuse the living Christ out of her.

"So," I said.

"So," she said. And clinked her ice cubes. "I was thinking a lot today about what we talked about the other night."

"Oh?"

"Yeah. I was. And I think I've decided that I was right." She took a drink and stared at me.

"OK."

"You don't remember what we were talking about?"

"Not really. Um. I'm sorry." Why was I apologizing?

"Man, that must have been better coke than I thought. We were talking about that movie, with Jim Carrey. *Eternal Sunshine of the Spotless Mind*. The end of it. Remember?"

"Yeah," I said. "I remember that movie."

"Do you remember what the last line is? After Kate Winslet hears the tape of him complaining about her and she runs out of the apartment and says all this stuff about how it's pointless because they're just going to drive each other crazy and everything's going to end badly? What he says next?"

I took a drink of my beer. Someone at the bar was handing the bartender what seemed to be a wind chime. It tinkled lazily until the killer hushed it with her palm. "I do remember, yeah."

"He says—"

"'OK.'"

"Exactly!" She stubbed out her cigarette. "And you think that he meant—"

"He meant OK, like, 'OK, I'm aware of that. But it's worth it. Let's give it another shot.' Like, 'Some things are inevitable and meant to be.'"

She snorted. "But why would he say that? They just found out that everything that they feel about each other is a lie—that everything is doomed to repeat itself and be miserable. The 'OK' was letting her leave."

I laughed. "No way! That's completely the opposite of what the movie was supposed to be about!"

"You almost had me convinced, dude. Almost. But this morning I called my aunt and she agreed with me. Face it. You're just wrong."

The jukebox shuddered and "Charlotte Sometimes" by the Cure started playing.

"Dude," she said. "I love this song."

I almost said, *I know*, but instead I said, "Cath, I have to tell you something kind of strange."

She scratched her arm. "Do you have herpes?"

"What? No!"

"OK then. What?"

I laughed and felt like my stomach was itching. "The person you were hanging out with the other night . . . that wasn't me."

"What are you talking about?"

"Yeah, I don't know what I'm talking about either. But listen: We've never met before."

"Dude, you're really starting to weird me out."

"*I'm* weirded out. *I* don't understand it. But I think . . . well, I don't know what I think. But it's like someone is impersonating me."

"If that wasn't you, how come you knew how to find me?"

"Because . . . well, because I read your livejournal and—"

She rolled her eyes. "Eeeeesh."

"And I read mine, too, and someone has been updating it for me. And it's really creepy, I know, but I need to figure out what's going on."

She lit another cigarette. "Look, David—I mean, what the fuck? Are you schizo? Seriously."

"No. I don't think so."

"Are you bipolar?"

"Look, I'm not lying to you. We've never met before. You said I look different—can't you tell that it wasn't me? That it was someone else?"

"Dude, you look different because it's daylight and you're not wearing leather pants. Also you shaved. But it was fucking you that was in my fucking bed! Jesus!"

"Cath, it wasn't me."

"If you didn't want to see me again, that's cool, but this mindfuck thing is getting really old."

"Listen to me: On Saturday night I watched the Mets game in my apartment by myself. I didn't go out. I don't know what to say either, but . . ."

She was fumbling through her bag now, frantically. I felt it all slipping away; it did sound ludicrous. I could feel my words melting in the humid air of the bar, dribbling all over the walls and floors.

"Look, David." She pulled out her cell phone and started flipping through the menus. "If you weren't with me on Saturday night, then who the fuck is this?" She thrust the phone into my face. There was a photo on the screen with Saturday's date in the bottom corner. It was of me. I had too much product in my hair, too much scruff on my cheeks, and a rolled up five-dollar bill wedged up my nose as I leaned in to snort something off of a red tabletop. But it was me.

I leaned back. "Whoa."

"Yeah, fucking whoa!" She snatched her phone back. "What the hell is wrong with you?"

It felt like a car accident, really. In the sense that car accidents are those things that you think so much about before they happen—the chaos, the fear, the slow motion—and then when you're actually in one, everything just kind of makes sense. There's a loud noise, maybe. But very little surprise, very little drama. It's just what they are. It's what *happens.* That's what this moment felt like: Weird as it all was, it wasn't surprising. It was just what was happening.

"I don't know what's wrong with me. Maybe something *is* wrong with me."

"Yeah! Maybe!" She finished her drink.

"Listen," I said. "Did he—did *I* give you any way to get in touch with me?"

"Yes. You gave me your cell-phone number. Listen—do you have episodes like this a lot?"

"OK," I said. I felt like MacGyver. "I want you to call me."

"You're sitting right across from me, fruitcake!"

I took my phone out of my pocket and laid it on the table. "No, really. Just do it. I have to see what happens."

"Fine," she said. Her face was flushed, with pink and red splotches across her nose. It looked like the Martian skyline, and it was awfully cute. "Fine."

She dialed the number.

"It's ringing," she said.

I stared at my phone. Nothing happened.

"Maybe you have bad service in here," she said. "It's still ringing."

I stared down. Still nothing.

"Look, you freak." She kicked at my heels below the table. "You probably gave me the wrong phone number anyway. That's probably your sty—hello?"

I looked up. Her face looked crinkled, confused.

"Who is this? David?"

I grabbed her wrist and mouthed, "Don't tell him!"

"Uhhh . . . yeah. Hi, David. This is Cath from the other night. Where are you? The Apple Store? Oh, that's cool. Yeah. I check my e-mail there all the time too."

My brain was numb. Suddenly, she was laughing.

"Yeah, I do still think I'm right. I was just talking . . . about . . . that." She paused and pulled her arm away from me. "Look, dude, what the hell? Do you have a twin brother or something? Because if you do, this is *so* not cool."

I grabbed the phone away from her. "Who the hell is this?"

A voice on the other end said, "This is David Gould. Who the hell is *this*?"

I said, "*This* is David Gould," but my tongue felt cottony, and even I didn't know if I believed myself anymore.

"Oh," said the voice. "Ha." Did I really sound like that? "Well," it said, "are you having fun yet?"

"What?" I was yelling now. "What the fuck does that mean? Who is this? How did you get my password?" I could hear the store behind him, people milling about, pricing iPods, speaking Italian.

"Because I certainly am." The voice practically purred. "Bye, David. Tell Cath to call me later. And don't be a stranger."

Click.

I held the phone to my ear longer than I should have, mainly because I knew that when I pulled it away I'd have to rejoin the planet again—a planet that was spinning away from me really rather quickly.

When I did, Cath was looking at her knees. "That wasn't you," she said.

"I know," I said.

"But it was." Her eyes were glistening.

"I know," I said, but quieter.

"I need another drink," she said. And for the first time that day, we agreed.

OH SHIT! WHAT! IS! Happening!

CHAPTER SIX: BOOKS WITH MORE THAN ONE AUTHOR

LATER, WHEN I THINK we were drunk, we hashed out a plan.

"So let's be clear." Cath listed a bit in her booth and slurred her words slightly. "You want to meet yourself."

"Yeah."

"And you want me to introduce you to yourself."

"Yeah, exactly."

"And you can't pay a therapist to do this for you?"

"Cath."

She shook her head and killed off her third Tom Collins. I'd often heard that gin made an angry drunk, but it seemed to have the opposite effect on Cath Kennedy: The more she drank, the gentler she appeared, the softer her hard edges seemed.

"So you're just another David that's gonna use me, huh?"

"What? No!"

She smiled. "I'm kidding. But this is really fucking weird."

"I know. Believe me, I know. The last thing I ever thought I'd be doing is sitting here with you."

She crunched an ice cube. "What? Why? What's wrong with me?"

"Nothing's wrong with you." I wanted to say, Other than the fact that you bite your nails and didn't call your father until you'd been in New York for three days. But I didn't. Instead I sipped more beer. "I just didn't know that you were real."

"Well, here I am," she said, frowning. Then she smiled. "Whoever you are, you were a really good kisser, you know."

My face got hot. "It wasn't me, Cath."

"So you say, so you say." She drummed her nibbled nails on the tabletop. "How long have you been reading my diary?"

"Um, I don't know. A year maybe?"

"OK. Why me?"

I paused.

"I don't know," I lied. "You're, um, very compelling. And you have good taste in music. And in books. You like Murakami."

Her face turned bright. "You like Murakami?"

"He's my favorite," I said.

"Mine too." She took a sip of Tom Collins. "Which one do you like best?"

"Dance, Dance, Dance," I said without hesitation.

Her eyebrows raised. "Are you serious? That's your favorite?"

"Yep," I said.

"But that's the one where nothing happens—the dude just wanders around haunted hotels and obsesses over a dead girl's ears. He's just a lonely guy getting mixed up in other people's lives."

"It's my favorite," I said.

"OK," she said, and shook her head. "Whatever. But wait: This whole time, you were writing a book about me? And you were going to tell me . . . when?"

"It's not a book about *you*, Cath. It's about online diaries. But you weren't going to be in it."

"Why not?" She seemed genuinely offended.

"Well, because . . ." I paused. "Reptilia" by the Strokes started up on the jukebox and I wanted to tell Cath that she loved this song, but I imagined she already knew. "Because you were private, you know? It was like having a favorite TV show that you don't want anyone else to know about."

She rubbed her eyes. "I'm glad my fucking life can be so entertaining."

"It's not like that."

"It's not?"

"Well . . . yeah, it is. But it's more than that too." I sighed. "Look, I'm sorry. I'm a little drunk. And more than a little freaked out."

"I can tell. Look, I'll help you. I like adventures. And plus, I thought I liked you—or at least the other you. *You* you I'm not so sure about."

I smiled and batted my eyes.

"But for God's sake you have to even the playing field, creepo. What's the address of *your* diary?"

I blinked. "Seriously?"

"Yeah fucking seriously! I usually don't like books with more than one author, but I'll see if I can make an exception."

"OK. That's fair." I was shuffling my empty beer glass between my hands like an air-hockey puck. "But . . . there's something you should know about it."

"Don't worry," she said. "I won't take the stuff about Saturday night personally since apparently you didn't write it."

"No," I said slowly. "It's not that. It's that my diary, the whole thing, it's . . . fake."

"Well, duh," she said.

"Excuse me?"

"That's the beauty of the creepy things, right? You can say anything you want and no one's gonna contradict you. Well, except in the comments but you can shut those off."

"No, I know that. I don't mean it's embellished. I mean it's fiction. I make it up. I've never done any of the stuff in it."

"That's weird."

"I know."

"Why would you take the time to do that? You're, like, a real writer. You get paid. You have a life."

"Yeah, but . . ." I felt the beer sloshing around in my brain, making me more than a little seasick. "There's stuff that I don't do in my life. That I can't do or whatever. And this way . . . at least I can write about it. I can live vicariously through it, you know? But now someone has *violated* that whole made-up life and is mocking me or whatever and it . . . sucks. It really, really sucks."

Cath was staring at me. "Dude, whoever David number two is, he's not mocking you."

"He's not?"

"Hell, no. It sounds to me like he's improving on you."

"He is."

"Yeah." Her eyes locked onto mine. "I mean, you talk a lot of game—write it, too. This guy—whoever the fuck he is—at least he has the balls to go through with it."

I looked away.

"I'm getting another drink." She stood up. "And then I'm going to see my friend DJ. You're welcome to come if you want. But I understand if you'd rather just go home and write about what you think it was like."

My head was in my hands before she'd even made it to the bar.

I reached for my wallet, steadied my hand, and followed her up for another drink.

Forty-five minutes later, I was following Cath down Essex Street in the fading sunlight. All around us were lazily handsome young people in thick-framed black glasses, artfully torn ringer Ts, and flowery sundresses. People leaned against buildings, sipped Sparks in front of bodegas, strummed guitars on the hoods of cars. Even the dawdling end-of-rush-hour traffic seemed tastefully color-coordinated. It was like hiking through an Urban Outfitters catalog.

Cath, in contrast, walked Manhattan's sidewalks like she was scaling a mountain: head back, center of gravity low, gulping up the pavement in comically huge swallows of steps. Her arms swung at her sides; her tiny hands balled into fists. It was hard to keep up.

"So, is your friend named DJ or is that what he's planning on doing tonight?"

"Cute," she said. And picked up the pace.

"Where are we going?"

"To a bar."

"OK. What makes this bar different from all other bars?"

"Tonight we recline instead of sitting upright." She smiled.

"Ah, Passover humor," I said appreciatively. "I didn't think they made Canadian Jews."

"They do, but I'm not one of them. My best friend in high school was a chosen person."

"Oh, yeah," I said. "Angie Gotbaum."

maybe you shouldn't put all of your life on blast like that on the internet

All of a sudden Cath stopped short and wheeled around into me.

"Look, creepo, I don't mind you knowing lots of stuff about me—well, I do mind, but I can live with it. But you don't have to *prove* that you know me. Not when there's two of you and I barely know either of your asses."

I couldn't think of a response to that, so she spun back around on her heels and took off east on Rivington.

"It's called the Satellite Heart," she said over her shoulder. "It doesn't have a sign. It's awesome."

Natch, I thought to myself. And picked up the pace.

From my early, drunken impressions of it, the Satellite Heart was indeed a bar, and it was also not quite like other bars. For one, it was fucking impossible to find. Located just off an alley that I had never even noticed, just off Rivington, just off Essex, the bar itself was below ground and, as (non)advertised, it did not have a sign. You had to step down a half-flight of metal stairs to reach the unmarked door; all that was visible from the street was the top of a wide window filled with red velvet curtains. At first sight, while my spinning head waited for my pupils to dilate, the Satellite Heart looked like David Lynch's idea of a fortune-teller's studio (minus the gypsy dwarf), but after a moment I could see that the red velvet couches gave way to the more staid exposed brick of the rear wall. The air-conditioning was cool and so was the mood of the place. The music was unobtrusive, the conversation a murmur. It felt a million miles away from the summer sweat of the city street behind us. The bar seemed to have its own curious personality; something throbbed through the place like blood.

The room itself was about double the size of my bedroom, with a handsome wood bar dominating the far wall. The bartender was a broad-shouldered Eastern European–looking man with a thick mustache and a playful grin who seemed to be taking in the atmosphere as he stood there with his thick arms crossed. To the right of the bar was a makeshift DJ booth where a toothpick-skinny black guy was spinning vinyl. It was a remix of a remix of a Rapture song.

"Hey, you!" I turned around with everyone else only to find that the bartender (who did have a rather impressive accent) was yelling at me.

"Yes?" I said, hating the sound of my voice.

"Close the damn door! I pay for the air-conditioning!"

"Oh," I said dumbly. "Right." And slammed it shut behind me. With the traffic noises removed, the hum of conversation from the low couches all around me swelled up to fill the void. I glanced around the room and saw no faces, just types: tight T-shirts, dark suit jackets, tousled bedhead, visible bra straps.

Cath had scampered ahead and was busily conferring with the DJ, who was, it seemed, actually her friend. I walked to the bar and had a seat.

"You," said the bartender.

"Yes?" I said.

"You were raised in—how you say it—a barn?"

"No," I said. "I was raised in Rhode Island."

"Very good!" he said, throwing back his head and roaring with laughter.

I hadn't meant to be funny, but gave an encouraging chuckle. Cath came up behind me and put her hand on my shoulder, which twitched a little at the contact.

"What are you laughing about?" she asked.

"Rhode Island," I said. "I think."

"Oh," she said. "That's funny?"

"Apparently."

"Franta," Cath said to the bartender, who was still wiping tears from his eyes, "this is David."

"Hallo, David!" said Franta. "I am Franta. This is my bar." He rummaged around for a moment before producing a highball glass full of ice and putting it in front of Cath. "You know this girl?"

I started to speak.

"Too well," Cath said.

"Ah!" said Franta, his eyes gleaming. "Very good, very good." He mixed a Tom Collins for Cath and poured it without ever glancing at what he was doing. "David, tonight you are going to drink whiskey."

"I am?" I said.

Cath leaned in close. "Let him choose. Just this first time. That way you get to come back."

I felt like a stranger in my own skin, not to mention my own city.

But I was all the way in now, so I licked my dry lips and nodded.

Franta clapped his hands together and theatrically dropped a single ice cube in a lowball glass. He set it in front of me with a flourish, then produced an unmarked brown bottle from somewhere below the bar.

"This is for you, David. It's very good. Very good!" Franta lifted the bottle high above his head and let it pour all over the lonely ice cube, filling the glass halfway before jerking the bottle back without spilling a single extra drop. "Now: Drink."

I raised the glass to my lips a bit unsteadily and sipped. The whiskey burned and tasted vaguely like licking mossy tree bark. But I felt a flash of warmth shoot through me, in spite of the AC, and I smiled. "Yes," I croaked. "Very good."

Franta clapped his hands again. "You see?"

Cath tugged at my elbow. "Come meet my friend."

"DJ?" I said, and she stuck her tongue out at me.

"David," Franta whispered as I stood up. "I was also not raised in barn. I was raised in Czech Republic!"

As I watched Franta's mustache twitch with mirth, I wondered if laughter was the appropriate response this time, too. Luckily, I didn't have to wonder long; Cath yanked me away and led me behind the DJ booth.

"Andre," Cath said to the skinny black kid as he slid the fader to the left and Wire's "The 15th" started to play, "this is David."

Andre slipped his headphones off. "Hey," he said in a voice far too deep and exhausted for such a small frame. "I know who he is."

"You do?" Cath looked puzzled.

"Sure," said Andre.

"I'm sorry," I said, swallowing another burn of whiskey. "Have we met?"

"Not officially," said Andre, shaking my hand with a grip as loose as a Hilton sister. "But you were really starting to piss me off at the Dark Room the other night."

The warmth of the whiskey was replaced with the arctic freeze of dread.

"I wasn't at the Da—"

Cath cut me off. "What did he do?"

"Kept trying to score off me while I was spinning, and then he wouldn't stop requesting Primal Scream songs. Even when I told him it was hip-hop night."

I felt winded suddenly. And old. "I'm sorry," I said. "I—"

Cath elbowed me in the side. "He hasn't been himself lately."

Andre smiled and lifted his headphones back to his ears. "Hey, it's cool. Who has?"

Cath and I took our drinks to one of the red couches against the wall as Andre segued into Primal Scream's "Miss Lucifer," ostensibly for me. I raised my glass to him in mock tribute and he saluted back. I didn't have the heart to tell him that I didn't even like this song.

Cath lit a cigarette. I glanced at Franta and saw that he was smoking too, so I let it go. I crossed and uncrossed my legs.

"It certainly seems as if you've been getting around," she said.

"It certainly does." I glanced at my glass and noticed that it was already empty.

"Don't worry," Cath said, pushing her hair behind her ears. "We'll fix this."

"We will?" I said, doubtful.

"Sure we will," she said. And smiled, really smiled at me, for the first time. "It's just . . ."

"What?"

"Let me fix something else first," she said, putting her drink down on the floor and rummaging through her bag. "Here we go." She had a bright orange tin of pomade in her hand and she smeared a healthy dollop across both palms.

"What are you doing?" I asked. "Your hair looks fine."

"I know it does, creepo," she said. "But yours doesn't."

She leaned forward and ran the mess through my hair, digging her fingers into my scalp, leaving an electric trail that tingled down to my spine. Her eyes were focused as she twisted and twirled her hands; her face was close to mine, her cheeks smooth. I closed my eyes; the pomade smelled like lemongrass.

After a minute more, she was done. I opened my eyes and saw her lean back with an appreciative look. "Much better," she said. "You're starting to look more like yourself already."

"That's what I'm afraid of," I said as I stood up for another round of drinks.

At the bar, Franta refilled my glass and poured one for himself.

"Nice kid," he said, nodding sagely to himself.

"Who?" I asked. "Cath?"

"Yes, yes. Her. The rest of them. These who walk in now." He pointed behind me and I swung around to see a shoulder bag–slung hipster trio breeze in and make their way over to where Cath was sitting. "They all good kids. So what they play music, make with the cigarettes. All of them, good kids."

"Yeah," I said, digging into my wallet to pay. "Most of them are."

"What about you, David?"

I glanced up. Franta scowled at me.

"What about me?"

"Are you good kid?"

I put some money on the bar. "I try, Franta. I try."

As night fell, the Satellite Heart started to beat faster. Franta let Andre turn the volume up and the dimmers down. The whiskey also had its effect. I found myself talking more, glancing at my watch less. I couldn't seem to remember the world outside of this strange, red little room. And that thought alone made me something close to giddy.

Cath's friends who had shown up were the ones she always referred to in her diary as the VSC. There was her roommate, little Stevie Lau, who wore an electric-blue jumpsuit and vintage Chucks and was Andre's boyfriend—or at least he was this week. There was Debra Silverstein, a hyperactive assistant copy editor at *Vanity Fair* and admitted Anglophile. And there was Ben There, the leader of the crew. He was six foot one and ghostly pale and if it weren't for the rainbow-colored tattoo of a hawk that circled his neck, he'd be indistinguishable from a cadaver, no doubt the victim of a mosh-pit riot he'd incited. Ben There had earned his name for his perpetually jaded attitude and earned his money from his deceased parents. According to

Cath, he slept all day in his Alphabet City loft before rising at six p.m. to eat waffles and play Xbox Live. Then he went out and partied until sunrise. Every night.

"So, David." Ben There smoked theatrically, and everyone shut up at the sound of his voice. "Didn't I see you last night at the Beauty Industry secret show? At the Delancey?"

Cath—long past drunk—let out a high-pitched giggle.

"I don't know," I said. "What was I doing?"

"Running around the dance floor like a great big crazy person, trying to bum a smoke off of every member of the band."

I sighed. "Unfortunately, that's beginning to sound like me, yeah."

Stevie piped up. "How was the show?"

Ben There stubbed out his cigarette, arched his eyebrows sarcastically, and gave Stevie a look.

"Oh," said Stevie.

When Debra began laying out the various options for the rest of the night—a gallery opening in DUMBO, an hour of free Red Stripe at Rothko, a GoGo Bordello show at Barrio—I leaned into Cath and felt a thrill when she leaned back.

"Cath," I said. My breath smelled like whiskey but I didn't care; hers smelled like Parliaments. "I've been meaning to ask you something."

"What is it?"

"What the hell does VSC mean? Does it stand for something?"

Ben There and Stevie announced that the first "part" of the night was up to Debra, but they were not going to miss the *Fader* party that started at three a.m.

"Isn't it obvious?" she giggled again. "They're the Vampire Social Club."

A wolf howl emanated from the couch across from me.

"Sorry!" said Debra, as she reached for her Sidekick and began typing into it frantically. "I have it programmed to make that noise when someone IMs me."

"Cute," I said as the wolf howled again.

These vampire socialites were only a few years younger than me, but I felt like their grandfather. Their very drunk grandfather. I turned back to Cath.

"How did you meet these people?"

"Oh, you know—online, mostly," she sipped her umpteenth drink demurely through a miniature straw. "Ben There used to hang out in the old AOL punk-rock chat rooms and brag about how unpunk the rest of us were, how we didn't know anything. He started liking me because I bought all the albums he told me to, like Indian Summer and Moss Icon."

"Yeah, but how did you, like, *meet him* meet him?"

"Oh, you mean IRL?" She laughed. "In real life? I road-tripped to New York when I was seventeen and stayed with him. My dad thought I was visiting Angie in Quebec."

"Wow," I said.

"Yeah," she said, her eyes shining. "It was pretty wild."

"You had no problem traveling to another country to sleep with some guy you'd never even met?"

She frowned. "Come on, dude—I'd met him. I mean, I *knew* him. Distance doesn't mean shit online, anyway; he was a hell of a lot cooler than the girls at Holy Cross." She sighed and looked at the tall, ghostly figure across from us as he smoked and shot down plan after plan from the other members of the VSC. "I think I knew him better then, really. Before I met him. Online he was just more . . . honest."

Behind us Andre started playing "Burning Photographs," the one Ryan Adams song I legitimately liked. I gave him a one-drink salute, which he returned with a sarcastic flourish.

"So are you really going to set up this meeting for me?"

"What," she said, "the one with yourself?"

"Yeah."

She lit a cigarette. "Yeah, of course. I already texted him about it."

"You did?"

"Yup."

"And what did he say?"

"Nothing." She exhaled a thin stream of ivory smoke. "He just sent me one of those winky emoticons."

I sat back. "Great."

Cath inhaled and her cigarette glowed as red as the room. "You know, for the same person, you two Davids are pretty fucking different."

Ben There leaned forward. "What are you two little birds twittering about?"

Cath blushed. "Nothing. David just wants to get to know himself a little better."

Ben There twisted his mouth. "And you're the person to help him do it?"

Cath stubbed out a half-smoked cigarette. "Maybe. Who the fuck knows." She stood and stumble-stepped to the bathroom.

Ben There watched her until we all heard the click of the bathroom lock. "She's quite the live one, our little Miss Misery."

"Yeah," I said, still looking at the bathroom door. "She's something."

Two minutes later, Cath came rocketing out of the bathroom, cell phone in hand.

"He wrote back again," she said.

I put my latest empty glass down, stopped smiling. "He did? What did he say?"

Cath collapsed on the couch next to me, tossed her phone in my lap. "See for yourself."

I flipped open the phone and looked at the message there.

```
1 New Text Message From: David
9:48 p.m.
Ask David how Amy is doing, would you?
```

I felt sweaty and sick and quickly closed the phone.

"Who's Amy?" said Cath, snatching her phone back.

"She's . . ." My tongue felt thick in my mouth. "She's my girlfriend."

Cath raised one eyebrow. "You guys share a girlfriend and her name is Amy?"

Just the mention of Amy's name in this place, on this night, felt like a stomach punch. I was suddenly sober and my ears were ringing. What the fuck was I doing with these people? In this life? When I still hadn't spoken to the person I loved most?

"Whoever this"—just the words sounded crazy in my throat—

"imposter person is, he definitely does not know my girlfriend."

Cath smirked. "How do you know? I mean, if you look the same, maybe she couldn't tell . . ."

"Stop it," I said.

"Why are you out with me anyway if you have a girlfriend? Shouldn't you be home with her?"

"She's not there."

"Where is she? Canoodling with you number two?"

"Stop. She's in The Hague."

"What the fuck is a Hague?"

"Not *a* Hague. *The* Hague. It's a city. In Europe."

Cath lit another cigarette. "Lucky Amy."

I hated the way her name sounded in Cath's mouth—like something small. Something tiny. Something to be mocked.

I stood up. "I have to go."

Debra looked up from her IM conversation. "You do?"

Ben There smiled lazily. "Better plans?"

"I just . . ." I felt wild standing there, out of control. I felt a thousand pairs of inebriated eyes boring holes into my body. "I just have to go. Nice to meet you all." I tripped slightly over the table, then walked quickly to the door. Behind me, I heard Debra's phone howling at the moon.

"Good-bye, David!" Franta yelled from the bar. "Don't go back to Rhode Island!"

I gave a halfhearted wave in his direction, then shot out and into the night. It felt like walking through an airlock—except that outside wasn't outer space, it was another dimension. The air was humid and thick; people's voices were loud and garish; the headlights of passing taxis seemed luridly yellow. I stood at the top of the steps, feeling my heart race in my chest. Feeling strangely guilty.

The door behind me opened and shut.

"So that's it?"

It was Cath, standing at the base of the stairs. I turned.

"Yeah, that's it. I have to go home."

"Huh." She stood with her arms crossed. She had a flat shine of perspiration on her forehead and flecks of ash on her white shirt.

"I don't know what's going on, Cath. You've been really nice to me. Thanks. But . . . I don't know you. I don't know these people."

She kicked at the metal stair. "I thought you knew me too well."

"Right. Well, one or the other."

We stood looking at each other. I ran my hands through my crinkly, suddenly stylish hair.

"Please set up some sort of meeting for me, Cath. I need to make this stop."

"OK, David." She turned to go. "But I'm not sure that's what you really need." She pulled the door open, and then she was gone.

The bright lights of the F train were making me nauseous, so I rode most of the way home with my eyes closed, pushing hard against the sockets with the heels of my hands until I saw nothing but skittering fireflies. So that was Miss Misery, I thought. No—that was Cath. They were both whirlwinds, but only one was real. And after just one night with her, I felt like the Kansas heartland, post-twister.

"My name is Sonny Payne. I'm homeless and I'm hungry."

I looked up. We were at the Jay Street stop, and Sonny—the oldest and most reliable of the F-train panhandlers—had entered my car and launched into his routine.

"If you don't got it, I understand because I don't got it. But if you could spare some change, some food, a piece of fruit . . ."

When he passed me, this little old black man with the snow-white beard who had been riding the trains with me ever since I moved to this city and would probably remain long after I had moved, I dropped a pocketful of change into his gnarled hand.

"God bless you," he said.

"Get home safe," I said, whatever that might mean.

"You too," he said. And moved on his way.

As I walked up the hill from the subway, I clenched and unclenched my left hand, wishing there was another hand there to fill my own. I loved Amy. I knew that. I thought of her, then: of the hundreds of times we'd made this walk together, what it felt like to laugh with her, sleep next to her, look after her. But below that was another feeling, a newer sensation that ran through my stomach like a zipper. It was the tangible memory of the evening that had just ended, the manic weightlessness of the VSC's world. Of strange new possibilities; of Cath's fingernails on my scalp.

I had wanted this, hadn't I? Recklessly, stupidly. And now I had to deal with it.

Back in my apartment, I deleted two messages from Watkins, drank three glasses of water, took four Tylenol, turned on the air conditioner, and got changed. I felt the early tremblings of a hangover in my skull and behind my eyes. With the lights still out, I flipped on my computer, signed onto Instant Messenger. A window popped open almost immediately.

TheWrongGirl87: hey

davidgould101: hey Ashleigh

davidgould101: what's up?

TheWrongGirl87: um

TheWrongGirl87: tell me what I have to do to have your life again?

davidgould101: :-P

davidgould101: wow

davidgould101: why does everybody want my life all of a sudden!

TheWrongGirl87: ???

davidgould101: Apparently my life is really easy to have—I'm not the only one who has it.

TheWrongGirl87: ???

davidgould101: Never mind. Strange day. What do you mean?

TheWrongGirl87: I cant do it i just cant do it anymore

TheWrongGirl87: its all unfair

TheWrongGirl87: sooooo unfair

davidgould101: what happened

TheWrongGirl87: my parents. they happened.

davidgould101: tell me

TheWrongGirl87: I brought home the lit mag today to show them. I thought that MAYBE if they saw my stuff printed they'd say something

TheWrongGirl87: like compliment me or something

TheWrongGirl87: yeah right

davidgould101: what did they do?

TheWrongGirl87: first? they screamed at me.

davidgould101: why? what poem did they read?

TheWrongGirl87: the one I sent you. 'in blood red.'

TheWrongGirl87: they called me dirty and blasfemous (sp?)

TheWrongGirl87: and they ripped up the whole magazine

davidgould101: no way that's horrible

TheWrongGirl87: it gets worse

TheWrongGirl87: then they called the principal and demanded that all the copies of the mag that were handed out at school get destroyed

davidgould101: :-o

davidgould101: no way

davidgould101: what happened?

TheWrongGirl87: I dunno. im not allowed to leave my room. I guess I'll find out tmw

TheWrongGirl87: its so stupid

TheWrongGirl87: so so stupid

davidgould101: ashleigh I'm really sorry. no one should have that happen. its unfair, but you're almost out of there right? one more year?

TheWrongGirl87: yeah

TheWrongGirl87: I guess.

TheWrongGirl87: I just wish I could have a different life, you know? I want everything to be different and I want it RIGHT NOW

davidgould101: be careful what you wish for.

TheWrongGirl87: why? everything sux. I want to leave.

TheWrongGirl87: yr so lucky you get to write anything

davidgould101: well, not anything

TheWrongGirl87: yeah anything. I wish I had freedom like that. like you.

davidgould101: be careful what you wish for, ashleigh. really.

TheWrongGirl87: darn im not supposed to be online either, here they come TTYL

"TheWrongGirl87 signed off at 11:04 p.m."

Alone again, I thought about checking my diary, but now—with something legitimate to write—I suddenly didn't feel like it. Besides, I didn't want to know what the other me was up to. God knows I'd hear about it soon enough.

There's something else you could do, I heard my brain whisper. You could call your girlfriend. It was a thought. An idea. A plan, even.

But I couldn't bring myself to do it. What would I tell her? What could I possibly say?

Get yourself together, she had told me the night before she left. For me. For both of us. How could I call her and tell her that I couldn't even get *that* right. That instead of pulling myself together, I'd actually completely fallen apart?

With the calming hum of the AC in my ears, I climbed into bed. Better to go to sleep. To prepare for whatever was to come. More than enough had happened already today. Enough for two people.

My phone chirped from the bedside table.

```
1 New Text Message From: Cath
11:14 p.m.
Hey creepo its on. U have a date w yourself. Tmw.
lunch. Dolphin Diner on 10th. High noon. Dont be
late. xoxo.
```

I shut my eyes and buried my face in a pillow. Amy's side of the bed was no longer warm, and I couldn't smell her shampoo anywhere. It was hours before I fell asleep.

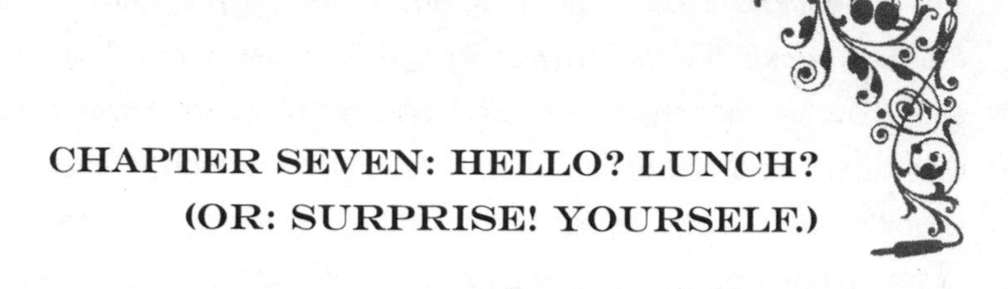

CHAPTER SEVEN: HELLO? LUNCH? (OR: SURPRISE! YOURSELF.)

<YOU HAVE FOUR NEW MESSAGES>

Hey bitch, it's Pedro. You screening your calls? Or do you not have to wake up in the morning now that you live all alone? Ha! Like that's stopping you. Look, dude, just wanted to say it was good seeing you out at that *Fader* party last night, and that chick you were with was super, super cute. Even for a fag like me. I'm glad you're not staying cooped up—and hey, your hair looked good too. Have you been working out? That's not me being queer; that's a compliment! Call me.

<TUESDAY, 9:12 A.M.>

David, it's me. It's really strange that you haven't called. I thought you would miss me. I miss you. . . . I'm on my lunch break and I'm sitting in my apartment here and I'm in another country and I feel like I'm losing you. Why won't you call me? I don't understand.

<TUESDAY, 9:56 A.M.>

Duuuuuude. Where the fuck are you, homes? It's Bryce. Do you know what time it is here in the City of Angels? It's seven in the morning, dude! I don't wake up this early. I don't drink smoothies and I don't go jogging. I don't even know what morning *looks* like. So why am I up? Because I just fielded a call from someone else's girlfriend who is in *Europe* for Chrissakes and is worried about her boyfriend who is either in Brooklyn or in massive denial. Or in the witness protection program. What's going on there, friend? Why is Amy calling *me*? Why are you calling no one? Inquiring minds, dude. What do they do? *They want to know.* OK. I'm going back to sleep.

<TUESDAY, 10:20 A.M.>

David! How's my favorite MIA author? Ha, ha! It's Thom and I—

<MESSAGE HAS BEEN DELETED>

<END OF MESSAGES>

The Dolphin Diner was located on Tenth Avenue in Manhattan in a neighborhood that is slightly between Chelsea and the Meatpacking District—in every possible sense. It was an odd choice for a meeting place—certainly not any location I would have chosen (even though, apparently, I did). I had only ever been there twice myself, and neither time had been intentional. Once was right before moving to the city. I had come down from college to look at apartments and then gone to Penn Station to meet Amy. We had been so excited to see each other that we had walked west instead of east and ended up, hungry and exhausted, on Tenth Avenue. The other time had been a stupid night a year ago when Amy was visiting her parents in St. Louis and Bryce had convinced me to get drunk and take half of a Vicodin he had stolen from his mother's medicine cabinet. It had felt great for about twenty minutes, during which time I had agreed to go into the city with him to some bridge-and-tunnel club on the West Side and watch him flirt with girls. But as we left the subway, I suddenly became overwhelmingly dizzy and almost blacked out on the sidewalk. He basically carried me into the Dolphin, where I had three glasses of water and then took a cab home. Good times.

As I walked out of the C/E stop at Twenty-second Street, I glanced at my watch. It was 12:15—late, but I didn't care. If I really was meeting myself, then wouldn't both of us be late? It was kind of a prerequisite for Gouldian authenticity. The day was sunny but humid, and I felt an unpleasant dampness creeping down my back. The forecast had called for rain and so I—awed supplicant of the Doppler 10,000—was wearing a black rain jacket despite the ample sunshine. Better to be safe than not-sweaty. The people on the wide sidewalks were an odd mix of leggy models and lushy businessmen. None of them carried umbrellas. Secure in my meteorological superiority, I raced from the subway and cut westward along Twenty-second Street, doing my best imitation of a car in a video racing game: tailgating dawdlers, applying an imaginary hand-brake for sudden turns. I was halfway across Ninth Avenue when my cell phone buzzed in my pocket.

```
1 New Text Message From: Cath
12:16 p.m.
Which David is this?
```

Great. Existentialism before lunch.

I cleared a pathway for myself under the shade of an apartment-building awning and typed while I walked.

The real one. Thanks for remembering.

I was waiting for the light at Tenth Avenue two minutes later when my pocket buzzed again.

1 New Text Message From: Cath
12:18 p.m.
Oh. never mind.

Not an auspicious start to the day, I thought as I neared the diner. One never wants to finish second when one is playing with oneself.

The Dolphin—acclaimed and frequented for its painfully hip retro design—is actually the oldest business on its block. To the left of it is the "discount" outlet of an Austrian furniture firm that doesn't believe in couches priced under three thousand dollars—or pillows. To the right of it is a store specializing in nanny-busting video cameras that come encased in stuffed bears. I've often thought that the only reason the Dolphin stays afloat is because half of its customers have been going there for years and the other half think that it might be ironic but are too nervous to ask.

I felt a hiccup of panic in my chest as I pulled open the glass door. Nearly all of the diner's pink vinyl booths were full, which relieved me slightly—I'd learned from spy movies that the hero is never shot when he meets his adversary in a public place—but it also increased the sense that I was being watched. I scanned the tops of the diners' heads, looking for my own. Maybe this diner was a gateway to Bizarro World.

Maybe I had been accidentally (and secretly) cast in a citywide remake of *The Prince and the Pauper.* Or maybe—please, God, maybe, I thought—this was all just a massive mistake.

"One for lunch?" I was at the counter now, and the largest, hairiest man I had ever seen was looking at me from behind a cash register that, underneath his meaty paws, looked like it was made by Fisher-Price. He had a name tag that read STAN, but I didn't believe it. If I had an impersonator, then clearly so did Bluto, Popeye's archnemesis.

"No . . . ," I stammered. "Not exactly. I'm meeting someone."

"Ah," said Stan/Bluto. "Your brother!"

Oh, Christ.

I started to say, "I don't have a brother," but instead I followed Bluto's swollen, carpeted forearm to where it was pointing: the last booth against the far wall, where I was sitting, smiling, waving at me.

I stumbled a little, but caught myself.

"You OK?" Bluto looked genuinely concerned.

"Ah," I said, but my mouth was dry. "Yeah." My voice cracked. "It's just that he's . . ."

The me at the booth was shrugging now, laughing behind his eyes. My eyes.

"I know how it is!" Bluto laughed and clapped me on the shoulder so hard I thought I felt my collarbone buckle.

"You do?"

"Brothers!" He laughed again. "Sometimes they don't get along so good!"

I swallowed hard and made my way down the aisle toward the booth.

• • •

Sitting across the table from yourself isn't anything like looking in the mirror. It should be, but it isn't. Have you ever tried to surprise yourself in a mirror? You can't. It's like trying to tickle yourself—no matter what you do, you always know what to expect. So looking in the mirror becomes, for better or worse, a con job. The best you can do is primp and preen, show off the most flattering views possible of yourself, showcase your finest expressions. We don't look in the mirror to be surprised. We look in the mirror to be reassured.

Which is the exact opposite of sitting across the table from yourself in a crowded diner on a sticky Tuesday, the third day of July. A mirror mimics you. A doppelgänger, however, mocks you.

The person who was sitting across from me *was* me in every appreciable way except reality. We were the same height, the same weight. Had the same shade of brown hair, the same dark brown eyes. We had the same knotty fingers and the same hard chin. We even had the same beard bald spot—a thin line along the left jawbone. We had the same voice, the same vocabulary, the same wave. We even had the same handshake.

"Hello, you," said my doppelgänger.

"Hello, me," I said. And felt like passing out.

The doppelgänger reached across the table and pinched my arm, hard.

"Ow!" I yelled. "Why the fuck did you do that?"

"Because you were wondering just then if you were dreaming, and I thought I'd disabuse you of that notion in the quickest way possible."

I rubbed my arm. It seemed that I was a bit of an asshole.

"So," I said as calmly as possible. "What the fuck is this?"

"This?" he said theatrically. "This is lunch."

I stared at the doppelgänger more closely then and started to make out the differences. For one, there was no way my ears were that big. There was also a hardness in his look that seemed unfamiliar to me. A cruel focus to his eyes, which were ringed by dark, purple circles of exhaustion. His stubble was quickly advancing to the far side of being a beard, and his hair was artfully collapsed and dribbled down the sides of his face in thick sideburns. His shirt was a flimsy white button-down with light blue stripes that looked cheap but was clearly obnoxiously expensive. Worst of all, I had a sneaking suspicion that underneath the table his pants were leather.

"Like what you see?" he asked. "Because I certainly don't."

"Nice," I said. "You need a shave. And some sleep."

"Thanks, Dad," he said.

"And a breath mint wouldn't hurt either. You smell like cigarettes. And rum."

"Kahlúa, actually," he said. "Disgusting, I know, but that's who sponsored that party last night. An open bar is an open bar."

"Who are you?"

"Isn't it obvious that I'm you?" The doppelgänger picked his teeth with a fork.

"No, that's ridiculous. *I'm* me. Where did you come from?"

"Jesus, you haven't gotten laid in a long time, have you?"

"What does that have to do with anything?"

The doppelgänger snorted and rubbed his nose with the back of his hand.

"Hello?" I said, trying to mask the quaver in my voice. "What does that have to do with anything?"

"Man, if you don't know . . ."

A beehived waitress arrived tableside bearing an enormous plate.

"Hey hon, here you go," she said, placing a platter of burger and fries in front of the doppelgänger. She turned to me. "Did you want to order anything? He said you wouldn't mind if he ate first." She paused. "Jesus, you two sure look alike!"

"Um," I said.

The doppelgänger speared a french fry with a knife. "You should get something," he said. "You look skinny."

"So do you," I said.

The doppelgänger winked. I turned to the waitress, who was slowly shifting her eyes from one version of me to the other.

"I'll just have a Coke, please."

When the waitress was gone, the doppelgänger upturned a bottle of ketchup and splashed red all over his plate.

"If you wanted coke, David, you should have just asked me."

I watched him lift the burger to his lips and take a sickeningly large bite. Bloody beef juices ran down his chin.

"Jesus," I said. "Is that a hamburger?"

"Oh, yes," he said, wiping undaintily at his mouth.

"B-but," I stammered.

"What?"

"I'm a vegetarian!"

I realized I had yelled this when all of the tables around us fell silent, knives and forks clattering. Directly behind me, a baby started to wail. I couldn't believe any of this was happening.

The doppelgänger looked around with amusement at the staring faces.

"It's OK, everyone," he said in an affected basso-profundo voice. "We're just working out some differences between us." He winked at me again. I wanted to punch him, but I bruise easily.

Slowly the diner began to hum again as people looked away from our table and back to their own. In the mirror behind the doppelgänger, I caught a glimpse of Bluto at the counter shaking his head sadly, mouthing the word "brothers" to himself.

"Look," I said as calmly as I could manage. "Where did you come from?"

"From you," he said, sounding bored. He hefted the dripping burger again and waved it at me. "You sure you don't want a bite? It's really good."

"Yes. I'm sure."

The doppelgänger shrugged. "You don't know what you're missing."

The waitress returned, dropped a glass of Coke and a straw in front of me, and stomped off in the direction of hungrier tables.

"What do you mean, from me?"

"Look, I don't know how to explain it, buddy." He paused as he chewed and swallowed. "All I know is that if you start creating a better life in your free time, someone's got to hurry up and start living it."

"You mean the diary? My diary?"

"Actually," said the doppelgänger as he reached for my straw, "I think it's more *my* diary." He ripped the straw open with his teeth and positioned it over my Coke. "Do you mind?"

"Go ahead."

"Thanks, chum." He dive-bombed the straw into the glass and drank half of its contents in one long pull. "Ahhh," he said. And belched.

"This can't be happening," I said.

"Oh, but it is." He sat back and smiled smugly. "How's Amy, by the way?"

I felt my blood boil. "Shut up about Amy."

"Why? You certainly have."

"Look, what do you want?"

The doppelgänger crossed his arms behind his head. "Oh, lots of things. Money, power, respect. Clubs to stay open past four a.m. Stalls with more privacy at the Dark Room. A paying DJ gig. Nothing that you can really offer me, though." He gestured at the windows facing the street. "Looks like it's gonna get nasty out there."

He was right. The street—so sunny when I had arrived—had grown dark and ominous. It was not yet one p.m., but it looked like the tail end of a winter evening.

"Good thing you brought a jacket, David." He grinned. "That's the thing about you that I really envy, you know? You're so responsible."

"I wish you'd just leave me alone," I said quietly.

The doppelgänger ignored me and kept talking. "You know? Like you're *so proud* of the fact that you always 'just say no'—like they give an award out for being boring! Or how you've had the same girl-friend since college and never once thought about cheating on her or even trying something new! That's ridiculous! How can you know you're happy with the prize package if you've never even tried for door number two?"

"And what you do is better?" I tried to reign in my temper. "You go out all night, every night? You do whatever drugs exist? You have no purpose, no job, no friends?"

He laughed. "I'm not perfect either, David. But at least the mistakes I make are intentional. Plus, you have to admit I'm having a lot more fun than you are."

I had nothing to say to that.

"Besides, I'm not doing anything that you wouldn't do. Believe me."

"And why's that?"

"Because I'm you!"

"You're not," I said, but I didn't even believe myself.

"I'm you, David. Except I'm the you who does all the things you're too scared to be doing. Like going out. And taking chances. And fucking Cath Kennedy."

"Jesus!" I yelled again. "You're disgusting."

"Am I?"

"Leave her out of this," I said. "She's just a kid."

"Oh yeah," he said, his voice harsh and ugly. "Like you know her all that well."

"And you do?"

"Who do you think she called last night after you bailed on her, David? Who do you think she spent the night with?"

I felt nauseous and sank backward in my seat.

"She likes you fine, David. She told me so. But she *wants* me."

I rubbed my face. Steadied myself on the table. Outside, the street was lit up by a strobe of lightning. People oohed, and the baby behind me resumed shrieking.

"Maybe you should stick to girls on the Internet—or in Europe."

"Fuck you," I said, and slowly stood up.

"You leaving?"

"I'm going to the bathroom. Eat your fucking burger. When I get back, we're going to settle this. Enough is enough."

The doppelgänger laughed and resumed eating. I walked as quickly as I could to the bathroom and locked the door behind me.

When I was a kid growing up in Providence, the upstairs bathroom had been my sanctuary: the one place in my liberal household that had a lock on the door. When I was sad or upset or just seeking some privacy, I would rush into the bathroom with a comic book or a magazine, twist the lock, and spend an hour or so sitting on the floor, leaning against the bathtub, reading. Recharging. This bathroom, however, offered no such relief. It was dank, unair-conditioned, and smelled like Pine-Sol. Half of the ceiling was missing, and pipes and bright pink insulation dangled low above my head. There were fruit flies buzzing lazily around the trash can, which was piled high with discarded towels. I leaned forward against the white sink, ran some cold water, and splashed my face. I looked in the streaky mirror and was half surprised to recognize myself in it. The old me. The real me.

I let the water drip off of my face as my heart throbbed a Rush-style drum solo in my chest. I hated confrontation. I hated fights of any kind—hell, polite disagreements in movies made me uncomfortable. And now I had this in my life? A Freudian breakdown over burgers? What were the possible outcomes of an episode like this? Would I have to arm-wrestle myself for my sanity? Had I lost some sort of galactic bet?

I just wanted to go home.

But the home I had wasn't the one I was imagining. I had three sets of locks on the door of my apartment, but they weren't doing a very good job of keeping me in or the world out. Up until six weeks ago, I had had stability. A life. A partner. But I had frittered it all away. And now I was left with . . . what? A vibrant answering machine, an uncommunicative pigeon in a planter, and a psychotic id rampaging around the city seducing twenty-two-year-olds with my face?

Hell, no.

I reached for a paper towel and rubbed my forehead dry. I needed to put a stop to this. I needed to be the strong one. I glanced in the mirror and almost surprised myself with how tough I looked. Almost.

I took a deep breath, unlatched the door, and crossed the room to the table in long, determined strides.

"Listen," I said as I slid into the seat. "You can't . . ." I stopped.

The other side of the booth was empty. I exhaled and sat back. Where could he have gone? I looked around the diner and didn't spot him. I glanced outside but the rain was pouring down in great diagonal sheets of gray, obscuring everything.

It was then I spied the note on the table. In my own handwriting it said: "Thanks for lunch, pal. Don't get in my way. Oh, and try to stay dry!"

I reached frantically around the bench and then under the table.

The bastard had stolen my rain jacket.

And then my heart leapt up to my throat.

My wallet had been in that jacket.

Fuuuuuck.

This whole exchange has me so confused & intrigued

CHAPTER EIGHT: THE REAL ONE

[from **http://users.livejournal.com /~thewronggirl87**]
Time: 2:19 p.m.
Mood: Miserable :'(
Music: Death Cab for Cutie, "Coney Island"

I think this is the saddest song I have which is just awesome because this is the saddest I've ever been. ::cries::

If I ever have a child I'm never going to yell. Or scream. Or hurt. Because what's the point?

All I did was words and all they said to me was words – so I guess we're even. But I wrote something that tried to be beautiful. ::still crying:: And all they did was try to hurt me.

When my mom yells her voice gets all scratchy and high like a chipmunk record and she throws her hands up over and over like 'how could you have done this to me' like she's so great and perfect and flawless (ha!). And when dad got home from work he started too. He's so big that when he yells he's scary - this vein in his forehead bulges out like he's gonna have a heart attack and he turns purple like the Hulk (no wait the Hulk was green, his pants were purple !! - ::laughs a little then keeps crying::)

very good taste in music

Tonight I was supposed to be seeing Senses Fail and My Chemical Romance in SLC but now I'm not. Apparently now I'm not doing anything except sitting here for a long long time. I HATE THEM SO MUCH!!!

HOW TEEN.

How can you not know your own daughter? Why can't they just let me be who I really am? I can't be who they want. They have one daughter like that already - Jessie is so perfect it makes me want to puke all over myself. I should probably just leave and let them get on with raising their real little angel. All I do is take things that are perfect and make them ugly. And everything that I find beautiful makes them sick. ::sobs:: I used to hate myself but now I know better. Now I just hate them.

I just threw a thing of lip balm across the room but it didn't shatter. I think I just dented the perfect white wall instead.

I don't fit in here. I tried. I'm going to be EIGHTEEN FREAKING YEARS OLD and it's still not good enough. No matter how much I try to bend and hide something always ends up sticking out and breaking something. Ruining everything.

I have to change: me, my life, my world. Anything, really. I have to see what it's like on the other side of this screen.

I think I have to go away.

"MzMisery signed on at 7:13 p.m."

davidgould101: HEY.

MzMisery: Hello?

davidgould101: It's David Gould.

davidgould101: The real one.

MzMisery: Oh hey

davidgould101: Yeah hey.

MzMisery: How was lunch?

davidgould101: What do you think?

MzMisery: I dunno. That's why I asked.

davidgould101: IT'S A FUCKING DISASTER THAT'S WHAT IT WAS.

MzMisery: whoa

MzMisery: no need to shout

davidgould101: really? there's no need to shout?

davidgould101: I'm living some lost episode of the fucking twilight zone

davidgould101: and you think I should LOWER MY VOICE?

MzMisery: . . .

davidgould101: fine ok sorry

davidgould101: thanks for telling me that you're still seeing him

MzMisery: who?

davidgould101: the OTHER ME

MzMisery: oh

MzMisery: him

MzMisery: yeah . . . sorry. it's just that he can be pretty persuasive.

davidgould101: I'll bet

MzMisery: he's a fun guy. look, I don't know what's going on! this is a weird city!

davidgould101: he's a total asshole!

MzMisery: he's not that bad

davidgould101: HE STOLE MY WALLET

MzMisery: LOL

MzMisery: really?

davidgould101: yes really!

MzMisery: whoa

MzMisery: what do you think he's doing with it?

davidgould101: from what little I know of him I imagine he's making both the salesmen at Barneys and the entire nation of Colombia extremely happy.

davidgould101: with my money

davidgould101: jesus

MzMisery: LOL

davidgould101: it's not funny cath

MzMisery: sorry.

MzMisery: look what do you want me to do about it?

davidgould101: I want you to stay away from him

MzMisery: why???

davidgould101: because he's some sort of supernatural asshole! because you can't trust him!

MzMisery: and I can trust you?

davidgould101: of course

MzMisery: you're the same person creepo!

davidgould101: please. we're not the same person.

MzMisery: you are totally the same person. neither of you will leave me alone!

davidgould101: . . .

MzMisery: I didn't sign up for this, dude

davidgould101: I know

davidgould101: neither did I

MzMisery: well maybe if you weren't so repressed all the time, none of this would be happening

davidgould101: oh, I'm repressed

MzMisery: um, hello? yes!?

davidgould101: this is great

davidgould101: you're just a kid!

MzMisery: yeah well yr just a grumpy old man

MzMisery: and besides, if I'm just a kid why were you so obsessed with me anyway?

davidgould101: I was not "obsessed" with you

MzMisery: that's not what you #2 says!

davidgould101: what he's TALKING about me now? fuck!

MzMisery: it's cool. it'd actually be kind of sweet if it wasn't so creepy!

davidgould101: cath please stop seeing him. he has to be stopped.

MzMisery: I dunno

MzMisery: what are you going to do for me in return?

davidgould101: I don't know. anything. I just want my life back.

MzMisery: I'll think about it. honest I will.

MzMisery: but I have to run

davidgould101: wait

davidgould101: are you seeing him tonight?

MzMisery: . . .

davidgould101: christ are you going to meet him NOW?

MzMisery: look I said I'll think about it but I'm not going to change my plans just like that

MzMisery: not for the version of you that suddenly is too scared to talk to me face to face

davidgould101: no no!

davidgould101: wait—I'll meet you. I'll do whatever. honest.

MzMisery: maybe . . .

davidgould101: please, just tell me where to go.

MzMisery: whoops! gotta run!

davidgould101: no! wait! is he there? don't go.

MzMisery: TTYL!

davidgould101: jesus! stop! don't go with him! and DON'T LET HIM SPEND ANY MONEY!

"MzMisery signed off at 7:21 p.m."

davidgould101: dammit.

I was sitting in my apartment with all of the lights out, staring at my computer screen, at the window where Miss Misery had just been. I was in my underwear, as my clothes were still completely drenched from my miserable post-lunch journey home. The thunderstorm had been ferocious, with rain that hammered the pavement like hailstones, leaving scores of people huddling under bus stops and awnings, flinching with each deafening clatter and roar that came booming from the sky. I had tried to stick to the sides of buildings, but the wind was blowing the rain at impossible angles; I was soaked through before I had even crossed the avenue. To get on the subway, I had had to borrow sixty-five cents from a red-haired girl with freckles and a Hello Kitty umbrella. Look on the bright side, I kept saying to myself as the water in my hair dripped down my face: At least you always keep your house keys in your pants pocket.

The storm had ended now and the sky was clearing, but I could still hear sirens in the distance, ferrying able men to trouble spots where they would soon be hard at work picking up the pieces of trees that had been forcefully removed from their rightful perches—

no doubt restoring electricity and cable service; restoring order.

I wished that one of the sirens could have rushed to my aid, but there was no knock at the door, no helpful call from the street below. In that numb moment, I would have settled for that infuriatingly chipper painter from earlier in the summer, or that damn bird in the herb garden. Heck, I would have even answered the phone.

But for once it didn't ring. I was alone, outdated, replaced. David Gould 2.0 was out running the streets now, taking over the city in a way I would never have dreamed. He had my money, my ID, my momentum. Heck, he even had the fantasy girl I wasn't even sure if I wanted. It was, in the words of Ben Grimm, a rather revolting development.

In the ghostly half-light of my dim office, I wondered if this was the end of the me that I had known. I felt my anger fading, along with my resolve and maybe the rest of me as well. I felt shimmery, indistinct. What if my boring, insignificant life was in the end no different from *Highlander*, that stupid movie with Sean Connery in a ponytail? What if there really could be only one?

Just then my laptop chimed like a bell, saving me from further self-pity or marginal film comparisons.

TheWrongGirl87: you there?

davidgould101: hey ashleigh.

TheWrongGirl87: hey

TheWrongGirl87: don't you want to know what happened today?

davidgould101: absolutely I do!

TheWrongGirl87: well you didn't ask!

davidgould101: oh. you mean with you. yeah, I want to know.

TheWrongGirl87: :-/

TheWrongGirl87: well I'm grounded again.

TheWrongGirl87: actually grounded for something I wrote. the only time I'm allowed out of the house for the foreseeable future is this weekend when I'm supposed to go on some stupid "potential applicant" visit to BYU.

davidgould101: god, that's horrible.

TheWrongGirl87: I dunno, BYU is supposed to be pretty nice.

davidgould101: no, I meant the grounding part

TheWrongGirl87: oh.

TheWrongGirl87: yeah. it sucks.

davidgould101: you should never get punished for something you wrote—or something you created. that's not fair at all.

TheWrongGirl87: yeah, well, tell that to my parents. they're freaking out. my mom doesn't even want me to hang out with my sister anymore. she's afraid I'll, like, 'ruin' her too.

TheWrongGirl87: I would do anything to get out of here. you know I said my parents were calling the principal

davidgould101: yeah

TheWrongGirl87: well he told them about the

other thing that happened—with the pictures?

davidgould101: what pictures?

TheWrongGirl87: I told you all about this!

davidgould101: I'm sorry . . . I've been a little bit all over the place

TheWrongGirl87: :-P

TheWrongGirl87: I took these pictures of Krystal—my best friend? when she just found out she was pregnant. and so she was crying and had mascara streaked on her face and some on her wrist. and I entered them into the photo exhibit at school. and when her bitchmom found out about them she showed up in the middle of the day and ripped them all down then tried to get me suspended. said I made her daughter look suicidal.

davidgould101: wow

TheWrongGirl87: it's like: newsflash lady! she WAS suicidal!

TheWrongGirl87: but whatever, I got out of it because I get good grades and they didn't tell my parents

TheWrongGirl87: but now it's out of the bag

TheWrongGirl87: they just hate the idea of me having my own thoughts you know? I'm a dark person and everything here is really really light. they refuse to admit who I actually AM.

davidgould101: uh huh

TheWrongGirl87: it's like there are two of me.

the perfect girl that used to have pigtails and is going to be a rich doctor and the me that I am now.

davidgould101: this sounds familiar

TheWrongGirl87: oh did you read my LJ from this afternoon? :-(

davidgould101: no I just mean it sounds familiar to me too

TheWrongGirl87: why? you're awesome

davidgould101: no I'm not

TheWrongGirl87: yeah you are you're like the coolest guy I know. you've got the perfect life

davidgould101: I wish

TheWrongGirl87: well at least yr not grounded

TheWrongGirl87: if there's something wrong you can go and fix it

davidgould101: yeah you're right

TheWrongGirl87: see? :) I got all the answers.

davidgould101: so what do you do if people have the wrong impression of you? if you want them to know who you really are?

TheWrongGirl87: yr asking me?

davidgould101: yeah I am

TheWrongGirl87: I'm just a kid!

davidgould101: so's everybody

TheWrongGirl87: well

TheWrongGirl87: I think you gotta go out and shake people up. if they think yr somebody else, prove 'em wrong. grab that person that they have fixed in their heads and kill him dead!

TheWrongGirl87: LOL

davidgould101: huh

davidgould101: you might be onto something

TheWrongGirl87: yeah? cooool

TheWrongGirl87: well I'm glad I helped you. what about me?

davidgould101: what about you?

TheWrongGirl87: hello? I'm the miserable emo kid here not you.

davidgould101: ha. right

TheWrongGirl87: I can't put up with them anymore or living in this house

davidgould101: well don't do anything rash

TheWrongGirl87: my eyes are sore from crying. they're all puffy. bleh.

davidgould101: I'm sure you look fine.

TheWrongGirl87: yeah?

davidgould101: seriously, ashleigh, the biggest difference between living at home and going out into the world is TIME. because when you're stuck at home you can't imagine there ever being a point when life isn't just like it is now. but it gets different, honest it does.

davidgould101: it gets better.

TheWrongGirl87: I dunno

TheWrongGirl87: they just have everything planned out for me, you know? nothing is ever gonna change.

TheWrongGirl87: I kind of thought I could try something else. I was going to tell you about it.

davidgould101: yeah? I'd like to hear it. but look. I'm sort of in the middle of something and I think you just gave me some good advice on how to finish it.

TheWrongGirl87: oh.

davidgould101: why don't you find me later? or tmw?

TheWrongGirl87: yeah . . . tomorrow.

davidgould101: ok, tomorrow. seriously thanks—hang in there. I'm sure it's not that bad!

"davidgould101 signed off at 7:49 p.m."

The seventeen-year-old on the other side of the country was right. I wasn't grounded. I wasn't in trouble unless I let myself be. If there was another me running around, it was time for him to find out who the boss was. It was time to go out.

I stood up and nearly tripped over a pile of CDs. I still wasn't wearing any clothes. OK, change of plan: It was time to get dressed. *Then* it was time to go out.

A few minutes later, racing down the stairs, clothed and anxious, I almost bowled over Mrs. Armando, who was standing in the dark hallway with her arms crossed.

"David," she said sternly, "you forget about somethin'?"

My brow furrowed as I racked my brain for some sort of plausible answer.

"Probably a lot of things, Mrs. Armando," I said, trying to mask the panic in my voice.

She tut-tutted under her breath.

"It's July, David, whole new month." She said "month" like "munt."

"Oh!" I slapped my head. "Rent. I'm sorry, Mrs. Armando. I guess I did forget. I'll get it to you first thing tomorrow."

"I don't know," she said as she slowly made her way through the dark toward her apartment. "Ever since Amy leaves, I don't know where you're at!"

You're not the only one, I thought as I raced out of the door and into the steamy night.

In my pocket I had all of the dollar bills and change I had found on my dresser and under my couch. I had my passport for identification and my iPod for a soundtrack. I also had the "emergencies only" credit card that my parents had given me when I had moved to New York. I had never used it, because this was the first time I had ever felt like I was experiencing an emergency.

In my head, in addition to a nonlocalized state of panic, I had the voices of the bank operators from a few moments before telling me that I did not have the authority to cancel my cards, as I had just recently called them and told them that they were to ignore me if I called back and told them to cancel everything. It seemed that in addition to my wallet, my pride, and my PIN, the doppelgänger had the most important tool of all in the world of telephone finance: my mother's maiden name. Bastard.

I was wearing my "fancy" jeans—that's what Amy called them, as they were the expensive and pre-scuffed pair I had bought in a fit of confidence one weekend the previous winter when she had been away. My standard-issue jeans were hanging in the shower, still drying from the complete soak they'd received on the way home from the diner this afternoon. I was also wearing a plain dark-green T-shirt—one of the few in my collection that didn't pimp for a criminally underappreciated indie-rock band on its front. These would be my work clothes for the night: I was on assignment again at last. Except that this wasn't an interview; this was a manhunt. I was going undercover. I was going to the Lower East Side. To prove my commitment to the mission, I had even pushed a dollop of Amy's product through my hair in an attempt to recreate the flickering hipness that Cath Kennedy had given me the night before.

Other than that, though, I had no plan, no confidence, and only a sputtering hold on my identity. I was—like thousands of post-college young people every year—going into the heart of Manhattan *to find myself.* The thought alone would have made me laugh if I hadn't felt like crying.

The sky was burning a dark shade of orange over Fifth Avenue as I walked briskly down the street toward the subway. The clouds were almost gone, and now the sun was dying. The sidewalks had dried from the afternoon's thunderstorm, but I could hear the rainwater continuing to pour down the drains by the curb. Tomorrow was trash day in the neighborhood, and the overflowing cans that marked my walk were ripe with a sickeningly sweet aroma. I raised my hand to my face and smelled that instead—warm and salty and, thankfully, familiar.

Down the hill, at the intersection of Fourth Avenue and Ninth

Street, Latino vendors were selling homemade popsicles and Ziploc bags full of sliced fruit out of the backs of navy-blue vans. The check-cashing spot hummed with activity, and the traffic, inching forward in both directions, was continuous. The F stop there was above ground, and after swiping my Metrocard I took the stairs two at a time and then hurried toward an empty spot near the end of the platform. It felt strange to stand still; my heart felt like it was about to cannonball out of my chest. I kicked at the ground and tried to slow my breathing.

It was possible to see the Statue of Liberty from where I stood, its familiar outline sheathed in the embers of the setting sun. Up here the air—an awkward marriage of exhaust and barbecue—somehow smelled cleaner, less heavy. For the first time that day I let my shoulders relax. God knows how many evenings I had stood in the same spot, seeing the same sights, hearing the tracks click and switch below me, smelling the air. And yet it still made me smile. New York was a beautiful city—you just had to have a different definition of beauty to appreciate it.

Eventually, the F train rumbled around the corner, out of the tunnel, and into the fading light, twisting and shrieking to a halt. I boarded a halfway full car and took a seat on the far side, away from the evening glare, up against the panel that separated the bench from the doorway. When I had first moved to Brooklyn, the F train had been my nemesis, always choosing my prime traveling times to stop running, to go express, to magically metamorphose into an entirely different train—a G, maybe, or an A. I quickly became bitter and mocked the train at length to Amy and my other friends; I became convinced that it was out to get me, that it knew the times I was in a hurry, the plans I had painstakingly made, and that it intentionally—no, maliciously—disrupted them. If I was ever out late on a weeknight, it would torment me by teasing me with lights in the distance of the tunnel that would upon arrival turn out to be mysterious cousins of the F that didn't even take passengers and that may or may not have been entirely mythological: a money train, or a windowless series of cars lined with lockers, or a yellow, stinking procession of emptied city Dumpsters. On weekend nights the F would cease servicing the stops I frequented—often without explanation. On Sundays it would make an appearance maybe once every half hour. In the summer it would break the air-conditioning in the car I was riding in. Year-round it would shut its doors in my face.

If the New York subway was the vibrant circulatory system of a living city, then the F train was, to me, a blocked artery.

Until, of course, I chilled out for a minute and allowed myself to learn something important: Your local subway doesn't have to be your friend; it just has to be respected. Despite my litany of complaints, the F had done a pretty good job of getting me home (eventually), and it had certainly provided me with a generous supply of anecdotes. The F, I had come to realize, didn't have to be an object of scorn or derision. It was more like the Mets—a lovable loser. More than that, it was *my* lovable loser. It was like an infuriating but irresistible friend or a quirky uncle: It was irrefutably in my life, and, surprisingly, when I returned to New England and the universe of cars for vacations or visits, I kind of missed it. But here's the crazy part: After that first year, I swear the F began to love me back. No longer did it transform itself mid-ride or not show up when I needed it. Sure, it occasionally ran express on weekends—but who among us doesn't? No, once I started being good to it, the F train started being good to me.

Which was, I thought—as I settled into my seat, pulled my iPod from my pocket, hung my headphones on my ears, and began fiddling with the dial in search of a good soundtrack to the strange night ahead—a pretty good metaphor for life in New York in general. There was a lesson to be learned in the frustrating quirks and vagaries of all aspects of city living, of the profound uncertainty of security alerts and armed guardsmen on street corners, of not knowing where your next paycheck was coming from, where your girlfriend was, or what drugs your friends might be doing in the bathroom. The lesson: Don't fight it. Fighting just points out the dissonance, the difficulty, the anger. It brings out the worst in people. Fighting made my heart beat too quickly in my chest, the volume of my voice rise to dangerous levels in public places. It was better to keep moving, to adapt. To deal with it. This was, I realized, the mantra that was ringing in my ears as the train approached Carroll Street and dipped its long silver head back below ground: Deal with it.

So I had a doppelgänger. That's OK. Some people had desk jobs or ponytails or tumors or jury duty. They'd dealt with them and so would I. That's what you did as a freelancer in New York. As a twentysomething. As a suddenly single person. You dealt with it.

My thumb spun the click wheel on my iPod until it settled on what I was looking for, a spindly pop song by Longwave called "Tidal Wave." I thought it was about getting pulled under by things out of your control and liking it. As I sped toward the city, I certainly hoped I was right.

CHAPTER NINE: DOESN'T THAT MEAN, LIKE, FLEXIBLE?

I CLIMBED THE STEPS and came aboveground on the south side of Houston Street, right where First Avenue becomes Allen. The sun was almost entirely gone now, but its heat seemed to have permeated the neighborhood. It was the day before a holiday—an extra weekend night!—and so the people scampering to beat blinking DON'T WALK signs had the manic energy of criminals or any other ne'er-do-well who had somehow pulled a fast one and gotten away with it. It had been some time since I had been out on a night like this, and I steeled myself before crossing the street. My iPod clicked over to "Victim of the Crime," a rhythmic track by a French band called Phoenix. As I fell into the flow of people on the cramped sidewalk in front of the falafel joint, I started to feel a hum in my legs, a buzzing in my head. I bobbed and weaved through an idling crowd of bridge-and-tunnelers, sped through a worry of crones. There was a beat to this sort of thing: walking the streets, surfing the crowd. An urban metronome that takes over your internal steering. I was good at it, I remembered now: cutting to the outside to avoid dawdlers, making empty parking spaces in the street my personal old-person passing lane. I even noticed a smile flirting with the corners of my mouth.

The positivity lasted about as far as the Mercury Lounge, on the corner of Houston and Essex. By the time I got there, reality had smacked me back: I didn't really have a destination. I was all fired up, with literally nowhere to go. I paused, then receded and let the pedestrian traffic overtake me. There was a line in front of the Mercury, and I did my best to make it clear that I wasn't cutting it.

Suddenly I felt a tap on my shoulder. I pulled my headphones from my ears and spun around.

Jack was standing right behind me, arms crossed, smile wide. "Fancy meeting you here," he said.

I shook his hand. "What's up?"

"You tell me, homey." He jammed his hands into his pockets. "From what I hear, you're quite the party-starter these days."

"That's what they tell me," I said, but tried to smile back.

"You here for the band?"

I shook my head. "Who's playing?"

"Some hardcore act from Boston. Crash Activated. Kind of derivative but the singer is supposed to be insane."

"Doesn't really sound like my thing," I said, and tried to check my watch surreptitiously. "Is Pedro with you?"

Jack looked surprised. "I though he was hanging out with you tonight."

I tried to play it cool. "Oh, yeah?"

Jack didn't blink. "Yeeeah."

"Well," I said, trying the words out in my mouth, "that's later."

"Ah," he said. His eyes were laughing.

I hit him on the arm. "What?"

"Nothing, dog!" He raised his hands in surrender. "It's just *you.* You've been holding out on us."

"Honestly," I said. "I haven't."

"Sure," he said. "It's just that . . ."

"What?"

"When wifey's away, the mouse will play . . . with lots of kitties, apparently."

I shook my head.

"C'mon, David!" Jack threw his arm around my shoulder. "It's cool! Are you smiling or blushing?"

I honestly wasn't sure. "I gotta go, Jack."

He pulled his arm away. "You meeting someone?"

I put my headphones back over my ears. "Looking for someone, actually."

"Anyone I know?"

I paused. "I don't know. I hope not."

"All right, then." He gave me a pound. "Peace. Let me know next time you're throwing one of your parties!"

I shook my head a final time, pressed PLAY on my iPod, and walked around the corner as quickly as I could.

A block down Essex Street, an idea began to form in my head. I pulled my cell from my pocket and texted Pedro as I walked:

```
Hey dude, I'm in the city. What's the plan?
```

I was headed southeast with the vague goal of finding the Satellite Heart, hoping that maybe—just maybe—Cath would be there. With *him.* Of course, what I would do with them when I found them was still a mystery.

I turned left onto Rivington and paused. The block was packed, with hordes of smokers gathered on opposite sides, clustered in front of rival bars—one group in front of the Magician on the north side and one in front of Welcome to the Johnsons on the south. The groups were nearly identical, yet they were glaring at each other across the street like metrosexual Jets and Sharks. I pushed past them on the north side (my allegiance, however flimsy, had always been with the Magician) and paused to look around. This was where Cath had led me the day before, but I couldn't seem to remember where the bar actually *was.* I spun around and got bumped and jostled on both sides by handbag-carrying Condé Nast types giggling and smoking en route to a birthday party. Across the street there was a tiny sandwich shop. I turned around again, still hoping to spy something familiar. It was only when I considered clicking my heels together that I noticed it. Just next to the sandwich shop (which was, it turned out, actually called the Tiny Sandwich Shop), obscured by a Dumpster, was the unmarked alley. I shot across the street—just narrowly avoiding a speeding cab—and into the alley. There it was: the metal steps down, the red velvet curtains. The Satellite Heart. I jammed my iPod and headphones in my pocket, ran my hand through my hair, and stepped down into the bar.

"You again!"

Franta threw his hands up in the air dramatically when he saw me enter. The mood of the place was the same as it had been the day before—hushed, intimate, glowing—but the music was not. Rubbery bass lines bounced off my eardrums, and I could feel the crack of the snare in the small of my back. I recognized the rapper's voice—it was Freeway—but not the beat. The DJ—hunched low over the turntables, desperately scratching some musical itch—was definitely not Andre. It was a small, bespectacled white kid whose red hair ran wild under a Detroit Tigers cap.

"Hello, Franta," I shouted over the music as I approached, scanning the couches for familiar faces. I spied plenty of beautiful young black-haired girls seated close to skinny guys with too much product in their hair, but not the two I was looking for.

"So," Franta bellowed as I took the stool in front of him. "You going to be polite this time?"

"What?" I yelled. "When was I not polite?"

The DJ segued smoothly into another bass-heavy track, this one by Cam'ron.

"Before!" Franta leaned in. "You come in here with girl; I say, 'hello, David!' And you don't say anything to Franta, sit all the way over there"—he pointed to the couch closest to the entrance—"and you make *girl* get you drinks."

"Oh," I said as Cam'ron's juvenile rhymes echoed around my skull: *God damn you / Cam'll blam blam you / Van Damme you / ram-a-lam-a-flim-flam you.* "I'm sorry, Franta. That's not like me."

"No problem," he said, clapping me on the shoulder. "Sometime you have to act funny with girl . . . and sometime girl make you act funny!" He chortled with laughter. "So," he said, composing himself, "what you doing now?"

"I'm looking for someone," I shouted. "Cath—that girl who brought me here yesterday. Have you seen her?"

"No, no," he said. "Not today. Nice girl, that one." He rummaged underneath the bar for a glass. "Here—if you look for someone, you gonna need some vodka." He scooped two ice cubes into the glass, then filled it nearly to the brim with Stolichnaya. "Detectiving is hard work. You want lime?"

I looked at the straight liquor in front of me and felt my stomach lurch. "Um," I said. "Yeah, I'd better take one."

He nodded and squeezed a wedge into the glass.

Cam and Santana / hit you with a bow hammer / send you back to Atlanta / with a glass of Fanta / banana-fana-fo-fana . . .

I glanced over at the DJ and watched him stab the air with his hands on every downbeat. Underneath his cap, he mouthed each lyric. Franta saw where I was looking and let out a hiss of disgust.

"This guy!" He gestured wildly in the direction of the DJ. "He think he is black rapper! I don't need this in my life." He shook his head sadly. "Usually have good kids in here, play rock and roll—who cares? Franta is a hip guy, you know! I like Velvet Underground! You know"—he sang loudly and off-key—"'it so cold in Alaska!' But this stuff." He pointed over again with his thumb. "'Hoo-hah, hoo-hah.' Who wants to give a few shits. You know?"

"Yeah," I said. "It is kinda loud."

Franta scrunched up his face. "What you say?"

I yelled again, "IT'S VERY LOUD!"

Franta stepped back. "What you yell for? I know it's loud." He pushed the drink toward me. "Here. Drink. Makes music quieter in brain."

I lifted the glass carefully, watching the clear liquid splash against the rim. Oh well, I thought. You've got to start sometime. I took a tentative sip. The vodka burned, icy and peppery, in my throat. I coughed and put the glass back down. I glanced up at Franta, embarrassed, but he was still looking at the DJ with something between horror and disgust registering on his broad face.

"I need new kid with records," he said. "And quickly."

I was choking down my second full sip of vodka when my phone buzzed in my pocket.

```
1 New Text Message From: Pedro
8:18 p.m.
"I dunno baby—don't you have to go on soon?"
```

What the hell could that possibly mean? Had my doppelgänger taken up summer stock? Would he soon be starring in a drug-addled Off-Off-Broadway production of *Pippin*? I was lost in thought when Franta put his meaty hand on my shoulder.

"David," Franta said wearily. "You like the music, right? In general?"

"Yeah, Franta," I said. "I like the music."

"You wanna come play it here some nights? I used to have nice kids like you do it. I can't take no more of this one. He make me sick in the head."

"Really?" I was actually pretty excited at the prospect. "Yeah, definitely. I'd love to. Thanks!"

"Is nothing," he said, and reached for the brown whiskey bottle. "For Franta this is matter of survival."

The thundering beats lifted for a precious moment while the DJ wrestled with the fader, and I lifted my drink to toast Franta. As I did so, I distinctly heard a wolf howl from somewhere behind me. I wheeled around on my stool and scanned the bar. Sure enough, there on one of couches against the far wall sat Debra Silverstein with a vodka cranberry in one hand and her Sidekick in the other, furiously texting into it with her thumb.

"Excuse me, Franta," I said. "I see someone I know."

He waved me off, and I picked up my drink and walked over to where Debra sat. She was wearing a tight black skirt and a black vintage Duran Duran tour T-shirt that was artfully ripped around the collar and at least two sizes too small for her ample chest. On her sleeve were two pins, one that said THE KILLERS and one that said I MADE OUT WITH ULTRAGRRRL. I stood directly over her, but she didn't seem to notice.

"Mind if I join you?"

She looked up with a start. "Oh! Hey! Sure!" She motioned to a spot next to her on the couch, then resumed typing.

I sat and took a drink while wolf howls filled the air between us.

"Sorry," she said. "Just figuring something out."

"That you have lycanthropy?"

She didn't look up. "What?"

"Nothing. Never mind."

I sat for a while and sipped; with the ice partly melted the drink wasn't nearly as strong. I watched Debra's thumb dance across the microscopic keyboard. A chorus of wolves bayed at the moon. I began to think that it would take a silver bullet to get this girl's attention for more than six seconds. Then, with a start, she snapped the Sidekick shut and turned to me.

"So!" she said. "Hey!"

"Hey, yourself."

"What are you doing here?" She sipped her vodka cranberry delicately through a tiny straw.

"I'm looking for Cath, actually. Have you seen her?"

"No, not tonight," she said, fiddling with her hair. "I was supposed to but I think I'm just gonna have one more drink then head home. I have to go to my parents' this weekend."

"Oh, yeah?"

"Yeah. My little sister is getting bat mitzvahed on Saturday."

"Mazel tov," I said. "Where's home?"

"Jersey," she said, rolling her eyes. "Kearny."

"Isn't that where My Chemical Romance is from?"

She nearly choked on her drink. "Holy shit, how do you know that?"

I laughed. "I have a friend who loves them."

"Holy shit," she said again. "I love them too. They're killer."

I nodded. Then she nodded back. So I nodded again. Then she nodded. It could have gone on all night if the wolf hadn't resumed howling.

"Sorry!" she said. "One sec!" She flipped open the Sidekick and started mashing buttons with her thumb.

"Sure," I said. "Gotta feed the dog."

"Ha, ha," she said, typing. "What?"

"Nothing," I said. "So, do you have any idea where she might be?"

Howl. Type. Howl. Type.

"Who?" she said, not listening to me.

"Cath," I said, patiently.

She laughed at something that appeared on her screen. "Oh," she said. "No. No idea! Sorry!"

"Right," I said. Back up by the bar the red-haired DJ wrapped up his Cam'ron set and launched into something even louder and vaguely crunk.

Debra snapped the Sidekick shut again and turned to me. I had a strong urge to grab it and drown the wolf to death in her vodka cranberry, but I resisted.

"God," she said. "Could the music in here suck any harder?"

"Probably," I said. "Give it time."

She rolled her eyes.

"Debra," I said, "could you do me a favor?"

"Totally," she said sweetly, sipping through the straw.

"Could you text Cath and ask where she is?"

Debra frowned. "Why don't you text her?"

I sat back. "Because I want to surprise her. You know how she is."

A devilish look came into Debra's round brown eyes. "Totally!" She flipped open her Sidekick again and thumbed out a message. It seemed that Debra really did know how Cath was—which was good because that made one of us. "She'll write back quick," she said. "She always does."

I killed off my vodka. Maybe things were looking up.

"Thanks, Debra," I said.

"So." She took another sip and leaned into me. "How come I've never seen you at Sorted?"

I shook my head. "What's that?"

"What's that?" she scoffed. "It's the party I throw every week! Carlos from Interpol spun last time, and before that was James Iha. And next time is the chubby guy from Franz Ferdinand!"

"Wow," I said with as much sincerity as I could muster.

"Yeah," she purred happily, "it's awesome. You should come! I'll stamp your hand and you can drink free Amaretto Sours until one a.m.!"

I gagged a little at the thought but tried to smile politely. I was trying to think of something productive to say when a howl interrupted me. I'd never been so relieved to hear the wolf. Debra scanned the message and looked back up at me.

"This doesn't make any sense."

"What?" I asked.

"She says she's watching you DJ."

"Me? Where?"

"The Madrox." Debra scrunched up her eyes and looked suspiciously at me. "How could you be here if you're DJing there?"

"Ah," I stammered. "Well . . ." I was interrupted by a thunderous crash from the bar that caused the record-player needle to leap entirely off the wax, blanketing the room in deafening silence. I turned around. The DJ was nowhere to be seen. Franta stood in his usual spot but with a look of terror on his face. He was staring straight down.

"What the hell?" said Debra.

I jumped up and ran over to the bar. Franta stood, frozen.

"Oh my, oh my," he said. "Franta is gonna get sued this time."

"What the hell happened?" I asked.

"David," Franta said without looking up. "David, you are witness.

I say I hate rapping music but I don't hate red-haired boy! Red-haired boy is OK with Franta!"

I heard a low groan of pain from behind the bar. I propped myself up with my hands and peered over the row of glasses toward Franta's feet. The trapdoor to the basement was open but the basement light was off, making the gaping hole in the floor nearly impossible to see unless you were looking for it. Lying in a heap on the wood stairs that led down was the red-haired DJ. He was conscious but not moving. He groaned again.

"Ryan!" Franta said to the DJ. "Why you gotta come back here when I'm working! Why you gotta fall through the floor like that!"

Ryan let out a low moan. "I needed something from my bag," he said slowly.

Franta knelt down. "What you need so badly?"

Ryan spoke softly and carefully, as if volume would finish the job on his spine that the stairs had started. "The new . . . Ghostface . . . record!"

"You almost die for this!" Franta said, slapping his forehead. "You almost die for black rapper!"

I figured now was as good a time as any to make my exit.

"Thanks for the drink, Franta," I said. "I'm gonna go."

But he didn't seem to hear me.

"I can't feel my lungs," Ryan said weakly.

With a wave to Debra, I turned and left the Satellite Heart.

The Madrox was located directly west of the Satellite Heart on Ludlow Street and was, generally speaking, its polar opposite. Its name (derived from some obscure Marvel Comics character) wasn't nearly as transparent as the names of some trendy East Village bars—say, the Hole, which was genuinely filthy, or the Cock, which was a pretty reliable place to find . . . well, you know—but it was equally underlit and profoundly underdecorated. Though only open for a few months, its instant hipness was a minor miracle of *Tipping Point*–style antimarketing. The first time I was there, a few weeks after it had opened, the walls were as clean as a dinner plate and the air smelled of Pledge. The second time—for Pedro's birthday party, two months or so after the first visit—it was a zoo specializing in that most elusive of species native to the East Coast of America: *Hipsterati alcoholicus.* It became, quite suddenly, the VSC's standard late-night spot, the number-one bar for indie-rock afterparties, the venue of choice for aging British rock-stars-turned-DJs, and the preferred place for squeaky-clean pop singers to be "accidentally" photographed canoodling with Canadian heavy-metal screamers. It was so perpetually crowded and cool that it was becoming almost uncool. It was, in a word, insufferable.

It wasn't even nine p.m. when I arrived, but the line to get in was already spilling onto the sidewalk. The door was blocked by a wall-like black man, as wide as he was tall, who was checking IDs like he was staring at a Magic Eye painting. But not even his massive girth could block the defibrillating levels of bass that poured out from behind him into the hot, crowded night. The glimpse inside I managed when the bouncer moved his mammoth arm to allow entry made me woozy: Tank-topped, sweaty-faced girls were three deep along the bar, waving twenties and clamoring for attention from the overwhelmed bartender. I was grateful, then, for the severity of Franta's cocktails.

Maybe he was right: Detective work did demand hard liquor. Entering the belly of the beast demanded a bellyful of something beastly. No wonder film-noir gumshoes were always knocking back shots of rye or other nasty-sounding, old-timey drinks in between trips to Lauren Bacall's house.

I felt a tap on my right shoulder.

"Hey, can I bum a smoke off of you?" I turned and the girl that faced me was as tall as I was but couldn't have been a day older than twenty-one. Her skin was a deeply burnished brown, her eyes were bigger than coasters, and if she was sweating to death in her red velvet blazer, she certainly wasn't showing it.

"Sorry," I mumbled. "I don't smoke."

"That's OK," she said, smiling. "I don't either."

"Oh," I said. "Then why did you ask?"

"Because I only smoke when I'm drinking." She let loose a throaty laugh that sounded caught somewhere between a hiccup and a gulp.

"Oh," I said. "Well."

She pushed her curly hair off of her forehead and halved the already tiny distance between us. "You were playing really good stuff in there."

Undercover, I said to myself. Gumshoe. Lauren Bacall.

"Thanks," I said. "I try."

"Yeah, it was really hot."

"It was?"

She hiccup-giggled again. "In there, I mean. Really hot in there."

"Yeah," I said sagely. "This place is hot."

"So," she said, and sort of rubbed my left arm.

"So!" I said back. I was close enough to play connect-the-dots with the freckles on her cheek. I heard a taxicab honk from the street, and people continued to push by us on the sidewalk in both directions.

"Do you have to, like, go back in there now?" she asked.

"Yeah," I said, half regretfully. "Right. I guess I do." I paused. Her giant eyes were still locked on mine. "Um," I started. "Have we met before?"

Hiccup-laugh. "I don't think so," she said, extending her right hand into the four and a half inches of space we had between us. "I'm Zaina."

I took her hand; it was roaringly hot and brittle like spun sugar. "I'm David," I said. "Zaina is a lovely name."

She blushed. "It's Persian."

"Cool," I said. "Like the cats."

"Yup," she said. "Or the empire."

"That too."

She squeezed my arm, leaving a red mark. "Bye, David. See you in there."

"OK," I said. "Nice to meet you."

My eyes lingered on her skinny frame for an extra moment as she rejoined her friends; then I stepped down two stairs and took up position in the back of the entrance line. Whatever my doppelgänger had done so far, I had to admit it wasn't all bad.

I wasn't waiting in the line for long.

"Hey!"

I glanced up and around.

"Hey!"

"Me?" I said meekly, peering around the line toward the front where the voice was coming from.

"Yeah, you!" It was the bouncer. "Get the hell up here!"

"OK," I said, giving sheepish looks to everyone I passed.

"I told you when you got here, Gould—you don't need to wait."

"Cool," I said. "Thanks, man."

The bouncer snatched a driver's license from a gawky blond mod at the front of the line and inspected it. "I know I'm a man," he said. "My name is Clarence."

"Thanks, Clarence," I said. And walked past him into the Madrox.

My first reaction was to the heat: It hit me like plastic sheeting, wrapping itself around every exposed inch of my body and instantly coating me with other people's sweat. Next was the smell: It was, I imagined, the odor of a baseball locker room after the pennant has been won, when the usual aroma of jockstraps is, however briefly, washed away under a tidal wave of cheap champagne. Finally was the noise: If I thought the red-haired kid had been generous with the volume at the Satellite Heart, my doppelgänger was an audio philanthropist on the level of the Rockefellers. "Jacqueline" by Franz Ferdinand buzzsawed through my eardrums and drew blood in my brain. I could feel the low end reverberating in the bottom of my sneakers. The empty beer bottles and glasses that lined the tables and the bar skipped and lurched with every downbeat, forcing them on a Bataan-style death march toward the floor.

The place was packed to such a degree that the words "fire

hazard" had long since lost their meaning and the sign on the wall noting the lawful occupancy as eighty-five seemed more like quaint, outdated advice than a binding legality. It was exactly the sort of scene that I, David Gould (the first), abhorred and avoided. Which of course made it exactly the scene that my double lived for. I pushed forward through the crowd in an attempt to buy a drink. I wondered, briefly, if they served shots of rye.

Eventually I made it to the front of the drink line and managed to make eye-contact with the tender, a sallow-faced young woman with mousy brown hair that framed her face in a '70s shag style. She was wearing a white and blue baseball T that said WINGER across the front in big, ironic lettering. I started to speak, when she leaned across the bar and gave me a lingering kiss on my cheek.

"Hey," she yelled over the music and the crowd. "Great set."

"Uh," I said. "Thanks."

I was about to order a beer when she disappeared for a moment, then returned with a lowball glass filled with clear liquid.

"Stoli rocks with a splash of tonic, right?"

Maybe this place did have something in common with the Satellite Heart. I nodded, then motioned her back and leaned in close to her ear. She smelled like bubble gum.

"Do you think I could get a lime, please?"

"Sure," she said, and gave me a flirtatious wink.

I moved away from the bar and slurped the first few centimeters off of my vodka. It wasn't a bad drink, really. It lacked the calming fire of whiskey and the solid, carb-filled grounding of beer, but it seemed to quiet the terror in my gut and provide a pleasant, energetic hum to my head. The air was cooler in the back, so I dodged the bathroom line and leaned against the wall. The Madrox was divided into two rooms, and the DJ booth was located in the other one. I decided to get my bearings for a bit, get another drink in me before risking a very public confrontation. Also, I still had no idea what I was going to say. "Shattered" by the Rolling Stones started up and I tapped my foot to the rhythm.

"There you fucking are! I've been looking all over you."

I turned and saw Pedro pushing through the crowd to get to me. His face was shining and his head was freshly shaved. Behind him was a miniature man who, as he approached, revealed himself to be the oldest person I had seen in months. His long face was lined with deep crevices, and the purplish skin that surrounded his eyes seemed to be crumbling away. He had three hoop earrings in each ear, a leather vest over his sunken chest, and a red bandanna tied around his upper left arm.

"Hey," I said. "Here I am."

"I thought you ran off, baby. I knew it couldn't take you that long to get cigarettes!" Pedro gave me a half hug, then threw his arm around his friend. "This is Screwie Louie."

I offered my hand and shook something clammy and calloused. "Nice to meet you," I said.

"Nice to meet you, David," said Screwie Louie in a high-pitched voice eerily reminiscent of Señor Wences. "I hear a lot about you."

Pedro grabbed my drink, took a big sip of it, then coughed dramatically. "What the hell is this? Vodka?"

"Yep," I said, taking it back from him.

"I thought it was water!"

Screwie Louie giggled like a schoolgirl.

"Yuck," said Pedro, wiping his mouth. "C'mon, finish that up and come with us."

"I just got it," I said.

"Finish it, bitch!"

I raised the glass to my lips and did as I was told.

"Good boy," said Pedro. "Now come with us."

He grabbed my wrist and led me toward the very back of the bar, past the line right up to the bathroom door. A guy on deck, dancing back and forth from leg to leg, grabbed at us as we passed.

"Hey!" he shouted. "There's a line here! What the fuck?"

"Sorry," said Screwie Louie, patting him on the back. "Health inspectors. We won't be long."

Without even pausing, Pedro led us all inside the tiny bathroom, then slammed the door shut and bolted the lock. I felt sweaty and more than a little drunk.

"Pedro," I said.

"Shhhh," said Pedro. "Don't worry. This is the good stuff I promised you."

Screwie Louie reached deep in the front pocket of his jeans and extracted a small plastic bag filled with white powder. He handed it to Pedro, who in turn handed Louie a wad of twenties.

"This *is* the good stuff, right, Louie? I don't want that baby-powder shit."

Screwie Louie giggled. "I promised you—don't get uptight."

Pedro removed his keys from his pocket and dug one of them deep into the bag. When he pulled the key out, it was crowned with a generous mound of white. In one quick motion he raised it to his right nostril and inhaled the entire pile. He fell back a bit, snorted air. Shook his head. Then he looked up at both of us with a maniacal grin.

"Oooooooh," he purred. "Mama likes!"

Screwie Louie smiled a toothy grin. "What'd I tell you?"

I had been around people who were on it, but I had never actually seen someone take cocaine before. It was—like fistfights, breakups, and the city of Los Angeles—almost depressingly the same as it was in the movies.

Pedro hit his other nostril, then offered me an equally generous bump. I stepped backward.

"No, no." I said. "Thanks. I'm cool."

Screwie Louie giggled. Pedro frowned.

"What do you mean, you're cool?" he said. "You asked me to go get it!"

"I did?"

"Of course you did!" The pile of white balanced precariously on the key between us. It was flaky and almost sparkled in the harsh bathroom light. "Whose money do you think that was, anyway?"

Jesus, I thought. Someone pounded on the door, causing Pedro's hand to shake, and a dusting of white fell onto the tile.

"Don't be a bitch, David." Pedro leaned in closer. "Time to take your medicine."

Undercover, I said to myself. Belly of the beast.

Tentatively, I hovered my nose over the key. The last thing I wanted to do was be like Woody Allen in *Annie Hall* and sneeze it over the entire room. I raised my hand to my face and pushed my left nostril closed as I had seen Pedro do, then sucked in the powder with my right.

Screwie Louie giggled.

I felt nothing at first, just a taste in my mouth like dissolved aspirin. Then a burn back in my sinuses and a trickle down my throat.

"Beautiful," said Pedro, as someone outside resumed pounding on the door. "Now one more for the road . . ."

I found it much easier to talk to Screwie Louie after our trip to the bathroom together. Actually, I found it much easier to talk to *everyone*. It's not that I felt particularly different from when I had arrived—though I noticed by the empty glasses that I had somehow put away two more vodkas in between return trips to the bathroom—I just seemed to be enjoying myself more. A lot more. Gone was the burning desire to go into the other half of the bar and confront my evil doppelgänger. Gone, in fact, was the burning desire to do anything other than sit here with my friends—old and new—and talk. About anything. At length. And at great speeds.

The DJ—me? Andre? the red-haired kid with the broken back?—was playing a tune called "Beating Heart Baby," and I had never heard it before but it seemed to be one of the two or three greatest songs ever recorded. Pedro was sitting to my left on the black banquette telling me about his latest conquest, the closeted lead singer of a screamo band that he was being paid to publicize. He kept rolling his eyes and laughing hysterically. He kept hitting my knee. I wasn't following the story—my brain was focused on the music and how I felt like the blood in my head was surging to the beat of the drums—but I agreed that whatever it was he was telling me was definitely hilarious.

I heard someone shout my name from the bathroom line, and I looked up. It was a tall, skinny Arab woman with curly hair and legs like skyscrapers. She said my name again and smiled and waved. I smiled dumbly and waved back. What was her name again? The one who didn't smoke? Cats. Empires. Zelda?

"How do you know Zaina?"

Zaina! That was it! I turned to face Screwie Louie on my right.

"I don't," I said. "I mean, I just met her outside. I think she thought I was someone else."

Screwie Louie giggled. "Who'd she think you were?"

"Oh . . . ," I said, mind racing. "I guess she thought I was some guy named David!" We both laughed.

"The thing about that girl," said Screwie Louie lasciviously, "is that from what I hear she's . . ." He leaned in close. "She's mad docile."

I paused. "Docile?"

Screwie Louie leered at me. "Yep. She's real docile."

I scratched my face, ran my tongue along the smooth fronts of my teeth. "You mean, like, obedient? She's obedient?"

Screwie Louie frowned. "No, man! She's docile. Look at those legs! She's docile."

I stared at him. He looked confused.

"Doesn't that mean, like, flexible?"

I laughed harder. "Nope!"

Screwie Louie's wrinkly face fell. "Damn . . . I've been telling *everybody* that."

I shook my head. I couldn't seem to stop laughing. There was a strange incessant ringing in my ears and a cottony thickness in my throat. Pedro gave my shoulder a push.

"You're not even listening to my story!"

"I'm sorry, dude," I said. "I'm just . . . all over the place."

"That's OK," he whispered. "I'm fucking high out of my mind right now!"

I laughed. "Is that what it is?"

"See what you've been missing? It's fun to leave the house sometimes, isn't it?"

"Yeah," I said. "It really is."

And I believed it. It was fun. It was, in fact, better than fun. It was fucking fantastic. The heat. The sweat. The volume. The shouting. The drinks. The girls. All of it seemed to make sense now—it was as if I had been living at the wrong rpm. Sped up as I was, I finally got it. So this is why people went out all the time. This is what it felt like. I could barely catch my breath for smiling.

A new song started then, a familiar rhythm and vocal line. It was the beginning of "Temptation" by New Order. Drugs or no, this was *absolutely* one of the two or three best songs of all time. I turned to Screwie Louie to make sure he knew it too.

"Holy shit," I yelled at him. "I love this song!"

Screwie Louie stopped talking to a girl twenty years his junior and put his arm around me. "I love this song too!" he yelled.

"Wait, wait." I scratched my head, rubbed my nose. "Someone else loves this song too."

"I love it," said Pedro. "What about me?"

"No, no," I said, darting my eyes around the room. "Not you. Someone else. Someone important. She's always talking about it."

I looked around more. The song was building and people around us were starting to hoot in recognition; some stood and began to dance. *Heaven. A gateway. A hope . . .*

And then I saw Cath Kennedy bearing down on me from the other side of the bar.

"Her!" I shouted excitedly. "This is *her* favorite song too."

Pedro looked up. "Her? The chick you were with the other night?"

Cath was wearing a white tank top with a red bra underneath. Her jeans were black and extremely tight, almost melting into her high-heeled boots. Her hair was swept up from her face and she was wearing giant hoop earrings that made her look like she was playing dress-up in her mom's closet. She looked ravishing. And she was headed straight for me.

When she arrived, she yelled.

"There you are! Where the fuck have you been?"

I smiled happily. "Hi, Cath."

"Don't fucking 'hi, Cath' me, creepo! I can't cover for you forever. This is *your* DJ night, remember?"

Something lurched in my chest. "Oh, yeah," I said. "I remember."

She leaned forward across the table and grabbed my arms.

"Come on!" She pulled and I let her lift me up off the couch.

I turned to Pedro and Screwie Louie.

"Bye, guys," I said. "I'll be in the other room. I'll be DJing."

"OK," said Pedro. "Bye!" Screwie Louie giggled.

Cath put her arm around me and cut a swath through the crowd toward the other side of the bar. She was taller in her boots; her head pushed against my shoulder. I liked the way her arm felt around my back, too; its pressure, warm and constant, reminded me of something, of someone, but I didn't have time to figure out what or whom. We kept walking; we kept moving.

"Cath," I said. "You totally love this song."

She laughed. "I know I love it, creepo. Why do you think I'm playing it?"

We ducked under a crowd of meatheads near the entrance and cut left.

"I love this song too!" I said.

"Well, I also love it because it's six minutes long, and that gave me enough time to scour this entire fucking place for you. Where the hell have you been? You left me there like forty minutes ago!"

I laughed. This was hilarious!

"Don't be a jerk." Cath slapped my side where her arm was resting, but it only made me laugh harder. "Seriously! God, I hate it when you do that."

The other side of the Madrox was much like the one I had been in, only darker and slightly more mysterious. The entire middle of the room, however, was filled with dancers—gyrating kids twirling, touching, jumping up and down to the beat. *Oh, you've got blue eyes / oh, you've got green eyes / oh, you've got graaaaay eyes.* Cath led me back to the DJ booth against the far wall, but I stopped her before we got there.

"Wait!" I said, giddy. "Dance with me!"

"What?" She turned red. "Are you high?"

"Maybe!" I yanked on her arm. "Come on! We've got like two whole minutes before we need another song."

I pulled her close to me and started dancing. She was shy at first, barely acknowledging the rhythm, just watching me, shaking her head. Then, slowly but surely, she started swaying. She danced precisely, almost behind the beat, with no wasted motion. Moving her waist and shoulders in different directions. Lifting her arms high above her head.

And I've never met anyone quite like you before . . .

She grabbed my hip and twisted her body into me. I ran my hands through my hair, then rested them on her hips. We slid into each other, mouthing the words. Her hair tickled my nose. Her face was resting on my shoulder. I felt her small breasts against my chest. We were dancing way too slowly now, our bodies tangled up tight. I felt a stirring in my lap. Her hand was on my thigh.

No, I've never met anyone quite like you before . . .

Her mouth moved up to my ear. "Hey," she said.

Then she stopped dancing altogether.

"Hey!" She pulled back. "When did you change your shirt?"

"I didn't," I stammered. "I didn't."

She looked confused. "Yes, you did."

"No, I didn't." I grabbed her by her bony shoulders. "Cath, it's me. David."

She shook her head. "I'm not talking about you. I'm talking about your shirt."

"No," I said. "It's me, David. The real one."

She slapped me in the chest, pushing me backward. "Oh fuck, not this *Freaky Friday* shit again."

"Yeah," I said. "Shazam."

Then the song ended and the entire bar fell silent.

All around us, people stopped dancing. Bottles rattled and clinked. Someone coughed. The quiet was punishing.

"Shit!" Cath squeaked. "Shit!"

She scrambled away from me, behind the DJ booth, and began flipping through a large book of CDs. Someone nudged me from behind. "Hey," said a voice. "Aren't *you*, like, the DJ?"

Oh yeah, I said to myself. *I guess I am.*

I walked quickly over to Cath, who was, quite literally, freaking out. "Fuck," she chirped. "Shit!"

"Just put something on," I whispered, feeling strangely calm. "Anything."

She flipped through more pages of discs. "You're going to get him fired. He's going to kill me."

"Don't worry about him," I said. "Here, play something off this." I handed her my iPod.

"Music!" yelled someone on the dance floor.

"One second!" I yelled back. "Technical difficulties!"

Cath was furiously spinning the click wheel. "Jesus," she said. "How much Fleetwood Mac can one person have?"

"You'd be surprised," I said, smiling.

"Here," she said. "Thank God." She jammed the connection wire into the headphone jack and suddenly the opening notes of Bloc Party's "She's Hearing Voices" filled the Madrox. The beat was thundering, paranoid, and inescapable. A sarcastic cheer went up from the crowd; then people began dancing again, quite unsarcastically.

Cath let out a deep breath. Then she punched me in the chest again. "Your battery better not fucking die, creepo."

"Don't worry," I said, my smile bigger. "I get all charged up before I see you."

She hit me again.

"What?" I started laughing again. I couldn't help myself. This time, this excitement, this music, this girl—it was all exciting and electrifying and there was a taste in my mouth like biting through steel.

Cath's lips were frowning, but her eyes weren't. I kept laughing and watched her face melt like an ice cube. Soon she was laughing too.

"See?" I said, wiping tears from my eyes. "It's funny."

"Fuck you," she said, but she didn't mean it.

I gestured toward the dance floor. "The secret is, you've got to make them wait for it. That way they want it more."

"What the hell has gotten into you, creepo?" She crossed her arms in front of her chest. "I thought you were the responsible one."

"Yeah, well," I said. "Nobody's perfect."

"Tell me about it."

"Maybe he won't come back," I said, more to myself than to her.

"Oh," she said, "he'll be back."

"Yeah?"

"You think he'd let *you* steal his night?"

"Cath," I said. "Where did he go?"

She shrugged. "He said something about going off to score some drugs. I told him it wouldn't be that hard in this place."

"I think you're right."

Cath cocked her head to the side. "There's really something different about you tonight."

"Oh?"

"Yeah." She grabbed my chin in her hand and turned my head left and right, inspecting me like she was on an archeological dig. "You look more like . . . him."

"Him."

"Yeah."

"I look more like him."

"That's what I'm saying!"

"Cath, we're supposed to look alike. He's a doppelgänger."

"He's German?"

"No . . . no. He's—never mind."

She let her hand fall down to my chest. I tensed for another smack—one more and it'd definitely leave a mark. "It's weird, but it suits you."

"Cath, you have to stop seeing him. We have to make him go away." I heard the words come out of my mouth, equally sanctimonious and desperate, and I would have done anything then to have grabbed them and shoved them back in my mouth. To have grabbed her and just started dancing again. But I couldn't. I was still me. And I was strangely jealous. "We have to do something."

"Mmmm."

"Cath."

"Start laughing again, David. You're easier to deal with that way."

"I'm serious."

"So am I. Whatever—here come your friends."

I turned and waved to Pedro and Screwie Louie as they cut across the dance floor, drinks in hand.

"Interesting technique," Pedro said when he arrived, cackling with glee. "DJ John Cage performs forty-five seconds of silence."

"Shut up," I said.

Pedro handed me a vodka. "And don't look now," he said, "but this song's almost over too."

"Shit," said Cath, and resumed spinning my iPod.

Pedro leaned in. "She's hot!"

I leaned back. "She's twenty-two!"

Pedro held out his hand. "Well, then," he said. "Congratulations."

I stared at his hand.

"Don't be rude!" He waggled his hand in the air impatiently.

I took it to shake, then felt him slide the small plastic bag into my palm. I looked up in surprise. Cath let out a squeal of excitement as she found what she was looking for, and "This Is Our Emergency," a song by Pretty Girls Make Graves, started up over the speakers.

Pedro winked at me. "Come on, baby," he said. "You're in it to win it."

I felt what was in my hand; it seemed hotter than the room, forbidden. Exciting. I was in. I did want to win. But it was more than that: I was the DJ now. This was my party. I could do what I wanted.

"Cath," I said. "I'll be right back. I'm just going to the bathroom."

Pedro winked again. "Don't worry about her. We'll keep her company."

• • •

Alone in the bathroom, illuminated under the harsh light, I felt, for a moment, insane. I didn't do things like this. I didn't *want* to do things like this. And yet here I was, ready, able, and poised to do them. I was free-falling now, miles away from the comfortable life I had scripted for myself. No girlfriend. No wallet. No control.

But then I thought of that other version of me updating the diary I had started, and I remembered something else: I was the writer here. I *had* scripted this life. If not for myself, then for whom? There was graffitti written across the streaked and filthy mirror: "KILL ME DEADER." I opened my palm, leaned back heavily against the locked door, and looked down. OK, I thought. Let's play.

I had just taken a bump up my left nostril when someone started pounding on the door.

"Just a second!" I yelled, fumbling with the baggie and my keys, trying to make myself presentable. My heart hammered in my chest. The person kept hammering on the door. Stupid. So stupid.

"Jesus!" I shouted, louder now. "Hold on to your . . ."

The door pushed inward and the lock gave way with a flimsy *click*. My doppelgänger walked into the bathroom and shut the door behind him.

". . . self," I finished.

"Hey," he said, taking two steps toward me.

"G-give me my wallet back," I said, rubbing my nose.

"Is that *cocaine* in your hand, David?" The doppelgänger took another step closer. "Did you just *snort cocaine*? I'm shocked!"

The doppelgänger had changed his clothes since lunch but hadn't showered; his hair stood at angles that did not exist in nature. His T-shirt was the same color green as mine, but more form-fitting; DETH KILLERS OF BUSHWICK was emblazoned across the front. His jeans were skintight and artfully frayed. They were also clearly brand-new. His shoes were bright orange with an argyle pattern dotting the sides.

I put my hand out to keep him back. "How much did those shoes cost, asshole?"

He stopped. "What, these? Don't worry. They were on sale."

"I'll bet."

"I'll lend 'em to you sometime—something tells me we're the same size."

"Fuck you."

He smiled. "You really need to keep more money in our checking account, David."

"I'll take that under advisement."

"Testy, testy!" He reached forward and snatched the baggie out of my hand. "Where'd you get this anyway? Did Pedro come through? I've been looking for him everywhere." He pulled the baggie open and dipped a finger into it, then ran it across his gums thoughtfully.

"I'm not going to give you my keys, if that's what you're thinking."

The doppelgänger laughed. "I wasn't—but that would have been good, wouldn't it?"

I took a step back. "Hilarious."

He reached into his jeans pocket and removed a silver sugar spoon. "Nice, isn't it? I stole it from the restaurant at dinner tonight." He dipped the spoon into the baggie and scooped out enough powder to improve ski conditions in the Poconos for a week. "Well," he said.

"Bottoms up." With a Herculean snort, he Hoovered up the contents of the spoon, then repeated the action three more times, twice in each nostril.

"Jesus Christ," I said. "You're going to give one of us a heart attack."

The doppelgänger wavered on his feet for a second. "Hooo," he said. "Whoa."

I watched him warily. "Get a hold of yourself."

The doppelgänger balled up his fists and pounded them on the sink. "Yeah!" He yelled. "I love doing what I want to do!"

"Look," I said. "Get out of here. Get out of my life. Give me my wallet." The drugs were in my veins now too, and I felt lightheaded and bulletproof at the same time.

He shook his head and turned to face me. "Look at yourself. You're not in your life anymore, little man. You're in *my* life. And I think it's time I asked *you* to leave."

"You!" My voice was shrill. "You don't *have* a life without me. You don't exist!"

"Au contraire," said the doppelgänger. "I was doing just fine tonight until you showed up, sticking your big nose in things that don't belong to you."

"We have the same nose!"

A timid knock came from the other side of the door.

"Go away!" My doppelgänger and I shouted in unison.

"Look," I said. "You're ruining everything."

"Am I?"

"There's only one of me. There can be only one!"

"That movie sucked. Anyway, you're the one that did this. Don't forget that. You locked yourself in that stupid apartment of yours and made yourself so lonely and self-pitying that you had to dream up a whole other you. And now you blame me for existing?" He took another step toward me. I could smell the liquor on his breath. "Please. You're not cut out for this shit. Go back to reading about your precious Miss Misery on your computer screen. And I'll go back to having sex with her."

I hadn't planned on punching the doppelgänger. I had never punched anyone before. But I couldn't help myself. My right arm reared back and connected, solidly, with his smug unshaven jaw. The noise was like the snapping of a twig. He fell backward, tripping over the toilet. I felt a fireworks of pain in my knuckles.

He sat down hard on the tile floor and rubbed at the red mark on his jaw.

"Well," he said.

And then he stood, brushed himself off, and almost casually walked over and punched me in the stomach.

I doubled over as all the air left my body, seeing stars and twinkling brown fuzzies around the corners of my eyes. I fought tears, and all the vodka I had downed seemed to be negotiating a potential retreat from my stomach. I swallowed hard and fell to my knees as the bathroom door opened and Cath Kennedy walked in.

"Holy shit!" she screamed, her hands flying to her face. "David, why are you hitting yourself?"

"S'funny," I said through gritted teeth, "I used to know a bully in second grade who was always asking me the same thing."

The doppelgänger smirked and took a few steps back. "Close the door, Cath," he said without taking his eyes off of me. "Join the party."

In the white light of the bathroom, Cath looked even younger than she was, all stick arms, stick legs, and bones. Her face was flushed, her expression panicked. She pushed the door shut like it was a living thing—carefully, meticulously—and made three quick steps toward where I knelt before she froze and backed up again.

"Ah," said the doppelgänger. "The dreaded choice."

I eased back on my haunches, leaned against the wall. My stomach felt cramped and tight, but my lungs were slowly beginning to accept the idea that they should fill themselves with air. My hand was pulsing with icicles of pain. "There is no choice, asshole," I said. "You don't exist."

"That's not what she'd say."

"Shut up, both of you," said Cath, quietly but firmly.

"Cath, please," I said. "I'm not really like him. Let's just get out of here."

"Boo-hoo," said the doppelgänger. "You think she doesn't know how you are? How I am? She made her choice a long time ago, you . . . *spectator.*" He spat the word like it was poison.

Cath put her hands on her hips. "I said, shut up."

The doppelgänger took a step toward her. "But . . ."

She smacked him so hard in the chest he sat down on the toilet.

"You two jokers don't get it, do you?" Her voice was high and tight. "This has nothing to do with knowing *you.* You idiots don't even know yourselves. This is about *me.* I'm a person too. And just because *you* like to cyberstalk me and *you* like to get me drugs and take me dancing doesn't mean that either of you has any idea who *I* am or what *I* want. And I'll tell you—*both* of you—that what I want right now is out of this fucking bizarro identity crisis. So stay the hell away from me. That goes for both of you."

She remained in the bathroom an extra moment with her finger outstretched, pointing, accusing—turning her glare from me to the doppelgänger and back again just to make sure we got the message. Then she turned gracefully on her heel and stormed out, slamming the door shut behind her.

"Fine!" yelled the doppelgänger at the door. "Fuck you, then! There are lots of other girls here—*young* girls—and all of them want me!" He stood up unsteadily. "I'm the DJ!"

Slowly, painfully, I pulled myself up off the floor. "Nicely played," I said. "Not at all desperate. Very believable."

For the first time since I'd met him, the other me seemed speechless. I walked over to the sink and ran my hands under the tap.

"And hey, slick—if you're the DJ, isn't that deafening silence out in the bar kind of *your* responsibility?"

"Shit," he said, rushing to the door. As he opened it, he turned and pointed at me. "This isn't over."

I dried my hands on a towel and inspected the knuckles where my skin was stinging, red, and broken. "I know," I said. And let him walk out into the bar alone.

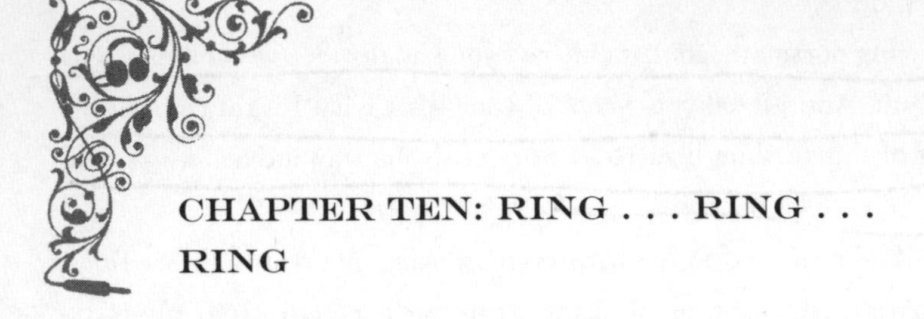

CHAPTER TEN: RING . . . RING . . . RING

I GOT SOME STRANGE LOOKS from the people waiting to use the bathroom when I emerged a few minutes later.

"Didn't you just . . . ?" stammered a bookish kid with thick glasses as I passed.

I winked at him and kept walking. He'd have his story for the night. Either that or he'd quit drinking for good. Out on the dance floor the crowd had thinned a bit, no doubt due to the on-again, off-again nature of the music. The one thing worse than a celebrity DJ was an inconsistent DJ. The doppelgänger was standing behind the fader, flipping wildly through the books of CDs. It was almost enough to make me feel sorry for him. Almost.

The song he was playing was "Mystery Achievement" by the Pretenders. Screwie Louie and Pedro stood to his side, laughing at some private joke. Neither of them noticed me as I passed, and Cath was, I was sure, long gone. I felt sober but hyperalert, like I had downed four cups of diner coffee with a Ritalin chaser. The pain in my right hand pulsed, and I tried to keep time to it as I walked.

I needed to get out of there. To clear my head. To catch my breath.

I pushed through the crowd and squeezed through the door out into the night.

"Man," said Clarence the bouncer as I passed. "I could sure use some of whatever it is you're on."

I froze. "What?"

He chuckled, waved a few more miniskirted twentysomethings inside. "The way you're coming and going here it's like there's two of you."

"Right," I said, and gave a friendly nervous laugh that came out more like a gurgle. "See ya."

I speed-walked to the corner of Ludlow and Rivington without pausing or looking behind me. Moving through the thick summer night felt like hugging a snowman after the dank humidity of the Madrox, and I even shivered a little. At the corner I stopped and surveyed the scene. Yellow cabs and livery cabs jockeyed for position in the street, honking and bleating in both directions as revelers decided to call it a night or move on to round two. There was a crowd in front of Pianos—bearded and scruffy rejects from Williamsburg central casting, chain-smoking and putting air quotes around their lives. I didn't want to go home, and I didn't know where to go. As my body processed the confrontation that had just occurred, I felt a thick thirst in the back of my throat. The night air seemed to hum all around me. I held my hand out flat in front of my face and watched it shake: tiny, indistinct vibrations rocketing through my body. What to do? What not to do?

That's the problem with choices, I thought. You can only ever choose one of them.

"Hey," someone called from behind me. I turned to see Zaina

sprinting down the street, her curly hair bobbing and weaving across her face. "I didn't think I was going to catch you."

And sometimes someone else chooses for you. I smiled and scratched at my face. "You caught me," I said.

She stopped in front of me and caught her breath. "I thought you were still DJing, then the next thing I knew you were flying out the door."

"I needed some air."

"Yeah, me too." She smiled a crooked smile.

"So," I said, nervous. "What are you up to?"

She put her hand on my arm and ran it up and down. "I was going to a friend's house to party some more. You want to come?"

Of course I didn't. I was a responsible person with someone who loved him and a mountain of work to do. But the sound of her voice made my blood jump like iron filings underneath a magnet, and I knew that for one night at least I didn't want to be me. I wanted to be him. So despite myself I said:

"Sure. Let's go."

[SECTION HAS BEEN DELETED]

The storm rolled back over the city that night; it had blown over after the afternoon rainfall but midway to the midwest stopped as if it had forgotten to turn the lights off. Sometime after three a.m. the sky started again with its ominous rumbling, and the air became thick and still.

The taxi driver was none too pleased about having to schlep me all the way out to Brooklyn, but I promised him a big tip, which I delivered even after he took the wrong bridge.

"It's gonna rain again," he said to me as I handed a twenty through the glass.

"Yeah?" I said, counting my change. "How's that for business?"

The driver snorted. "Business is business," he said. "Always gonna be some crazy kids like you who need to get home in a hurry."

I thought about responding, but he revved the engine and lightning cut across the sky, so I hopped out and sprinted across the dampening sidewalk to my house.

The keys shook in the lock and I dropped them twice, but I managed to make it into my building before the storm broke again. Safe in the foyer, I turned and watched as the world was illuminated by ferocious shards of lightning. There was no one on the street. There was no one anywhere at all. No witnesses. No one to know where I had been or what I had done. No one to verify it for me later, in case I doubted it. I rubbed my still-smarting fist. No scars, either—just bruises. I clicked the lock and tiptoed up the stairs to my apartment.

<YOU HAVE THREE NEW MESSAGES>

Hello, this is a message for Mr. David Gould. I'm calling from Chase Manhattan Bank. Mr. Gould, we've noticed an abnormally large number of withdrawals from your checking account today and wanted to make sure that your ATM card is still in your possession. For your security please give us a call at your convenience at 1-800-KL5-0439.

<WEDNESDAY, 5:55 P.M.>

Mr. Gould, this is Carol Fitzgerald from the Pendant Publishing legal department. I'm calling under the advisement of a junior editor here, Thom Watkins. Mr. Gould, it is my duty to remind you that you are under contract to Pendant Publishing to deliver a manuscript in a timely fashion. Some lateness is to be expected, but Mr. Watkins has alerted me that you have not been in contact with him for over two months. Please be advised that we will take the necessary legal action against you if you do not make an attempt to contact Mr. Watkins after this holiday weekend. Thank you for your time.

<WEDNESDAY, 6:11 P.M.>

David, it's me. I know you're hearing these messages, so I'll just say it into the machine. It's not that different from talking to you anyway—or at least to you the way you were before I left. Anyway, look: I just want you to know that I get it. I understand. I know what you're doing—what you're doing in a really creepy fucking passive-aggressive way—but I know what it is that you're doing. And what I want you to know is: I'm doing it too. I'm moving on. I feel I owe you that—that you should know. There's someone that I've met here and . . . well, he's not you, but at least he'll call me back. I love you so much. I miss you. But I can't be doing all of this alone. It's not fair . . . (crying) . . . All I ever wanted from you was some effort. But if you don't know what you want, well . . . I love you. Happy Independence Day. Good-bye.

<WEDNESDAY, 8:18 P.M.>

<END OF MESSAGES>

There are scenes in films when the villain is shot and he doesn't realize it at first. He continues making his pompous, self-referential speeches or laughing at the seemingly inevitable doom of the hero that he has cornered. Perhaps he'll continue to fiddle with the elaborate mechanism he's constructed to take over the Earth, or he'll draw back the hammer on his own weapon, delighting in the bullet he is about to fire into his opponent. But gradually a shadow will cross his face: Something isn't right; something has gone wrong. The villain feels something—probably something like a prick or a sting, something nowhere near the magnitude of what it actually feels like to be shot—and he'll look down and see that blood is pouring down his shirt. He'll be confused at first, or possibly mildly annoyed. *Whose blood is this?* his face says. *How much will this cost to be dry-cleaned?* But then the sting will turn into an ache or a burn, and he'll frantically push aside the clothing to discover what we, the audience, have known all along: There is a hole in his body. And whether he has seen it or not, his life is escaping out of it. Then and only then does he collapse to the floor and die.

That's how I felt in those first horrible seconds after listening to the message from Amy, with the lights in my apartment all turned off but the thunderstorm illuminating the room every few moments like a strobe on quaaludes. There was a hole in me—had been for months—and I had ignored it. And now my life had escaped.

The coffee table was covered in newspapers and chopstick wrappers, and I dove into the pile with a ferocity that surprised me; my arms flailing and flying, I threw papers in all directions, scrabbling and searching for what I knew lay at the bottom of it all. When I found it, I held it up to the window and caught the staccato illumination of the storm. It was a sticky pad that Amy had rescued from her childhood bedroom the previous Christmas; in neon pink eighties bubble type it read A NOTE FROM

AMY. On it, in her calm, immaculate script, were three lines of numbers. Her numbers, set off by odd European exchanges and area codes. My hands were shaking and my face was wet with panic and tears. I wondered if this was how suicides feel when they jump off tall buildings—is it possible to convince yourself the entire way down that you're flying, not falling? If so, the only thing that convinces you of the truth is the impact, but by then it's too late to offer much of a rebuttal.

I picked up the phone and began to dial. I needed her. I needed her voice. I needed her to tell me that everything was going to be all right. Outside, the thunder sounded like a jet plane crashing into a mountain. The whole house seemed to shake. The storm was getting closer.

I couldn't seem to make the buttons push the right way—too many sevens, not enough eights—but eventually I heard the call click through and the ringing begin. It was ringing in another language: that strange European double-tracked ring, where the second one begins before the first one has ended, the rings cascading out of the receiver, stepping on each other's toes, making me feel small and insignificant. *RingRING . . . RingRING . . . RingRING.*

She wasn't picking up. I looked at the clock above the TV. It was nearly five in the morning. What time was it there? Ten? Eleven? Would the Dutch be aware it was Independence Day? Was it a holiday for them? For her? For *him*?

RingRING . . . RingRING . . . RingRING.

I was mouthing her name, shaking my head, pounding my fists into the futon-couch. I couldn't lose her. I couldn't *lose.*

RingRING . . . RingRING . . . RingRING.

Could one night of drug abuse give you a heart attack? A nervous breakdown? The lightning was closer and closer, the thunderclaps reverberating into my skull. The building itself seemed to be giving way, giving in. I know who I am, I said to myself. I know who I am. I never should have doubted it. Over the hissy static of the receiver I felt I could actually hear the pounds and pounds of freezing water washing over the telephone lines. An entire ocean, and below, the rocks. Submerged.

RingRING . . . RingRING . . . RingRING.

She wouldn't answer. Oh, Amy, I thought. I'm sorry. I did it this time, didn't I? I really screwed it up. I'm so, so, sorry.

But all the phone said was, *RingRING . . . RingRING . . . RingRING.*

I hung up and with tentative steps took the phone with me into the bedroom. I lay down, clutching the phone to my chest, and called back every two or three minutes. She didn't pick up. No one did. Lying on my back, listening to the rain hammer the city, I stared at the ceiling and laughed in spite of myself. The ceiling fan spun lazily above me—a sight I had never paid much attention to with Amy next to me. And I remembered something she had said when we moved in: You know, on those British makeover shows, there's only one constant—the ceiling fan is always the first thing to go.

But no, Amy, you were wrong. The ceiling fan wasn't the first to go after all. You were.

RingRING . . . RingRING . . . RingRING.

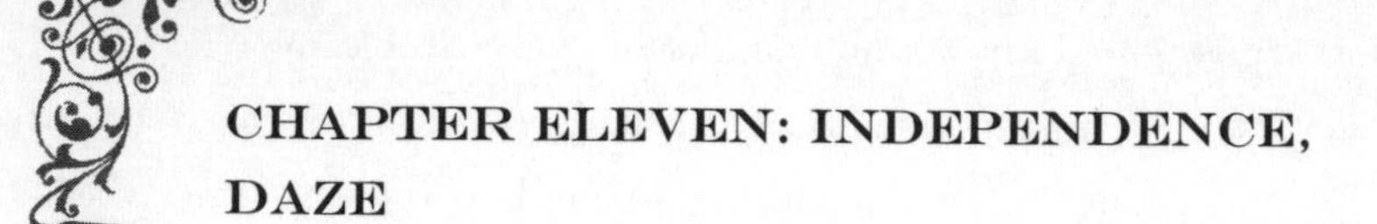

CHAPTER ELEVEN: INDEPENDENCE, DAZE

```
1 New Text Message From: Bryce
12:19 p.m.
Did you see the Post today? Page six? What the
hell are you up to?
```

MY BRAIN WOKE UP before my eyes did. I could feel it lumbering its way into consciousness, clawing its way through the mud and fog I had drowned it in the night before. Freed, finally, of sleep and excess, it lay there in my skull curled up like a turtle stripped of its shell, huddled and afraid. Good morning, it said to me in shallow, gasping breaths. Please don't ever do that to us again. And for good measure it sent the stabbing pain of a hangover headache rocketing through my nerves.

I opened my eyes. The digital readout on my alarm clock said 12:28 p.m. It was the Fourth of July and bright sunlight was streaming into my room. I wiggled a finger to see if my body still worked. Pleased with the result, I dispatched a distress call to my entire arm: Wake up, the message said. Reach for the glass of water on the table and bring it to our mouth. We need to drink something productive for a change. After some muscular grumbling, my arm obeyed, and I tipped the water glass to my lips without sitting up. Better, I thought.

I swallowed and returned the glass to the table. As I did so, I noticed the raw and cracked redness of my knuckles. Oh yes—my introduction to the "sweet science" the night before. I wiggled my fingers, which grudgingly obliged. No harm done. To my hand, that is. I sat up and instantly regretted it, as the headache chose that moment to turn itself up to eleven. I slunk back down to the pillows.

In addition to the roar in my skull, there was a small niggling pain in my palm; a sharp woodwind note to contrast with the timpani between my ears. I held my hand up to my eyes. The pain centered on a tiny black spear embedded in the meat of my palm, just above my wisdom line. A splinter, I thought. How the hell did I manage to get a splinter? In addition to bathroom fistfights, drug abuse, and ill-advised flirtation had I also been chopping wood? Unlikely, but so was everything about my life these days. I resolved to get to the bottom of it.

But not right away. I tabled the issue by closing my eyes and attempting to go back to sleep.

This worked for about thirty seconds, during which time I remembered not only Amy's message but also my crazed and desperate response to it. The uncomfortable lump of plastic underneath my right shoulder was, I realized, the telephone. On what must have been my thirty-fifth day of waking up alone, I finally surrendered to the reality of it: to the unconscionable ache, the tsunami of sadness and regret. I raised my hand to my face to block the tears that wouldn't come but should have and managed to smash the splinter farther into my skin. The pain was so severe and specific that my eyes actually watered. "You're a wreck," I said out loud. And slowly—very slowly—I pulled myself out of bed and stumbled toward the bathroom.

• • •

I hadn't shaved in days, and my hair was a Ph.D. dissertation on scatter art. There were purplish circles under both of my eyes, and my pupils were swimming in a white sea flecked with blood. But I recognized myself in the mirror. That was a start.

I pulled open the medicine cabinet and let my eyes adjust to the chaos. There were shelves of facial creams and facial washes. Exfoliating agents and defoliating agents. Toothbrushes, tooth flossers, and toothpastes. Prescription bottles that had expired years before and small blocks of foam whose purposes were obscure even to me. This was the realm of Amy, and I was utterly lost in it. But these were desperate times. I had a splinter—an injury that I had assumed disappeared after puberty like loose teeth, skinned knees, and chicken pox—and if there was an instrument in the house to cure me of it, it was lurking somewhere in this cabinet. I took a breath and dove in.

Five minutes later, I had overturned a box of Q-tips, knocked tampons all over the sink, and found a pair of sunglasses I thought I had lost back in college. But no tweezers. Amy had eight different brushes, and even now hair scrunchies were scattered on every table and every counter in the house, but she didn't have tweezers? I looked at the splinter, embedded in me and throbbing, redder and angrier by the moment. My God, I thought, I really am helpless.

I took a step back and considered my options:

1. The emergency room. Pros: effective, hygienic, responsible. Cons: public-humiliation factor quite high.
2. Calling a female friend. Pros: unusually sociable! Cons: public humiliation guaranteed.
3. Ignoring the injury. Pros: consistent with recent behavior,

would increase the chance of eating something large, greasy, and hangover-killing within the hour. Cons: eventual death by gangrene.

Dissatisfied with the options before me, I opted to go with number four: Make do with what you've got and gouge the motherfucker out of there. Reaching underneath a box of butterfly bandages, I chose my weapon: a pocket fingernail trimmer. Lacking the traditional bullet to bite down on, I steeled myself, armed the trimmer, and went in for the kill. Using my left hand, I managed to get the splinter between the teeth of the trimmer, and, bracing myself for the pain, I squeezed. *Snap.* I opened my eyes. The trimmer had done the job it was created for: It had trimmed the splinter, leaving the rest of it tucked comfortably inside my epidermis. Fuck!

I sat down on the toilet and took another deep breath. Focus, I said to myself. Just do something right. Try again. And ever so carefully, I positioned the trimmer for another strike, squeezing gently this time and pulling away from my pierced hand. Slowly but surely, I felt the splinter leave my body. I looked down. I was free. I had done it.

I'd like to blame the wildly fluctuating levels of serotonin in my brain for the ecstatic rapture I felt in that moment, but that would probably be inaccurate. What I felt then, more than anything else, was a supremely satisfying sense of *competence.* I hadn't run. I hadn't hid. And I most definitely hadn't gone to the emergency room.

Today truly was Independence Day.

After a shower, four Tylenol, and a gargantuan egg-and-cheese sandwich from the bagel store, I was once again feeling close to human.

There was still an odd hollow echo in the back of my head and a rough patch at the back of my throat to remind me of the night before—but it wasn't like I needed reminding.

I had bought a copy of the *Post* when I was out and opened it now on the coffee table. Bryce had been reacting to something on the gossip page, "Page Six." I scanned through the barren holiday dish: apparently Paris Hilton had slept with someone, P. Diddy had attended some sort of party, and human beings still inhaled oxygen and exhaled carbon dioxide for survival. But there, on the bottom right-hand corner of the page, underneath the headline SPOTTED! I read:

> . . . bad-boy writer/party promoter DAVID GOULD acting awfully cozy with PATTY REX, flame-haired guitarist from Detroit rock 'n' rollers THE ESQUIRE BABYS, at downtown hot spot the Madrox last night . . .

I sat back on the couch. What was more embarrassing? I wondered: to have an asshole doppelgänger hooking up with almost-famous rock stars or to be labeled a party promoter by the *New York Post*? Truly a modern dilemma.

I laughed a little, but it was a sick laugh, sad and tiny. I desperately hoped that the *Post* didn't get picked up by a wire service in the Netherlands. I rubbed my sore right hand. What to do?

I had tried beating him. I had tried joining him. Neither had worked, and both had left me poorer—emotionally, physically, and financially—than I was when I started. What was left? Killing him? I didn't have the stomach for that, and I had a sinking feeling that when Jack referred to his "friends" in the Russian Mafia of Sheepshead Bay he was kidding. Besides, I was opposed to assisted suicide. Rimshot. *Sigh*.

What about retirement? Retreat back to these safe apartment walls and let the doppelgänger live—or ruin—my life at his own pace? No one would notice I was gone, and the few friends I had would probably end up being like Pedro and prefer the new me to the old. I felt empty, hollow, and washed-up. Yes, retirement and surrender were probably my best bet. Why mess things up further?

Just when I was beginning to get some real traction in feeling sorry for myself, my cell phone beeped from the next room.

1 New Text Message From: Cath
1:37 p.m.
Dear creepo: I have your iPod. Let me know if you want it.

It seemed that her David vacation hadn't even lasted twenty-four hours. Forcing my thumbs to do my bidding, I texted her back:

I do want it. Can I pick it up from you somehow?

A moment passed, and then:

1 New Text Message From: Cath
1:41 p.m.
Well, my roommate is sort of having a 4th of July

party. You could come if you wanted . . . It starts at 7.

I felt strangely elated. I was back on the grid; the lights were on. But I had to be sure. I wrote:

I'd love to. You do know which one this is, right?

The answer arrived almost immediately.

1 New Text Message From: Cath
1:43 p.m.
Of course I do. I wouldn't have invited otherwise. :-P

I leaned back on the couch and felt something strange and unfamiliar on my face: a smile. I was invited to a party—me, not the other version of me, not somebody's misconception or bad idea brought to life. Hungover, circle-eyed, recently de-splintered me.

I should thank Cath, I thought. Really thank her. She had been put through the ringer by me—and by the other me. And for her to reach out was something special. She deserved a present. Something to show my appreciation. But what would a newly lonely, skinny, sardonic media professional in New York City give a woman as a gift?

That's easy: a mix CD.

I brushed the crumbs off the coffee table and hummed to myself, awash in all the exciting possibilities.

With the sunlight pouring in through my windows and the air-conditioning providing a calming wave of white noise, I sat down at my desk. Self-consciously, I slid the picture of Amy under some papers so it couldn't see what I was doing. Europe or no, she'd never approve of me making a mix CD for another woman. I put my headphones on and opened up iTunes on the computer. I felt another strange rush of contentment; maybe it was chemical, but I didn't mind. It felt good to have a task again, to be productive. I rubbed my hands together and started in earnest.

Four hours later I was done. This was the mix I made for Miss Misery:

1. **"The Trial of the Century"—French Kicks**
   (A quietly pulsing, insistent opener. Sets the mood: pensive but still vaguely groovy. Nice quasi reference in the title. Message: It's been hard but we've seen it through. Subtler message: I care!)
2. **"The Two Sides of Monsieur Valentine"—Spoon**
   (Topical! Relevant! Obscure! Irresistible!)
3. **"I Know I'm Not Wrong"—Fleetwood Mac**
   (An all-time favorite, poppy and just shy of insane. She made a joke about all the Mac on my iPod at the club; little does she know what she's in for! Sets a pleasant, workable mood.)
4. **"Cinnamon"—The Long Winters**
   (Overlooked pop gem—nice segue from the Mac—acoustic but with a little oomph to it. Also: Lyrics about skin, marriage, honeymoons, etc. are flirtatious but in a genteel, nonthreatening way. Work that Gouldian charm!)
5. **"Head Full of Steam"—The Go-Betweens**
   (This one took a while—it's always difficult to pick one song by a

favorite band. Can't get too obscure; can't try to impress. Better to be safe: Pick a popular number and hope it leads to an interest to hear more. Relevant lyric: "To chase her/a fool's dream." Apologetic and forward at the same time—story of my life!)

6. "If You Knew Her As I Know Her"—The Mendoza Line

(Who could resist the title? Goal: admitting the fact that I am kind of stalkerish but repositioning it as a POSITIVE. I am blessed with perspective! And canny musical taste! Right? Right??!?)

7. "July, July!"—The Decemberists

(Helpful tempo quickener—short but sweet. Also deft reminder of when the CD was made . . .)

8. "Fourth of July"—Galaxie 500

(Spacey and weird—total tempo change. But come on, who could resist the title? This is the sound of NYC sometimes: bizarre and droning and a little bit haunted. If Cath doesn't recognize it by now, she will before the summer is over.)

9. "There's Glory In Your Story"—Idlewild

(Gloriously poppy B-side from underappreciated Scottish band. Choice lyric: "Independence Day comes when you're down.")

10. "Sympathy"—The Get Up Kids

(Ashleigh turned me onto this one, actually—I'm not usually much of an emo fan. But there's something churning and yearning about this song that gets me; I listened to it on repeat in the days after Amy left.)

11. "Y Control"—Yeah Yeah Yeahs

(Purpose number one: Look! I'm hip! Purpose number two: This is what I thought nights out sounded like before I actually experienced one. Now I know that they sound noisy and sweaty and

that the music sounds good no matter what it is. But I still like the way I think this makes me think I feel. Or something.)

12. **"Ladyflash"—The Go! Team**

    (This song is punky and funky and exciting and mysterious—and if I ever get the chance to dance with Miss Misery again, I want it to be to this song.)

13. **"Calm Before the Storm"—The Bats**

    (Another all-time favorite and a nice stroll back down-tempo before the close.)

14. **"Look Up"—Stars**

    (A bold move on two counts. One: It's Canadian, so she might know it—or even worse, she might hate it. Two: It's sappy and hopeful and romantic and all of the things that I am but try not to be. I had this song on and off the CD seven times before burning it. But if I go down, at least I go down my way.)

With the disc burned, I rifled through copies of *Esquire* and *GQ*, searching for a suitably vague and cool-seeming image to gank for a cover. I found one near the back of a year-old issue of *GQ* with Jake Gyllenhaal on the front. It was a two-page ad for expensive watches, but all I was interested in was the background: a moody shot of the old TWA terminal at JFK Airport, aglow with strange hues of green and gold. I snipped it out and stuck it in an empty jewel box. Looking good. All I lacked was a title. I thought for a moment, then without hesitating uncapped a Sharpie and wrote across the disc: "INDEPENDENCE, DAZE." What girl didn't love puns? I slammed the case shut, threw it in my bag, then went to get changed. I was feeling peppy and I had a party to go to.

• • •

When I raced out of my apartment a short time later, Mrs. Armando was waiting for me at the foot of the stairs, sweeping up great clouds of nothing in the dim indoor light. The entire first floor smelled like a pine forest, and I did my best to avoid any spots she may have already tended to.

"David!" she said without looking up at me. "What time you get in last night?"

"Last night?" I said, playing dumb and charming at the same time. "I don't know, Mrs. Armando. Late?" I smiled as broadly as I could. I was moving again. I wasn't going to be dragged down by this.

"I don't know where your head is at," she said in the direction of the floor. She coughed, and I thought I was free, but then: "You gonna watch the explosions tonight?"

I paused. "The explosions?"

"You know, the flag, the lights, all lit up in the sky? Whaddya call it."

"Fireworks?"

"That's it, that's it. You gonna watch?"

"I'm gonna watch, Mrs. Armando. Are you?"

"Oh . . ." She fussed with something on the corner of the rug. "You never know, you never know."

I took that as my cue to push past her and open the door.

When I left the house for the second time that day, the quality of the sky seemed to have improved even more: Where once there had been gauzy puffs of clouds, now there was nothing but a deep, burnished blue. The sun was glaring and hot, focused down to a tight coin perched precariously above the Manhattan skyline. Everything seemed richer, more profound: the loose soil spilling onto the sidewalk in front of the house, the reggaeton blaring from the open windows of a passing Honda, the smile from the unknown bearded neighbor out walking his three-legged Great Dane. I smoothed my T-shirt out, felt the first tickle of sweat in the small of my spine. Even the air smelled decadent, like wood chips and hot dogs; thick not with humidity but with nostalgia for summer days remembered from sleepaway-camp photo books and family-vacation videotapes. Without my iPod to blanket my ears, I focused instead on smaller sounds: a baby crying, children playing catch in the middle of the street, the tinkly chime of a Mister Softee truck blocks away, and everywhere the quiet, calming hum of a thousand air conditioners at full tilt. I put my sunglasses on and stepped off the landing, staring upward for a change at the deep leafy green of the few trees that lined the street—dyed a strange golden yellow by my UV-protection lenses.

As I headed toward the avenue, I felt a spring in my step, a twittering hiccup in my chest. I felt poised for something, a strange miasma of anticipation coating my entire body as if I too were playing catch in traffic—with both the ball and an eighteen-wheeler barreling my way. It was excitement and nerves and fear and all of those things, but it was also something new: It was freedom. It was a holiday in every sense—from work, from responsibilities, from life. I felt like I was bursting out of my own skin, like I was walking quickly downhill after weeks of uphill trudgery. I clenched and unclenched my fists at my sides and imagined, as I often did on this walk, how much easier and more pleasant things would be if I could fly.

I couldn't, of course—I was just impatient—so I kept walking until Fifth Avenue, then hung an aggressive left and headed toward the subway. The sunlight bashed itself into glass storefronts and spilled messily onto the pavement. Everywhere children were running, Super Soakers filled and dripping; pizza slices were folded over and eaten; beer was purchased; cars were double-parked and other cars were honking before slowly and grudgingly double-parking themselves. A trio of do-ragged black guys swept down the sidewalk like a wave, smoking Newports, pushing one another and throwing noisemakers down at their feet as they walked, *pop-pop-pop*. A pigeon flew low over my head; instinctively I ducked and then wondered if it was my old friend. No, I decided—too pale. All that greenery would have had to have improved a bird's health.

I wondered what the sky was like in the Netherlands—dark by then, probably—and if the expats had paid for fireworks of their own or if that was too ostentatious for Americans abroad these days, most of whom were tripping over each other pretending to be Canadian. But I didn't like the room this thought led to in my mind, so I quietly shut that particular door and stopped thinking about it.

Instead I double-timed my steps and nearly sprinted down the hill and up the stairs to the train. My legs felt hot and claustrophobic in my jeans, but I didn't mind. The day was well and truly spectacular.

Up on the platform again, I walked to the end as I always did and stared out over the Gowanus Canal at the shimmery image of the Statue of Liberty, as small as a tourist's statue of it from this distance, standing stock-still and ramrod straight. It was, as always, strange to see see something so famous, so recognizable in the mundanity of public transportation. It was like coming face-to-face with a supermodel in the DMV, almost unbelievable in its reality. But it also made me calm. I turned 180 degrees and stared out over Downtown Brooklyn—the avenues and warehouses, the impossibly phallic Williamsburgh Savings Bank building forever thrusting itself into the sky—and then past it to the curve of Manhattan, as stoic as a mountain range, from the self-important skyscrapers at its southernmost tip all the way to another unreal familiar landmark, the Empire State Building, where Amy had once worked and where I would wait in endless security lines and forever elevator queues just to sneak in a wordless visit during her lunch hour. Hello city, I said silently. I wonder if you've changed this year too.

"David? Is that you?"

I turned, and it wasn't the city made flesh, responding to my sun-drenched whimsy. It was Agnes, a former colleague of Amy's from another summer job, this one at Amnesty International. Agnes was only five years our senior but decades apart from us in demeanor. She was prim and tidy, even today wearing gray slacks and a polo shirt just red enough to highlight the lack of blood in her neck and just loose enough to accommodate the baby that was growing in her belly. She had mousy hair that mushroomed in all directions and an accent that, to my ears at least, caromed dangerously between Swedish and French.

"Hello, Agnes. Long time no see."

"Yes, I knew that it was you!" She clasped my left hand clumsily and then made some attempt to lean into me, brushing my cheeks in a sloppy recreation of a European greeting.

I smiled dumbly, taking in the sight of her. "Yes," I said. "Here I am."

"You are looking a little tired, no?"

"Maybe," I said in halfhearted cheerfulness. "Maybe." I ran a hand through my hair, let the backs of my fingers brush my face. Once again I had forgotten to shave.

"Paul and I were just speaking of you," she said referring to her husband, a professional percussionist at Broadway shows. "We were thinking that we wish Amy were here for when the baby comes. She always said she'd help with the babysitting. And what a delight it would be with you both in the neighborhood!"

I smiled but it came out like a grimace. "Oh, I'm sure she would have loved that."

Agnes took my left hand again in her own clammy paw. "Oh, you poor dear. She really left you all alone, didn't she?"

I took my hand back as gently as I could. "It's not so bad. I'm managing."

Agnes clucked, and the tendons in her neck seemed to make a desperate lunge for freedom. "*Managing*! We shouldn't have to *manage*!"

"No," I said, feeling torn in two. "We shouldn't."

We stood there then, feeling the sun beat down on our heads, with not a single thing more to say to each other. Why hadn't I noticed her first? Then I would have been able to do the sensible thing: pretend I hadn't seen her and walk farther away until awkward pauses like this one—in fact, entire awkward conversations like this one—would have been an impossibility.

When the weight of the silence became overwhelming, we both made efforts to repel it.

"Have you—?" Agnes said.

"What is—?" I said.

"Go ahead," Agnes said, bored and blushing.

"No, no," I said, rubbing my palms against my jeans. "You."

"Have you been following Amy's case in the papers? They've been doing an awfully good job of reporting it."

"Amy's case," I repeated, with no inflection.

"Yes—Radzic's trial? Did you see that he's insisting on representing himself and has been calling everyone—*everyone*—in as a witness? Yesterday he called Bill Clinton, Kofi Annan, and the Pope, but when none of them miraculously appeared, he settled for his prison guard and his anesthesiologist."

I shook my head. All of a sudden I wanted to grab this poor mousy pregnant woman and shake her and bury my face in her shoulder and cry and beg her to tell me everything she knew about the person I should have given up everything for. Instead all I said was, "Crazy."

"Yes," she said, believing it. "Very crazy."

My phone buzzed in my pocket. It was only an incoming text, but I took it out and regarded it like it was the phone call I'd been waiting for half my life. I glanced up at Agnes with a look of extreme concern on my face. "I'm sorry to be rude," I said. "I'm afraid I have to take this call."

"It is no problem," Agnes said, waving me away as she would a mosquito. "When Amy returns we will all have to get dinner again. This time at a place with high chairs!" She rubbed her swollen belly as if a genie would pop out and grant us each three wishes.

"Absolutely," I said. "Absolutely. Take care." And I headed off down the platform, still clutching my phone like it was a grenade with its pin removed. When I was well out of earshot, I actually opened the phone, held it to my ear and mimed speaking to someone for a moment, but I needn't have bothered. Agnes was headed off to the other end of the platform, no doubt as grateful for the interruption as I would have been had it been genuine. Feeling disgusted with myself, I slid the phone from my ear and looked at the screen. It read:

```
1 New Text Message From: David
6:22 p.m.
Rock stars love us. ;-)
```

I felt fury rise in my throat, and I slammed the phone shut. Up and down, up and down. I rubbed at my forehead, felt the sweat that had begun to appear there, as if massaging my skull could make my brain divulge the mysteries of its massive mood swings.

The papers have been doing a good job of reporting it. I hadn't looked at the papers; I hadn't even known what Amy was doing over there. I hadn't picked up the phone, and I certainly hadn't bothered to ask. There was no mystery to that realization, only shame. A shame that burned even brighter when I felt the almost imperceptible weight in my shoulder bag: the mix CD I had made for someone else.

I felt—no. Finish the thought:

A mix CD made for a twenty-two-year-old you barely know that you are racing to see. While another version of you laughs and preens and snorts and flirts and scores. Really, I thought to myself, it's enough to give someone some sort of breakdown. The idle G train stalled in the middle of the station rumbled to life then, and I looked down the tunnel to see the faint light of an approaching F. Time to go; time to keep moving.

My phone buzzed in my hand:

```
1 New Text Message From: Cath
6:25 p.m.
To: Creepo. From: Stalkee. Please bring beer.
That is all.
```

I smiled in spite of myself. I felt that tickle in my sternum again as the train approached and opened its doors wide. Independence Day. I hoped I wasn't lying to myself and I hoped I wasn't making a mistake, but in that quick pause before I stepped aboard I reached up and pulled down a curtain on my brain. I forgot about Agnes and her baby and the international court case that I knew nothing about and the doppelgänger and the state of my checking account and the sad little yank of loneliness that threatened to pull me back onto the platform and down the stairs and up the street and back to the four dull walls of my apartment.

I had been invited to a party and I had accepted. I needed to buy beer because they had run out of it and because I, for one, planned on drinking some.

The train rolled on into the city.

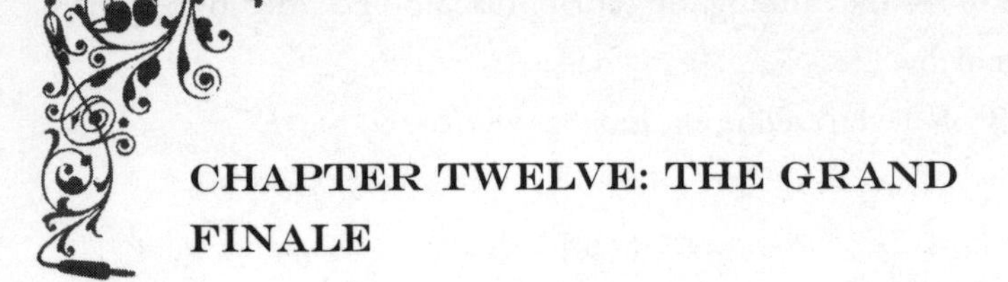

CHAPTER TWELVE: THE GRAND FINALE

THE FIRST THING THAT HAPPENED in Manhattan was that I got lost. Actually, that was second. First, I managed to successfully purchase a six-pack at a bodega on the corner of Sixth Street and Avenue C, though that hadn't been without its own drama. Beer choice is as important for a party as the music, and for a time—standing dumbstruck before the altar of refrigerated shelves—I was overwhelmed by the decision and considered fleeing back to Brooklyn. Corona? Too girlie. Tsingtao? Too exotic. Wine coolers? Too trashy. Asahi? Too expensive. Bud? Too cheap. I opened one of the sliding doors, felt the cool blast hug my face, then closed it again. At the counter, neighborhood kids taunted the clerk in Spanish—something about hot dogs and fire hydrants. Come on, Gould—get it together. It's only a simple choice.

The Miss Misery I spent hours reading about would probably have appreciated the urban poetry of a guest arriving exactly on time with nothing but two forties of Olde English and a leering grin on his face. But Cath Kennedy probably wouldn't have liked it. Some things are funny only in theory—not so much when you actually have to drink them.

Finally, with the weight of the inebriated world on my bony shoulders, I slid open the door and removed a six-pack of Stella. No one actually *liked* Stella, of course, but no one actively disliked it either—which made it, for my purposes, perfect.

I paid eleven dollars to the clerk, who asked for ID (*por favor*) and then looked at my passport like he would an unwanted card in a low-stakes game of gin rummy before returning it. He never bothered to look at my face.

Alphabet City was giddy and eager with the holiday. As the blazing day started to recede into a serene and faultless evening, hipsters and natives alike crisscrossed the avenues en route to their various parties and events. On days such as this, even the most brutal-looking blocks of Manhattan—graffiti-scarred Pentecostal churches, bombed-out bodegas—could appear almost pastoral. There was a warmth and vibrancy to the air that made me feel that my intensive exercise in self-deception was going to work. It was at precisely these moments—the in-betweens, the almosts, the about-tos—that I knew I should be reflecting on the uniqueness of my situation. I should be mulling and stewing, thinking and deciding. Firing up the machinery two decades of education had installed in my brain and let the creaking, unoiled behemoth heave and shudder to life. It was in the walking and the traveling—the expository paragraphs—where the protagonists of books I loved and admired came to know themselves and by extension reveal themselves to their devoted readers. But I had no such desire to reflect, to reveal, to consider, to decide. All I wanted in that moment was to be at this party, and I wanted to be there as myself.

I walked up Avenue C past the German beer-and-schnitzel *haus* and the Basque tapas bar—little flowers of gentrification in an otherwise untended garden—and turned eastward on Eighth Street. This was the block where Cath Kennedy lived with Stevie Lau, but the building numbers seemed to get bored and give up halfway down it. There was a dry cleaner on the corner and a fortune-teller, and at the far end was a lighting-fixture store, but there were apartment buildings everywhere—each with its own family out front barbecuing on hibachis placed haphazardly on the stone steps. Boom boxes were out in force: more reggaeton, some dance hall, and from the corner of Avenue D the almost wistful crooning of Tony Bennett. I walked up and down the street three times, getting stranger looks from the families on each pass, before I paused and checked the address again. Was it possible to be in the right place and still be lost? If it was, I had no doubt that I had managed to do it.

"You need help, kid?"

I turned to face a small brown-skinned woman seated on a folding chair that had a paisley scarf draped over it. This was, I gathered, the fortune-teller. She seemed enormously bored, and I wasn't sure if she was working or just enjoying the day; seated outside as she was, but behind a small card table with a box of tarot cards and an incense candle on it, the answer was probably both.

"Yeah," I said. "I'm looking for 358."

She smiled a feline little smile. She could have been thirty or she could have been eighteen. "This is 358," she said. "Are you looking for me?"

I smiled back, not because I wanted to but because I had nothing else to offer in return. "No . . . ah, no. I'm looking for 358 East Eighth Street. Apartment three-B."

The fortune-teller whistled. "Oh, the apartments. That's upstairs.

You have to cut through here." And with that she gestured lazily behind her at a door draped with more paisley scarves.

"I see," I said. The incense was picked up by the breeze and wafted up my nostrils—clove, maybe, or cinnamon. "Thanks."

She cocked her head at me. "You sure you don't want a reading? Holiday special. Only two bucks."

"I thought you'd charge something like $17.76," I said, trying to be merry.

She stared. "That's way too expensive."

"Oh," I said, crushed slightly. "I guess you're right."

She leaned forward. "Something is troubling you," she said portentously. "There are two paths laid out but you cannot choose."

My ears felt hot. "Really?"

She nodded and took my hand. "You try to deny what's best, but the only person that hurts is you."

I stared.

"It's your boss, isn't it? He places demands on you that cannot be met."

I pulled my hand back. "I don't have a boss," I said.

She shrugged and lit a cigarette. "Oh, well," she said. "I was just making that shit up, anyway."

I blinked. She exhaled extravagantly.

"It's a holiday—who wants to work?"

I pushed past her into the building.

The stairway was grim and narrow, as if constructed for a fantastical race of metropolitan pygmy people slightly shorter and leaner than normal Homo sapiens. There were cigarette butts on the linoleum and the smell of fatty chicken soup in the air. Apartment three-B was on the third floor, marked by a steel door with wilting paint the color of blush, an embossed numeral, and a sticker advertising a 1-800 number that only charged $3.99 a minute for dirty talk with a "real live" transsexual. I knocked twice and waited.

When the door opened there was no one I knew behind it—just a random NYU type with a massive jewfro and thin metal glasses over a pimply face. His T-shirt said JESUS IS MY HOMEBOY, and in his hand was a half-empty bottle of Miller High Life dripping condensation onto his black Umbro shorts and flip-flops. From the long hallway behind him I could hear the muffled sounds of hip-hop, laughter, and the steady whirring of a Cuisinart.

"Hi," I said. "Is Cath in?"

He stared at me dumbly for a moment.

"I'm a friend," I said. "I'm here for the party?"

Without taking his eyes off me, he shouted over his shoulder, "Cath! Someone's here!"

There was no answer. Lacking anything better to do, I coughed.

Jesus' homeboy turned around fully this time before bellowing *"Cath!"* again and stomping off. Alone in the doorway, I heard the Cuisinart stop, and then Cath popped her head around into the hallway. "Aha," she said. "It's you. One second." Her head disappeared for a moment and then was replaced with her whole body walking the length of the hallway in those great, gulping strides of hers. She was wearing a sky-blue skirt and a tangerine-colored ringer T-shirt with bands of pure orange at the neck and arms. She was rubbing her hands with a red-and-white-checked kitchen towel. And clomping on the uncovered wood floor were violet cowboy boots that ended mid-calf. All those colors together shouldn't have worked, but against the white walls and drab hallway the effect was like an Alka-Seltzer dropped into a plastic cup of dingy tap water.

She walked right up to me and kissed me on the cheek. "Don't touch me," she said. "I've been making dip."

"OK," I said.

She turned and started back up the hall. "Well, come on! Follow me!"

I did as I was told. The hallway was decorated with wrinkled Morrissey posters and lined with cast-off shoes—filthy New Balance sneakers, leather sandals, leather boots, round canvas Campers—and it stretched the length of the apartment. Off of it was a door to the bathroom, a pathetic little closet, and the cramped kitchen. Then the hallway became some sort of common room, and behind that were the two bedrooms. There were people gathered in the common room and Mobb Deep was playing on the stereo, but I glanced quickly and didn't recognize anyone. I followed Cath into the kitchen instead.

"Here," I said. "I brought beer."

She turned and took the bag from me. "Thanks."

I was nervous, so I babbled. "I was going to bring forties, but I thought that might have been too gangsta for you."

Cath put the Stella in the refrigerator. I caught a glimpse of Chinese take-out boxes and ginger-ale bottles. "That would have been awesome," she said. "You totally should have."

"Yeah," I said. And put my hands in my pockets.

The kitchen was no bigger than the bathroom in my own apartment, but what it lacked in size, it made up for in cabinets, which were piled on top of one another almost all the way up to the ceiling. The fixtures were new—gold handles, $8.99 at Home Depot—and everything else was white. Everything, that is, except for the counter, which was splattered with salsa and avocado and God knows what else. It looked like Jackson Pollock's midnight snack. In the center of it all stood the Cuisinart—proud, useful, grubby—and next to that a casserole dish, full and spackled with more colors than either Cath or the counter.

"What are you making here, exactly?" I asked.

"It's a seven-layer dip!" Cath beamed like Sandra Lee at a Tupperware party. "My mom used to make it on New Year's when I was a kid."

"It's very impressive," I said, leaning my hands against the refrigerator. "Very colorful."

Cath smacked me.

"I was being serious!" I said, smiling.

"I didn't like your tone," she said. But she was smiling too.

"Well," I said. "Is it done? Can I try it?"

Cath regarded her creation with a critical eye. "I suppose you can. It's only got six layers, though. At present."

I took a step toward the counter and lifted a chip out of an open bag of Tostitos. "And which layers would they be?"

Cath counted on her fingers as she recited. "Black beans, jalapeños, salsa, guacamole, tomatoes, and jack cheese."

"Goodness," I said, chip poised and at the ready. "What could possibly be missing from that?"

"Sour cream," said Cath, like it was the most obvious thing in the world. "But go ahead. Sample. Be my guest."

I scooped inward, doing my best to get some of all six layers. En route to my mouth, a suicidal black bean leapt to its death on the floor below.

"It's OK," she said. "I'm going to have a lot of cleaning up to do tonight anyway."

I bit down and the chip began to crack, so I panicked and shoveled the whole mess into my mouth. It tasted all right—Mexicany, or at least a Canadian's version of Mexicany—but then the rosy glow of spice on my tongue and at the back of my throat exploded into a full-scale mouth inferno. "Gah," I said, waving my hand in front of my face. "S'hot."

Cath looked troubled. "It is? But I took the skins off the peppers. That's where the heat is."

I was sweating, and my mouth was like Chicago in 1871. I tried swallowing some more. It didn't help. "No, no," I said sloppily. "Thheaithinthetheeds!"

Cath cocked her head. "What?"

"Theat's in the theeds!"

"I can't understand you, David. Do you want something to drink?"

I choked and swallowed the last of it. "The seeds! The heat is in the seeds, not the skin!"

Cath pulled one of my Stellas out of the fridge, popped the top, and handed it to me. "Really?"

I laughed and tears were in my eyes. I drained half the beer and felt my insides cool off and return to normal. "Really! I promise you!"

Cath crossed her arms and regarded the dip. "Huh," she said. "I had no idea!"

I took another sip of beer. It was cold, good. "Cath, your dip is lethal."

"That's just what the dance instructor told me."

"What are you going to do about it?"

She twisted her mouth in thought. "Well, I guess I'm going to serve it and then wait for the fireworks."

"In your guests or in the sky?"

She smacked me again, but I knew it was coming this time.

"Am I early?" I asked. "There don't seem to be many people here."

"Everyone's on the roof," she said. "We have a great view."

"Cool," I said. And we looked at each other for a half beat too long.

Cath blinked first and opened the fridge. "Come on," she said, opening a beer for herself. "Let me get you your iPod."

The dip-making apparently now concluded, Cath grabbed my hand in hers and led me out of the kitchen and through the common room. Jesus' homeboy was there, sitting cross-legged on the purple and white throw rug. There was a futon as well, with a boy and a girl on it. Ben There was sitting moodily on top of a dining-room chair that had no table to keep it company. There was an enormous black and white poster of Ian Curtis on the wall and a dead spider plant on the windowsill. The room wasn't air-conditioned, so the street noise wafted up from behind the plant. Cigarette smoke was heavy in the air.

I nodded at Ben There, but Cath didn't stop for any of them. She led me up to and through a white door with a whiteboard on it that said, in giant blue block lettering, "HAPPY."

"Is that a question or a statement?" I asked.

"Is what what?" she said, and dropped my hand. We were in her bedroom now, and she closed the door behind her. The lighting was muted here: soft, gauzy. The blinds were down and a small air conditioner hummed and shook in the boxy window. The room was smaller than the kitchen. Just a mattress spread out on the floor with a tousled red duvet on top of it and a cracked wooden desk groaning under the weight of a laptop, a typewriter, and a dozen coffee mugs filled with varying levels of room-temperature coffee and cigarette butts. The floor was littered with clothing—T-shirts, skirts, brassieres—which made sense, seeing as there wasn't a closet. My eyes lingered on a stack of well-worn paperbacks: Greene, Murakami, Didion, Pelecanos, and assorted manga. On the floor next to the mattress was an old Sony stereo system with loose CDs stacked high on top of it and a small shoebox filled with jewel boxes to its right. The walls were bare except for a framed print above the bed, a delicate painted image of a woman draped in black, and a photo taped above her desk.

"The word on your door," I said, getting my bearings. "'Happy.' Is that a question or a statement?"

"Oh." Cath laughed. "It's neither. I just think it's the strangest word—don't you? Have you ever actually *looked* at it?"

"Well, all words look dumb when you repeat them enough."

Cath plunged into the hysteria that was her desk. "Not *that* dumb."

"Huh," I said. "I guess not."

"Here it is." Cath extracted my iPod from the mess and handed it to me. It was none the worse for wear. "Even I couldn't have lost something in less than twenty-four hours."

"Thanks," I said, sliding it into my bag and noticing what else was in there. "I have something for you, too."

Cath fluttered her eyes. "For little old me? You shouldn't have!" She kicked at a skirt on the floor and sat down on the edge of the mattress. "It's not like a mixtape or something corny like that, is it?"

I flushed. "Ha, ha. Of course not. Why would you say that?"

Cath took out a cigarette and pushed the shoebox of CDs over to me with her foot. "Take a look."

I picked up the box and examined the contents. They were all mix CDs, each adorned with different masculine handwriting. They had names like *Everywhere* and *The Wish for Thunderstorms* and even *The New Sound of Missing You.* Some had elaborately designed covers. Others just had text.

Cath lit her cigarette and exhaled a little laughter with her smoke. "It's what boys do. They always do it. It's like they're genetically incapable of giving a girl something other than their own taste in music." She pretended to gag. "I knew you wouldn't be that cliché!"

I was frozen, still thumbing through the CDs. God, how corny! How predictable! "How did you know?" I asked.

"Well, for starters, you already made me one."

I looked up. "Excuse me?"

Cath reached under a pile of socks and winged a jewel box my way. "You know," she said. "You—the other you."

I caught the jewel box in my right hand and put the shoebox back down on the floor. In my hand was a mix CD made by me—but I hadn't made it. The cover was a photo of the Chrysler Building at night, unevenly sliced out of a men's fashion magazine, and on the CD itself a shakier version of my own handwriting had scrawled, "Nicotine Stains." Classy title. My eyes scanned the track list: Cabaret Voltaire? LCD Soundsystem? Jandek? Who was he trying to impress, anyhow? The Boredoms? Royal Trux? Superpitcher? Freaking *Bauhaus?* This was terrible! Worst of all, it showed no flair for sequencing, for dramatics. I was embarrassed for my own good name. I couldn't take my eyes off it. "He made you this?" I asked, my voice cracking.

Cath was making a brave effort to straighten out her sheets. "Yup."

"How? He doesn't even have a place to live, does he?"

"He made it here, actually. Just downloaded the songs when I was at work."

I sputtered. "He made you a mix on your own computer?"

"Yup." Cath stopped and turned to me. "What, does that break the boy code or something?"

"No, no. It's just . . ."

Cath laughed. "Look at you! You're actually offended! It's—"

I cut her off. "What offends me is the . . . I don't know, the lack of *style.*"

"Really? I thought the transition from Siouxsie and the Banshees into the Wiley/Dizzee Rascal remix was pretty good."

Under my breath I muttered, "Dizzee Rascal remix!"

Cath was staring at me as one would at a mildly autistic puppy. "This makes you so mad, doesn't it? It's actually kind of cute."

I dropped the CD onto the bed. "Whatever."

Cath beckoned for me to sit next to her. "So what do *you* have for me? Frankincense? Myrrh?"

"Oh," I said. "You know what? I think I'll give it to you later. It'll, uh, make more sense then."

Cath frowned. "OK, but don't make me wait *too* long."

I sat, gauging the distance between us carefully.

"So," I said. "Now that I have my iPod, should I leave? I mean, you are supposed to be staying the hell away from any and all David Goulds. Or so you said last night."

"Yeah," she said, suddenly fiddling with the loose discs atop her stereo. "I meant it too."

"OK," I said. "What changed?"

Cath seemed flustered. "I don't know." She hit EJECT and winged whatever had been in the stereo across the room, replacing it with something new. "Do you know this band? Dubstar? Totally cheesy and totally underappreciated. English." Shimmery synthpop filled the small room.

"I don't know them," I said.

"No one does." Cath smiled. "I love them." And she hummed along.

"Cath," I said, remembering that I was the older of the two of us. "What changed?"

"Nothing changed, creepo," she said without looking at me. "I just . . . wanted to invite someone to Stevie's party. I don't know many people in this city, remember."

"Why me, though?"

She stubbed out her cigarette. "Because you're nice, I guess.

And I liked dancing with you. And . . . you seemed lonely."

"Huh," I said.

"Whereas the other you just seems desperate."

"What's the difference?" I asked.

"Probably a few drinks." Cath raised her beer in mock salute. We clinked bottles.

"Yeah," I said. "Probably. Still, I'm glad you invited me."

"You know, I still wasn't sure I believed you until I saw that little scene in the men's room last night. About you not being the same person."

"No?"

"Like Batman and Bruce Wayne, you know? No one's ever seen them in the same room."

"We're not the same, Cath. How could one person be so . . . extreme?"

"I don't know." She shrugged and lit another cigarette. "It doesn't seem that far-fetched to me."

"Well, it does to me," I said. "And I need to do something about it. But I'm all out of ideas."

"Well," Cath said, exhaling a stream of smoke. "I guess you could call the police."

"And tell them what, exactly?"

"That you have a stalker? Identity fraud? Grand Theft Emo? I don't know."

"Yeah," I said. "Exactly." I took a sip of beer. "Besides, I think Bloomberg shut down the local X-Files chapter. Budget cuts, you understand."

Cath stuck her tongue out at me. "Funny."

"Look, the truth is . . . I don't really care one way or another."

Cath looked surprised. I was rather surprised myself. She said, "You don't?"

"No. I really don't. I'm doing too badly with my own life to worry about someone else's."

"But he's you, right? Isn't that your life too?"

"No," I said. "Why should it have to be?"

"It shouldn't," she said. "Sometimes it just seems like you want it to be."

We didn't say anything for a while after that—just sat there, drinking beer and watching Cath's cigarette smoke weave its way up to the ceiling. Eventually my eyes fell on the photograph Scotch-taped to the wall above the desk. I stood up and walked over to it.

"What's this?" I asked. "Is this you?"

The picture was of a three- or four-year-old girl who looked suspiciously like Cath wearing a Burger King crown and mugging for the camera. She was in the arms of a beautiful woman with sapphires for eyes and shoulder-length black hair.

"Yes," Cath said in a strange, small voice. "That's me and my mom."

The woman looked almost exactly like Cath, but somehow *fuller*: Her face was longer, and there was a strength to her gaze, her arms, her shoulders, that Cath lacked—a certainty of purpose, a gravity. I could see why Cath had chosen this picture to display.

"She's beautiful," I said.

"She's dead."

"I know," I said. "I'm sorry."

"It's OK." Cath took a long drag of beer. "You didn't do it." She gave me a half smile. "You're a freak, but I don't think you're cancerous."

"How old were you?" I asked.

"Um," said Cath. "I was eleven."

"That must have been horrible."

"It was. I mean, it is. But—and I think about this all time—what would be really strange is to have had her live. Like, sometimes I think about this shadow me that split off the minute she died. This totally happy girl that grew up with both parents and never went through a bad period or being such a bitch."

"There's that word again."

"What? 'Shadow'? 'Bitch'?"

"No," I said. "'Happy.'"

She laughed. "Right."

"But you get along with your dad, don't you? He seems like a good guy."

Cath's face melted a little, like I had been holding it too close to a flame. "He's the best guy. He's wonderful. He put up with *everything*—the times I ran away, the times I came home high or drunk or with funny-looking cuts on my arms. I mean, in high school there would be weeks when I wouldn't talk to him. Or if I did I would just totally curse him out. And he would just shake his head and smile to himself. He never stopped making me breakfast. He never got mad. *Ever.* And eventually I stopped trying to wind him up, because what's the point?" She sucked in nicotine and sputtered. "God, he's so good at being a dad—at being *my* dad. And look at me now—I still left him."

I sat down again. "Cath, that's what kids do. They leave. They have to."

"I know." She rubbed at her nose and then at her eyes. "It's just . . ."

"What?"

"When we're together we just have this . . . what do you call it? Banter. Like, that's how we communicate. Like I'll come home from making out with a boy and covering the entire downtown area with stickers that have random words printed on them like 'roar' or 'lion' or whatever, and he'll be asleep on the couch listening to his batshit crazy modernist classical crap. And he'll pretend he wasn't asleep and then he'll pretend that he wasn't waiting up for me. And we'll do this dance, and I don't have to tell him what I was doing because he knows, and he doesn't have to tell me he loves me because I know. But we never say anything, you know? We never say it."

Cath's face was red now and her eyes wouldn't leave the floor. She placed her cigarette on the edge of a mug that had a picture of a bear on it, and I watched the fire eat away at the filter. The music was still playing—it was cheerful and bouncy and totally inappropriate.

"Hey," I said. "I'm sorry to make you talk about this. That wasn't fair of me."

She didn't listen. "I have dreams now, you know? I have dreams of him dying, and it's the scariest thing in the world to me—it literally makes me unable to breathe to the point where I think *I'm* dying too. But I could never say anything about it to him. And I'm still living here doing stupid things like making dip."

I put my arm around her. Her shoulders were flushed and hot. "Sometimes it's hard to say stuff to the people who mean the most to you," I said. "Sometimes it's easier to say it to total strangers. It doesn't mean you're wrong, and it doesn't mean you shouldn't try."

"I know," she said. "I know."

"I mean, why else would you be telling *me,* right? No one is stranger than me."

She laughed. "Great party, huh?"

"I dunno," I said. "I've barely seen it."

"Let's go upstairs. I'll show you the roof." She started to stand. "Wait, are my eyes all red?"

I looked up at her—at the sharp chin, the tendons in her neck, the tiny wrists. It was a marvel, really, that she'd made it this far in life without snapping in two. "A little bit, but no one will notice."

She rubbed at her face. "Great—now everyone will think you made me cry."

"Nah," I said. "Just tell them it was the dip."

She smacked me, and I knew that everything would be OK.

Up on the roof, the party was, indeed, in full swing. People I recognized from the VSC and dozens of others I didn't were scattered everywhere, drinking beer and margaritas, and listening to the Chameleons play from a dinky boom box wedged on top of an exhaust grate. From this vantage, the East Village was a giant game of Q*Bert, all diagonal boxes and squares that appeared—in the fading summer light and mild alcoholic haze that enveloped me—eminently jumpable. All across the neighborhood, young and old had taken to the roofs and were celebrating and waving to one another in a gregarious manner they would never repeat on the grimier streets below. Cath was beside me, taking in the scene, balancing her homicidal dip on her bare knee. I gestured at the humble balustrade that edged the roof, intended to keep us from plunging to our deaths but instead drafted into service as a buffet table. Jesus' homeboy and other scraggly sophomores were manning a tailgating grill in the shape of a football.

"Is there anything for me to eat over there?" I asked. "I'm a vegetarian."

Cath rolled her eyes. "It's the twenty-first century, dude," she said. "We don't have anything here that wasn't slaughtered out of soy."

"Well," I said, "I hope the beans were killed humanely."

"Always," she said. "Always." And then she went off to add her dip to the food offerings spread out before us.

I drank another beer and then a third and watched happily as the evening eased its way into night. I got into a conversation with a nineteen-year-old Korean girl named Sunny about collegiate topics I knew nothing about, like eighteenth-century French painting and the benefits of study abroad. I let Jesus' homeboy—whose name was actually Keith—ruminate at length about the relative merits of nylon guitar strings versus steel. Andre ambled over, shook my hand with a firm grip, and called me Ryan Adams. We all laughed at that. I had another beer, ate some potato chips, and then downed still another can—Tecate this time, watery and sweet.

Standing on a rooftop, talking to these kids made me feel caffeinated and nostalgic, as if I had stepped through a wormhole and were back at one of my own gawky freshman parties, clutching an illict can of Beck's outside the only fraternity that didn't check IDs, sneakers toeing a clumpy root underneath a maple tree. Feeling out which of all these strange new people would be friends for the next phase of life (those with Guided By Voices boxed sets in their rooms and Replacements posters on their walls) and which would merely be faces in the alumni magazine for decades to come. Flirting shyly with the curly haired girl from my American Literature course who had a My Little Pony pencil case and liked Adrienne Rich a little too much. Finding out if the high-school charm still worked in the new setting or if college required advanced placement in wooing.

This time, however, I was older than everyone else: I had all the answers. I could see the game; I could see the strings. I knew which comments would provoke laughter and which would provoke nods. I knew which girls thought I was cute and which weren't listening. I was in control of it, so when Keith brought me another beer I accepted it gladly and made a joke, and Sunny laughed and they all laughed and I laughed too. This was all so easy. It was all so clear.

I was drunk and happy and the city air felt warm and clean on my face. I was funny. I was on. I was, in fact, so enraptured by the moment that when I felt my phone buzz in my pocket, I actually picked it up and answered it.

"Hello?"

"Holy shit, the enigma lives!"

It was Bryce. I should have guessed.

"Hey, man," I said.

"Don't 'hey, man' me, you great big crazy person. Where the hell have you been? I haven't heard from you in weeks!"

I heard his voice in my ear, but my eyes followed Cath Kennedy as she strode across the roof, empty beer bottles gathered in her hands, and made her way back down the stairs to the apartment, Ben There following somberly behind, his arm perched lazily and worryingly on her shoulder.

"I've been . . . well, all over the place, really."

"Yeah, no shit! Country mouse is suddenly city mouse!"

My head felt thick. "What?"

"Nothing. Where are you? I hear other human people. That doesn't seem like you."

"I'm at a party."

"One of the ones you 'promoted'? You bad boy rock writer, you?"

"Ha. No. A friend's."

"OK, OK. Now we're getting somewhere."

"Good."

"So you have friends now."

"What the hell do you think *you* are, dude?"

Bryce chuckled. "I don't know! You tell me!"

"Bryce, you're my best friend."

"I know that. Just wanted to hear you say it. So where the hell have you been?"

I took a deep breath and walked away from the crowd of people who stood chatting around the cooler of beer. I walked to the opposite side of the roof and looked out over Eighth Street. One of the families had provided its children with bottle rockets and noisemakers, and they were making liberal use of them in between the parked cars below.

"Bryce, have you ever felt split—like there are two of you and you don't know which one is right?"

"All the time, dude."

"Really?"

"Except that with me there are like four or five people, and one wants to go for a drive and one wants to eat and another wants to call that girl who winked at me in the bar on La Cienega the other night and one just wants to go play tennis. Oh—and the fifth one is happily getting shitfaced with you in New York right now, glad he never left to move to this crazy place."

"So what do you do?"

Bryce laughed again. Behind his voice I could hear traffic noises: cars accelerating and decelerating, honking and steering, braking and swerving on the other side of the country. "Depends on the day, dude. Depends on the day."

"I guess so."

"What the hell happened with Amy?"

The name was like a knife in my heart. "She left."

"I know that, nimrod. And you stayed."

"Yep."

"And that's all there is to it? You aren't speaking to her anymore now too?"

Then the words tumbled out. "What am I going to say to her, Bryce? What do I have left to say? All I did was talk for years and I never once backed up any of the bullshit I said. So I could call her and pretend to be in fantasyland and still hopelessly in love, but the simple truth of it is that I'm here and she's there and that's it."

"Hit a nerve, did I?"

"I guess so." I was out of breath.

"But David . . ."

"Yeah?"

"You do love her."

I sighed. "I know I do."

I heard a car door slam; Bryce must have gotten to where he was going. "Listen," he said. "Do you remember the Fourth of July four—no, Jesus, *five* years ago?"

"What?" I said. "In Philly?"

"Yep."

"When we went to the baseball game and sat out on the field to watch the fireworks afterward? That was great."

"Do you remember who my date was?"

"Sure—Stacy Ackerman."

"What a cow!"

"She wasn't that bad—but you only liked her because of her dad's car collection."

Bryce snorted. "And the marble floors in her parents' house."

"Of course. How silly of me. Marble floors can be very important to the life and general well-being of a recent college graduate."

There was a pause. All of America rotated and buzzed between us. "I miss you, buddy," he said.

"Yeah," I said, feeling a catch in the back of my throat. "I miss you too. I could really have used you out here this summer."

"It sounds to me like you've got it figured out."

"It does?"

"At least you're doing something, man. Listen—I love Amy to death and I think you should never walk away from something like that. But if you're going to do something, you should do it all the way."

"Maybe so."

"Why do you think I moved across the country?"

"Because the women out there are hotter and your sister offered you a job?"

"Yeah—but no, dude. No. I did it because I could sit around with you in New York all year, broke, with my thumb up my ass and daydreaming about going, or I could pack the car and *go.* You fucking think too much. That's why you're smart but that's why you're stupid."

"Thanks, pal."

"You know it, chum."

"Listen," I said. "I gotta get back to the party."

"OK, sure. Don't be a stranger, huh?"

"To me or to you?"

"What?"

"Nothing. Take care. Send me a postcard."

"I will." Bryce coughed again. "And listen, when you get a chance, I really might need to borrow a couple . . ."

"Good-*bye*, Bryce." I laughed. He'd owed me $425 for the last nine and a half years.

"Just thought I'd try it. Stay frosty."

"You too."

Click.

And just like that I was back on the roof of a strange party in a dark, festive city. I turned away from the edge of the roof and walked halfway back to the conversation I had left. It was still going, of course, ice-skating from quasi-ironic nostalgia ("Who was the genius who greenlit *The Golden Girls*? What production chief in L.A. was sitting around going, 'Get me a quartet of menopausal hags and let the comedy ensue'?") to fully nostalgic irony ("Remember when the coolest thing you could say about something was that it was 'decent'? What was that about?"). I shook my head. The same conversation, the same party, a thousand times all over the city. I felt old.

After a few minutes, Keith must have noticed me feeling sorry for myself, as he waved me back over.

"Hey, professor, where are the fireworks gonna be? I don't want to be facing the wrong way."

"Over the river," I said, helping myself to another beer.

There was a pause. "Which way is that?"

"East," I said, taking a sip.

Blank stares greeted me.

"That way." I pointed. Everyone cheered.

I wasn't just the oldest person there, I was apparently also the only person with a sense of direction.

Beer after beer, I bullshitted with the kids. The more empties I piled up on the edge of the roof, the less drunk I felt. It was more like turning up the volume on a radio without an antenna: The staticky hum just grew louder in my ears, helping to mask the thought of anything other than this rooftop, this party, this conversation. Except one thing, of course: Cath. The thought of her itched in my mind, causing my eyes to dart to the door anytime someone new came upstairs. Where had she gone? And why had she been gone for so *long*?

I was busy explaining to Keith why nineties R.E.M. was not, in fact, better than eighties R.E.M. when Stevie Lau burst through the doorway screaming bloody murder.

"Ew!" he shouted. People turned. Stevie was wearing a burgundy Puma tracksuit and his hair was a thousand points of spikes. "In my bed! *Ew!*"

The various groupings on the roof dissipated and circled around him. He was steaming; he was loving the attention. Surveying the crowd, he began his story. "*Someone* up here—I won't name names, *Andre*—accidentally pitches my favorite lighter—the one with the hula dancer—off of the roof, so I go downstairs to get some matches. And while I'm down there, I have the temerity"—all around me people who had no idea what that word meant murmured to themselves—"to go into my own bedroom. And what do I see there but *people*." He paused for dramatic effect. "*Straight* people. Having sex on *my* bed!" He caught his breath. His tiny face was the same color as his tracksuit. "Naked!" There was some hubbub, but the story was clearly winding down. Stevie waved his arms like propellers. "Rutting! Like animals!" Andre, head bowed with the gravity of the situation, came over to his boyfriend to provide comfort. Stevie let out one final peep: "And they didn't even ask permission!"

No one thought to ask the most important question: Who was it? My heart raced. I was making a move to rush down the stairs when someone tapped me on the shoulder. I turned.

"Hi!" It was Debra Silverstein. She was grinning, carrying a paper plate filled with food, and wearing a ripped B-52s T-shirt advertising a concert I had actually and quite unironically attended in 1989.

"Oh," I said. "Hi, Debra." I paused. She kept grinning.

"Hi!" she said again.

"I thought you were going to be in New Jersey. Isn't your sister getting bat mitzvahed?"

Debra rolled her eyes. "Ohmigod, what *drama*! The whole thing is canceled."

"You can cancel a bat mitzvah?"

"Well, not canceled, but, like, postponed?"

"Ah," I said, hoping that that would be enough for me to break away. But it wasn't.

"Yeah," she said, still smiling. "It's a huge shitstorm. Basically, my sister? Nikki? She didn't like her Torah portion."

"You mean the story from the Torah that she's supposed to recite."

"Mm-hmm." Debra bit down on a tofu pup with such ferocity I thought she would leave teeth marks in her hand.

"But you don't choose those—you just read whatever comes up the week you get bat mitzvahed."

"Exactly," Debra agreed. "But Nikki's portion? Was, like, really lame? It was about goat herding or something. Totally dull. So she refused to do it."

"She refused to do it."

"Well, between you and me she totally didn't like her shoes either."

"Her shoes."

"They didn't match her dress."

"Oh," I said, trying my best to look considerate. "That sounds really . . . unfortunate."

Debra nodded enthusiastically, thrilled to have found an ally. "I mean, goat herding! Yuck! She's gonna wait until it's time to talk about something more awesome, like, I dunno . . . when that dude turns into salt?"

I shook my head with deep compassion, then said, "Listen, Debra, have you seen Cath?"

Debra looked puzzled. "You're always asking me that!" She laughed, so I laughed too.

"I guess I am," I said. "So you haven't seen her?"

"No," she said. "Sorry."

A loud wail of a police siren started up, almost causing me to leap out of my shoes. "Jesus," I said. "Did Stevie call the police?"

"Ha, ha," said Debra. "No!" She pulled her Sidekick out of her pocket. "That's my new ring tone! I got sick of the wolves." She silenced the police with a press of her thumb. "Sorry if I scared you!"

"It's OK," I said. "Listen, Debra, I'm going to—"

"What's your Hebrew name?"

"Excuse me?"

"Your Hebrew name? You, like, have one, don't you?"

"Oh," I said. "Yeah. Um, it's Yosef. After an uncle who died before I was born."

"Neat," said Debra.

And she stood in front of me, rocking back and forth, just waiting for me to ask. So I did. "OK, what's yours?"

"It's Malkah Surah," she said proudly. "It means 'Queen Sarah.'" She beamed.

I was just about to make an inappropriate remark when a giant seagull swooped down from nowhere and snagged an entire hot-dog bun from Queen Sarah's plate. Debra screamed.

"What the hell is that?"

"It's a bird," I said.

"Yeah, obviously, but what is it?"

I paused. "It's like a plane, but with blood."

Debra stared. I killed my beer and walked off in search of Cath.

Cath's room was empty and so was Stevie's, so I locked myself in the bathroom to get some air. I sat down on the edge of the bathtub. Why was I so jealous? I had no claim to this girl—I had no claim to anyone. Halfheartedly, I picked up a few of the dozens of bottles that lined the white shelves of the bathroom: Kiehl's products for every possible cleansing need. I wondered which roommate they belonged to or if the two of them had a time-share agreement. The floor was littered with two-year-old issues of oversize fashion magazines like *V* and *W*, all promising the secret of the new looks in London. The sink was full of cat.

Wait—what?

I stood up. In the sink, playfully batting at a thin stream of water, was an undersized gray and black mottled cat. It noticed me, said, "Mrowr," then began bashing its tiny forehead into the water.

"What are you doing?" I said. "Cats hate water."

But the cat didn't listen—in fact it twisted its body in liquid-inspired ecstasy, lolling around the entire sink and ignoring me entirely. Sufficiently confused, I unlocked and opened the bathroom door, and Cath Kennedy was standing on the other side.

"There you are," she said, taking my arm. "I've been looking all over for you."

"You have a cat in your sink," I said.

"Oh! You met Sinky!" She dropped my arm and rushed into the bathroom to give the cat a damp pat on the head. "He loves it in here. We have to keep the faucet turned on for him."

"I thought cats hate water," I said.

"I thought people didn't have evil twins!" she said, sticking her tongue out at me.

"Point," I said. I watched her pet Sinky for a moment, then said, "I was looking for you, too."

"You were?"

"I was."

"I was dealing with Ben There and then helping him into a cab," she said.

"'Dealing' . . . like in Stevie's room dealing?"

Cath laughed. "Ohmigod, gross! No—that was our neighbors. We didn't even invite them to the party. They're exhibitionists." Sinky was licking happily at her wrist. "Anyway, he was in a bad mood. I don't think he likes you very much. I think he might even have been jealous."

I raised my eyebrows. "Jealous of *me*? Why?"

Cath shrugged. "I suppose he gets jealous whenever a strange older man who isn't him takes an interest in me." Sinky was purring loudly now, his tiny eyes closed in private passion. "How come you didn't pet Sinky?"

"Oh," I said. "I guess I'm out of the habit. I used to love cats, but

Amy"—I watched Cath's face for any reaction, but there was none—"Amy was allergic, so I had to keep away."

Cath grabbed my hand and pulled me into the bathroom. "Well she's not here now. Come on—who could resist that face?"

I looked down and felt myself resisting, then giving in. I gave Sinky a light tap on the forehead—which was soaked and fuzzy—and then a full stroke from front to back. The cat arched its furry spine in appreciation. "Cute," I said.

"Well done," said Cath, taking my arm again. "Now come on. I don't want to miss the fireworks."

And so I let her lead me back up the stairs. Up on the roof, night had fallen completely and the chatter and laughter that emerged from our party seemed to blend and mingle with similar sounds from the top of every building in the city.

We walked past the rest of the guests—arranged around the boom box and the food—and made our way to the opposite end of the roof. It was unspoken, our walk, but somehow exhilarating: We were together now and didn't much care who knew it. We crouched down behind the air-conditioning unit, just hidden from plain sight, faced east, and waited for everything to begin. We didn't have to wait long. A hush fell over the city, and the prerecorded string music started up from a radio perched on someone else's rooftop. And then, before long, the *whoosh* of rockets was audible and the first fireworks of Independence Day lit up the night.

"Wow," said Cath. "That's beautiful."

And it was. As the lights exploded all around us, I felt outside of myself for the first time in days. The city was beautiful, illuminated, shining. The only sounds were the staccato bursts of exploding fireworks and the multitracked oohs of appreciation echoing from every rooftop, from everywhere.

"These are my favorites," I whispered, as a cascade of slowly bursting green lit up the night.

Behind us, I could hear Keith laughing about something and Debra squealing, Stevie's high-pitched complaining and Andre's muttered shushing. But none of it mattered. White flashed, then orange. The vague sound of strings and snippets of political speeches: Lincoln, Roosevelt, Kennedy. I turned slightly and watched the glare illuminate Cath's face. Her eyes were wide open and seemed never to blink. She looked innocent, awestruck.

Eventually there was a pause. Somewhere someone whistled and someone else applauded.

Cath leaned into me. "Is that it?"

"No way," I said. "It wouldn't be the Fourth of July without the grand finale."

"God," said Cath. "That's so *American.*"

But as the pops and flashes began again—louder than before and with greater frequency, reds and whites and blues oozing and melting over one another in a relentless cacophony of noise and color—I felt Cath Kennedy snake her small bony palm into my own, felt her body push into my side. I squeezed her hand as the last dying embers exploded in the sky and she squeezed it back. I turned and found her looking at me strangely, her eyes reflecting the colors of the flag, sparks like fireflies dancing in her pupils.

"Cath," I said.

"Shut up," she said, and pulled my head down to hers and kissed me on the mouth.

It was a good kiss, too, completely free of awkward fumbling or closed-mouth half starts. It was as if we had done this before, even as the unfamiliar curve of her thin lips and the surprising taste of cigarettes on her tiny, darting tongue sent a shivery thrill running through my body. I turned into her and raised my arm to her ear. She squeezed my side, those furious fingers working their way under my T-shirt, when a cry came up from behind us, interrupting everything.

"Holy shit! What the hell is in this dip?"

Cath giggled and took my head in her hands. "Let's go back downstairs," she whispered, and I nodded in agreement.

Back in her room now, with only the desk lamp on, we tried kissing again and it seemed to work, so we kept at it, her leading me backward in half steps until she was sitting down on the bed and I was standing awkwardly above her, trying to kneel down and kick my shoes off, and she was scooting backward trying to make room for me, our mouths still connected, while she raised her arms over her head and worked her T-shirt up and—whoops, had to stop kissing for a moment—off, and there went the T-shirt and I was lying on the bed with her, trying not to be on top of her but more off to the side because this was going awfully fast, hoping she would take the lead and put me wherever I needed to be. The air conditioner was on way too high and it made the small hairs on her arms stand up and the soft skin along her stomach rise in goose bumps. I ran my palm along it and she made a noise in my ear, something soft and sudden like "oooom," and so I did it again. She wrapped a leg around my waist and let her mouth wander away from mine now, across my cheek and up to my ear, her small tongue at my lobe now, but all of a sudden it didn't feel sexy so much as it felt *young*—like this was a move from *Seventeen* magazine and we were making out in her father's Toyota Camry. Carefully I moved her mouth back to mine, and she sat me up slightly and started to lift my shirt off, her hands tickling and wheedling their way up my sides to my rib cage. The only noise in the room aside from the rustling of her sheets and the tangling of our limbs was the hum of the air conditioner, and I wished now for that synthpop music of hers—anything to cover up the silence, to give me a soundtrack for doing whatever it was we were doing. She tugged at my shirt again and I gave in, raising my arms above my head, and while my eyes were covered she sat up all the way and ran her lips along my collarbone, her tongue down my sternum. I pulled my shirt the rest of the way off and looked down at her fine black hair as her head danced delicately along my body. I lay back down with her then and saw her small chest, the almost comical lace of her white bra against the sharp angles of her shoulder blades, her nothing biceps—and then I felt the passion leave me in one giant rush.

"Cath," I whispered as gently as I could manage, half hoping she wouldn't hear me.

"Mmmm," she breathed, kissing my neck, rubbing her hand—oh, God—along my waist and ever so slightly lower.

I closed my eyes. "Cath," I said again. "Cath, I can't do this."

All of a sudden she was alert to me, and her soft body turned rigid.

"What are you talking about?" She spoke at full volume. What *was* I talking about?

"This," I said, pulling back slightly. "This is fast . . . we should . . . talk about this."

Cath pushed me off her and sat up. "What do you want to talk about?"

"I'm just not sure if this . . . is what we should be doing."

Cath crossed her arms in front of her chest. "Why not? You don't want me?"

I blushed. "No, that's not it, I . . ."

She kicked at my crotch. "Because I can tell that you do."

"Yeah, Cath," I said, "I do. I really do. It's just that . . ." She stared, a flush in her cheeks. "I have a girlfriend, still. It still means something to me. I'm sorry."

"You're sorry?" She reached around on the bed for her shirt, found mine instead, and pulled it over her body. Now she was navy blue and the slogan on her chest advertised a favorite band of mine that was entirely inappropriate for the situation: The Jealous Sound. "I don't fucking get you, creepo. I really don't." She stood up and retrieved a pack of cigarettes from her desk, extracted one, and lit it. "If you have a girlfriend, why aren't you with her? If she means that much to you, why are you here with me?"

I sat up, feeling vulnerable with no shirt on. "I don't know."

"If you're so faithful, why did you start a secret diary about being so fucking unfaithful?"

"You read it?"

"Of course I read it. And you know what? I couldn't tell where the one you started and the other began." She exhaled and leaned against the wall. I said nothing. "You wanted this life all the time—yet you managed to still be in la-la land with Annie?"

"Amy," I said feebly.

"Whatever." Cath stomped across the small room, back and forth, back and forth, pointing her cigarette at me like a pistol. "Seriously, tell me—if you even know. If you are so sure that you can't betray her or whatever, why aren't you over there with her now?"

I knotted my hands in my lap and stared down at my knuckles. The skin on my right fist was still chapped and raw from the punch I had thrown the night before. "I always told her that we'd be together forever. She was the one who had doubts. I was completely certain. About us. About the future." I looked up at Cath, who was staring back at me. "I guess the only way to describe it is . . . it's like I carried the future in front of me like a carrot on a stick. The closer I got to it in terms of years or situation or life or whatever, it was always the same distance away. Like I was never going to actually reach it."

Cath let out a bitter laugh. "You're comparing your girlfriend to a carrot."

"No! No. Well, maybe. It's just that I knew the path I was on and what I wanted it to be, but I was never prepared for it to actually *happen.* You know?" I sighed. "Maybe it's for the best, her leaving. I promised her a future for years, but it was never going to stop being the future. It was never going to become the present."

Cath stopped pacing and sat down on the bed across from me. "Mm-hmm."

I rubbed my forehead. "It's just . . . when I talk about it, I feel like

I'm running in place. No, not in place; like in one of those—what were they? Those exercise balls you'd put a gerbil in? So it can run around on the floor but never actually escape?"

"David," Cath said.

I looked up. "Yes?"

"Are you drunk?"

"What? No!"

"First your girlfriend is a carrot, now you're a gerbil in a plastic ball. Hello? Why can't you talk about this like a human being?"

I shook my head. "Yeah, but . . ."

"But what?"

"Gerbils really like carrots."

She smacked me in the shoulder.

"You have got to do something about that aggression," I said, staring at the red, Cath's-hand-sized mark that was forming on my body.

"Yeah, well, you've got to do something about your psychological meltdown."

"I know it."

"So seriously, why did you start that diary?"

I considered the question, maybe for the first time. "I guess I bound up so much of my life in her that when she left . . . it's like I was nothing. And I had this urge to be *something*, to do something. And all of the lives that I was reading about seemed so much fuller than mine. Full of all these things that seemed so appealing. So impossible."

"David, they're not like that. They're just the parts people choose to share."

"I know."

"And look at the parts you chose to share."

Silence.

"But what about you, Cath? The long nights? The drinking? The sex? That's what you were presenting to everyone—what did that mean about you? What does that say about you?"

She threw up her hands. "What does it say about me? I'll tell you: whatever I want it to! I don't care! It's my actual life, David—it's what I've got. It's not some walk-on-the-wild-side fantasy. I'd fucking love to have what you apparently threw out, and until I get it I can do whatever I fucking want." She paused, lowered her voice. "You're just running and running, but you're not running *to* anything." She stubbed out her cigarette, considered her words. "I'm not a plot device for you, David. I'm not some evil harpy thrown into your life to cause your downfall. I'm just me. And I deserve better than this."

"You're right," I said. "You're right." She leaned back, stretching one leg across mine, and I felt all the heaviness of the past week in that solitary contact. "I guess I want everything. But I just don't want to deal with the consequences."

"David," she said, sounding suddenly more tired and old than she had any right to, "you need to figure this out. Quickly. You can't be two people, David. It doesn't work that way."

"I know," I said.

"You either want to or you don't. There's nothing else to it."

"I know," I said.

"Decide," she said.

• • •

But I didn't decide, not then. I couldn't. The more I pushed away from Cath Kennedy, the more I wanted her to pull me back. And the more I tried to eliminate the doppelgänger, the more divided I felt. We talked a bit longer and we even made out some more, but the passion was gone and the reason for doing so even more lost. I had wanted Miss Misery, but I had met Cath Kennedy instead. And the funny thing was that maybe after everything, I wanted Cath Kennedy more. But wanting and doing are two separate things—each with its own set of responsibilities and consequences. There was no Miss Misery. There was only Cath, and she was real and made of bones and feelings and not to be trifled with. Not halfheartedly. Not without fixing myself first.

So eventually I got up to leave, and Cath let me—I put my shirt back on and even turned away as she changed into one of her own. I knew I had to call Amy again. And I knew I couldn't hang up until everything was resolved.

At the door Cath said, "Thanks for coming."

And I said, "Thank you for inviting me. I really had a wonderful time."

We stood a little longer, awkward in the formality of the moment. Then Cath's face brightened. "I almost forgot!" She reached into her skirt pocket, pulled out my driver's license, and handed it to me.

"How—how did you get this?"

Cath beamed, shrugged. "I found it on the floor of the Madrox last night on my way out. I guess the other you was too fucked up to remember to hold onto it."

"Wow," I said, staring at it. David Gould. Five feet nine inches.

Brown eyes. Organ donor. Never before had I been so happy to see the simple details of my life in front of me. "Thank you."

"No problem," said Cath, kissing me on the cheek and pushing me gently out the door. "Try not to lose it again—and try not to forget it either."

It was after midnight when I got off the subway in Brooklyn, and the streets were quiet. Walking home, I turned my face up and closed my eyes; tried to catch the warmth of the night in my mouth, tried to swallow it and trap it and make it part of me, the only calm part left. Sooner or later, this craziness had to come to an end. I realized, maybe for the first time, that only I could end it.

As I neared my building it appeared that someone had left some luggage on the top step. Was someone moving out? But no, it wasn't luggage—it was a person, huddled over and keeping still. A bum? A locked-out member of the Armando family? It wasn't—oh, God—it wasn't the doppelgänger, was it? Bringing my nightmare quite literally to my doorstep? But no, it wasn't him either. I approached quietly, swinging open the gate, and only then realized that the huddled figure was, in fact, a teenage girl with long blond hair. The girl was wearing a gray sweatshirt with a unicorn on it and listening intently to headphones, which she threw off as she caught sight of me. No way, I thought. It couldn't be. I rubbed my eyes.

"Ashleigh?"

The blond girl on the steps sprung up. "I thought you'd be taller," she said, and threw her arms around me.

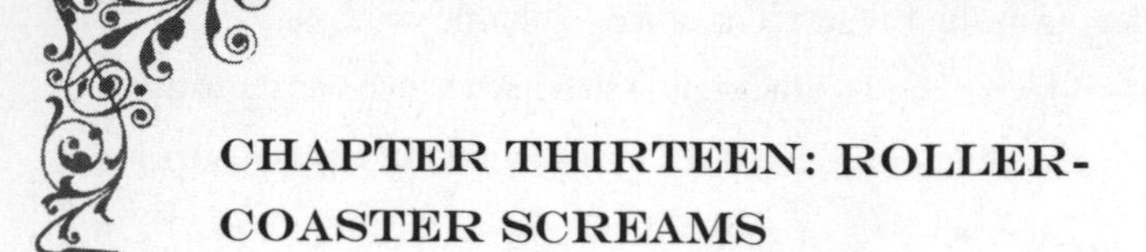

CHAPTER THIRTEEN: ROLLER-COASTER SCREAMS

[from **http://users.livejournal.com/~thewronggirl87**]
Time: 8:11 a.m.
Mood: Decided
Music: Dashboard Confessional, "This Bitter Pill"

I reserved the ticket and I just finished packing my bag and that's it. I'm outta here. I'm done. They think I'm catching a ride with Jonathan Howland and his family but by the time they figure out the truth, I'll be across the country.

I am tired of living a lie. I am tired of having the people who made me and are supposed to love me the most hate me, undercut me, try to hurt me. And I am tired of lying to them. Having to be two people – the good one and the real one. Leading a double life. I'm so freaking sick of it. I know that this seems like a crazy thing to say but all I want is a life that's *less* complicated. And I can't get it here. Mom coming in here last night and searching under my bed and taking every CD that she found – every notebook, every scrap of paper. That was the last straw. When she touched the parts of me that I had created, that I'm responsible for . . . when she balled up the papers and ripped some and clenched them in her furious hands it was like she was doing that to *me*. Balling me up and ripping me and throwing me away. It hurt so deep.

So I'm leaving. I'm leaving everything. My family doesn't know me and they don't want to know me so I'm going to the one person I don't have to lie to. The one person who understands me better than anyone else. And the one city where you're allowed to start all over.

This isn't like that poem we read in school last year about the two roads in the forest. My life has never been like that. My life has been nothing but dark, miserable forest. And what I'm doing today is the first time I even saw a road.

If anyone ever finds this and reads this just know that I'm happier – maybe even happy. I'm sorry for all the hurt I caused everyone and mostly I'm sorry for letting everyone down. I'm sorry Jessie that I won't see you grow up but you're perfect and light and all I could ever do was mess you up, make you dark, or drag you down. Maybe one day we'll know each other again and you'll forgive me.

Good-bye. Good-bye. Good-bye. ::crying:: Good-bye.

In my dream, I was sitting in the chorus room at my old high school. I thought I was waiting for Mr. Davis, the beloved music teacher, but in fact I was waiting for the dentist. It seemed that one of my teeth—my favorite tooth, actually, the sharp incisor on the right side—was loose, and I was waiting for him to show up and examine it. But there was a bowling alley next door, and the noise was so loud that my tooth started rattling around in my mouth, and then it fell out. For a while I thought it was OK because it was just a baby tooth, but then I remembered that I'd lost all my baby teeth twenty years before, so this one was really gone. Gone for good. So I was swallowing blood and waiting for the hygienist—Cath Kennedy dressed as a candy striper—to notice that one and now two and then three of my grown-ass adult teeth were falling out of my mouth. And she wouldn't notice. No one would. My teeth were like rock candy—brittle and crunchy—and they fell out of my mouth in packs of two or three. But then someone was calling my name (finally!) and I turned but it wasn't Cath Kennedy or any member of my high-school faculty. It was someone else, someone young, saying, "David. David. David."

"David."

I opened my eyes. I was in bed. And Ashleigh Bortch was standing in the doorway repeating my name. I turned.

"Good morning!" she said merrily.

I rubbed my face. "Good morning, Ashleigh," I said.

She was dressed as she had been the night before, and she was sipping a glass of orange juice. "Why do you have a pigeon feeder in your window?"

"I don't," I said, struggling to get a firm grip on consciousness.

"Then what is it?"

"It's . . ." I cleared my throat, sat up. "Never mind. It's a pigeon feeder. What time is it?"

"It's eight a.m.," she said sprightly. "It's when I always wake up."

"Even during the summer?"

"Oh, yeah," she said. "I keep my alarm on year-round."

"Fantastic," I said. "Um, I'm going to take a shower. And then we're going to talk."

"OK," said Ashleigh.

"You can't stay here, Ashleigh. You have to go home." I did my best to look stern, sitting as I was amid my unmade bed wearing a bright red T-shirt with a picture of Tintin on it.

But all she said was, "You're out of OJ!" And then she scampered back to the living room.

Ashleigh Bortch had run away from home, and the only place she had felt safe running to was here. To New York City. To my apartment. To me. She had tried to explain all of this the night before, sitting in my kitchen, clutching the mug of chamomile tea that I had made for her and doing her best not to cry. In turn, I did my best to reason with her, tried telling her that she didn't know me, that she couldn't run away from her own life—that it's better to stay and fight and deal with it. That she was breaking the law—or worse, that I was breaking it by even having her here with me. But she didn't listen to any of that. All she said was, "But you know me better than anyone else!" And her eyes got red and weepy and I could tell how tired and scared she was, and I looked in the mirror and my own eyes were red and exhausted. So I told her she could sleep on the futon for one night—but that tomorrow we'd have to work on sending her back home.

Her parents were under the impression that she was spending the weekend at a prospective pre-med student program at BYU, safely ensconced with no one but ardent fellow Mormons to entertain her; Mr. and Mrs. Bortch wouldn't worry about their daughter until she didn't show up at home again on Sunday. Ashleigh had pawned her stereo the day before and then used the cash—plus all the money she had in her bank account—to buy a one-way ticket from Salt Lake City to JFK. From there she had taken a bus and two subways and walked. She had gotten my address from the phone book.

I was impressed, of course, but also mortified. This girl didn't know me, and I certainly had no idea what to do with her. The fear and loneliness and unhappiness that had propelled her to fly to the other side of the country were as foreign to me as Cantonese. I wasn't a runner—I was a dedicated wallower—and my own teenage years had been generally spotless. For me to act as a confidante, let alone as guardian, to someone nearly a decade my junior was just impossible to comprehend. Not to mention incredibly inconvenient. For the longest time I had had nothing better to do than screw up my own life. Now, when I was finally gathering the necessary strength to work on fixing it, other people kept crashing their own problematic lives into mine. I felt like the only bumper car in the ring with its power turned off.

As I showered, I considered the various things I could say to Ashleigh, but all of them were subtle variations on the phrase "get out!" I sighed and rinsed the shampoo from my hair, letting the water run all over my face. It wasn't waking me up, particularly, but it was making me feel peaceful. The rhythm of the water was warm, dreamlike. Too nice, actually. I twisted the faucet and the water slowed to a trickle, then disappeared. Dripping and goose-bumped, I stared lazily out the window. Another beautiful day, bright blue and brilliant. Mrs. Armando's garden was an explosion of green below me, and in the backyard next to hers two young boys splashed in an inflatable kiddie pool. I couldn't kick this girl out. She had turned to me. I couldn't turn away.

I dried myself as best I could, threw the Tintin T-shirt back on, wrapped my towel around my waist, and walked out into the kitchen. Ashleigh was sitting at the kitchen table poring over old issues of *Transmission.* In her lap was a box of Kix cereal that had to have been at least a year old.

"This is stale," she said, popping another handful into her mouth.

"I know," I said. "But please—help yourself."

She looked up at me with giant shining blue eyes. "Thanks," she said. I couldn't be mean to this kid—she was living and dying on everything I said.

"I'll just be a second," I said. "I'm going to get dressed, and then we are going to have a talk."

"OK," she said, turning back to the magazines. But I could feel her eyes back on me as I passed her en route to the bedroom. "Man," she said. "You look just like all the emo boys in my high school."

I froze. "I what, now?"

"Yeah," she said. "All the emo boys are super skinny like you. Of course, they all have eating disorders, so they can wear girls'-size jeans. Like this guy I was crushing on for a second? Bert? He had a smaller waist than I did. That totally sucked."

"Huh," I said. "I'm gonna go get dressed now. I promise I won't wear any girls' jeans. You can check."

"OK!" Ashleigh resumed crunching the stale cereal and I made it to the bedroom without further incident.

After I was dressed—in men's jeans and a plain gray T-shirt—I asked Ashleigh to sit with me in the living room. She took the futon, still covered in sheets from the bed I had made for her the night before. I pulled a chair in from the kitchen and sat on it facing her to make the whole thing seem more official.

"Golly," said Ashleigh. "You sure have a lot of newspapers lying around."

"Did you just say 'golly'?"

She blushed. "Yeah, sorry. My parents make us say stuff like that. So we don't get in the habit of cursing or blaspheming or anything."

"Gotcha," I said. "I hope I don't offend you if I curse."

She grinned. "No way."

It was odd and disconcerting to be around someone so completely and totally *young*—but no, it was more than that. The kids at the party yesterday were young, but they were familiar—they were basically the same as me. This girl came from an entirely different planet. Her skin was whiter than white, and her hair was the sort of washed-out, straw-colored blond usually attainable only through multiple bleachings. She wasn't chubby, but she definitely wasn't skinny, either; her round and freckled cheeks seemed woefully out of place on such a tall frame. In fact, her body and head seemed to belong to two different people. Her body was that of a grown woman, but her movements belied her age: She fidgeted constantly, as if a small but distinguishable current were being run through her nerve endings. Her face was as wide open as the full moon, and her blue eyes had a hunger to them that was almost uncomfortable to look at. She giggled and talked bigger than she was, but having her in the room felt like playing host to a deer—something wild and willful and prepared to bolt at any moment.

"OK, Ashleigh," I said. "Why did you run away from home?"

She frowned, and when she did so her lower lip stuck out almost comically from her face, as if it had been stung by some ornery wasp. "I told you all about this. I thought you were listening."

"I'm sure I was listening," I said as patiently as possible. "But why don't you tell me again just so we can have everything on the table."

She glanced at the chaotic coffee table in front of her. "It looks like you've got plenty on the table already."

"Cute," I said.

She smiled then, but as she began to talk, the smile washed away from her face like a sand castle at high tide. "I hate my life, basically. I hate it so much. And I just got sick of it, you know? Fed up. They treat me so badly, and they didn't just invade my privacy this time. They freaking destroyed it. And so after all of that all I could think about was what we talked about. And I just wanted to do it for myself."

I was confused. "What we talked about?"

"Yes!" She balled up one of the newspapers on the table and winged it at my head. Why were these younger women always trying to hit me? "Sorry," she said. "I just don't want to know that you weren't listening. Nobody ever listens to me."

"Don't worry," I said. "I listen to you. I just want you to remind me what we talked about."

"The other day," she began, picking at her fingernails, "when we were online. We were talking about what you do if the entire world thinks of you as a different person. If you're totally misunderstood or not, like, you know . . . appreciated."

My mind raced backward. It sounded familiar. But I thought we had been talking about *me*.

She went on. "And I realized that when I was giving advice to you, I was really talking about myself. That you had to shake those other people. You had to take the false image of you that they carried in their brains and kill it dead. You had to, like, take it over."

"Uh-huh." I nodded.

"So when my mom tore my room apart the other night, something in me snapped. And I realized—she can't do this. She can do all she wants to the imaginary me, the one who loves church and obeys them and is going to get married and go on a mission and blah blah blah. But when she comes in *here* . . ." Her cheeks were red and her eyes were moist. "I mean, when she goes in *there*, that's out of her, like—what's the word? For places a policeman is in control of?"

"Precinct?" I said. "Jurisdiction?"

"Yeah." She nodded. "That one. That's just not her business. I won't let her mess with my real self anymore. It doesn't belong to her. It belongs to me."

"OK," I said. "That sounds reasonable. But why did you get on a plane? For God's sake, Ashleigh, why did you come *here*?"

She blushed more deeply. "Once I knew I had to protect the real me, I got even more upset. Because I realized that no one *knew* the real me. Only maybe Krystal—she's my best friend—but she's as powerless as I am. I told an older girl that I knew once about how I really feel and how I don't believe in the church or in God and stuff—and she stopped speaking to me. But not until after she told my mom what I had told her. Which was majorly not fun. So I was thinking that I only get to be my real self online, with the people I meet there. And the person that I thought of . . ." Her voice went all small and her eyes didn't leave the rug. "The person I thought of was you."

"Me," I repeated dumbly.

"Yeah," she said shyly, her eyes desperately seeking out mine. "You."

"Ashleigh, I'm sorry, but why me? We've never even met."

She groaned. "Don't you get it? That's, like, exactly what I'm saying! If you *knew me* knew me, all you'd see is what the rest of them see. But online you listened and you . . . I dunno, you took me seriously. And you have this freaking amazing life where you get to listen to free CDs and meet rock stars and, like, *write books*." She said the latter as if she were quoting from scripture, like she was saying I had the power to bend steel or shoot beams of force from my eyes. "It's all that I've ever wanted, and I just had to get away. I had to come get it. Before . . . I dunno. Before it was just, like, *too late*." A single tear traveled the lonely road over her freckles and down to the bottom of her face.

"Hey," I said. "Hey, don't cry." I got up and retrieved a box of tissues from my bedroom. "I get it. I hear you. I do." She blew her nose noisily into a tissue. "I'm . . . flattered, really."

She looked up at me, eyes alight, nose still buried in yellow tissue. "You are?"

I smiled at the sight. "Yeah. I am."

"So this is gonna work?" She snuffled again, balled the tissue up in her left hand. "You'll help me?"

"Yeah," I said, hearing it aloud myself for the first time. "I'll help you."

She was practically levitating off the futon. "I can stay?"

I raised my hand. "No, Ashleigh. You can't stay." She deflated. "You're going to have to go home somehow—before you get found out or I get arrested. But we'll figure it out together, OK? Together?"

Her face went in a hundred different directions. "OK. But . . ."

"But what?"

"I just . . . before you do anything with me, there's one thing I've really always wanted to see."

"What, in New York?"

"Yeah."

"OK, name it. Anything."

Her face lit up again. "Are you anywhere near Coney Island?"

On the raised subway platform, waiting for the F to arrive at Fourth Avenue, Ashleigh tore through a cinnamon bun I had bought for her at my local coffee place and stared expectantly down the track.

"Haven't you heard that watched pots never boil?" I asked her, but she ignored me. I felt sorry that we were on the Brooklyn-bound side of the tracks. It was impossible to see the Statue of Liberty from here, and I knew she would have appreciated it.

During the half-hour ride out, Ashleigh bopped from one end of the car to the other, staring at maps and the ads for Captain Morgan Spiced Rum and trying hard *not* to stare at our fellow passengers. Across the aisle from where I sat and where Ashleigh occasionally joined me were two Russian women speaking animatedly to each other. One was older, her thick eye makeup lacquered on her wrinkled face like icing on a cake. She wore a white sundress with red poppies stitched into the fabric. Her companion was much younger—probably my age exactly—and tall and lean and blond. She wore tight acid-washed jeans and a white blouse with a wide, lacy neck. She was, in fact, incredibly beautiful, with a haughty air to her; the only thing standing between her and perfection was a remarkably angled nose that mimicked a double-black-diamond ski slope. I took the two to be mother and daughter. Ashleigh took them to be fascinating.

"What language are they speaking?" she asked me in a hushed whisper.

"I think it's Russian," I said.

"Wow." Ashleigh's eyes registered respect and amazement.

"There are a lot of Russians in Coney Island and Brighton Beach; it's like the primary language spoken out there."

The women seemed to sense that we were speaking about them, and they turned and faced Ashleigh, the older one giving her a broad wink. Ashleigh turned ten shades of purple and dropped her face to her hands.

When her embarrassment passed and the train was outside again, elevated and passing the lettered avenues, I asked her, "Why is it that you want to go to Coney Island so badly, anyway?"

"It's, like, my favorite song. By Death Cab. Do you know it?"

"I'm not sure I do."

She sang tentatively, swallowing every other word. "'Everything was closed at Coney Island . . . I couldn't help from smiling!' Or something like that." She blushed again.

"Well," I said. "Nothing is going to be closed on a holiday weekend in the summer, I'll tell you that much."

"Oh, yeah," she said. "I didn't think of that."

"You might even get a chance to ride the Cyclone."

"What's that?"

"It's like the oldest roller coaster in the country. It's super old, super wooden, and super scary. Like this cross between an amusement-park ride and a medieval torture device."

Ashleigh's eyes widened. "Cool."

I had to admit I was having fun. Despite the potential illegality of all of this—and despite my still not having dealt with the doppelgänger drama—I realized that this was the first summer day I had taken for myself in ages. Showing off New York, having a visitor—even a runaway Mormon visitor—allowed me to step back, to relax. To do all the things that were only a subway ride away from my daily life but usually felt farther from me than Utah.

"You were right, by the way," she said. "It is hot here."

"I told you."

"It's different hot back at home. It's less . . . soupy."

"That's what I've heard."

At Avenue U, Ashleigh ran to the window and stared out over the boundless urban landscape in front of her: row house after row house, life after life, all passing beneath the solitary train car. She ran back and took her seat next to me. "It's so . . . huge."

"And just think," I said, "this is only one fraction of one borough of the entire city."

She shook her head. "Where I live, everything is just flat. You can see it all in one look, and if you can't, there are always the mountains."

"That sounds nice."

She shook her head harder. "It's not when you live there. For tourists and stuff the mountains are beautiful, or they mean, like, skiing or whatever. For me, they're always at the edge of everything I do. Like a barricade or something."

"Keeping the world out?"

"No," she said. "Keeping me in."

Right before we arrived Ashleigh elbowed me in the side and said, "By the way, the phone rang when you were in the shower."

"It did? It tends to do that."

"I picked it up."

"You what?"

She raised her hands in mock surrender. "That's what people do, right? When phones ring, they answer them?"

I rubbed my brow. "Not everyone."

"Sorry."

"It's OK. Who was it?" My mind churned. A long-lost relative? The juvenile-crimes division of the NYPD? Amy? That would be perfect—just the thing she needed to hear was a female voice at the end of the line.

"It was weird—just some guy. He asked for you and I said you were in the shower. Then he just laughed and hung up."

"That's creepy, Ashleigh. What did he sound like?"

"That's the thing. He sounded just like you."

The F train dead-ends at Coney Island. With its long journey (from the farthest edge of Queens, through the arteries of Manhattan, and then straight down across Brooklyn) completed, the train shuddered, groaned once, and then fell silent. Ashleigh and I joined the rest of the early thrill seekers—a motley assortment of young and old, pale and dark, most clutching towels and sand pails and beach chairs for the long sunny day ahead—and headed down the stairs. I've often thought that the Coney Island subway station resembles a giant, open mouth—constantly spewing its contents into the bizarro universe of Astroland, the boardwalk, and the beach. The smell of sand and salt water filled the air as we hit the sidewalk, and even now, at just before ten in the morning, the rumble and rattle of the Cyclone was audible and with it, every few moments, a symphony of shrill roller-coaster screams.

"This place is freaking crazy," said Ashleigh, and I couldn't think of any better way to put it myself.

We jaywalked Surf Avenue with the rest of the crowd and plunged ourselves into the cacophony waiting for us on the other side. "Stay close," I said to Ashleigh, and then chuckled at my weirdly parental tone. There were street vendors everywhere hawking sunglasses and balloons: Spider-Man, Pokémon, SpongeBob by the hundreds. The day was just beginning, but the sticky heat was out in full force; the humidity was less noticeable here by the ocean, but it already felt more oppressive than the day before. We cut left and tried to maneuver past a gaggle of slow-moving moms and kids waving and pointing at the cheap toys for sale all around us. Ashleigh gawked down each alleyway at the midway games and flashing arcade lights. Rides whooshed and children wailed; a posse of shirtless black men with white do-rags wrapped around their heads walked by chomping on morning hot dogs from Nathan's, daintily picking at thick-cut cheese fries with tiny red plastic forks. A bald Chinese man offered back massages on a special chair just off the curb, an island in the midst of roaring pedestrian waters. I tried to imagine what this was like for Ashleigh—like going from a sensory deprivation tank into a carnival dunk tank, probably. Her eyes were wild with delight, and she kept turning back to look at me, to make sure I'd seen whatever she had seen too, that I could somehow verify it as real, as actually happening.

It was something close to exhilarating witnessing this glorious, noisy chaos through someone else's wide and unjaded eyes. Part of living in New York—even the neighborhoods far less gaudy and circus-like than this one—is losing yourself in crowds, subsuming yourself and your better nature under the currents of the city streets. What it took me until that moment to realize was that it was also quite possible to *find* yourself in that same loud thrum, to become alive to yourself only when surrounded by countless others. In my mind I juxtaposed Ashleigh's lonely cursor blinking on a computer screen—hers or mine or anyone's—with this glittery blond ball of *something*—energy, potential, nerves, whatever—that was bouncing around in front of me. The two were inextricably related but powerfully different—like a world-class athlete and his pale weakling of a shadow.

Forward and forward we pushed through the crowd. The only thing that could finally bring Ashleigh Bortch to a complete standstill—to shock her out of her New York rhapsody—was the sight of the Cyclone. It looked, as it always did, like a long-forgotten erector set, something as old as the Pilgrims and as dangerous as one of their smallpox-laden blankets. The car rushing along its dipping tracks sounded like a skeleton in a hurricane—rattling and clattering and about as far from reassuring as you could imagine. Even before noon, there was a snaking line of gawping Brooklynites waiting to test their luck against the great beast. Everyone knew the thing had to topple sometime. But they also knew that the odds of it happening on their heads were remote.

Ashleigh whistled. "Whoa," she said.

"Yup," I said.

"That's . . . that's *crazy.*"

"I know it."

"I'm scared just looking at it."

"To be honest, so am I." We stood for a moment, heads tilted, mouths open. Annoyed thrill seekers pushed at our backs and sighed loudly as they navigated around us. "Hey, Ashleigh, why don't we get a snack and go check out the boardwalk? That might help us build up our courage."

"OK," she said, turning. "I'm starving."

"You did just have breakfast, didn't you?"

"That was nothing," she said. "I'm a big eater. You had like no food in your house. You totally have an eating disorder."

I led her along the Astroland fence toward the ocean. "That's crazy. I do not."

"Then why don't you have any food in your house?"

"Because . . . because I'm lazy and don't eat at home very much."

She skipped ahead. "Mormons have to keep a year's supply of food in their pantries at all times—that way we're prepared for tough times."

"Yeah? Well, this is New York. My apartment doesn't have a pantry. My apartment barely has a bedroom."

Up on the boardwalk we dodged oncoming Rollerbladers and approached the food stall closest to us. Ashleigh seemed overwhelmed by the choices—everything from cotton candy to shrimp platters with a side of corn on the cob. Luckily for me, not even Ashleigh's boundless appetite was up to a fried clam roll before noon. I steered her toward a funnel cake instead and let her carry it—steaming hot and smothered with powdered sugar—over to one of the wooden benches facing the ocean. We sat and picked at the scorching dough, and soon our fingers were slick and powdery with sugar. I should have brought sunglasses, I realized, as I felt the sun draw a trickle of sweat from my brow. The sky over the beach was washed-out, white-hot, and blank, and the ocean roared and tumbled in a long gray-blue expanse before us. A seagull pimp-strutted along the railing that separates the wood from the sand and eyed our snack suspiciously. I kicked at the air to make it fly off; I wasn't looking for a repeat of yesterday's airborne snatch-and-grab on the roof.

"Wow," Ashleigh said. "I've never seen the ocean up close before."

"You haven't?"

Her voice was small. "Nope."

We sat for a while and took in the sight.

"This is totally fun," said Ashleigh.

"Is it what you expected?"

She licked her fingers. "Not at all."

"Sometimes that can be a good thing, though, right?"

"Yeah, I guess so." She smiled. "Sometimes."

"Ashleigh, I have to ask you. What did you think you were going to do here? Just start an entire new life? You didn't even bring anything with you."

"That was the point, kind of." She turned her face to the ocean. "I mean, I brought my Discman. I brought a few T-shirts and, like, some underwear. I brought some money and some goldfish crackers. And I brought Bear."

"You brought what?"

She blushed. "Bear. He's a—it's a stuffed animal. Shut up, OK?"

"Hey," I said, tearing at the cake, "whatever gets you through. I used to have a stuffed animal too. I wouldn't sleep without it."

"What was it called?"

"Well . . . it was a rabbit. So . . ."

Ashleigh flicked powdered sugar at my eye. "What was it *called*?"

I sighed. "Honey Bunny."

Ashleigh laughed so hard she snorted. "Ohmigosh. That is *so cute*."

"I'm glad you find it amusing."

"When was this?"

"Ohhh, I dunno." I acted like I was casting my memory way back into the past. "A long time ago. Like when I was . . . nineteen?"

She kicked at my shins. "Come on."

"I'm kidding. When I was like two or three, I guess."

"I bet you were a happy little kid."

"Yeah, I guess I was."

"Lucky."

I looked at her, squinting my eyes in the glare. Behind us three boys clattered by on scooters, hooting and exhorting one another to go faster, faster, faster. "Yeah, I guess I was that too."

Neither of us said anything for a time, just watched the ocean pull back and roll in, pull back and roll in. A bored, bronzed lifeguard sounded his whistle occasionally, but for the most part the morning bathers behaved themselves, splashing gaily in the shallows or floating lazily on inflatable tubes shaped like crocodiles.

"OK, I'll admit that I didn't think all that much. I just did it. I figured that . . . that other people would help me with the hard part."

"Ashleigh," I said, still staring at the horizon. "The hard part is the life you just left."

"Yeah?"

"Yeah," I said. "You are seventeen years old, and you have an entire life in front of you. I know it's impossible to imagine, but there is so much out there. There is so much life beyond those mountains. And you can have it, if you really want it. But the sucky part is that you just can't have it yet."

"But I can't survive there. I can't. I just can't."

"You can, Ashleigh. You will, believe me. You have no idea how fast time really is. Between when I first started talking to you online last year and now—that must have felt like an entire lifetime for you. A different grade, a different set of problems, different dreams. Hell—sorry, *heck*—last year you told me you still listened to Britney Spears."

She blushed horribly and pushed my side. "Just to be, like, funny! Not for real!"

"Whatever you say." I laughed. "But all that time for you was like a blink for me. When we started talking I had my air conditioner on, and when you showed up yesterday I had it on again. That's a full human year. And by the time you get to be my age it goes like *that.*" I snapped my fingers. "And I bet when you're twice my age it goes twice as fast as that."

"Weird," she said.

"Yeah, I know it. Life is long, kiddo. But it goes really fast. You can't mess up your future now by staying here. Not when you haven't even gotten to it yet."

She chewed more funnel cake, then chewed my words over in her mind. "You shouldn't just let a year go by like that," she said finally.

"What? We're not talking about me, Ashleigh. This is about you."

"Well it can be about *youuu*"—she drew out the word, making fun of me—"too. You're not *that* much older than me, you know. You're not like my parents."

"I certainly hope not."

"Don't worry—you're not. They're not nearly as messy as you."

She stuck her tongue out at me, then got serious. "But if what you're saying is true and time is so super fast, then shouldn't you be doing more with it? If I had the freedom you have—if I could, like, decide to hop on a train and come out here every day, or go to concerts when I wanted to, or just sit in a park and daydream—I would totally use it. I wouldn't just think about whether my stupid air conditioner is on or not. That's not how I'd want to keep track of my life."

It's a humbling feeling being put in your place by a seventeen-year-old, but it's not altogether unpleasant. I just let her words penetrate my skull; I didn't stop them at the border of my brain because she was twirling her hair in her fingers or because she dotted her *I*s with hearts. I remembered the way she had struck me online, and I tried to see that phantom person in the young girl with powdered sugar on her face sitting next to me. And I could. Somewhere in this young body was a serious person who I had met in a serious way. And she had just seriously stuck it to me. "You're right," I said.

"Really? Well, maybe we both are."

"OK, deal," I said, and held out my hand to shake. Her palm was sticky but warm.

"Deal," she said. "Now what about that roller coaster?"

It wasn't until they were actually strapping us into the second car from the front that I remembered that, for all my tough talk, I had never actually ridden the Cyclone myself. I decided not to share that with Ashleigh, since she looked to be about two or three shallow breaths away from full-fledged hyperventilation. Instead I let my heart attempt to jackhammer its way out of my ribs in relative silence and tried to put on a brave face. The girl behind us was quietly sobbing, and it was starting to get to me too. "You sure you're all right with this?" I asked.

"I think so," Ashleigh said. "I mean, I'm not usually the kind of person who likes roller coasters."

"But?"

"But, like, I'm not usually the kind of person who runs away to New York City either."

Under our feet we felt the car grumble to life. The groaning, unsteady response of the ageless white wood supporting us would have been audible to a deaf man. "You know what, Ashleigh?"

"What?" Her hands gripped at the sticky metal bar that was going to keep us from being flung to our deaths. At least in theory.

"I think you're wrong. I think you're *exactly* the type of person who likes roller coasters."

She flashed me a brilliant smile as we shuddered into the first incline.

Up, up, and up we went, like patients in a sadistic dentist's chair. To our right, Coney Island was spread out before us, a view that stretched all the way to the ocean. The sun felt hot on the back of my neck. I tried to remember the last time I had been on a roller coaster but couldn't.

"Look!" Ashleigh was elbowing me in the side. "Look down there!"

I turned. She was pointing excitedly to the crowd gathered near the entrance to the Cyclone.

"Doesn't that guy look just like you?"

I did my best to sit up and peer over the rail. At first I saw only a

Dude STALKMUCH!?!

mess of people, tiny as ants. But I followed Ashleigh's outstretched finger until I saw a solitary figure, hair running wild, standing apart from the crowd in his sunglasses and staring directly at us with an enormous shit-eating grin on his face. It couldn't be.

"Wow," said Ashleigh. "That guy is totally you!"

I leaned over more, trying to get a better glimpse. It couldn't be, really. It didn't make any sense. Just when things were starting to make sense. The figure pulled his right hand out of his pocket and started to wave, and that was when we reached the summit and spilled forward, racing down, down, down and then twisting around the track with all the subtlety of a punch in the face.

My stomach did a triple lutz, then made a nosedive for my ankles, and my hip began smarting from bashing against the side of the car on every turn. Ashleigh was screaming, a high-pitched primal yawp, and soon she was clutching my arm harder than she was the safety bar. The coaster didn't so much take us for a ride as it rode *us*—every twist, every roll penetrated to the bone. The sea air rushed against my face, and my eyes were full of tears. It was utterly punishing, this feeling: being totally at the mercy of something inanimate and huge and ferocious and unrelenting. I felt like I was shaking more than the wooden structure, and I squeezed my eyelids shut as we whooshed and galloped. It seemed like it would never ever end.

But all of a sudden it was over. We slowed and rattled and came to an ungraceful stop back where we had started. Ashleigh had yet to let go of my arm, and when she did her fingernails left a flurry of scratches on my bicep like malicious paper cuts. I gasped for breath and opened my eyes. We had survived. We were safe.

"That was incredible!" Ashleigh yelled. "Can we do it again?" Her face was a lusty shade of crimson. Even the mookish attendant let out a chuckle as he helped lift her out of the car.

Unsteadily, I climbed out and joined her on the platform. "Maybe in a few minutes," I said. "I think I dropped my intestines somewhere over the second dip."

It's hard to explain, but as I followed the skipping seventeen-year-old back out to the sidewalk and felt my legs reassert themselves under me, it seemed like I really had dropped something up on the coaster, something that had been weighing me down. It wasn't my intestines and it wasn't my pride, either. With each wobbly step I felt, if not reborn then certainly reimagined, as if the new, ocean-and-exhaust-scented air that had pushed into me had been an oil change for my soul. All the tiny hairs on my arms were standing ramrod straight. I cracked my knuckles and got my bearings. Ashleigh was jumping up and down in place, clapping her hands, reliving every one of the two hundred or so seconds we had spent on the Cyclone. My eyes—dry now, thankfully—scanned the crowd for the doppelgänger but turned up nothing. Had he really been here? And what could he have wanted?

"What are you looking for?" Ashleigh finally seemed to be settling back to Earth.

"That person you saw from up there," I said, my pupils moving from face to face. "The one you said looked like me."

"Come on," said Ashleigh. "Don't be so, like, full of yourself!"

"I'm not," I said, though I didn't believe it.

"Well don't be so paranoid, then. Come on—let's get something else to eat!"

• • •

We stayed at Coney Island until just past noon, strolling the midways, playing Skee-Ball, and even taking a turn on the strange Matterhorn-themed ride that spins riders past spray-painted images of the Swiss Alps and giant rest-in-peace portraits of Tupac Shakur and Biggie Smalls, while blasting hip-hop from Hot 97 at eardrum-exploding volume. Ashleigh managed to put away a tub of popcorn, a stick of cotton candy, and a twisty rainbow-colored lollipop that was longer than my forearm. A few times as we walked Ashleigh tried to hold my hand, but I managed to slip away from her grasp. There was no sign of the doppelgänger, and after a while I forgot to keep looking for him. I felt the hint of a sunburn on the bridge of my nose and the memory of the Cyclone wind on my brow. It had turned out to be a pretty good morning.

But on the F back to my apartment, I told Ashleigh that she had to go home.

"OK," she said.

I was stunned. "Really? 'OK'? That's it?"

She kicked at the peeling linoleum floor. "Yeah, I guess. I mean, I hate it there. But it wouldn't really work with me here. You don't have enough room in your apartment."

"Uh, no. No, I don't."

"We can still be friends, though, right? I mean . . ." She blushed. "We are, like, friends, right? In real life?"

"Absolutely," I said. "You're a good friend, Ashleigh."

She blushed more deeply. "And I can still write to you and complain about stuff, right? Because I'm serious. I'm going to have a life just like yours. I'm going to do it."

I laughed. "I don't think my life is one to shoot for, Ashleigh. Aim higher."

"Ok, I promise." She sat silently for a time, staring out through the glare at the streets passing below us, her body leaning gently on my side. "I feel better," she said suddenly. "I guess it just helps knowing that all of this is out there."

"I'm glad," I said. "Sometimes it's hard to get outside of yourself, or to imagine anything outside of your daily routine."

"Yeah. That's why you've gotta shake it up sometimes, right?"

"That's right," I said. "That's exactly right."

Back at my apartment Ashleigh took a shower while I searched the Internet for flight information. There was a plane leaving JFK for Salt Lake at 5:15 p.m., and for a little over eight hundred dollars it was possible to buy a one-way ticket. Ashleigh, of course, had no money left, so I typed in my emergency credit card number on the purchase screen. My parents hadn't specified *whose* emergency the card was for. And it was better than getting hauled in for aiding and abetting.

I heard Ashleigh rustling around in the living room, so I called out to her. "OK, you're all set. I'll get you a car service, but you'll have to head to the airport pretty soon."

She came through the door wearing a sky blue T-shirt that said INSIDE WE ARE ALL BROKEN on it and holding the mix CD I had made for Cath Kennedy. "What's this?" she asked.

"Oh . . . it's just a CD I made."

"Can I take it for the plane? I don't have anything new to listen to."

"Sure," I said, pushing back from my desk. "Be my guest."

"Just one more thing," she said, lightly resting her hand on my shoulder. "I don't want to go alone. Would you please just come with me?"

I sighed. "OK, Ashleigh. I'll come with you to the airport. But you have to get right on the plane."

"Who's this?" Her hand left my shoulder and darted underneath the stack of papers where I had partially hidden the photo of Amy sipping a cup of coffee. She grabbed the photo and held it up to the light. "Is this your girlfriend? She's pretty."

"Thanks," I said, feeling the constriction in the back of my throat. "Not that I can take any credit for that."

But Ashleigh was still staring at the photo. "She looks . . . she looks like a real grown-up."

Gently, I took the picture from her. "She is, Ashleigh. That's exactly what she is."

An hour or so later the car service pulled up out front, and Ashleigh and I hurried down the stairs. Waiting for us at the bottom was Mrs. Armando.

"David!" she yelled, even though I was less than three feet away from her. "You gotta get that bucket off the window!"

"Bucket?" I tried to hurry Ashleigh out the door. "What bucket?"

"You got a bucket of dirt and birds on the fire escape and it's a-spilling into my garden. You gotta get rid of it!"

The herb garden. Of course. "OK, Mrs. Armando, I will. I promise. As soon as I get back."

The old lady nodded but didn't move out of our way. She just stared at Ashleigh, who was nervously shuffling her feet and twirling her hair in her fingers. "And who are you?" Mrs. Armando said with trademark bluntness.

"A-Ashleigh."

"This is my cousin, Mrs. Armando. She stayed me with me for a night. She's heading home now."

"Uh-huh."

I saw her eyes looking from the bright blond hair to my own dark tangle. "We're cousins by marriage."

"Whatever," said Mrs. Armando. "As long as you not catting around!" She pointed at me as she turned back to her own apartment. "No catting, David!"

"No, Mrs. Armando, I promise. No catting." And with that we rushed out into the waiting town car.

Traffic was light on the way out to JFK. Even so, the driver stuck to the back roads, taking Atlantic Avenue through the rough-and-tumble intersections of East New York and eventually paralleling the Van Wyck Expressway in Queens. Ashleigh didn't say much along the way; she just stared at the window and listened to her Discman. Just before we pulled up to the gate, she hit STOP and took her headphones off. "This mix you made," she said.

"Yes?" I smiled expectantly.

"It's kinda boring."

"Thanks," I said, shaking my head.

When we pulled up to Departures, I told the driver to wait for me, and I carried Ashleigh's backpack into the terminal. There weren't many people standing around at that time of day, so it was a relative snap to retrieve her e-ticket from a self-serve kiosk and then find our way to the security line.

"OK," I said. "This is the end of the road. You take care, OK?"

I made a half move to hug her, but she just stared at me.

"What?" I said. "Do you have enough money for a snack? For magazines?"

She kept staring, a mottled pink flush on her cheeks.

"Ashleigh, you've got to go. The car is waiting for me. Your parents are waiting for you. If you go now, there's a chance they might never know you were gone."

"B-but . . ."

"But what, Ashleigh? This is serious!"

She balled her fists. "But I *told* you. I said I'd go, but only if you came with me."

"Come on, Ashleigh." I started to laugh and then spied the steely resolve in her blue eyes. "I came to the airport with you! You didn't mean . . ."

She cocked an eyebrow.

"You didn't mean I had to come with you to Utah, did you?"

But that's exactly what she meant.

Oh, boy.

SHIT BOY! YOU gonna get arrested.

CHAPTER FOURTEEN: GREAT! SALT LAKE!

THE WOMAN WAS WEARING far too much eye makeup and seemed to hold me personally responisble for her having to work on such a beautiful day. I glanced at her name tag. It read MARY-BETH and was decorated with two smiley-face stickers that in no way resembled the grim look on her actual face. Her long, palm-tree-decorated fingernails danced on the keyboard in front of her mysteriously. I leaned my elbows on the counter, trying to catch a glimpse of whatever was occurring on the other side.

"Yes, sir," Mary-beth said eventually, her voice a monotone. "It is possible to return the same night."

"It is? Great. That's a relief."

"Well," she said. *Type-type-type.* "Not *technically* the same night, sir. There is a red-eye from Salt Lake City back to JFK that departs at eleven p.m. mountain time. It lands at JFK at seven thirty-one a.m. tomorrow."

"OK." I glanced over my shoulder to where Ashleigh was standing, arms crossed, backpack at her feet. Her face was draped in a truly Oscar-worthy pout, the kind that would cause a bankrupt father to purchase ponies if she so much as looked his way. I turned back to Mary-beth, whose lips were now puckering as if she had taken a secret suck on a lemon. "How much?"

"For the entire trip?" *Type-type-type.* "Due to the last-minute nature of your purchase, there are no discounts." *Type-type-type.* "The total is $1,273. Will that be cash or charge?"

My heart sank, but I handed her the emergency credit card and my driver's license. In for a penny, in for twelve thousand pennies, that's what I always say. As Mary-beth extracted the money from the plastic, I looked around the terminal. There was a pigeon swooping around the antiseptic white columns above our heads, and to my left a lonely Pakistani man pushed a cart with approximately seventeen pieces of overstuffed luggage strapped to it. He walked under a sign that said INTERNATIONAL GATES and disappeared. International gates. I drummed my fingers on the counter and turned back to Mary-beth.

"By the way, how much is a ticket to The Hague?"

Type-type-type—PAUSE. Her eyes slowly rolled up to meet mine. "Sir? I thought you said Salt Lake City."

"I did, I did. I was just . . . wondering. How much would a ticket be to The Hague?"

Mary-beth sighed theatrically, then resumed typing. "Sir, this airline does not fly to The Hague."

"Oh," I said, unsure how to feel.

"We fly to Amsterdam, and then you can connect to The Hague through one of our One Planet Alliance partner carriers."

I tried to picture Mary-beth's personal partner carrier, shuddered, then tried to imagine myself in Amsterdam. It was a hard fit. "Does that flight leave daily?"

Exaggerated sigh. "Yes, sir. In fact, our flight to Amsterdam leaves in just three hours' time. Would you like me to book you on *that* flight, sir?"

It would be so easy. So, so easy. But I felt Ashleigh's beady, resolute stare on my back, and I knew what I had to do. "Ah, no. No thank you, Mary-beth. Please book the Salt Lake City flight."

Mary-beth looked as if her head were about to explode into a thousand tiny, furious pieces. *"Sir."* She typed some more, handed me my cards and some papers, and it was done.

Ashleigh watched me warily as I turned away from the counter and walked over to her.

"Well," I said. "I hope you're happy." And I waved my ticket in front of her nose.

She responded by throwing her arms around me and squealing, so I took that to mean she was, indeed, happy. When I managed to extricate myself from her viselike embrace, I walked out to the drop-off area, where huddled clumps of smokers were taking their last, pathos-soaked puffs, and I told the waiting driver that his trip was a one-way after all. I signed the receipt and gave him a generous tip. If I was going to go in the red, I figured I might as well do it in style.

Ashleigh and I made it through security with no real trouble, though I was forced to remove my shoes twice even though no alarm had sounded. I brushed it off with the thought that there were few things more suspicious than someone flying across the country in the middle of the day with no luggage. We still had half an hour to kill before the flight boarded, so while Ashleigh decamped to a pay phone to try and finagle a ride home from the Salt Lake City airport, I wandered past the cookie-cutter Sbarros and Cinnabons and into the terminal's flimsy bookstore. There was an impressive wall of self-help books—the one called *Getting to Know the Real You In Six Easy Steps* caught my eye for obvious reasons, but at this point I was already on step fourteen and nowhere near the promised land, so I kept browsing. Tucked in the travel section, I found a yellowed paperback called, simply, *Utah!* and written by one Rulon Barber. I liked—and envied—the simple-hearted enthusiasm of the title, so I scraped together my pocket change and bought it, along with a pack of cards and some sugarless gum. With Ashleigh nowhere in sight, I walked to the golf-themed sports bar, took a seat at a two-top on the "putting green," and ordered a draft lager. I didn't want my body to go into alcohol-deprived shock at thirty-five thousand feet—and certainly not in an infamously dry state like Utah.

I paid for the $8.99 disposable cup of Sam Adams with the emergency plastic and sipped it slowly, watching the glum-faced janitors power-clean the terminal's white, shiny floors. The row of TVs behind me showed a college football game from sometime in the mid-eighties. So I was going to Utah—home of John Stockton, Robert Redford, and polygamy. A place I'd never twice thought of and never once thought I'd visit. And I was going for approximately two hours to escort a seventeen-year-old runaway back to her Mike-and-Carol-Brady prison-warden parents. I couldn't make this stuff up if I tried. I took another long sip of beer and chased it with a handful of snack mix that tasted vaguely of sawdust. As entertaining and unpredictable as the past week had been, I couldn't shake the feeling that I was still half-assing it. I was caught up in drama and momentum all right, but it was still borrowed. It wasn't earned. I was becoming adept at maneuvering the pitfalls and eddies of other people's lives; to Ashleigh I seemed downright impetuous! But to Ashleigh I probably seemed like all sorts of things: competent, successful, together, happy. It was nice to catch some of the reflected glow from her exalted image of me—hell, it was nice to be needed. But it also made me feel like a charlatan, an imposter in my own life. This roller coaster had been a fun ride. But I had to be prepared for it to end. Rides always do.

"Are you, like, an alcoholic?" Ashleigh hopped into the seat across from me, a stack of newly purchased music magazines in her hand.

"Possibly. But don't worry. I'm not flying the plane."

She stuck her tongue out at me. "So I had a hard time reaching anybody. But Krystal said she'll probably be able to sneak out with the car around seven and pick us up."

"Pick *you* up."

"Right, that's what I said!"

"And what's this 'probably'?"

Ashleigh shrugged. "She's my best friend. She should be able to do it."

"Did she ask why you would be at the airport?"

"Duh. Yeah."

"What did you tell her?"

"I didn't. I said I'd tell her later. She was talking about herself, mostly anyway. Boy drama."

I rolled my eyes. "Isn't it always."

"What'd you buy?" Ashleigh picked up my book and started flipping through it.

I swallowed another sip of beer. "I figured I should know something about the place I'm going to."

"Great." Ashleigh stuck her finger in her mouth and pretended to gag. "I don't see a chapter on boring, fake, religious, hypocrite people and their love of shallow, stupid things like fashion and skiing."

I took the book back from her. "You probably just didn't look in the index."

She stuck her tongue out at me again, then buried her nose in *Rolling Stone*.

The plane boarded on time and was only half full. Our seats were just behind the right wing. Ashleigh took the window; I took the aisle.

"You know," I said, looking around, "since it's not that crowded, we could probably spread out, take a whole row."

Ashleigh looked at me as if I had suggested rubbing two sticks together to better ignite the bomb in my shoe. "No way! We're flying *together*!"

"OK, OK. No problem. It was just a suggestion."

"Is everything all right over here?" A stewardess with exhausted eyes loomed large over our row.

"Yes," I said. "Everything's fine." But the stewardess lingered a moment, noticing Ashleigh's age, my five-hours-past-five o'clock shadow. "She's my—"

"Fiancée!" Ashleigh bounced in her seat and hooked her arm through mine. "We're engaged!"

My heart sank. I looked up at the stewardess, waiting for her to call the authorities, ground the plane, have me carted away. But she didn't do any of those things. Instead, she beamed. "Well, congratulations! That's just wonderful. I love having young lovebirds on my flights!" And she wandered off completely reenergized, nattering to herself about the majesty of romance.

When she was safely out of sight, I yanked my arm back. "What the hell did you do that for? That was crazy!"

Ashleigh looked hurt. "I was just having fun!"

"This isn't about fun, Ashleigh! This is all way too serious to be fun!" My voice was harsher than I had intended. I took a few deep breaths and stared at the cover of the in-flight magazine, which was awkwardly jammed in the seatback in front of me. "101 Things to Do in Phoenix." I'd never been there, but I couldn't think of *one.*

"I'm sorry."

"I mean, how old are you supposed to be, anyway?"

"Mormon women are supposed to get married young."

"Oh yeah?" I gave in, smiled. "I must not have gotten to that chapter yet."

As I watched the little computer airplane make its path over the foldout screen's digitized United States, I tried to remember the last time I had been on a plane. It had been with Amy, of course—visiting her cousins in San Francisco almost two years before. I shook my head. Flying always made me feel strange; the idea of waking up in one place and casually flying thousands of miles away to fall asleep in another still didn't make sense to me. So the idea of doing so with no preparation—no buildup time to get used to the idea of winging your body across the continent—was even more unfathomable. The entire day had been about doing things—as opposed to most days that summer, which had concerned themselves with the opposite. The little plane was making its way away from the East Coast now. Soon the big blue smear that was the Atlantic Ocean wouldn't even be visible on the map. All I could think was that once again I was traveling in the wrong direction.

"What are you listening to?" Ashleigh was clutching her headphones tightly to her ears, rocking back and forth and mouthing along with all her adolescent might. It took three tries to get her to notice I was asking a question; she finally hit PAUSE and heard me on the fourth.

"What? Oh." She lifted her headphones off her ears, cradled them in her fingers. "It's a mix."

"Not mine; I know that." I smiled.

"No, one I made for myself."

"What was the song?"

Ashleigh blushed. "Could you hear it? I always play these things too loudly."

"I couldn't hear it. You just seemed to be enjoying it. A lot."

"It was Jimmy Eat World." She gave me a shy look. "Do you like them?"

"Um," I said truthfully. "They're OK." I rifled through the audio reference library in my head until I came up with a match: giant soaring guitars, plaintive sensitive lyrics. Emo, basically.

Ashleigh shook her head. "They're a lot better than OK."

"And why is that?"

"Because they, like, *get it.* You know? There aren't that many bands that do."

I thought about that for a while, about the bands I loved and whether I would ever give "getting it" as a reason for allowing their songs to jam themselves in my head as the soundtrack for my increasingly convoluted life. I didn't think that I would. I tended to let my life dictate my music, not the other way around. And ever since I had started writing about records professionally, I tended to listen exclusively to new releases. Despite the giant bookshelves of CDs in my apartment, the only ones that had gotten play in the last few desperate months had been recent discoveries, advance copies, and pirated downloads. I craved the freshness more than the message. The songs I had on my iPod kept me company, but they didn't keep me going.

"Here." Ashleigh lifted her headphones over my head like she was knighting me. "See what you think."

She had the volume up way too loud, of course, and I had to gesture wildly to make her lower it. But once she did, I could hear a gently plucked guitar line and some appropriately soppy vocals about only once letting me or only asking once or something like that. It reminded me of the "next week on . . ." preview at the end of overheated teen soap operas or the music from jeans commercials on cable, all spinning wheels and dusty roads and too much lip gloss. But there was a catch in the voice, a wobble and a waver to the shimmering melody, and I had to admit it wasn't unpleasant. I started to make a so-so gesture to Ashleigh, but she was looking at me with the intensity of a fourth-generation monk, so I dropped my hand. Some things were too important to joke about.

Then the chorus hit me like a brass-knuckled punch to the heart, and my throat went dry and I closed my eyes. It was technicolor and it was big and it was shameless. *Can we take a ride? / Get out of this place while we still have time?* And then it went tumbling over a waterfall of cascading *oh-ohs* before plunging me into another level of icy cool chorus beneath it. I had to get outside of myself to hear it, really hear it. This song was about escape, but not in the sense I could recognize. I had been locked in a room for months, but the locks were on my side of the door. I could have left at any time, but I made sure all three latches stayed firmly in place. Any romantic desperation, any keening choruses or sweeping nostalgia had been carefully balled up and placed on top of an already full trash can in my mind. Ashleigh, on the other hand, had been so desperate to get out that she had broken the door down with her own weak arms, taking nothing but a stuffed bear and some crackers with her. A song like this wasn't a passive soundtrack; it was hope personified. It was a promise. It was an escape much more real than the one I was turning her right back around from.

I wanted to tell her all of this, that the song had gotten to me, but it wasn't over yet, and I had a funny catch in the back of my throat, besides. When it did finally end, the last notes still ringing in my ears over the thrum of the airplane, I took the headphones off and handed them back with a smile.

"Did you like it?"

"I liked it," I said. "You were right. They get it."

Ashleigh grinned. "I told you."

"Yeah, I just didn't listen."

About two hours into the trip, the movie started. I hadn't expected anything worth watching, and my low expectations were rewarded with a "tear-jerking" romantic comedy about a cocky womanizer who finally meets his match in a spunky single mother whose bug-eyed, camera-mugging offspring happens to be a basketball prodigy who may or may not be able to talk to cats. Or at least that's what it appeared to be about without sound. Ashleigh clapped her hands eagerly and jammed her headphones into the armrest. I sighed and flipped through my book. Rulon Barber had a golly-gee-whiz tone to his writing but managed to cram a number of interesting facts into each sentence. I read about Brigham Young's settling of Salt Lake City in 1867 with the words "this is the right place," the state's pride in its rapidly expanding population, and the light-rail system that connects the University of Utah with downtown. I glanced at the annual calendar in the front of the book and saw that every Fourth of July weekend something called the Northern Ute Pow-Wow was held in someplace called Fort Duchesne. Barber called it "one of the biggest pow-wows in the West." Big words, Rulon, I thought. It's a shame I'll have to miss it. I read on from Barber's overheated introduction:

> *From its gold-kissed and sandy deserts to the lapping shores of the Great Salt Lake, Utah, boxy and proud, may well be the most splendiferous state in the union . . . Founded on a dream, cultivated by a promise, Utah faces the twenty-first century strong in its faith, proud of its heritage, excited for its limitless future. Verily and truly, this* is *the place!*

I tut-tutted and closed the cover. Easy on the exclamation points, Rulon. You're providing a service, not selling mattresses. I checked out Barber's photo on the back of the book and found pretty much what I expected: middle-aged man in a crew cut with a neck as thick as his head wearing aviator shades and a shit-eating grin. Ah, Rulon, I thought. It's the glamorous writer's life for us, isn't it?

Still, I had nothing better to do and no love for crossword puzzles, so I read on, trying my best to familiarize myself with the LDS Church, which so thoroughly dominated the state. I did some due diligence on Brigham Young University, where Ashleigh's parents thought she was spending the weekend. It was located about sixty miles to the south of Salt Lake in the town of Provo and sounded like the least collegiate university in America: There was no drinking, no smoking, no caffeine, and no fraternizing with the opposite sex. Seeing how those were the four pillars of most people's higher education, I was at a loss trying to imagine what being a student there would entail. I imagined there was a lot of studying. And masturbation.

Throughout the movie, Ashleigh laughed uproariously and occasionally shook my arm to draw my attention to the screen. I just smiled and nodded. For such an unhappy person, she certainly laughed a lot. The stewardess had taken a shine to us ever since she'd found out we were "engaged," so she kept Ashleigh flush with caffeine-free soda and me flush with Amstel Light. Eventually, I even managed to doze off.

I woke up an hour or so before we landed when a passing thunderstorm caused a neck-snapping bout of turbulence. It reminded me of the roller coaster from the morning, the same dipping and slipping, the same churning sensation in the pit of my gut. Ashleigh didn't take it well, clamping her lower lip firmly underneath her teeth and making a worried, mewling sound. She turned up the volume on her Discman, grabbed my arm, and buried her face in it. As always, traveling with a nervous flyer made me more calm. It had always been that way. Being cast in the role of the brave one made me try harder to live up to it. I stroked Ashleigh's arm in what I hoped was a paternal way and waited for the bumpiness to stop.

I don't know for sure what I was expecting to see when we stepped off the jetway and into Salt Lake City International Airport, but I suppose the image in my mind was something between a John Wayne movie and the Rapture. What greeted us instead was an airport, no different from the one we had left five-plus hours before. The same newsstands, the same crappy theme restaurants. Even the same Grovestand health-food kiosk selling what looked to be the same decades-old mixed nuts. The typical American mass-transit innocuous inoculation. I yawned and stretched and watched Ashleigh's bag while she went to the bathroom.

It was seven p.m. local time. Through the windows I could see a fiery sun just beginning its descent on what I took to be the western horizon. Unlike JFK, the airport was positively bustling, with wide-waisted families plodding in every possible direction. One clearly related crew all sporting matching leather cowboy hats—even the toddler in the stroller—was the only real sign that we had crossed into the West.

"I can't believe I'm back." Ashleigh took her backpack from me and finished drying her hands on her sky-blue jeans.

"I can't believe I'm here," I said.

"What? It's a nice airport."

"An oxymoron." We started walking toward the baggage claim

where Krystal was due to meet us. We rode the moving walkways and stared at the *Tribute to the American Indian* photo exhibit that lined the walls. Near the security check was a store called West of Brooklyn. "You're kidding me," I said to Ashleigh, gesturing toward it.

"I thought of you yesterday when I passed by it," she said.

"Why would they call a store that?"

"Why not? It's accurate, isn't it?"

"Well, technically." I glanced inside as we passed by: just the usual assortment of beauty magazines, paperweights, and oversize wolf T-shirts. Why did stores continue to sell wolf T-shirts? Did anyone actually wear them? "We're west of a lot of things," I said. "St. Louis, Chicago, Kuala Lumpur . . ."

"Maybe it's a tribute to you."

"Huh," I said. "Maybe."

Down in the heavily air-conditioned baggage claim there was no sign of Krystal—though no shortage of people who could legitimately be *named* Krystal.

"Do you think she's on her way?" I asked, starting to get a nervous feeling in the pit of my stomach.

"Maybe." Ashleigh, was back in full-on deer mode, her eyes wide and darting around the crowd. "Oh gosh, that guy is totally from our church!"

"What? Where?"

Ashleigh darted behind me and lifted up the hood on her sweatshirt. "The *guy*! The blond guy!"

My eyes scanned the entire length and breadth of the baggage-claim hall trying to pinpoint the exact blond "guy" who had Ashleigh so agitated. That was probably when I first noticed: *all* the guys were blond guys. There was a creepy monotony to the face of every adult male around us: freshly scrubbed, apple-cheeked, hair perfectly coiffed, and a shiny blue, matte finish to the eyes that made it look like either the pupils were made out of glass or kept under a protective coating of it. Still, I tried to act reassuring, and I let my vision settle on a harried-looking fellow who was making his way through the revolving doors. "Don't worry," I said as his proud blond mane disappeared into a waiting cab. "Um, he's gone."

"He is?" Ashleigh peeked around from behind me.

"I think so."

I must have picked the correct head of hair, because Ashleigh seemed genuinely relieved. "That was close! I'm gonna go call Krys's cell phone. She should be here by now."

"OK," I said. And while I waited, I flipped through some more of Rulon's choice passages:

> *Nestled into the warm embrace of the Wasatch Mountains is Salt Lake City, the state capital and a shining gateway for hundreds of thousands en route to a better life. Salt Lake City is also the spiritual and physical home to the glorious LDS Church, situated in the beating heart of downtown, Temple Square. Walk through the handsomely paved square and greet the fresh-faced missionaries stationed there, tour the actual home built by Brigham Young for one of his families, and hear the wondrous voices of the world-famous Mormon*

Tabernacle Choir lift your soul—and your quickly beating heart—straight up to heaven with their majestic song.

Phew. I was tired just reading all of that. Still, it did seem pretty—and more than a little interesting. It was a shame that I wasn't going to be able to see any of this city that I had just paid a fortune to fly to. Oh, well. Maybe another time.

But then I caught sight of Ashleigh walking back toward me, a warily apologetic half-smile on her face. And I wondered if I wasn't going to get a chance to prove Rulon wrong after all.

"She had to go to the dentist?"

Ashleigh was explaining to me why Krystal wasn't at the airport and wouldn't, in fact, be coming to the airport at all. But it was taking an inordinate amount of time to sink in.

"Yes." Ashleigh chewed her fingernail thoughtfully.

"Because she hurt herself."

"No, because her brother hurt himself."

"In the teeth."

"Yeah." She tried to smile. "In the teeth."

"Why would anyone try to skateboard on their hands?"

"There's not that much to do here."

"I guess not." I rubbed my forehead. "But really he should have tried to land on something other than his mouth."

Ashleigh shook her head. "He's an idiot."

"Well, he's screwed us, that's for sure. How are we going to get you home?" Ashleigh flashed me her pony-buying pout. "Aw, man . . ."

• • •

It was surprisingly easy to rent a car in Salt Lake City, and if the people at the emergency credit card company minded this sudden flurry of activity, they didn't let me or the twenty-year-old ski bum manning the counter know about it. I had walked the length of rental-car hall—located across the street from the terminal—watching the names go from classy to ashy. Thrifty. Budget. Dollar. I had peeked around a corner looking for Busted, Cheap-Ass, or Broke, but, not seeing them, had settled for Dollar. After declining the insurance in triplicate, I walked with Ashleigh out the back door into a sweltering garage full of bland rental vehicles, most of which were outfitted with racks and hooks for ski equipment. All the license plates said "Utah!" just like my guidebook, and I shook my head. The only state in the union that felt the need to stick on an exclamation point right after its name for extra flash, and I was stuck in it.

"What'd we get? A convertible?"

Ashleigh seemed determined to milk every possible drop of fun out of this strange little adventure before she made it back home. She skipped at my heels like a wound-up puppy. "No, we didn't get a convertible. I think I've spent enough money today."

"Is it an SUV?"

"No, it's not an SUV." I shook my head and tried to navigate a clear path to space K-26.

"My parents drive an SUV. It's an Escalade. I told them it was bad for the earth but they told me that Utah highways are bad for their peace of mind."

"Uh-huh." I stopped short as someone who clearly had shelled out extra for a red Mustang convertible gunned his way past us toward the exit.

"I know I'm not supposed to like it, but it's pretty cool to sit that high up all the time."

"Here we go." Parked glumly in space K-26 was a beige hump of an automobile so devoid of personality it was hard to tell where it ended and the asphalt began. The inside fixtures were oversize and over-rounded black plastic, and there was a prim little American-flag decal affixed to the rear window. The Ford Tempo, pride of the Dollar fleet. "C'mon," I said. "Hop in."

Ashleigh face fell. "Ew."

"Ashleigh, it's not very punk-rock to care about cars."

She stuck her tongue out at me. "I'm not punk rock. I'm emo. And this car *breaks my fragile heart.*" But she pulled open the door and hopped in anyway, which relieved me to no end.

It takes about fifteen seconds after exiting the rental-car parking garage at the Salt Lake City airport to realize—officially and definitively—that you are in the American West. Nowhere else is that flat, first of all. The single snaking roadway in front of us felt like a random squiggly line drawn on an otherwise blank canvas. All around us was dark nothingness with a sprinkling of hard bright lights in the distance. The other dead giveaway was the sign that said DOWNTOWN, TAKE EXIT 1A. Only out here, in the land of boxy city maps and endless space, could a functioning international airport be located so close to the heart of downtown. I squinted in the nearly gone light and shifted lanes. As I did so, I caught the faintest glimpse of the ridiculous mountain ranges that hemmed in the horizon on all sides. They were craggy and snow-capped even now, and I felt their presence all around me even when the sun dipped farther and I could no longer make them out. They lurked and loomed, like uncapped teeth poised for a vicious, one-sided bite. I could see what Ashleigh meant about having them around all the time. They gave me the creeps.

Ashleigh was fiddling with the radio. "Hey," I said. "So where do you live, anyway? And please tell me it's close."

She looked up. "It's not that far, don't worry. It's like, a suburb?"

"OK," I said. "A suburb. Where do I go?"

"Get off here and head into town," she said. "My parents are going to be out until like ten or eleven tonight. They have meetings at the church. We could drive past Temple Square and, like, get something to eat."

I steered the car toward the exit ramp, the red glow of brake lights shining in my retinas. "Are you sure? I'd kind of feel better if I just dropped you safely at home. I don't want to push it."

"Come on! You're on vacation. Let's just go for a quick tour around. It'll be fun, I promise. I don't want you to get caught either."

I sighed. Some vacation. But what the hell—Rulon had gotten me all in a tizzy about Salt Lake, so I figured I might as well see what all his fuss was about. "OK," I said. "But quickly."

Ashleigh clapped her hands and slid a CD from her bag into the car stereo. Jagged, jangly orchestral rock poured out of the speakers.

"What's this?" I asked.

"It's the Used," she said, twisting the air conditioner up higher and rolling her seat back. "They're from here, so I figured they'd make good backing music."

The song that spilled out into the space between us was pompous and catchy, and it seemed somehow fitting. The perfectly skewed accompaniment to a truly bizarre evening. The highway ended abruptly, and soon we were on a four-lane strip that could have been the road to Anytown, Anywhere. Roast-beef take-out joints, cheap motels, and expensive gas stations lined my vision. Billboards advertised smooth country radio stations and more divorce attorneys than I figured there could possibly be divorces in such a God-fearing state. As we waited for a light, Ashleigh squealed. "Oooooh, gosh, there's my dad."

My heart did a cliff dive. "What? Where?"

Ashleigh didn't seem too phased. "Up there." She leaned forward and pointed straight up. I followed her gaze to a billboard perched over the traffic light, which read TIRED? OVERWEIGHT? UNDER-APPRECIATED? GET BORTCHED! There was a phone number, a list of addresses, and an elephantine, airbrushed image of a slick, smiling blond guy like the ones we had seen at the airport, the gleam of his white teeth matching the polish on his cheeks and the dead-eyed enthusiasm of his gaze. Underneath the ghoulish head were the words ROGER BORTCH, FOUNDER AND CEO, BORTCH PHYSICAL WELLNESS CENTERS.

An angry honk from a truck behind me snapped me out of my reverie and through the green light. Ashleigh turned up the volume on the stereo, and I leaned forward and wheeled it back down again. "Holy shit," I said.

"Hey, I was listening to that!" Ashleigh leaned forward to turn the volume back up, but I beat her to it and snapped the entire thing off. "Hey!"

"'Get Bortched'?" I glanced over at Ashleigh, who had her arms crossed in front of her chest. "'Get Bortched'?"

"He's really proud of that. He thinks it's what made him so successful." She turned her head toward the window. "I think it sounds gross. So does Mom. But he won't listen."

"Ashleigh, if that man finds out that I have his precious daughter, he's going to Bortch me until I can't walk anymore."

"He's not gonna find out."

I clenched and unclenched my fingers on the wheel. "Jesus, let's hope not." We drove in silence for a while, following the signs for Temple Square. "You never told me he was such a big deal."

"He has four rehab clinics and an ad on local morning TV. That's not that big a deal."

"Still," I said. "That's a pretty big billboard. His head is ginormous."

"It is in real life, too."

"Wonderful," I said.

"Yeah, it's great." Ashleigh put her feet up on the dash. "He cares so much about his precious little 'centers.' They're like his real kids."

I was still preoccupied with visions of what being Bortched by Roger would entail. One should never mess with the progeny of physical-fitness freaks. "So is he really buff or something?"

Ashleigh pushed air through her teeth, making a dismissive, whistling sound. "Oh, he benches like three-fifty, but he's never even gotten in a fight."

I quivered a little in my seat. "That's comforting," I said. "That's very, very comforting." Ashleigh snapped the stereo back on and I didn't stop her. The Used bellowed something about cutting so deep that it didn't even bleed. I tried to tune out the music in my head and remember that I was just a visitor here. But it proved an awfully difficult thing to do. Mostly, I hoped I would make it back to Brooklyn without being Bortched. Ashleigh sang along to the song on the stereo unselfconsciously, drumming her palms on the dashboard as downtown Salt Lake City ambled into view. Who was I kidding? I'd already been Bortched. There was no turning back now.

Downtown Salt Lake seemed plausible enough at first glance. There was a refreshing age to most things, a pleasant lived-in look to many of the storefronts. As Rulon had promised, there was indeed an efficient little train zipping along South Temple Street, making left turns difficult, but local life easier, no doubt. The road into town led us past the Delta Center, where the Utah Jazz play and where the Neville Brothers seemed to be performing that very night, and in the rearview mirror I caught sight of what looked to be an old train station.

"Is that an old train station?" I asked Ashleigh, visions of faded gold-rush glamour filling my head. "I love train stations."

"It used to be," she answered without looking back. "Now it's a mall. They built it for the Olympics."

I wanted to ask: Why would the Olympics need a mall? But some questions are better left unanswered.

"Temple Square is just up on the left," Ashleigh said. "If you want to see it, let's park here."

I steered the rental into an empty space on the south side of the street. Across the street, past the light-rail stop, a plain-Jane Best Western stuck its blunted snout into the purplish sky. The car made a hospital-like dinging noise to remind me I'd left the lights on. As soon as the AC went off, the famous dry heat penetrated my bones. There were shockingly few people on the street.

"Where is everyone?" I said.

"Home, probably." Ashleigh undid her seat belt and opened the door. "Where do you want them to be?"

Where, indeed. I locked up the car and followed Ashleigh across the street to the walled-in square. The air was hot but still—almost enjoyable. As soon as we set foot on the curb, two mousy-looking young women with name tags and ankle-length black skirts approached us, smiling as if they were auditioning for an orthodontist's catalog. Squinting in the glare of their megawatt teeth, I'd never felt more New York—or more Jewish—in my life.

"They're missionaries," Ashleigh hissed. "Total wack jobs."

The two swooped down on us like God-fearing vultures. They even walked in sync, their legs pistoning over the stone ground in easy steps. There was no similarity between them in looks—one was tall and blond; the other was stumpy and Asian—but their plasticine expressions united them in creepy Stepford sisterhood. I wanted to turn around and run, but they were already upon us.

"Good evening!" said Stepford sister number one. "Welcome to Temple Square! May we be of assistance?"

"Um," I said, feeling somehow guilty even though I hadn't done anything. "No, thanks. We're all right."

"There's a screening of a film beginning in ten minutes," said Stepford number two, smoothing out the pleats in her skirt. "It explains the glorious history of Brigham Young and the Church of Jesus Christ of Latter-day Saints." Her eyes brimmed with God-loving tears. "Would you like us to show you where the screening is?"

"Ah," I said. "No, no. We're just, um, browsing." The two smiled serenely. I started to blurt out another ridiculous pleasantry when Ashleigh grabbed my arm and steered me away from them and toward the giant, glowing temple.

"For a writer, you sure can be sucky with words."

"Writers don't have to speak out loud, Ashleigh. They are allowed to be mute."

"Whatever."

A gentle breeze pushed through the square, moving the hot air around and making me feel the thousands of miles between me and my humid home. Small groups of stern, anachronistic bald men in suits strolled by in every direction, muttering church business into one another's ears. There didn't seem to be many tourists. Ashleigh pointed out the giant round tabernacle building to the left and then steered us toward the burbling fountain at the foot of the imposing, bone-white temple. The turrets were lit from below by muted, glowing spotlights, and they pointed toward the star-filled sky with a stern austerity of purpose.

I gazed upward and thought: a story. A story traveled here and built this. No matter what my personal beliefs were, in that moment I was duly humbled and impressed. All of this for a story. Now that's dedication. Or good storytelling. I turned to Ashleigh, who seemed bored. "Can we go in?"

Ashleigh shook her head. "Only members of the church can go in. And even then, not always."

I felt the eyes of the missionaries with the lacquered smiles on us so I steered Ashleigh around the square to another corner of the temple. "Have you ever been in there?"

She sighed. "Once. When I was like seven. The whole family got sealed in there."

I frowned. "You were sealed in there? Did you have to, like, fight your way out? Indiana Jones–style?" I pictured Ashleigh, mud-streaked and panting, dodging rolling boulders and blowgun darts with trusty Short Round at her side.

Ashleigh sighed again, with infinite patience. "No, dummy. It's what the LDS Church does. It's a ceremony for the totally true believers. If you get your family sealed together, then you'll always be together, even after death."

"So if something were to happen to you and your parents, you'd be reunited with them in heaven or whatever?"

"Yep."

"You're stuck with your family for all eternity?" I shuddered.

"Now you see why I ran away."

"God, yeah." I whistled. "Eternity is a long time. If you had told me all this before, I would have at least let you go on a few more rides this afternoon. You deserved the break."

"Thanks a lot."

"C'mon," I said. "Let's go get something to eat." But as we walked, I stopped again. "Like, *eternity* eternity?"

She rolled her eyes. "I told you, yes."

"Man, oh man. Bortched for all eternity. That's something else." I dodged Ashleigh's kick, then raced her back to the rental car.

• • •

As we drove east, Ashleigh pointed out the landmarks we didn't have time to see up close: the grand old Joseph Smith Memorial Building, formerly the first hotel in Salt Lake City, named for the brilliant confidence man Joe Smith, who witnessed a vision from the angel Moroni in upstate New York and received golden tablets straight from God telling him about the ancient white civilizations of North America and leading him to found the LDS Church. Smith got dozens of people to believe his tale and even more to follow him across the country and marry him multiple times, all before getting himself shot to death in suspicious circumstances by angry nonbelievers in Ohio. Rulon had written a particularly florid passage about Smith, as well as about the impressive genealogy library housed inside the building that bears his name. As interested as I was in seeing what sort of record of Gouldian life might be found here in a practically Jewproof state, I drove on. We also passed the Beehive House, one of the creatively designed abodes of Smith's successor, Brigham Young. We also passed two malls and a Borders.

"Where are we going now?" Ashleigh was skipping tracks on the CD player, seemingly nonplussed by my rubbernecking tourism.

"Turn right up here," she said. "I'll take you to, like, the only cool place in this dumb city."

"Sounds good to me." And I did as I was told.

Driving Salt Lake was actually pretty simple, once Ashleigh explained the road system to me. It was another one of ol' Brigham's brainstorms: Everything was labeled in terms of its relationship to the temple. The east–west road that was two blocks south of the temple was 200 South. The north–south road that we were currently on, four blocks east of the temple, was 400 East. For a man who believed in a prophet named Ether, it seemed like a crushingly unpoetic solution, but it was darn efficient. We passed all the signs of modern American sprawl: fast-food joints, movie-rental chains, electronic wholesalers. We also passed a take-out pastry shop called Sconecutters.

"You know why the streets are so wide?" Ashleigh was staring out the window.

"Because there's a lot of space to use up around here?"

"No, the rumor is that it was so Brigham Young could walk arm in arm with all of his wives."

"Huh." I looked around—the streets were wide, though no one seemed to be walking anywhere with any of their wives. "Is that true?"

"Who knows. Sometimes it's hard to tell what to believe. They keep changing their story."

"That's the beauty of stories, isn't it?"

"Maybe." Suddenly, Ashleigh snapped upright. "What do *you* believe in?"

I laughed. "What, you mean like religion?"

"Sure. Why are you laughing?"

"I don't know. I guess I just don't spend much time thinking about it. I don't really believe in God or any of that."

"But aren't you, like, Jewish?"

"More than 'like,' Ashleigh. I am a full-fledged Jew."

"So doesn't that mean anything to you?"

I honked at a mammoth SUV that didn't seem interested in proceeding through the green light. For people with such big cars and wide roads, the locals certainly were lousy drivers. "Sure, it means something. But it doesn't affect my beliefs, really. Other than my natural cynicism—and charm."

"That must be nice."

I looked over. Ashleigh seemed to be losing enthusiasm the farther south we drove. "What do you believe, Ashleigh?"

She nibbled on her thumbnail. "I don't know. I used to believe in the church, you know? It's *everything* here, and it meant so much to my parents and, well, there's just nothing else. Like when I was a kid, not having the church would have been like not having sunshine or something. But when I got older, I started asking questions. And people wouldn't answer my questions, which I thought was just rude, at first, but then it seemed creepy. Like, why can't you answer these questions? Why do you have to make me feel like a freak for asking them? I used to pray to God to make me normal and have normal thoughts and not ask things all the time. But I couldn't help it. It's like when you tell someone not to think about an elephant. You know? Like what are you thinking about right now?"

"Right now I'm thinking about getting out of this turn lane. But I'm sure as soon as I manage to navigate that, I'm going to have a richly detailed elephant in my brain."

"Don't be a dork. I'm serious."

"I know. Sorry. So what happened?"

"Well, when I was fourteen we got America Online, and one night when I was in my room and didn't have any more homework to do, I went to this Web site about this TV show I really liked and saw that they had, like, a FAQ. You know, like the list of questions?"

"I know what a FAQ is! Oh, go through the light! No!" I braked abruptly as the Mazda I was trailing suddenly pulled up lame at a yellow. "What show was it?"

Ashleigh blushed. *"Seventh Heaven."*

"Ha!"

"Shut up!"

"Sorry, go on."

"Well it got me thinking. If you can get answers to questions about TV shows online, why not, like, religion? So I did a search and . . . well, it all kinda fell apart from there."

"Why did it fall apart?"

"I found all these sites, right? Where people could ask questions about the church and real people would answer them. There's even a giant site called Exmormon.org where people who got excommunicated tell their stories. And it was just . . . brutal. I cried and cried all night. I wasn't the only one who had questions. And when I read the answers—I couldn't unread them, you know? I read all this stuff about Freemasons and Mormons and how the twelve witnesses were all close friends of Joseph Smith and just all this terrible stuff. And I couldn't believe it anymore."

"Yeah, but Ashleigh, all religions are inconsistent. I mean, my family used to have a rabbi who ate a ham sandwich for lunch every day."

"It wasn't about it being inconsistent. It was about being part of something that wouldn't let me ask questions—that I couldn't stand. That's just not who I am."

I glanced over again at Ashleigh, feeling strangely proud of her. "No, I wouldn't want that either."

"It's funny," she said, lost in her own world. "The Internet opened me up to so many things, you know? New people, poetry, music . . . life. But it totally closed me off from the life my parents set out for me. Which just totally sucks."

"The Internet was just the tool you had, Ashleigh," I said. "It was like a shovel, but you're the one who dug your way out. Face it: You're just not a closed-off person. Which is a wonderful thing. There are far too many closed-off people in the world today. If you hadn't had that shovel, you would have just dug the hole with your hands. And then totally messed up your nails."

She punched my shoulder. "What are you *talking* about? Digging holes?"

"I don't know. Maybe all this mountain air makes me poetic."

"Well, quit it."

And so I did.

After a twenty-minute drive south and east, past a minor league baseball stadium, a state park, and some upscale shopping centers, Ashleigh had me pull into the parking lot of the Blue Plate Diner on 2100 East. The mountains loomed large in front of us, and when I cut the engine, the faint sound of crickets filled the air. Still, I was feeling antsy. "Are you sure we have time for this?"

"I promise," she said. "Plus, I'm starving!"

The diner was, in the end, worth visiting. Located on the east side of Salt Lake, closer to the university, it had that retro-funky, relaxed vibe familiar in all college towns. There were a few tables scattered outside, filled with recognizable boys with too much stubble drinking coffee too seriously next to white girls sporting trust-fund dreadlocks.

I felt instantly comfortable—here was an oasis of liberalism in a conservative sea—and predicted (correctly, as it turned out) that inside the fixtures would be vintage, the coffee mugs would be oversize (and bottomless), the local alt weekly would be available to browse, and some variation on a vegan tofu scramble would be on the menu. The woman who led us to a booth in the back had cat's-eye glasses and a cute, sardonic smile. I felt like we had stumbled into a completely different movie.

When we were seated and had both ordered drinks, Ashleigh leaned across the Formica tabletop and whispered, "I love this place."

"It's really nice." The gaggle of indie-rock boys seated at the middle table let out a wild guffaw and clinked their glasses. They were a familiar bunch: hooded sweatshirts up over their heads, spiked belts, and Dickies pants with shredded cuffs. The "bad boys" of any town, who were actually good boys, just bored out of their skulls. I saw Ashleigh watching them longingly and asked, "Do you know any of them?"

She blushed two shades of crimson. "What? No! I don't even live around here."

"Well," I said, shuffling the ketchup bottle between my hands. "I think they like you." More hooting and whispering from the table of boys.

Ashleigh kicked my shin under the table. Another day of girls like this one and I'd be covered in bruises. "Shut up! No they don't."

"I think they might," I said, raising my eyebrows. "That one with the nose ring has an Against Me! T-shirt on. Isn't that one of those rock-and-roller groups you're always IMing me about?"

"God, *Dad*, you're so embarrassing." But she was smiling, too.

I stopped teasing her then, hoping her good mood would last until I was able to drop her off, and concentrated on the menu. When the waitress came back, Ashleigh ordered the chicken sandwich and fries, and I got the veggie burger. The food came quickly and was awfully good, so we concentrated on eating. Which is to say I concentrated on eating, while Ashleigh concentrated on the table of boys. I took advantage of her distraction to lead a vicious raid on her french fries. I was remorseless. I took many prisoners.

"You could have ordered your own, you know."

"I know, but it's more of a challenge this way."

Ashleigh smiled, but the smile faded quickly. "Do we really have to do this?"

"I'm afraid we do, Ashleigh. It's the rules of dinner. I am charged by divine law to steal your fries and you are compelled by the almighty to defend them."

"No, I'm talking about *this*. Me, here. Do you really have to take me home?"

I wiped my mouth and took a swig of Coke. "Yeah, Ashleigh. I really do. This has been fun. Strange and prohibitively expensive, but fun. But it has to end before either of us gets into serious trouble."

"This has just been so . . . different. Like even though I'm back here already, I still feel free. I don't want to lose that."

"I know." I licked a dollop of ketchup off my finger. "You have to hold on to the feeling. You have to remember that even if you're trapped here—for the moment—you are and always will be as free as you want to be." I hummed a fragment of "Free to Be You and Me" for good measure.

"Tell that to my parents."

"No, I won't. But you should."

She laughed, but it was a bitter sound. "Right."

"Ashleigh, the most important thing for you to remember is that they're your parents. You have to love them, because as rough as they are on you, I'm willing to bet it's just because they love you. And because they're scared of losing you. But loving them doesn't mean you have to *like* them right now."

"That's not a problem."

"Look, don't forget about any of this, OK? The places we've been today. How far it's possible to travel."

"How could I forget?"

"And the most important thing for you to do is never give up fighting for yourself. Hold on to those poems or diary entries or CDs or stuffed bears or whatever matters most to you. You have to hold on to those things, because they're a part of you. You have to be confident in that. Don't conform. And if your parents really love you—which I bet they do—ultimately they'll figure it out and support you."

Ashleigh nodded slowly and popped a fry in her mouth. "OK. That makes sense. But we have to make a deal."

I raised my eyebrows. "Oh? I haven't done enough?"

"You better listen to your own advice."

I frowned. "Me?"

"Yeah you, Mr. Hotshot. I saw the way you hid that picture of your girlfriend. You miss her, don't you?"

I felt a pang in my lungs and wanted to change the subject, but one look into those irony-free blue eyes across from me and I knew I had to respond. "Yeah—yes. Yes, I miss her. A lot."

"So you'd better do something about it. Stop doing things for other people and do something for yourself. Get out there and fight. If I can't run away from my life then neither can you."

I nodded. "Deal."

"You know what?" Ashleigh dragged a fry back and forth through a puddle of ketchup like she was waxing a window. "You're not at all like I expected."

"Oh, no?"

She smiled. "Nope."

"Ah. The height thing."

"No, more than that. I mean, I just pictured you always as, like, this *adult*. Someone who had all the answers."

She popped the fry in her mouth as I let out a low chuckle. "And now?" I asked.

"I guess I realize that that was more about what I needed to see than about what you really are. I mean, you've been really great to me, don't get me wrong. But . . ."

"It's more complicated in real life, isn't it?"

"Yeah. But not in, like, a bad way."

I smiled. "Agreed."

"Good." Ashleigh looked pleased with herself. "Now I have to go pee."

"Thanks for the info," I said, shaking my head as she left the table.

While Ashleigh was gone I asked for the check, then felt my cell phone buzz in my pocket. I had almost forgotten it was there—it seemed strange that it still worked so far away from everything that was familiar.

```
1 New Text Message From: Cath
11:33 p.m.
How come you're not at home?
```

I shook my head with a grin. It was nice to be missed. But then a cloud passed through my mind. How did she know I wasn't home? Had she called my landline? Had she *stopped by*? God, I hoped not. Our awkward fumbling on her bed felt like a lifetime ago, so gauzy and unreal in my memory I wondered if it had even happened at all. I closed my eyes and tried to feel the push of her thin lips on mine, the jut of her bony hip. It had happened, all right. And I hadn't fought it. I shook my head. No wonder I was all over the place. A fighter picks his battle and sticks to it. When I got back to New York, I'd make some changes. I had to.

"Daydreaming about Brigham Young again?"

I snapped out of it, opened my eyes, and saw Ashleigh's smirking face. I jammed my phone back in my pocket. I'd answer Cath later. "No, just his polygamist ways." Ashleigh sat back down, but I stood up and gestured for her to do the same. "Come on, let's get moving. You have a home to be returned to and so do I."

Ashleigh was quiet as we pulled out of the parking lot and headed due south. The Bortch family lived in a suburb called South Jordan, which was, in the inimitably literal geography of the state, located just south of the suburb of Jordan. Ashleigh said it was about twenty-five minutes away, a straight shot down Main Street. I figured I had just enough time to drop her off safely at home, pull a U-turn, and race back to the airport for my flight. The road we were on turned brutally dull in a hurry: just another faceless dribble of early twenty-first century consumption. The same fast-food places, the same Barnes & Noble with the same dropped-in-from-nowhere boxy architecture. It all seemed to go on forever. I kept glancing to my left and right, trying to imagine the pockets of real, hot-blooded feeling that might exist in this flat valley, just off the road maybe, or just behind the next ridge. But it was hard to do. Mostly, I just felt trapped and vaguely claustrophobic. How could anyone grow up in such blankness? Seeing her now, questioning and fighting despite incredible odds, Ashleigh Bortch shone like a firefly in a coal mine. As I drove, I watched her eyes reflecting the glare of the oncoming traffic, taking it all in, never blinking, never backing down from what was to come.

She was a good kid. She had some screwed-up stuff to deal with, but who didn't these days? This wasn't some lark for her, some random, easily dismissed life hiccup. This was all she had. I switched lanes and thought about all the other young lives I had read about online during the past year, how their foibles and misadventures had provided me with a sort of detached entertainment, and in one great regretful rush I felt sorry for what I had done. Every one of those head-scratchingly epic suburban dramas had been fueled with real pathos, real pain. Every single one. How had I presumed to write a book about these kids without ever taking the time to meet any of them, to experience their day-to-day reality? I was years and worlds away from them, and—not for the first time since the doppelgänger had shown up—I felt like a fraud. Diarists like Ashleigh and her peers may have been painfully unsubtle, overly earnest, and dangerously impetuous, but at least they were trying something. At least they were fighting.

We passed a long line of cars with left-hand blinkers flashing, waiting for the signal and their chance to turn into a gargantuan, windowless structure just off the road. "That's Jordan Commons," said Ashleigh as if it were as familiar as the Louvre. "We're almost there now."

I shook my head to clear away the thought cobwebs that had gathered in the silence. "What's Jordan Commons?"

"It's like a really big deal around here. The guy who owns the Jazz built it. It's a giant movie theater with tons of screens, and the lobby is like a little town with lots of snack places and, like, arcades. They also have this giant TV that's always playing Fox News or something boring like that. Some old people just spend the whole day in there, seeing movies and eating."

"Sounds like a blast."

"There are also lots of big restaurants. There's, like, a Chinese place and a crab place. They're pretty good. The biggest one is the Mayan. I used to love it when I was a kid. We went there on my birthdays. They serve Mexican food and have a waterfall and Mexican guys jumping off of it."

I shook my head. "Mexican guys jumping off a waterfall? In a restaurant? Is that healthy?"

"It's entertainment. It's pretty cool."

"Wild," I said, trying to picture it in my mind. Just up the road, Ashleigh pointed out the turnoff and I steered the car underneath a highway and past two or three 7-Elevens.

"We're almost there," said Ashleigh.

Off the main road, everything was remarkably dark. There were no streetlights, and every third plot seemed to be empty, as if the suburbs had only managed to get one claw dug in this far south. "It's kind of spooky," I said.

Ashleigh crossed her arms. "What did I tell you? There's nothing here. Nothing at all."

"I guess you weren't kidding."

At a wide intersection, we turned right onto an even darker road. This was the town of South Jordan. After a half mile or so of nothing, we passed a building so illuminated that it seemed gaudy compared to the shadows that surrounded it. One glance at the angelic steeple and I knew what sort of building it was. "Is that your temple?" I asked as we drove by.

"Yup," she said. "That's where my folks are right now. Get ready to turn again, we live right behind the temple."

She wasn't kidding. Not a hundred yards down the road from the South Jordan Temple was an unlit turnoff into a housing development marked only by a shiny billboard that read REUNION VILLAGE: A MAINTENANCE AND WORRY FREE COMMUNITY.

"What have they got to worry about?" I said under my breath as I slowed the car to a crawl. Reunion Village was like a Foucauldian suburban nightmare, a perfectly manufactured and manicured "neighborhood" that looked like a cross between Green Acres and Leavenworth. The main road was a cul-de-sac; each "street" was an individually gated alleyway with white "modern" homes that were connected, three at a time. White fences made of some space-age metallic polymer rose six feet high in every direction. There were no trees. The stars glowed brightly overhead, as did the steeple of the temple. I was convinced we were being videotaped.

"This place is creepy, Ashleigh."

"I know it."

"What are all the gates supposed to protect you from? There's nobody within five miles of this place."

"I dunno. I guess it's supposed to keep us in."

I shuddered. "Well, punch in the security code. I want to get out of here before the sheriff of Mayberry shows up and runs me out of town himself."

The Bortch family lived on Homecoming Avenue. While Ashleigh got out of the car to open the gate, I did my best to quiet the wild jackhammering of my heart. This entire place made me nervous, and it took every bit of restraint I had not to throw the rental into reverse and peel out of there right then while the getting was good. Even the high-pitched *beep* of the security system accepting Ashleigh's password made me jump up in my seat as if some furious cowboy were shooting at my shoes.

"OK," she said as she hopped back in. "Just up the road and I'm back."

I drove like an elderly woman past three connected homes with no lights on, and then we reached the Bortch house. It was exactly like all the others: white, stone, and stucco, a pile of pointy lines and wide windows. I couldn't help but notice that it was also the house closest to the temple, which loomed over the entire street like a vengeful night watchman. I cut the lights and turned to Ashleigh.

"Well," I said. "Here we are. The end of the road."

"Yup." She stared at her hands.

"I don't get a hug or anything?"

Ashleigh snapped to attention. "You're just gonna leave me? You won't even see me *inside*?"

"Jesus, Ashleigh, haven't we pushed this thing enough? I have to get back to the airport. And you have to make like you've never been gone."

She turned and stared out the window at the dark house. "I just . . . it's important to me, OK? I want you to know where it is I ran away from. So that when I complain or talk about it . . . someone will know, OK?" And then she flashed me another one of those pony-purchasing looks, throwing in a quivering bottom lip for added spice and persuasion. I closed my eyes and sighed. Then I snapped the ignition off and threw the car into park.

"Fine. But in and out, OK? I am *not* getting caught here."

She nodded, and I followed her obediently across the front lawn, which was so neatly trimmed it looked like Astroturf. The air was still and deathly quiet. "How much time before they get home, anyway? And won't your sister be there?" I whispered and kept my head down, as if the bushes were lined with snipers. My eyes came to rest on a bright green mat laid out in front of the door that read WELCOME TO OUR HOME. Funny, it didn't make me feel any more welcome.

Ashleigh fumbled with her key. "Jessie had a sleepover birthday party at her best friend's tonight. That's why my parents are staying out so late." She opened the door with a soft *click*. "Relax, will you? They won't be home for another two hours. I promise." She reached out in the dark and flipped on a light, which was fine for a second until the high-pitched scream of an alarm ripped through the house and out the still-open door.

"Jesus!" I yelped, slamming the door shut behind me. "Shut that off!" Ashleigh seemed nonplussed and jabbed at a glowing green panel on the wall. The siren stopped, though my ears were left ringing. "Well, now that the CIA have been alerted to my presence, can I go?"

"Will you relax? Gosh, you are so dramatic. That happens every time anyone comes home."

I rubbed at my ears. "That's good for the nerves." Ashleigh threw her backpack down underneath a fake-stone mail table and walked into what I could now see was a living room that had apparently seen very little living. Everything was white or just barely off-white: the walls, the throw rug, the people in the pictures that crowded the mantel over the fireplace. The floors were imitation marble and reflected the harsh track lighting with an unforgiving glare. The air was heavily air-conditioned and smelled like potpourri. Everything was modulated; everything was sterile. Even the matching love seat and chair set seemed never to have been touched by a human. It was like a biohazard quarantine room as designed by Pottery Barn.

"Nice," I said, feeling like a stain on a wedding dress.

"No it isn't," said Ashleigh, clomping down a hallway toward the back of the house, throwing on lights wherever she went. I wandered over to the mantel, taking care not to step on the rug, and examined the pictures on display in their gold-edged frames. Ashleigh and a tinier, even blonder version of herself—Jessie, I imagined—smiling on a ski lift, mugging in front of a giraffe, being clutched by old people who must have been grandparents. And in the center of them all was a three-part folding frame that housed professional portraits of a truly ridiculous-looking white dog. "Uh," I said. "Is this your dog?"

Ashleigh popped back into the room with a can of caffeine-free Dr. Pepper in her hand. "Yeah. That's Nancy. She's a Maltese."

"Is she dead or something?"

"What? No! That's horrible. She's probably out back."

I wasn't sure what irked me more, pets with human names or pet owners with framed shrines to still-living animals.

Ashleigh took a long sip of soda. "Do you want to meet her? I can bring her in."

"Nah, that's OK. I don't really get along with dogs."

"What are you talking about? Everyone gets along with dogs. She's a sweetheart."

"No, really," I said, backing away from the mantel. "It's weird—they really don't like me. When I was in Mexico once, all the dogs in the town actually organized a dog gang against me. They would form a mob every time I tried to walk down one of their streets." I shivered at the memory.

Ashleigh was staring. "A dog gang?"

"Yeah, like a gang. But of dogs."

She shook her head. "You really are weird. C'mon, I'll give you a tour."

The rest of the house was similar to the front room: gaudy, faux-sophisticated fixtures; glorious, framed celebrations of family at every turn; and not a single *thing* anywhere. No books. No magazines. No records. No sign of human life—or at least interesting human life.

Other than a loaf of white bread on the "island" in the kitchen, I didn't even see any food. I tread lightly, feeling like the entire place would shatter with one wrong step.

"It's horrible, isn't it? My father calls it his castle. I try to spend as little time as possible out of my room."

Ashleigh led me up the softly carpeted stairs. The second floor was just a long hallway with a number of doors off of it, all of which were blank and closed except for the last one, farthest away from the stairs, which was decorated by a piece of white paper with a red heart drawn on it with a rough brush. "That's my room," she said, walking toward the heart. "Krystal painted that for me. I told my parents it was about love and friendship, and they let me put it up. But it's called 'Shattered Trash.'"

"Nice," I said.

When we reached the door, Ashleigh turned and said, "Wait out here for a second, OK? I want to tidy up. Super quick."

"Fine, but be fast, OK? I have to get out of here. I'm more than a little freaked out."

She rolled her eyes, then slipped in her room, shutting the door in my face. I heard the snap as the light went on and then the gentle strum of an acoustic guitar. Dashboard Confessional's plaintive sound filled the second floor.

I knocked on the door. "I thought you sold your stereo."

Ashleigh's voice was muffled through the door. "It's on my computer, dummy."

"Well hurry up, OK?" And then to myself I added, "This is ridiculous." I paced the soft carpet and then cracked open the door that

I figured was the bathroom to answer a bet I had made with myself. I flipped the light on. Yep—the toilet seat was cushioned. Amazing. I shook my head and closed the door. What was I doing here? How did I end up in this totally random, truly horrible house in the middle of nowhere? But nothing was truly random or nowhere these days. Roger Bortch had built himself a castle all right, but no security system, moat, or dog named Nancy could keep the world away. There were electric lines and cables and Ethernet cords snaking through all of these pristine walls, a digital escape route that his elder daughter clung to like a lifeline and that she had used like a lasso to rope me in. You can't build the walls high enough, Roger. I may have brought her back, but she's already long gone.

Just then Ashleigh's door opened a crack, and I heard her say, "OK, you can come in now."

I turned around and walked back toward her voice. "Fine, but one look around and then I have to get out of here. I—"

Ashleigh's bedroom was lit only by a halogen lamp in the corner; covered now by a purple scarf, it cast the entire room in a hazy, possibly flammable reddish glow. The walls were wallpapered with small images of lilacs and peppered with a few neatly organized band posters and photos cut out of magazines. The bed in the corner was a frilly canopy number, and beside it was an orderly desk with a boxy PC on top of it. Two bulky speakers sat next to the computer, and the voice of Dashboard's Chris Carrabba poured out of them, wailing something about chasing a ghost of a good thing. There was a window above the computer looking out into inky black nothingness.

I said, "Ashleigh?" She didn't seem to be in the room, but then I felt her come up behind me, wrap her arms around my chest. "What are you doing?" I pulled her hands away and turned. She had changed into polka-dotted pajama bottoms with only a frilly white bra on top. "Whoa," I said, and then she threw herself at me, smashing her lips into mine with such force that I stumbled two steps backward, my arms flailing as I tried to balance. It wasn't a kiss—more of a face-punch. I managed to pull my head away and untangle my torso from her grasping arms and hands. "Hey," I said. "Stop. Stop!"

She crossed her arms in front of her chest. "What? I thought . . ."

"I think you thought wrong, Ashleigh." I took another step back toward the wall. "I'm sorry."

Her eyes were wet and she flushed crimson. "Why not?"

"Ashleigh." I spoke quietly, taking a step toward her. "You're a great girl. But I'm way too old for you! We're friends, remember? Good friends."

"It's not fair," she said. "It's not fair."

I was about to tell her why fair had nothing to do with it when something faint but insistent tickled my eardrums. "What's that noise?"

Ashleigh was still covering herself. "Don't change the subject."

I walked to the computer and turned down the volume. "No, really—I hear a dog barking. Don't you?"

"No, I don't hear anyth—"

"Shh! Listen!" It was definitely a dog barking; I could hear it even over the hum of the central air. Ashleigh opened her mouth as if to respond, when suddenly the air-raid-siren alarm burst through the house.

"Oh, no!" Ashleigh's hands flew to her face. "My parents!"

"You're kidding." My face grew hot and my vision wavered. I felt like I was going to faint, vomit, or both.

Ashleigh looked rabid. "No!" she hissed. "It's them! They must have come home early!"

I could barely form words. "What do we do? What the hell are we going to do?" My mind spun. I was dead. I was a dead man. So much promise, and to what end? Murdered by a vengeful fitness-obsessed Mormon in a tacky tract house in Utah. It didn't seem fair. I felt like crying. "Ashleigh!" She seemed frozen in terror. I shook her shoulders. "Ashleigh! Get dressed!"

The alarm stopped suddenly, and the silence that took its place seemed even louder. But it was enough to snap Ashleigh out of her fear coma. She dove onto the bed and pulled a sweatshirt out from under the pillows, threw it over her head. "Don't just stand there," she whispered. "Hide!"

"I can't! They've already seen my car—it's right out front!"

"Shoot . . . well then go in the bathroom! Quick! We'll figure something out."

I said, "We will?" But she was already pushing me out the door and down the hall.

I heard footsteps below. A deep male voice bellowed up the stairs. "Hello? Ashleigh? Is that you, sweetie? Are you home early?" My vision blurred around the edges and my feet started to drag on the carpet. I felt like the elderly wolf in a Jack London novel, ready to give up and surrender to the cold and relative certainty of death.

But Ashleigh wouldn't let me die. "Move it!" she hissed, and shoved me into the bathroom and shut the door. I heard her yell,

"Daddy, it's me. I'm home early!" And I spun around in a circle three times and collapsed on the cushioned toilet seat, my head in my hands.

Through the door I heard Nancy bark, and then a woman's voice said, "Honey, why didn't you call us? Is everything all right?" I opened my eyes and stared at my unshaven reflection in the mirror. I wondered what it would feel like to be hit, stabbed, strangled, or just generally killed at the hands of Roger Bortch. Would he show any tenderness? Mormon mercy? My guidebook had said that the LDS Church had abandoned the practice of blood debt earlier in the century. I hoped news of that particular revision had trickled down to South Jordan.

I heard Ashleigh thump her way down the stairs, then say, "I'm fine. I just had to come home early because I, um, forgot my contact lens solution."

The male voice again then: "Whose car is that parked outside?"

I clamped my eyes shut again and reached for the door to lock it—only to discover that there was no lock. Downstairs, Ashleigh was a maestro of improvisation. "A BYU student," I heard her say. "On the, uh, orientation committee. He was heading up here to town and offered to drive me."

"A student?" said the woman's voice.

"He?" said the male. "Where is *he* now?"

"He's in the bathroom," said Ashleigh, extra loudly as if she were playing to the cheap seats. Which, in fact, she was. I realized that that was my cue, so after flushing the toilet as loudly as I could, I took a deep breath and stepped out of the bathroom and then down the stairs. I felt the curious, burning eyes of the Bortches the entire way down. As

I carefully navigated the steps, I saw the Bortch family appear in slow motion from the bottom up, as if a curtain were being raised on them. High-top sneakers, legs like ornery treestumps, and then the big reveal: Roger Bortch, recognizable from his billboard, standing impressively at the foot of the stairs, his waxy blond mane golden in the bright light. He was wearing a blue and black Sergio Tacchini tracksuit and had a wingspan like an eagle; his thick, sunburned neck gave way to rolling shoulders and muscular arms that were wrapped around a confused, yelping mound of white dog. Gleaming in his left ear was a tiny hoop earring that fell somewhere between midlife crisis and pirate. To his right stood Mrs. Bortch, a tiny skeleton of a woman with a judgmental nose and Ashleigh's apple cheeks. She had loud, clattery doorknob earrings of her own and wore a gray sweatshirt that said MOMS RULE! in plaid stitching. I took my time with the steps, gripping the bannister so tightly I thought maybe it would explode into a diamond.

"Hello, folks," I said with as much homespun charm as I could muster. "Hope you don't mind that I stopped in to use your facilities."

The Bortches stared at me like I had just beamed down from the *Enterprise.* Ashleigh had somehow managed to change into jeans—though she was still suspiciously barefoot—and she leaned against a chair with a "don't you dare fuck this up" expression on her face. "Not at all," said Roger Bortch with a tight smile on his face. "Anything for a fellow BYU man." He adjusted the dog, who was emitting a low growl in my general direction, and held his hand out to shake. "Roger Bortch," he said. His hand was bearlike and squishy. "This is my wife, Emily."

"Nice to meet you both," I said, grinning like a mentally deficient chimpanzee. My cheeks were burning underneath my totally inappropriate week's worth of stubble.

"And you are . . . ?" Emily Bortch gave me an encouraging smile.

"Yes," I said hopefully, returning the smile. She smiled more broadly, so I nodded and smiled.

"Yes, what?" Roger Bortch was no longer smiling.

"Hmmm?" I was still standing on the second to last step, oddly above the Bortches, like I was on display.

"What's your name, son?"

I froze. "My name." I didn't say it as a question, really. More like a resigned sigh.

"Yes, that's right. Your name. You've got one, right?"

"Oh yes, sir. I certainly do." I gazed into the eternal golden blankness of Roger Bortch and somehow found a lifeline. "The name is Rulon. Uh, Rulon Barber."

There was a pause so pregnant I feared in another nanosecond it would go into labor. I could hear Ashleigh not breathing, practically see the dubious thoughts coursing through her father's veins. But all of a sudden Roger Bortch broke into a trusting, masculine grin. "A pleasure to meet you, Rulon. A fine old-fashioned name you've got. Would you care to join us for a cup of coffee?"

My blood screamed: Get out! Now! Run for the door! Never look back! But my mouth said, "Thank you, sir. I'd love to."

I sat on the white couch as calmly as I could, while beside me Emily Bortch poured lukewarm Sanka into a BYU mug.

"So, Ashleigh tells us you're a student." Roger Bortch sat in the broad-backed easy chair directly to my left, legs spread wide, master of his off-white domain.

"Yes, sir," I said, hoping my voice wouldn't crack. "Actually, a graduate student."

"Really!" Emily Bortch seemed impressed and stirred an extra splash of half-and-half into her coffee.

"What do you study?"

I took a long sip of Sanka and turned back to my inquisitor. "Oh, ah . . . creative writing!" From her terrified perch against the fireplace, Ashleigh let out a squeak. My cell phone buzzed angrily in my pocket, and I did my best to silence it through my jeans.

A stormcloud darkened Roger Bortch's healthy features. "Creative writing?" He rolled the words around on his tongue as if they were a foul-tasting lozenge. "I didn't think my alma mater would offer graduate study in *that*."

"Well," I said, hoping my brain would be able to keep pace with my mouth, "it's a fairly new program. But, ah, we're making some great progress and attracting some very talented students just now. Such as your daughter."

Ashleigh squeaked again, louder this time. I couldn't bring myself to even peek in her direction. Roger harrumphed and leaned forward. "My daughter? My daughter is premed. She doesn't have time for any nonsense."

"I'm sure she'll be a fine doctor," I said, figuring, *screw it—what else have I got to lose?* "But her writing isn't nonsense. It's very evocative and, um . . . worshipful."

Roger placed his coffee mug down on the table. Emily scurried forward like a mouse and slid a coaster under it. "Worshipful, you say. My little girl?"

He was buying it. I had no idea why or how, but he was buying it. "Yes, sir," I said. "After all, our great . . . ah, leader Brigham Young had a full library of poetry and literature in all of his homes. He even entertained Mark Twain here in Salt Lake!" My mind was flipping through the pages of Rulon I had skimmed on the plane. Why hadn't I finished that chapter? "Individual expression is a truly wonderful way to, um, know God?" My voice cracked, but I covered it with a lusty swig of Sanka.

"Well, I must say it's nice to have a religious and respectful young man like yourself talking to my daughter." Roger shot Ashleigh a look. "And to hear that her . . . pursuits aren't leading her in the wrong direction." He sighed and shook his head. "Sometimes I feel like she was put on this earth just to test us."

I watched Roger Bortch's giant, overly muscled eyes soften. I felt as if our roles had become muddled—that I was now the parent with all the answers and he was the needy child. "I'm sure that's how all parents feel about their kids, sir." I drank more of the coffee. It was grainy and bitter. "That's the gift and the challenge."

Emily Bortch seemed shocked and thrilled to find the conversation going so smoothly. She wasn't the only one. She placed a skinny hand on my arm and asked, "Are you from around here, Rulon?"

"Ah, no, ma'am," I said. "I'm from, uh . . . Fort Duchesne." I gripped the sofa with my right hand. It was the only other town I could remember and my pronunciation of it was a wild guess.

Roger Bortch clapped his hands together. "Fort Duchesne! Why, you've got the biggest and best pow-wow in the West!"

I grinned stupidly. "Yes sir, that's right!"

Roger turned serious. "Rulon, did you do a mission?"

I took a breath and then nodded. "Yes, sir, I did. I believe it's an important thing for all young men to do." I peeked at Ashleigh, who was clenching her fists so tightly I was afraid she'd draw blood.

Emily refilled my coffee mug. "Where did you serve?"

I was ready for that one. "In New York City!"

Both Bortches gasped as if I had said a dirty word. "New York City?"

"Yes, sir," I said, starting to enjoy myself. "Might as well go to where the evil is, wouldn't you agree?" LOL! DUDE... YOU ARE SO FULL OF SHIT BUT QUICK ON YOUR FEET

Ashleigh burst out laughing, and then so did Roger. I laughed too, and Nancy the dog started howling, which made Emily giggle—and soon we were all laughing until we had tears in our eyes, even though for the life of me I wasn't sure just what they found so funny.

"Wonderful, wonderful." Roger Bortch wiped at his eyes. "Is that your car parked out there, son?"

"Ah, yes, sir."

Roger nodded as if I had confirmed his most private wishes. "The Ford Tempo. That's a very reliable automobile right there. I like the look of it, too."

"It's the best, sir," I said, biting my cheek to keep from laughing. "Listen, folks, you've been too kind, but I should be going. I'm staying with my brother tonight in town and I hate to keep him up too late."

Emily Bortch stood with me. "So soon? Why not stay for a moment—we have some pound cake I could defrost . . ."

"Oh, no thank you, ma'am. I couldn't trouble you any more."

Roger stood. "No trouble at all, son." He offered his meaty paw and I shook it. "Thank you for driving our daughter home. And for *steering her straight.*" He held my gaze and nodded sagely. I tried to look properly pious and nodded back. "And listen here, if you ever have any sort of physical injury or need to rehab, feel free to give me a call." He reached into his pocket and pulled out a business card, which he pressed into my palm. The card said GET BORTCHED! I exhaled slowly. "You do work out, don't you, son?"

I opened and closed my mouth. "Try to!" I said hopefully. "Try to!"

"It's the most important thing in the world." Roger flexed his shoulders. "I always say, we are given two temples in life. The one we pray in and the one we live in!" He pounded on his chest for emphasis. I kept nodding and tried to maneuver my way to the door.

But before I made it there, Ashleigh leapt forward and took my hand. "Good-bye, Rulon!" she said. "Thank you for getting me home safe." Her eyes were huge and hungry.

I shook her hand tightly, holding it for an extra minute. "My pleasure," I said, trying to make my look say things like *Be strong; be good; be careful.* But all I said out loud was, "Anytime." I opened the door. "Good night Mr. Bortch, Mrs. Bortch." I paused, felt their eyes still raking me, desperate for more information. I knew then that tough as it might be in the future, Ashleigh was going to be just fine. As desperate as she was to hide herself from her parents, that was exactly how desperate they were to find her. I turned back to them and said, "You have a very fine daughter."

Emily Bortch beamed and threw her arm around Ashleigh, who

flinched at the contact. "We know. We are extremely blessed!"

I smiled at the family, thinking, You have no idea what you've got. Then I stepped out into the warm night air and nearly sprinted to the car. I pulled a U-turn so quickly I fishtailed in the middle of Homecoming Avenue, then roared out of the open security gate without so much as looking back.

When Reunion Village was more than a mile behind me and the lights of the temple were just a faint, glowing smudge in the rearview mirror, I pulled over to the side of the road, flicked on my hazards with still shaking fingers, and laughed and laughed and laughed.

CHAPTER FIFTEEN: NEW ORDERS FROM MISSION CONTROL

THANKS TO THE EFFICIENT city planning of the estimable Brigham Young, I had no trouble steering the Tempo back to the airport and checking in for my red-eye flight with time to spare. I left the guidebook in the glove compartment. I figured I had had enough Rulon Barber in one night to last a lifetime. Better to offer his florid services to someone else.

Despite the late hour, the departure terminal of SLC International was still buzzing with the harried mania of travel. On my way to the gate, I stood leisurely on the moving walkway—letting it do all the work for a change—while commuters in business suits and overwhelmed young parents pushed by me, peppering my ears with exasperated sighs as they passed. It felt good to stand still and still be moving for a change. With the adrenaline wearing off, I realized that I was exhausted. My legs felt like two dumbbells sutured onto my torso for the express purpose of weighing me down, and I felt a creaking tightness in my shoulders and neck. As I approached the end of the walkway, I reached backward and made a feeble attempt to massage myself. Maybe I should have stuck around for a few days, taken Roger Bortch up on his offer of free rehab. The thought made me laugh out loud, and I earned a "you're hopelessly insane" look from a passing, prim stewardess.

As I waited to board, I picked out a stack of magazines from the newsstand, but I changed my mind just before paying and put them all back on the rack. I didn't need to read about the "100 Most Rock 'n' Roll Events of Rock 'n' Roll" or the "100 Songs to Download Before You Die." I picked up a box of sleeping pills and a bottle of water. What I needed was to rest.

The plane took off on time and without incident. I had an entire row to myself, so I stretched out by the window and stared out over the wing as we climbed through the stratosphere. I tried to get the lay of the land, but all I could see was blinking lights, then clouds, then nothing. Good-bye, Utah. Or, as I realized I should say, Good-bye, Utah! I never had gotten a good glimpse of the mountains, but I was happy to be rid of them; I felt like they had gotten more than a good enough glimpse of *me*.

When the FASTEN SEAT BELTS sign went off, I stretched and lay out across my row before realizing I had forgotten to switch my cell phone off. Red-faced—and certain that the federal government had somehow been made aware of my lapse in judgment and would be waiting at JFK to drag me off to Guantanamo in handcuffs—I pulled it out and saw that I had a message. Oh, yes—the ill-timed buzz at the Bortches'. I flipped open the screen.

```
1 New Text Message From: David
1:10 a.m.
Just don't say you weren't invited, ok?
```

I scratched at my stubble. What the hell could he mean? What was he up to now? I felt a twinge of anxiety and then shook it off.

Whatever it was, it could wait until morning. Or so I hoped.

When the stewardess came by with drinks, I paid four dollars for a lukewarm Heineken, then used it to chase the sleeping pills. I balled up two pillows, shut the window screen, and closed my eyes. I thought of Ashleigh Bortch, then, and how she must have been both the most successful and least successful runaway in history. I chuckled to myself, then felt a pang of missing her. The thought that someone had chosen me as a destination, as a place to run away *to* instead of *from*—well, to be honest, it boggled my mind. I wondered if I'd ever see her again and figured that chances were that I would. Something had bound us together across miles and cultures and years. And it was the sort of thing that proved awfully hard to untie. My relationship with Ashleigh—like nearly all the relationships in my life—had started loosely and then had suddenly gone taut. I never did seem to notice the gravity of things until it was too late. I was just glad I had been able to fulfill my half of the bargain this time, even though I hadn't been aware of making said bargain to begin with.

Thing was, there were real consequences to talking to people, to involving yourself with their lives. There was nothing casual about communication, no matter what form it took. I felt the sleeping pills pulling me down into sleep and I didn't fight them. I was like a row-boat shot full of holes. The water came up to greet me and then sank me down into its warm liquid embrace.

I dreamed about Amy. Which was odd, really, because she rarely figured in my dreams—almost as if my subconscious assumed that if I was sleeping she was right there next to me, so why not give other characters a shot? But not this time. The details were hazy and kept shifting: I was on some sort of barge traveling between islands. The water was more like a swamp than the sea, and the air was thick and humid. Every so often my passenger would be Amy, and she'd smile helpfully, as she was the one doing all the work. But then other times I was alone on the boat, and I knew that she was on one of the islands—either the one I was rowing toward or the one I was just leaving; it was hard to keep track. Near the end of the dream there was a procession of puppies marching through the swamp. The first group looked like foxes and the second looked like Nancy—the Bortches' pristine pile of *yip*. I had a new passenger then—a female one, though I couldn't tell her identity. She shook me by the arm gently and I turned to see who it could possibly be.

But it was only the stewardess, with her hand on my arm, calling me sir and telling me that we would be landing shortly. My mouth tasted like ashes, and my hair felt like greasy straw. There was a heavy weight behind my eyes, and my stomach churned with hunger. I was nowhere near rested, but I thanked her and somehow managed to sit up straight and open the window shade, letting in a piercing beam of sunlight. It was morning. I was home.

My eyes were bleary and bloodshot as I stumbled past the early-morning line at Au Bon Pain, the desperate scrum in the baggage claim. I had a funny tickle of a thought in my brain that felt like freedom: I owed no one anything; I was off the grid. But even then I felt the responsibility hood snap down on my brain, nudging me into the taxi line, pushing me roughly toward routine. I pretended I was back on the moving walkway again and directed the cheery Sikh driver toward Brooklyn.

Looking back on it now, I realize it should have been obvious that something was wrong, even before I entered my building. The taxi ride from the airport had been too smooth, too easy. There had been no traffic, no delays, and no feigned confusion on the part of the driver pertaining to the quickest—which is to say cheapest—route to my neighborhood. When I stepped out of the cab, I saw no clouds in the sky, and I felt the faintest rustle of a cooling breeze blow through the trees. It felt like the photo negative of the moment before a thunderstorm. Everything was so perfect, it felt ominous. It was then I noticed that my bedroom light was on and the windows were open wide.

If there was one habit that Amy had drilled into my skull it was never to leave any lights on, so my heart skipped at double time as I unlocked the doors. I walked straight into Mrs. Armando standing stock-still in the middle of the foyer. She had her arms crossed and she wasn't smiling.

"You used to be a good kid, David," she said.

"Good morning, Mrs. Armando." I tried to look cheerful.

"Don't you 'good morning' me. After what you do last night, I should throw you out right now."

"What I did?"

"Don't act like that to me. I let you live here in my house! I pay for it, I own it! And you disrespectin' it. Have wild people over, keep up half the block with the crashing and yelling. I'm scared to see what you do to my third floor."

Oh, God. I wasn't even back for five minutes and everything had already fallen apart. "Mrs. Armando," I said, my hands out in front of me in a sorry attempt to appease her. "How did he . . . how did I get in?"

She cocked her head. "You foolin'?"

"No . . . I'm sorry. I wish I was. But I'm not fooling."

She let out an exasperated sigh. "You ask me for the key! First you say you lose the key—meaning I gotta change the locks—and I give you a spare because you always used to be a good kid, David. None of this noise and nonsense."

He was here. In this house. In my home. "I'm so sorry, Mrs. Armando. I promise it won't happen again."

"I'm not cleaning up no more messes for you, David. I tell you to throw out that bucket and you throw it into my garden? Mess up my tomatoes?" She shook her head at the inhumanity of it all.

I started up the steps. "I'm sorry," I stammered. "I'm so, so sorry." I felt violated, terrified.

"I give you another chance, but only because of Amy. I always like her!"

But I was already halfway gone. I galloped the steps two at a time, reached the third floor, and turned the doorknob. It was unlocked. I pushed open the door, and what I saw sent my stomach into freefall.

Everything was wrecked. My living room looked like a vengeful TV cop had blown through the place sans warrant, overturning everything just because he could. The mail table was upside down, the easy chair was ripped down the middle, its cheap, fluffy intestines spilling out like it had seen the business end of a bayonet. The floor was littered with crushed beer cans, some still leaking their sticky, flat contents. There were fast-food wrappers and empty bags of Doritos. The coffee table was a graveyard of red plastic cups, some of which overflowed with cheap vodka and soggy cigarette butts. There was a thin film of smoke in the air, and the entire place smelled like the inside of the Marlboro Man's left lung. There was a nasty, jagged hole in the middle of the television set. The mirror that used to hang by the front closet was lying face up on the far end of the futon, its surface covered with a fine dusting of white powder. And crumpled up on the other end of the futon, her legs barely brushing the edge of the mirror and her pale arms wrapped around a throw pillow stitched by Amy's mother, was Cath Kennedy.

I raced over to her, crushing cans and kicking over an empty bottle of Popov en route. I could hear music playing faintly in my office. "Trouble" by Lindsey Buckingham.

I shook her arm. Her skin was clammy, and there was a thin film of sweat on her brow and upper lip. "Cath." I shook her harder. "Cath!" Was she even alive?

Yes, she was. But she didn't seem happy about it. She let out a low groan, and I could see her eyes swimming around behind her closed lids like fish beneath a frozen pond, desperate for sunlight. I shook her again, shouted out her name. Finally, her eyes fluttered open. She looked confused, startled. Then she flashed me a lazy smile of recognition. "Heyyyy," she said breathily, sinking deeper into the couch and stretching out her legs like a house cat. "You came back."

"Cath." I shook her again. "What the hell happened? *Where the hell is he?*"

She sat up, rubbed at her brow. "Who?"

I stood up, stomped toward where the music was coming from.

"Me!" I yelled, unable to see straight from anger. "The other me!" My office was a sea of CDs and wide-open jewel boxes, and my desk was lined with a barricade of empty Budweiser bottles. My laptop was open and on, a screen saver languidly flashing across its screen. I snapped off the stereo, steeled myself, then threw open the sliding wooden doors to my bedroom.

It was empty. The contents of my dresser were spread out across the floor like an extra layer of carpeting, and an innocent breeze blew in from the open windows. But no one was there. I felt the sheets. They were cool and untouched. I spun around and stormed back into the living room. I sputtered at Cath, impotent with rage. She was sitting upright now, taking small sips from a bottle of 7-Up. She looked like she had been thrown from the back of a horse, her hair sticking out wildly to the left, her face pinched and battered.

"He's not here," she said in a small voice. "He left."

I took two deep breaths, kicked a can of Rolling Rock across the floor, then sat down amid the ruined innards of the easy chair. "Cath," I said, more sad now than angry. "What happened?"

She blinked. "What time is it?"

I looked at my watch. "It's eight fifteen a.m."

She groaned and sat back. "There was a party."

"I can see that." From where I was sitting, I could see into the kitchen. The floor was a Picasso of swirled, dirty footprints, and the far window was, as I had feared, completely devoid of herb garden.

"He called me, invited me over last night."

"What time?"

She scratched at her arm. "I dunno. Maybe nine? He said he was at your apartment. That the two of you had made some sort of agreement. Like a truce. And that you both wanted me to come over."

"Uh-huh."

"So I had nothing better to do. So I came. And it was totally out of control. The entire VSC was here. Some band that I saw play at Lit once—from Detroit—they were all here and so were their roadies. That creepy dude with bleached hair—the Asian guy from Smashing Pumpkins who's always hanging around the East Village?"

I rubbed my eyes hard, until I saw stars. "James Iha?"

"Yeah, that dude was here all night. And you—the other you . . . he was completely out of control. He was drinking everything in sight, snorting drugs, making out with strangers. He had his shirt off and was just, like, *cackling* with laughter. He kept repeating, 'Why not? Why not?' Over and over again. It was kind of scary."

I tried to picture it in my mind. "So what did you do?"

"Well, I tried to find you. But it was hard—it was so packed in here, and things kept shattering and more people kept showing up. It took me almost an hour to go through the whole apartment. And people kept handing me drinks and . . . you know how it is."

"I do?"

She gave me a look. "Yeah, you do. But when I made it to the bedroom and saw for sure that you weren't here, that's when I sent you a text. I didn't understand where you could be. But you never wrote back."

"I know. I should have."

"Where *were* you?"

I sat back with a sigh. "Utah."

Cath looked confused. "Utah?"

"Yep."

"Like, *Utah* Utah?"

"The very one."

Cath laughed. "You really get around, you know that?"

"So I've been told. What happened next?"

"Well, I waited for you to write back. But it kept getting later and later. And I was drinking a lot—actually I was still probably drunk from the night before. And then you—*other you*—offered me drugs and I figured that I shouldn't leave. That someone responsible had to be here." She looked around at the destruction, gave a helpless shrug. "I'm sorry. I tried to be the responsible one but . . . I guess I just fucked it all up. As usual."

The cute and by now familiar band of red blossomed across the bridge of her nose. I felt tired and used up. I was no longer angry. "Cath, where did he go?"

She took another sip of 7-Up and continued. "It was around three or four a.m. People were still raging and you number two had somehow got me cornered in the bedroom. He had his hands all over me, rubbing my legs and my shoulders. He was nibbling at my ears and kept trying to kiss me. I was pretty far gone, but I knew enough to push him away. And finally I just exploded, made some joke about how it was like the exact opposite of the night before—you know, with *you.* And it was like he got hit by lightning. He just went stiff and cold and pulled away from me and started yelling, like, 'What happened?' and what had I done with you. He was scary." She reached around on the floor, found a paper towel and blew her nose into it. She inspected the results, smiled, and said, "Ha. No blood." Then she balled up the towel in her tiny fist.

"What did you tell him?"

"The truth! Just that I had invited you to a party and we had a good time together. That we, you know, hooked up a little."

"And what was his reaction?"

"He started saying, 'You invited *him,*' over and over. And he stood up suddenly and walked away from me, and it was like something changed in him."

"What do you mean 'changed'?"

"I don't know how to describe it." She shook her head, shivered a little. "Like I said, I was pretty wasted. But it was like . . . like watching a candle melt, but sped up. Like he was melting a little from the inside."

"Melting?"

"God, I don't know. That sounds so weird. It was like his insides were *soft* or something. Like he was changing from the inside out. Like everything was shifting, like sand after high tide. But then he snapped back, and anything that had been soft hardened up again. When it was over, his eyes were different. And he started moving differently too. Like he had just been radioed new orders from mission control. That's when he attacked your clothes in there." She gestured toward the bedroom. "He put on that T-shirt you were wearing the day I met you. And he kicked everyone out."

"And what did you do?"

"Well, it took a while for everyone to leave. So I lay down on the couch here to wait for them. Like I said, I didn't want to leave him alone here. But . . . I guess I fell asleep. I heard the door slam shut at some point, but I don't remember when." She looked up at me with moist eyes. "I'm really sorry, David."

"It's OK," I said. "It's OK." But I didn't feel like I was telling the truth. I stood up, starting walking back toward the bedroom. I felt like I was made of eggshells. Like I was already cracked and empty.

Cath called out to me. "What are you going to do?"

I didn't even turn around. "I don't know anymore. I don't have anything left."

"What are you talking about?"

But I ignored her. I was broken. Nothing that I cared for or held close was mine anymore. Everything was gone. There was nothing left. I kicked off my shoes and stripped off my jeans. A wave of blackness and sadness washed over me, and I was asleep before my head hit the pillow.

Sometime during the morning Cath Kennedy joined me in bed, pulled the covers over us both, and rested her head in the crook of my arm. She wore only her underwear, and she twitched with dreams as she slept. It was those tiny movements that woke me. I didn't move, didn't pull her close. Just felt her presence and pressure up against me. It wasn't unpleasant, but it wasn't anything greater than that either. I felt like we were all alone together, adrift, like abandoned cosmonauts in some forgotten satellite. There was a hollow feeling in my chest where my heart usually was, and I realized: This isn't the end of sadness. It's the beginning. Sadness and loneliness aren't destinations. They're roads that lead us away from everything we once loved. I had felt desperate and sorry for myself on that lost, wild night after the Madrox, thinking I had finally bottomed out. But that wildness in my bones had just been the start of it all, not the end. I was falling now. And there was no bottom.

I blinked my eyes open and they stung with tears. As if she could read my mind, Cath sighed and snuggled in closer to me. "There was something else," she murmured into my ear.

"What?" I whispered, staring at the ceiling fan as it made its lazy revolutions in the breeze.

"Right before he left, I heard him next to me on the futon. He was on the phone. He was talking quietly—so much so that I didn't recognize his voice. He was talking all lovey-dovey to someone. I couldn't make out much before he hung up. Then he was gone."

I sat up like I had been electrocuted. "On the phone."

Cath groaned and rolled away from me. "Yes."

"Oh my God," I said, leaping to my feet.

"Where are you going?" Cath whined and jammed a pillow over her head. "It's time to sleep still."

I ignored her and raced through the chaos to the living room. I pulled the phone from its holster and hit the redial button. There was only one number displayed. An international exchange. The Netherlands. Amy.

"No," I said out loud and threw the phone onto the futon.

From the other room I could hear Cath Kennedy rustling the covers. "What is it?" she said from under the pillow.

I ran into the office and swept the beer bottles onto the floor with a vicious crash.

Cath was sitting up now. "What's gotten into you? What are you doing?"

I buried my hands in the stacks of paper that covered my desk. The photo was missing. The photo of Amy was gone. I bashed at the keys of the computer and the screen saver blinked off. A Web page was open. Travelocity, thanking user David Gould for confirming his booking: JFK to Amsterdam, then a commuter flight to The Hague. The itinerary had been paid for by credit card. The flight was leaving today. I checked my watch. It was nearly two p.m. The plane was due to leave at six-twenty with a required check-in at four. Two hours. I had two hours.

I stood up with a start and raced to my dresser, ran my hand through the bottom of the sock drawer like a wild man. My hands skittered across the liner like a rabid spider. It was gone. My passport was gone. I turned to Cath Kennedy, who held a pillow balled up in front of her for protection and was staring at me like I was insane. Maybe I was. "Come on," I said, throwing her a T-shirt. "Get up. Get dressed. We have to get moving."

She didn't move. "Where are we going?"

I jumped into my jeans. "We're going to end this."

She just nodded shakily and pulled the T-shirt over her head. "OK," she said. But I was already dressed and sitting back at the computer. "Wait, what are you doing now?"

"One last thing to do here before we go," I said over my shoulder. Then I called up a different Web site, cracked my knuckles, and placed my fingers on the keys.

Cath asked, "What?"

"It's time to tell the truth," I said. And then I started typing.

CHAPTER SIXTEEN: (TRY AGAIN)

[from **http://users.livejournal.com/~davidgould101**]

Time: 1:58 p.m.

Mood: Honest

Music: None

This is me writing now. Me: David Gould. The only one. It's time to set some things straight. For who? you might ask, since this diary has pretty much never been read by anyone except for me and, well, other less-polite versions of me. Please think of it as an undelivered letter to the future - and especially to the two people I've been lying to for so long: to Amy and to myself.

I started this thing as a fantasy, then sat around passively as it turned into first a comedy and then a tragedy. No longer. True stories can be more than one thing at any time and so can people. I know that now. So let's tackle the unpleasant stuff, the half-truths, the clever omissions. Let's fill in the convenient blanks, particularly those from the other night when even though I was falling I still had to somehow feel like the hero. I came close to the truth, then backed away from it. So let's fix that now and then fix the rest. First on the screen, then in the world.

So, to review, what happened after the fistfight in the bathroom was:

1. Clarence, the bouncer, did not make a glib comment about there being two of me. He saw me sprint past him, yelled "Hey!" and that was the last I heard of him.

2. When the doppelgänger was speechless in the bathroom and just before I washed my hands I took the baggie full of drugs away from him and put it in my pocket. He offered no resistance.

3. Zaina did not follow me out of the club. I saw her leave and ran after *her.* I did that. Only me.

4. Because the truth of it is: I knew what I was doing the whole time. That's the thing about the way the drugs made me feel: I wasn't out of my head, I just found a different part of it to hang out in. I objectively knew that this was wrong, that this was cheating, that I was betraying something or someone - Amy, myself. But there was a new vibration in my blood that seemed to quiet

any doubts, seemed to justify anything that I wanted as being worthwhile. So what happened was we:

5. Walked hand in hand to Orchard and then down south of Delancey. We stopped at a bodega to buy a six-pack of beer. Zaina also bought a giant bottle of water with one of those pully-straw-things at the top. I pretended to walk away and look at the magazines while she paid, but she also bought cigarettes, sugarless gum, and condoms. The she led me down another street to the border of Chinatown - the streets were still damp and the air smelled vaguely of seafood. At a graffiti-scarred door we stopped and she rang a bell. We were buzzed in, walked up four flights of stairs, and entered a loft that was all white - the only thing on the walls was a complete set of Monaco Grand Prix posters from the years 1972-1985. Beyond those few flashes of color were a bare-bones kitchenette, a black couch, and an enormous cheap wood-grain entertainment center with a flat-screen TV, stereo, PlayStation, and shelves of CDs. There was a loft area over the kitchenette with a futon and a dresser. The stereo was blasting music; I recognized fragments here and there: Out Hud, Pinback, Little Brother, Ms Dynamite. The floor was hardwood but cracked and mildewed. The air was crisp and humming with central AC. The sink was full of dirty dishes. Someone had apparently attempted to cook a curry and failed.

6. The loft was owned by a girl who was currently sleeping off a tequila drunk up on the loft futon. We were told this by her boyfriend, a barrel-chested Australian with a ponytail and a goatee whose name I never caught. He was playing the role of host and told us to shush when we arrived, but never once thought to lower his own voice or the music. He took the beer and greeted Zaina with a kiss on the cheek. Seated on the couch was a tough-looking Asian girl with spangly ribbons in her hair and a bearded indie-rocker who I took to be her boyfriend who kept rubbing his face in his hands and moaning about how wasted he was. There was also a thick-armed girl with long black curly hair dancing alone to the music in the center of the floor.

7. The Australian guy was keeping everyone entertained - or trying to - by talking about the heavy-metal band he used to front back at home in Brisbane called 'Chaotic Neutral.' I made a joke about Dungeons and Dragons and he didn't seem to find it funny. He was sipping Red Bull and vodka and it was one of those parties where long pauses are appropriate, where the hour is so late that no one feels much motivated to fill the silence but no one wants to give up and go home.

8. Every so often Zaina would give me a look and we'd pretend like we were going to get a drink from the

fridge but instead we'd go to the bathroom and giggle and point out the expensive hair products and jars full of cotton balls and we'd do bumps and then try to hide what we'd done by swigging beer and running our fingers under the faucet then wiping at our nostrils. We were allies and so everything we did seemed to be hilarious.

9. It was the Australian who finally noticed what we were doing. He was pounding on the bathroom door because he had offered to trim the wasted boyfriend's raggedy beard into a goatee like his own. This all seemed incredibly homoerotic to us and perhaps to the guy's girlfriend too, but the Australian seemed very Iron John about it all. When he saw what we were doing his eyes got glazed and he licked his lips and he starting talking about how it had been ages since he'd done any and could he please etc. etc. etc. We offered him some and then soon the Asian girl wanted in and then everyone did except for the sleeping girlfriend upstairs who somehow stayed unconscious. It was the Australian guy who wanted to call for more. It was nearly 3 a.m. at this point but I was the hero and I was the go-to guy and I wasn't myself tonight, remember? So I called Pedro - who was safely home in bed - and got Screwie Louie's number.

10. Screwie Louie answered but he was back home too. He lived in Washington Heights at the very top of Manhattan. But yes he'd come but it would be a while. I hung up and told people the news and everyone pooled their money and there was energy and excitement and a renewed round of drinking.

11. But an hour passed. And then another. And he didn't show. And I kept calling and he kept promising soon, soon, soon. But something was wearing off and the party felt more and more like a hospital waiting room. The black-haired girl fell asleep on the floor and the Australian, in his boredom, had managed to shave all of the boyfriend's beard off and maybe tried to kiss him too. The music had stopped and no one had any inclination to start it up again. I was lying on the couch staring at the ceiling and Zaina was next to me sort of tickling my arm but the things she was saying just weren't funny anymore and there was a serrated edge to my thoughts, like a bread knife cleaving through my cerebellum. Back and forth. Back and forth. I didn't laugh at her and barely bothered to respond. This wasn't clever and it wasn't exciting. It was shallow and stupid. And I hated myself for believing otherwise.

12. So I gave up. I stood up, walked out, and ignored people's cries of "where are you going" and "for god's

sake leave us the number." I walked down the stairs and on the 2nd floor realized that I had left my iPod at the Madrox and on the 1st floor heard Zaina taking the steps behind me two at a time. She joined me on the sidewalk - I knew I had to find a taxi, that I couldn't still be out when the sun came up. But she pulled me close and I put my hand on her side and we awkwardly hugged good-bye, but she lingered and pushed her face close to mine and I realized I was supposed to kiss her. Her cheek was soft and my heart pounded as I sort of half-nuzzled it and she didn't seem to know what to do either so she rubbed her face against mine. And I almost did it, really I did. But instead I pulled away just as I saw a cab drive by. The driver didn't see me and I stepped in a puddle and slipped and I fell on my ass in front of a girl who I was too nervous to kiss good-bye. And I scrabbled to get to my feet and I slipped again and my face burned and she laughed and looked at me with something like pity.

13. And I got in another passing cab and I took it home. And there was nothing glamorous about any of it. Not at all. I was livid with regret before I even heard the messages blinking on my machine.

14. Oh, and: the only way I fell asleep that night was with some sleeping pills I found in the medicine

cabinet. Amy had bought them once for a flight back from Mexico. That's how I knew what brand to buy in the Salt Lake airport. Also, the phone number left by the concerned bank employee didn't really begin with KL5. That's a fancier way of saying "555," which is a fictional telephone exchange used only in movies and tv shows so people in the audience won't start calling the characters and bugging a real person, a la "Jenny" from that old Tommy Tutone song.

Which brings us all up to date, except for the biggest lie: Amy. She's been the ghost haunting this entire diary and I've never even paused to explain her or get a grip on my feelings. But sometimes what you leave out turns into the most important thing of all. There are so many details that I've never written down, just assumed could stay a part of me even after she left. How her intelligence and grace humbled me, how her jokes left me wiping away tears. And all the little, silly things that add up to something greater: like how she would snack on cereal while reading in bed and wake up with bran flakes stuck to her beautiful shoulders. How she pored over the *New York Review of Books* and *Melrose Place* reruns with equal gusto. How holding hands with her and sleeping next to her and just simply being with her filled me with a happiness so deep that I knew I'd never reach the bottom of it.

So let's say what I've never been able to say on here - or anywhere else - these past few weeks: that I love my girlfriend. That all the things I tried to do - and tried not to do - were about me and my failings, not hers. It wasn't that she closed me off, turned me into a prematurely old housebound bore. It's that I wasn't confident enough to share an entire half of myself with her. Instead, I locked it up, denied it, until it came - quite literally - crashing out of me.

I recognize it now. It's all me. All of it. I can be bad. I can fail.

And it's time for the person I love to know all of that. This is my diary, after all, and I'm back in control of it. And now I'm signing off. Enough writing - I've wasted far too much time sitting here as it is. It's time for doing.

Oh, and the punch I threw at the doppelgänger? I think I hurt myself more than I hurt him. The truth is, he barely flinched.

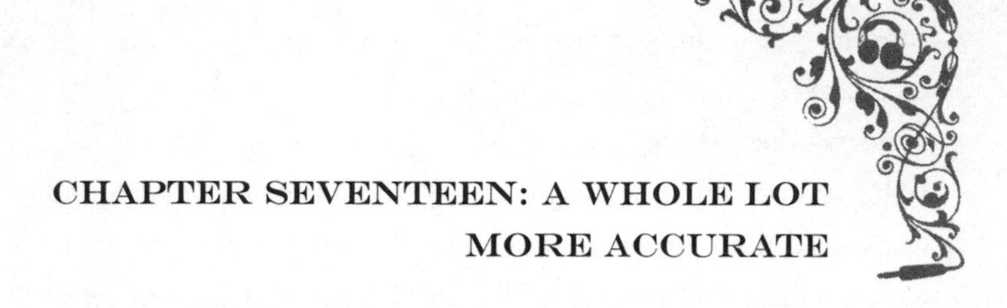

CHAPTER SEVENTEEN: A WHOLE LOT MORE ACCURATE

"I DON'T GET IT," she said. "So he's you now?"

"No, Cath," I said. "He's always been me. And I've always been him. That's the problem."

There were plenty of seats on the Manhattan-bound F train, but we were standing. I had too much anxious energy in me to sit: Tiny insects of nervousness were crawling up and down my legs, leaving an itching, tingling sensation that I desperately wanted to scratch. I needed to move, to sprint. But instead we were stuck between stations, held by the dispatcher. I clenched the overhead bar until my knuckles turned white. I had so little time. I had wasted so much.

"But he's *acting* like you now."

"Yeah."

Cath rubbed her forehead. "This metaphysical stuff is giving me a headache."

"Look," I said. "It's crazy, but it's not complicated. He showed up because I couldn't keep him down anymore. That's why he did all the things I wanted to do."

"Like me."

I nodded. "Not to be crude, but yeah. When you told him about us hooking up, though, he . . . well, he swapped roles with me."

"So he's the boring one now."

"Thanks."

"Sorry—keep going."

"If I wanted you, then he had to want what I had given up. He had to want Amy. It was all a matter of choice."

Cath still looked confused. "Doesn't he know what you really want?"

"Why should he? Until today I didn't know what I really wanted either."

Cath sighed. "So it's all some weird Freudian yin/yang thing."

"Yep." I smiled wanly. "Or Jekyll and Hyde."

"Laurel and Hardy?"

"Starsky and Hutch."

She smiled. "Mary-Kate and Ashley."

"Oh, God," I said. "That's enough of that."

Finally the train lurched back into service. I copped a piece of sugarless gum from Cath and chewed it ferociously, chewed until my jawbone ached. We were still five stops away.

"You know that stuff you wrote before we left?" Cath had read over my shoulder while I was typing but had kept quiet. When I had finished, I had hit POST and then we had sprinted out of there without even bothering to pick up the shards of broken glass on the floor or close any of the windows.

"Yeah. What about it?"

"That was pretty fucking emo. You know that, right?"

I closed my eyes and laughed. "Yeah, I know. That's the lingua franca of the Internet, right?"

"The what, now?"

"Never mind. I've just been hanging out with some very emo people lately and it must have rubbed off."

Cath looked thoughtful. She had one arm hanging on the bar above her and I could see white streaks of deodorant underneath her pale arms. "Nah. Anything honest on the Internet comes off as over-the-top. I learned that the hard way."

"I guess we all did."

"Yeah." Cath spit her gum out into its wrapper. "I can't stand it when the flavor wears off."

"You lack patience, my child."

"Hey, you're the one who's freaking out! I'm totally zen over here. Where are we going, anyway?"

"I thought we'd head to the Lower East Side. That's his stomping ground, right? If he's leaving town, I figured he might stop by the Madrox to pick up a paycheck or something." We had tried calling the doppelgänger before boarding the subway, but his phone had been disconnected. Not a good sign.

Cath tried her best to be encouraging. "That's a good plan. Plus, there's that bartender there he was sleeping with. Don't look so surprised!"

"What, the one with the Farrah Fawcett hairdo and the bad heavy-metal T-shirts? Miss Ironic Hipster of the year?"

"Jodie. Yeah. Her."

"God. I certainly got around, didn't I?"

"You can be surprisingly charming when you feel like it."

"Thanks, kid. You're not so bad yourself."

Cath shot me a wink, then linked her arm through mine. The train passed under the East River.

Manhattan was vibrant and glowing in the afternoon summer sun. We stepped out of the train on the south side of Houston Street and immediately had to dodge a gang of cheerful Rollerbladers and a swooping battalion of furious pigeons. On the corner of Orchard Street a gangly dreadlocked man had set up a rickety boom box and was popping and locking on a piece of flattened cardboard that had once held bottles of Clorox bleach. It took every ounce of resolve I had to keep pushing forward and not just grab Cath's hand, steer her to a park bench, and proceed to waste away the day. But I thought of Amy and all that I had done, and I kept walking.

The outside of the Madrox looked filthy and silly in the daytime, its all-black paint job standing out like a winter coat at the beach. The door was closed and locked—it wouldn't open for another four hours at least—but inside the lights were on. I knocked on the door and peered through the submarinelike peephole in the middle of it. When no one answered, I pounded harder and reopened the scabs on my knuckles in the process. I was licking a trickle of blood from the back of my hand when the door opened and the bartender I had seen the other night was on the other side of it. Jodie.

"You again! I thought you left." She had her hand cocked suggestively on her hip and was wearing a STRYPER '88 tour T-shirt that barely made it to the top of her pierced belly button.

I smiled. "I came back."

Cath, who had been kicking her heels on the sidewalk, rushed over and took her place by my side, causing the bartender's face to darken. "What's *she* doing here?"

"Hadn't you heard? We're together." Cath smiled sweetly and batted her eyes.

The bartender snarled, "That's not what he said ten minutes ago."

I wanted to say, "Girls, girls you're both pretty!" But instead I pulled my arm back from Cath and said, "Can we come in for a second?"

Jodie sighed. "Fine. But make it fast." She held the door open wider and we slipped in.

Empty and air-conditioned, with its bright work lights on, the Madrox seemed oddly tiny and hollow. I could hear the sound of a vacuum cleaner in the next room, and behind the bar a serious-looking older man was busily removing plastic wrap from the mouths of liquor bottles. "Look, Jodie," I said, leaning slightly against the banquette nearest to the door, "this is going to sound weird, but just go with me on it, OK?"

"Sure," she said, lighting a cigarette with a bright pink Bic. "Lay it on me."

"By the way, I *looove* your T-shirt," said Cath. "It's like, *so* ironic, right?"

Jodie shot Cath a withering look. "Fuck off, bitch. Shouldn't you be in, like, nursery school right now?"

"Hey!" I shouted. "Quit it. I just have one question and we'll be out of here."

Cath muttered, "I'll school *you.*"

I turned to her. "You. Wait outside. Now."

She stuck her tongue out at me and left.

Jodie blew smoke rings. "Way to ditch the pip-squeak."

I ignored her. "Jodie, was I here earlier today?"

She crinkled up her nose. "Did you get hit by a truck? Of course you were here."

"OK." I took a deep breath. "Look, you probably won't believe me, but that wasn't me. It was . . . someone else who is trying to take over my life. I need to find him."

"Mmm-hm." Jodie took a long pull on her cigarette. "Drug abuse can make you paranoid, you know."

My frustration was quickly morphing into exasperation. "OK, fine—I honestly don't care if you believe me. Just tell me what happened when I was here."

"You are a fucking fruitcake, Gould. Marcos warned me about getting involved with the entertainment."

The guy behind the bar nodded his head. "What I tell you, Jodie?"

She didn't turn around. "Shut up, Marcos."

He nodded again. "OK! I shut up now!"

"Jodie," I said. "Please."

She exhaled loudly and dropped her cigarette to the floor, stubbing out the ashes with the heel of her boot. "Yes, you were here. Yes, I gave you the money that we owed you for DJing. Yes, I tried to get you to fuck me in the bathroom, and yes, you rejected me like the fucking asshole crazy person you apparently are!"

I took a step back. She continued. "Does this get you off? Hearing me tell you about things that just happened? Jesus."

"Jodie, where was I going?"

"To hell for all I care."

"Jodie. Tell me and I'll leave."

She clicked her tongue against her teeth noisily and glared. "You said you were going to that lame speakeasy bar the Satellite Heart. And that you'd be leaving town for a while and would miss your next gig." She took another step toward me. "And *I* said that if that was the case, you could feel free to miss all your gigs, as I had had just enough of skinny, self-obsessed rock-critic lameos to last a lifetime!"

Her face was inches from mine, and I could see the wrinkles at the corners of her eyes; she was clearly much older than I had first thought. Her breath smelled like Marlboros and Jim Beam and I inched my way back to the door. "OK," I said, grasping for the knob, "that's all I needed. I'm sorry for what he—" She took a menacing step toward me. "For what I did to you." I had the door open now. "You've been very, ah . . . helpful." Sunlight streamed into the bar and I stepped lightly across the doorway.

"Get. Out." She growled.

"Right," I said. "Good-bye, Jodie." She slammed the door in my face and I heard her lock it in triplicate.

I turned to Cath, who was leaning against a parking meter. "Nice girl," I said.

She raised an eyebrow. "You sure know how to pick 'em."

"Give me a break, will you? Come on. He's at the Satellite Heart."

"Oh, good," said Cath. "All of this excitement has made me awfully thirsty."

"Let's go," I said, pushing Cath lightly on the back. "Let your liver lead the way."

• • •

Walking into the Satellite Heart was like a surprise party in reverse: Everyone in the bar looked shocked to see *me*. The couches in the back were full of early happy-hour types finishing their first pints of whatever and talking too loudly about their plans for the evening. Ryan, the red-haired DJ who had fallen through the floor, was again behind the turntables, manfully trying to mix a Jadakiss song with one arm in a heavy plaster cast. Debra Silverstein and Ben There were huddled around the bar and I knew from their confused faces that we had caught up with the doppelgänger.

Debra spoke first. "Is there, like, a back door?"

"Hey," I said. "What?"

Ben There fought to regain his trademark disinterest. "There must be, Debra. He also must keep a change of clothes in the alley."

Cath came up behind me. "What are you talking about?"

Ben There arched his eyebrows. "Your boyfriend here just went into the bathroom."

"I did?"

"But how could he be here *and* there?" Debra looked as if her head was going to explode.

"We found him," I said, feeling a flutter of anticipation in my chest.

"Uh-oh," said Cath. "I guess I'm not going to get that drink."

"What's going on here?" Ben There smiled slyly. "Is this another one of your little games?"

"It's no game, dorkface." Cath crossed her arms. "There's two of him."

Ben There looked delighted. "Really! How kinky."

"Like, a good one and a bad one?" Debra seemed thrilled. "Like that cartoon in *Mad* magazine? With the birds in hats that always try and kill each other?"

I peered around the bar toward the bathroom to see if he was listening. "You mean 'Spy versus Spy'?"

Debra clapped her hands. "Yes! Wait. Which one is the good one and which is the bad one?"

Cath smirked. "Depends on the day."

Ben There sipped his drink and turned to face me. "Are you going to try and kill each other? Should we get some plastic wrap to protect ourselves from blood stains?"

"What? No."

Cath put her hand on my shoulder. "You're not going to get in a fistfight again, are you? That didn't work out so well last time."

I shook off her hand. "Will you all please be quiet? How long ago did he go in there?"

Ben There chuckled. "Relax, Rambo. He just went in there a minute ago. He did say he was in a hurry, though."

I walked away from the group and headed toward the back bathroom. He had walked in on me once. Time for me to return the favor. But before I made it to the door, Franta stepped in front of me, his bald, imposing bulk blocking both my path and my vision.

"David," he said. "Where you going?"

"Franta," I said. "I have to go to the bathroom."

"Ah-ah." He shook his stubby index finger in front of me. "There is somebody already in there."

"Is there?" I tried to sound casual. "Let me check."

I reached for the doorknob, but Franta gently pushed my hand away and whispered, "Doppelgänger, eh? He give you trouble?"

I was too stunned to speak.

"Oh, don't look so surprised. Franta been around for a long time. I seen some crazy things like you wouldn't believe."

"You know what's going on?"

"Sure."

"You've seen something like this . . . before?"

"Ho boy, yes."

I felt weak and woozy and steadied myself on the edge of the bar. "Well, then . . . what should I . . . what do I do?"

Franta chuckled and rested his meaty paw on my shoulder. "I watch you, I watch him run in and out of this place all week. I look you in the eye right now and I think—this boy figure it out on his own. He get it now. He knows what he has to be doing."

"I do?"

Franta grinned. "David, you know what you want?"

I nodded.

"Then you go get it. You don't look back. You don't let anybody stand in your way. Not Franta. Not these kids. And not your own self."

"OK."

"And if you come back around, I still need a new kid to play records. This one with the rappers and the broken bones can't even move! I need one with softer music and two arms that work."

I smiled. "Thanks, Franta. Really."

"Is no problem. Now, like I promise, I get out of your way."

Franta turned and walked back around the bar. Behind where he had been standing was the doppelgänger, drying his hands on a paper towel and staring straight at me. He was wearing the same ironic softball T-shirt I had worn to meet Cath and an old, loose-fitting pair of my jeans. Also, he was clean-shaven, which made him look younger than me and downright innocent. "Well, hello," he said, throwing the towel away. "Fancy meeting you here."

"Give me my passport. It's over."

The doppelgänger looked shocked. "What are you talking about? You made your choice—now get out of my way and let me make mine." He pushed past me into the bar, and I grabbed his arm as he passed.

"You've done enough. Give me my passport. And my wallet. And everything else you've taken from me."

"Why would I do a thing like that?" He yanked his arm away and stood still in the middle of the bar. As I turned to face him, I felt all of the eyes in the Satellite Heart trained on me and my double.

"Holy shit!" Debra squeaked.

"This is awfully freaky," purred Ben There, his head swiveling from one version of me to the other. "Cath, you've outdone yourself this time. An honest-to-goodness identity crisis!"

Only then did the doppelgänger seem to notice Cath. "Well, I certainly hope *you're* happy." He sneered.

She took a step forward. "Just give him back what's his."

"He doesn't even know what's his anymore!"

I also took a step forward. "This ends now," I said. "I'm taking it back—all of it. Just give me what belongs to me."

The doppelgänger swung his head frantically from me to Cath

and back again. "This is ridiculous," he said. "What are you going to do, hit me again? Call the cops? Like they'd believe you." He took a step toward the door. "I don't have any of your stuff on me. Why can't you just make up your mind like normal people? Jesus!"

"I'm telling you that I *have* made up my mind."

The doppelgänger looked panicked. "Well, so have I! I have a wonderful girlfriend! And a quiet, happy life!" He seemed shaky, unsure, weak. "And I wish you'd stop trying to foul it all up!"

"Look," I said, taking another step toward him, showing him my open palms. "I'm not going to—"

A loud police siren ripped through the bar. The doppelgänger almost jumped out of his skin. "Holy shit! You did call the cops. You're crazy. I'm gone!" And with that, he pulled open the door and sprinted up the stairs and down the street.

I turned back to the bar. "Jesus Christ, Debra, why can't you just choose a *normal* ring tone?"

Debra meekly punched a key on her Sidekick and quieted the siren. "Sorry!"

"What do we do now?" Cath grabbed my arm.

"We follow him," I said. And together we raced out of the Satellite Heart.

A crowd was forming at the corner of Rivington, where the other me had pushed past an old lady, knocking her basket of groceries into the street. A bunch of chivalrous local toughs, revenge on their minds, shouted "Hey!" as I passed, but we ignored them and kept running. The trail ran cold back at Houston—there were too many people pouring out of the subway, running to catch the uptown bus, and mingling in front of bars for us to be able to make out one fleeing doppelgänger in the midst of them. Cath stepped off the curb and peered in all directions. I doubled over to catch my breath. It had been a long time since I had run that fast, and I felt a nasty cramp forming in the pit of my stomach. "Do you see anything?" I panted.

"No." Cath walked up to me and rubbed my back. "God, old man, don't die on me now."

I stood up and wheezed. "You should be so lucky. Where do you think he went?"

"Well, he said he didn't have your passport. So he must have stashed it somewhere. Someplace nearby."

"He's a homeless extension of my troubled psyche," I said. "Where could he have possibly felt safe? Bellevue?" I looked at my watch. It was three o'clock. I felt everything slipping through my fingers.

But then we figured it out at the same time.

"Your apartment," I said.

"My apartment," said Cath, and she sprinted across the street just as the light turned yellow.

"Wait up!" I took off after her and nearly died under the bicycle of a Chinese delivery guy before making it across the street. As I jogged up Avenue A, I made a quiet resolution that if this craziness ever ended, I would really definitely consider joining a gym.

We knew we had guessed right when the fortune-teller seated in front of Cath's building took one look at my red-faced, gasping form and burst out laughing.

Cath stopped short of the door with her keys in her hand. "What is it, Stacey?"

The fortune-teller wiped at her eyes. "Oh boy," she said. "I'll tell this friend of yours the same thing I told his twin—today just isn't your day."

Cath grabbed the fortune-teller by the shoulders. "Is he here? Is he still here?"

Meanwhile, I finally caught the ragged edge of my breath. "Stacey?" I wheezed. "Stacey the fortune-teller?"

Stacey gave me the finger. "It pays the bills, jackass. Yeah, he just went up. I think he works out more than you do; he was running pretty fast."

"Thanks for the observation."

"Hey, no problem. By the way, I predict a heart attack in your future unless you get your white ass to a gym!"

But we were already up the first flight of stairs. As we climbed, we planned.

"I'll go in first and try to reason with him," Cath said, her thick heels making a racket on the cheap linoleum. "You wait in the hall in case he tries to make a break for it."

"That's a good plan," I said. "Where'd you pick that one up?"

"*Law and Order.* They give away all the best tricks."

"Huh," I said. "You ever notice on that show how the people the cops interview never stop moving or doing their jobs? There's always all this *business.* If I was ever being questioned by cops, I would definitely take a break from waiting tables or fixing a tailpipe."

We reached Cath's floor and trod lightly down the hall. "A keen observation," Cath whispered. "Good to know your pop-culture radar is still functioning."

I chuckled under my breath. "When I lose that, I've lost the will to live."

We reached her apartment, and I leaned my back against the wall just to the right of the door in order to remain out of sight. Before turning the lock, Cath made a series of elaborate gestures with her fingers that seemed half SWAT team and half third-base coach. "What are you doing?" I mouthed.

"Making sure you stay sharp!" she mouthed back. I gave her a look, and she took one long index finger and laid it across my lips with a grin. "Shhhhh," she said. Then she opened the door and went inside.

The door swung shut behind her with a smooth *click*, and I strained my ears to hear inside the apartment to no avail. The wall I was leaning against was plaster, two-toned, and filthy. From behind the door of another apartment I could hear the sounds of Spanish-language TV blasting at full volume. I closed my eyes and let my head fall back against the wall, which was surprisingly cool for such a hot day. My breath was slowly returning to normal. And I felt that my life would soon do the same—if only I could catch up to myself. I tried to picture daily life in the Netherlands—all pot-smoking, justice, and socialized medicine—but a loud crash from Cath's apartment shook me from my reverie.

"Cath?" I yelled. "Cath? I'm coming in!"

I pushed the door open as hard as I could, figuring that if the doppelgänger was going to make a move in my direction, I might as well smack him back into the apartment. But the only person I saw was

Andre, standing with one foot still in the bathroom, wearing nothing but a bright red towel wrapped around his waist.

"What the hell is going on?" he murmured in his sonorous voice.

I took two steps past him into the apartment. "Cath?" I shouted. "What the hell *is* going on?"

When she answered, she sounded desperate. "Hurry! Help me!"

I took the rest of the hallway in three long strides, expecting to see the doppelgänger holding Cath at gunpoint—or worse—but when I reached the living room, he was nowhere to be found. There was movement in the far bedroom, and I caught a glimpse of a naked Stevie Lau diving under the covers to hide himself, thick plumes of sweet marijuana smoke billowing through his door. Cath, however, was halfway out the living-room window, one leg splayed comically in the air, wrestling with something—or someone—out on the fire escape.

"Hurry up!" she squeaked. "Help!"

"Is it him?" I scurried to her side. "Did you catch him?" But as I peered out the window, I saw that what was scurrying and straining in Cath's desperate grasp wasn't my double. It was Sinky, the water-loving cat.

I reached my hands out the window and wrapped them around the cat's furry chest. I could feel its tiny feline heart hammering away either in terror or the thrill of escape. "I've got him," I said. "Bring him in slowly." In response, Sinky yowled theatrically, but he didn't put up much more of a fight.

When we had him safely back on the sill, Andre came up behind us and nimbly slid the window closed. "You never should have given *him* a key," he muttered before spinning on his heel and flouncing back into Stevie's room. The door slammed shut behind him.

Cath sat down on the floor with her legs spread out in front of her, holding the wild-eyed Sinky to her face. "Poor baby," she breathed. "Poor, poor baby. Shhhh." Her face was flushed crimson.

I joined her on the floor. "I guess he never figured out that he was four stories up." Cath let the cat go, and he slinked off toward the bathroom, presumably for a post-traumatic dip under the faucet. I touched her shoulder. "What happened?"

"He was here."

I stood. "What? He was? Where did he go?"

Cath sighed. "I tried to get him to stop; he had your passport in his hand. But when he saw me, all he said was, 'You missed out.' And then he opened the window and started climbing down the fire escape. I tried to follow him, but so did Sinky."

I rushed back to the window and peered out of it. "He did what?"

"He took the fire escape down!"

I opened the window again—checking behind me for the cat—and crawled out onto the ledge. The summer city air wobbled around me and so did the metal railing. My heart lurched—I've never been good with heights. With one hand on the brick wall of the building I craned my neck straight down and caught sight of the doppelgänger leaping off the final ladder down onto the sidewalk. He brushed himself off, looked back up at me, and saluted grandly. Then he sprinted off toward Avenue C.

I eased myself back into the apartment. "Come on," I said. "We've got to follow him."

Cath exhaled loudly. "I was afraid you were going to say that."

"Don't worry," I said, closing the window and heading toward the door. "We'll take the stairs."

"My hero."

Stacey the fortune-teller was still cackling with laughter when we burst out of the front door a few moments later. We dodged an overworked dog-walker and his dozen yelping charges and headed for the corner of Avenue C, where I could see the doppelgänger standing just off the curb, raising his hand at passing cabs.

"The airport," I said. "He's going to the airport."

He was still waiting as we neared, aware of our presence and checking frantically over his shoulder, but then I heard Cath cry out behind me and I tore my eyes off him and turned toward her.

She had tripped over some uneven pavement and was clutching at her knee in pain. "Go on!" she yelled when she saw me pause. "I'll be fine."

I hesitated, looked to see the doppelgänger flag down a taxi and leap into the backseat, and then looked back at Cath. *Damn.*

"What are you doing?" she said when I knelt down beside her. "He's getting away."

"We'll catch him," I said, moving her hands from her knee. "Let's see the damage."

It wasn't bad—just a ferocious scrape rimmed with red, familiar to anyone who ever had a BMX bike and no appreciable balance. "Damn it." Cath bit her lip and one tear spilled out of her left eye. "That is going to leave a hellacious bruise."

I stood and helped her up. "You're going to survive, tiger. Now do you want to go home or do you want to continue the chase?"

"Did Samwise Gamgee abandon Frodo when the going got tough?" Cath scoffed.

I threw her arm around my neck, and we three-legged-raced our way to the corner and raised our hands to flag down a cab of our own. "Cath," I said, "we're not gay hobbits."

She elbowed me in the side. "Speak for yourself, creepo."

I looked up the street and saw the doppelgänger's cab stopped at a red light, just one block away. We were lucky—luckier still when a taxi screeched to a halt in front of us. I helped Cath in, then raced around to the other side and took a seat behind the driver, a young African guy with chipmunk cheeks and a shaved head. "Where to?" he said in a thickly accented voice.

I leaned forward and pointed through the safety screen that separated the front and back seats. "Do you see that cab up there? The one stopped at the light?"

"Yes, sir."

"I need you to follow it."

We stayed parked.

"Sir?" The cab driver seemed puzzled.

"That cab," I said urgently. "Please—I need you to follow it. Now."

He turned to face me. "Seriously?"

Through the grimy windshield I saw the traffic light change to green. I felt wildly impotent. "Yes!" I yelped, my voice cracking. "Please! Follow that cab!"

The driver flexed his fingers around the wheel. "Like in the movies?"

I was near tears. "Yes! Just like in the movies! Please!" But we didn't move, and I slumped back against the seat.

The driver, whose ID said his name was Demba Diop, turned back to face us gravely. "Sir," he said, "I have been driving this taxi for sixteen years. *Sixteen years.* And I have been waiting every single one of them for just this occasion." He flooded the engine with gas. "I will not let you down!"

And with a violent screech we tore away from the curb, leaving a symphony of honking horns in our wake.

Cath and I fought the g-forces that were pinning us to the seat and reached wildly for our safety belts. When they were properly fastened, she let out a low whistle. "Man," she said, "so this is how it all ends? With a wild chase scene? Talk about your clichés."

"Hey," I said, "don't knock it. Clichés get overused for a reason." I grimaced as we caught air going over a manhole at Thirteenth Street. "Besides"—I turned toward her, but her eyes were shut tight and she was yanking on the handle above the window like it was a parachute rip cord—"you have to admit this is kind of exciting."

The cab's tires squealed on the asphalt as we hung a violent right on Fourteenth Street. Cath didn't open her eyes. "Wake me when we're not dead, OK, hotshot?"

The driver was hooting with laughter. "I think he is going for the FDR Drive, sir!"

I swallowed my stomach back down as we shot a yellow light, and leaned forward. "He's probably heading to the airport!" I shouted. "JFK."

"No problem, sir. I know all the shortcuts!"

"That's what I was afraid of!" I said, and sunk back into the seat. The doppelgänger's cab was still in sight when we zoomed up the on-ramp to the FDR, but by the time we had merged into the ocean of northbound cars it was gone. As if he could sense my tension, the driver hammered down on the wheel and the taxi shimmied across two lanes of speeding traffic before easing balletically and near-suicidally into the left lane, neatly cutting off an eighteen-wheeler. The doppelgänger was two cars in front. Our driver would be lethal at Tetris, I thought. The insulted truck let out a furious honk, and Cath's hand skittered across the seat, found my hand, and squeezed it. I squeezed back.

We took the Queens Midtown Tunnel to the LIE, but traffic backed up again as we approached the Van Wyck. Our driver noticed the doppelgänger's cab slowly cutting across lanes, heading to the right side of the highway. We followed and at one point got nearly close enough to make eye contact, but unlike us, he seemed unconcerned about the chase. He was sitting calmly, eyes forward. Cath rolled down her window and shouted out to him, but he didn't react at all.

She said, "For someone who just crawled out of a window, he seems awfully chill."

"That's because he thinks he's got it all figured out. What does he have to worry about?"

Cath turned to me. "Does he?"

I shook my head. "Nope. He's got nothing at all."

But then his cab took a random eastbound exit and was gone. "Damn!" I shouted. "We lost him!"

Our driver seemed unperturbed. "Sir, please sit back and enjoy the ride. I promised you I would not fail, and I do not make promises lightly."

We lurched off the road onto the shoulder and sped down the next exit ramp. I watched through the safety glass as the speedometer flirted with seventy-five. The driver steered us onto some awfully suburban-looking streets, and for the first time since we had left my apartment I felt a twinge of fear. What if we didn't catch him? What if it didn't end tonight? He was heading to The Hague. He had called Amy and said God knows what. This was a deeper violation than anything he had done before. The leather-clad life he had been swimming in—with its drugs, DJing, and divas—had merely been a distraction. It was an unreal part of myself that he had made painfully real. But now he was headed straight for the realest thing I'd ever had—rocketing toward it like some sort of vindictive missile. If he were to get on that plane, all I'd be left with was the mess he'd made. Something shallow. Something tawdry and unkempt. A daze of nights. Half a life.

I leaned forward. "We have to catch that cab."

The driver shook his head and sped up a side street, then skidded through a ferocious turn. "You, my young friend, worry too much." The brakes squealed as we stopped at a light adjacent to the expressway. "Here is your prey." He gestured to the taxi that was idling just in front of us. Through the windshield I saw the back of my own head. It was him. "We have caught him," said the driver. "Now: What would you like to do? In one film I saw—a very good film!—the one taxi drove the other one into a ditch by ramming it in the side like this!" He clapped his palms together loudly.

"No! I mean—no. That won't be necessary. Let's just get to the airport at the same time."

"You're sure, sir? We could easily ram them—"

I LOVE THIS CAB DRIVER!

"Yes," I said firmly. "Very sure."

The driver shrugged. "Whatever you say, sir." The light changed and we drove on at a more humane speed.

Cath tugged at my arm. "It doesn't seem like he's noticed us."

We could still make out the doppelgänger's form staring blankly at the road ahead. "No, you're right."

"Why do you think that is?"

"Maybe he doesn't care. Maybe he just doesn't believe that we can stop him. Or that we'd want to."

"Are you going to fight him again? Is it going to be like that weird movie with Sean Connery in the skirt and the French guy who has that giant sword and . . ."

"*Highlander.* And no—I already tried that line of thinking. No violence."

"But then how are you going to stop him?"

"I've already stopped him," I said calmly. "He just doesn't know it yet."

When we reached the outskirts of JFK, I had the strangest feeling of déjà vu. And then I realized that I was actually the *third* version of me to be at the airport that day. I wondered if there was a separate French phrase for just such a scenario.

Our driver had dutifully avoided ramming the doppelgänger's cab during the rest of the ride, and now he kept a respectful distance as we took the exit for the international terminal.

"You are leaving the country, sir?" asked the driver.

"One of us is," I said. Cath gave me a surprised look but kept quiet. The doppelgänger directed his taxi to pull over in front of the same airline I had flown to Utah—I guess great minds think alike—and I directed our driver to do the same. I handed two twenties—the last cash I had on me—through the partition and told him to keep the change.

"Thank you, sir. And thank you both for allowing me to realize my most longed-for American dream."

"The pleasure was all ours," I said as we slid out of the backseat. "And if I ever need to ram someone, I will be sure to flag you down."

We could still hear the driver's laughter after we shut the door. All around us, skycaps buzzed like wasps, checking baggage, opening limo doors, and pushing trolleys piled high with suitcases. The doppelgänger took his time counting his change before opening the door and stepping out onto the sidewalk. He slammed the door behind him and then stretched grandly as if he were only now greeting the dawn. He didn't even turn around.

"Hey!" I shouted out to him.

Slowly he turned with a look of total confusion on his face. It wasn't just that he was surprised, it was as if he were seeing us in a different language. Cath, getting into the swing of things, put her hands on her hips like an Old West sheriff and yelled, "End of the line, asshole!"

The doppelgänger's shoulders slumped. He seemed more disappointed than scared. He said one word—"Why?"—and then sprinted across the street, dodging taxis, heading away from the terminal and toward the parking garage.

"Oh, Christ," said Cath. "Here we go again!"

"No." I put a steadying hand on her arm. "You wait here. I don't want you running on that knee."

"Thanks, Rex Gordon, but I'm fine."

I looked in her blue eyes. "Wait for me here. I have to do this alone."

She started to protest, but then her eyes softened and she nodded. I took off toward the garage.

The first level of parking was lousy with SUVs, white Lexus whales, and Fords better suited to paramilitary operations than escorting plastic surgeons and their families back to Long Island. I cut up row A, then ducked down behind a gaudy yellow Hummer and followed the steady *clip-clop* of the doppelgänger's footsteps over to row G. I thought I had him then, and I leapt out from behind a space-age Suburu only to scare about five years off the life of a hobbled and bearded Hasidic Jew. "Sorry," I said, patting him on his frail shoulders as I caught a glimpse of the doppelgänger cutting up a set of cement stairs to the second floor.

I took the stairs three at a time, my heart in a brutal race with my lungs. The second floor was full near the stairs and then thinned out toward the ramp up to the roof. I saw the doppelgänger almost get mowed down by a Jeep that was backing out in a hurry and then watched him take off toward the ramp. He was running the way I was taught in gym class: knees high, arms steadily swinging at the sides. I shouted out to him to stop, but my voice echoed off the low ceiling, and what ricocheted back into my ears sounded tinny and hollow. I saw him break into the sunlight of the ramp and ran after him, knowing that this time *for sure* I would join that gym.

I caught up to him on the roof, which was empty save for an unoccupied police van and a gang of pigeons snacking on a smashed bag of Herr's potato chips in the shade of the far wall. The sounds of jet planes were everywhere, and the sun beat down bluntly on the exposed asphalt, making the air shiny and sticky with reflected light and heat. He stood in the middle of the roof, hands on knees, catching his breath. I felt for him—I wanted to do the exact same thing. There was a burn in my throat from breathing so hard, and my feet ached.

He watched me approach but didn't make any effort to escape; he just slowly regained his breath and uncurled his back to stand straight and face me. We stared at each other for a time, through the looking glass that wasn't there, until he spoke first. "You look different," he said.

"Yeah," I said. "I know."

"So you made up your mind after all."

"That's right."

"What was it? The party? The plane ticket?"

"The phone call," I said.

The doppelgänger snapped his fingers. "Right! Right. The phone call. She was very sweet, you know. She was very excited to see . . . well, one of us. She said we were finally making an effort. Finally ready to move on to the next stage."

I nodded. "She's right. I am."

He looked forlorn. "Yeah. She's always right, isn't she?"

"That she is."

"Oh, well." He reached into his pocket and handed me my passport. "You'd better hurry," he said. "You've got about ten minutes left to check in."

"Thanks. The rest of it?"

The doppelgänger chuckled. "Can't blame me for trying." He dug around in his back pocket and produced the extra keys, my wallet, and finally the folded-over photo of Amy. "I wouldn't use the Visa for a while if I were you. I think it's, ah . . . overdrawn."

"I'll keep it in mind."

The doppelgänger flickered a little, like a television during a thunderstorm. "You know, I really thought there was a chance for both of us."

I shook my head. "Come on, now. 'A house divided against itself' and all that."

He nodded, blinking on and off like a light switch. "You're right, you're right. Can't be all one thing all the time, I guess. Oh, well." He turned and started to walk toward the far part of the wall where the pigeons were feasting, the only part darkened by shadows. Then he stopped and turned back to me, a wistful look on his face. "Don't forget about me, now."

I laughed. "How could I?"

He flashed me the shit-eating grin of old. "There's no way in hell you could." Then he walked, diminishing with every step, into the shadows.

When I got back to where I'd left her, Cath was smoking a cigarette and flirting with a meaty skycap who looked like an extra from the Gotti crime-family picnic. She was wearing his hat, and her face was twisted up and her hands dancing, the way she always was when she was telling a particularly juicy story. I smiled at the sight of it.

"Hey!" she shouted when she saw me walking across the street. She snapped the cap back on her new friend's prodigious head, crushed the cigarette under her foot, and ran over to me, grabbing at my arms the way one would a long-lost relative. "Are you OK? What happened?"

"I'm great," I said, throwing my arm around her shoulders and walking her back up onto the curb. "I'm better than I've been in a long, long time."

"Yeah?" She squinted up at my face. "Yeah. You look it. But what happened to *him*?"

"We don't need to worry about him anymore."

"Jesus, that sounds ominous! What, did you kill him? Has he been officially 'disappeared'?"

I smiled. "He can't disappear. He's right here. I just . . . what's the phrase? Pulled myself together."

Cath smiled back. "Wild. That was like a *kumate.*"

"A what, now?"

She gave me a playful shove. "You know—a *kumate.* Like in those Asian kickboxing movies? 'Two men enter . . . one man leave!'"

I laughed. "I think that actually does pretty much sum it up."

"So now what? You sweep me off my feet? Now that you've vanquished your ne'er-do-well rival, we ride off together into the sunset?"

I looked at the ground. "Actually," I said, "what happens now is I get on a plane."

The words hung in the air between us for an extra moment, and then Cath simply shrugged. "Yeah, I figured as much. What was it my mom told me when I was a little girl? 'Never fall for the nerdy sweet guys with girlfriends and raging, externalized ids'?"

I looked up at her. "She was a wise lady."

"Yup. She was." Cath tweaked my nose with her thumb and forefinger. "So you're just going to fly off to Europe now with no baggage?"

"That's the idea."

She nodded. "I hope you fix things up with Annie."

"Amy."

"Riiiiiight. Her. I bet you will."

"Thanks. I hope so. You know what? I bet she'd like you."

Cath's eyebrows shot up. "Really?"

"Well, maybe. Eventually. Once she got to know you. After a few drinks, perhaps."

Cath gave my chest a last hearty smack. "One to grow on, creepo. So you're really going to tell her all about this? All about me?"

"You know it," I said. "I'm not making the same mistake again. From now on, I'm an open book." I spread my arms out wide.

"It's funny," said Cath, turning thoughtful. "If you were ever to write this all down, I bet it'd be just as crazy and exciting and wild as all the diaries you used to spend all your time reading."

I nodded. "Probably more so."

"Well, then, you finally get it. What's been a total clusterfuck of an emotional nightmare for you can always be exciting and, like, *other*ing for somebody else. These things that people write, the stories they tell . . . they're never just entertainment."

"Oh, no? Then why are you smiling like that?"

"Well, *I've* been pretty fucking entertained." She raised her arms to my shoulders, like we were slow-dancing in middle school. "I'm going to miss you, creepo. You're something else."

I kissed her cheek and held her close. "*You're* something else, Cath Kennedy." When she pulled away, my arms lingered around her waist. "I spent all that time being obsessed with Miss Misery, but she's got nothing on you."

Cath blushed. "Thanks. Don't you dare be a stranger."

"Never again." I held her stare for a moment longer, then smiled and started to walk away. "Oh," I said, turning back. "One last thing." I handed her the extra set of keys. "Would you hold on to these and maybe check in on the place for me? I might have left some lights on, and I don't know how long I'll be gone."

She looked unsure. "You trust me that much?"

"Yeah," I said. "I really do."

As I walked through the air-conditioned airport, I held my head high, my shoulders straight. I felt strong. I felt sure. And I liked it. Once again I got some funny looks from the security staff when they noticed I had no luggage, and I laughed to myself about how unlike me all this spontaneity was.

But when it was time to board, I thought of all that had happened and all that had ended on that roof, and I came to the realization that it *was* like me after all.

I had been wrong, you see. My life hadn't been lived as an exercise in responsibility. What it had been was an exercise in convenience: Everything worked perfectly, so being responsible wasn't a test; it was a given. Until the day that Amy left, shattering my plans, upsetting my routine. Then, faced with a deviation from whatever path my subconscious had set out for me, I resisted. All of the demons I had sat on for years came bubbling to the surface, and I backslid into immaturity. Into peevish selfishness. Into no one but myself.

But no longer. Flying to Europe on a moment's notice wasn't to right some wrong or aid some damsel in distress. It had nothing to do with lives outside my own. It was about me and it was about my life. It was about living it instead of fearing it for a change. It was about going out instead of staying in. It wasn't about dealing or fighting or any of the convenient buzzwords I had placated my subconscious with over the past few hectic days—it was about accepting.

I had just made it to the start of the jetway, and the smiling stewardess held out her hand to take my ticket and send me on my way. But instead I hesitated and took myself out of the line. There was one last thing to do before I boarded.

I pulled my cell phone from my pocket and dialed a number I hadn't dialed in a very long time. It rang once. Then twice. Three times.

"Hello, you've reached the office of Thom Watkins at Pendant Publishing. Please leave a message after the tone."

Voice mail. How appropriate.

"Hi, Thom," I said as I reentered the line and handed my ticket to the attendant. "It's your long-lost writer, David Gould. Just wanted to check in with you now that I've been found. Listen, Thom, the book is going to be a little bit different than I imagined. Hope that's OK. It turns out it's going to be a novel."

I had reached the end of the jetway, and I ran my fingers along the cold hull of the airplane for luck. Then I stepped aboard, ready for whatever would come next.

"You see, Thom, I've realized something about these diaries. They may be true, but they don't always tell the truth. Because reality can be much crazier than fiction. And fiction, well . . . sometimes it can just end up being a whole lot more accurate than the truth."

The day I left was perfect—at least in terms of weather. When night fell, all of the windows in my apartment were still open. And I was gone.

ACKNOWLEDGMENTS

This book, like everything I endeavor to do, would have been impossible without the constant support, love, wit, and inspiration of my friends and family. There are a select few, though, to whom I am especially indebted.

First and foremost, thanks are due to my steadfast agent, Jim Fitzgerald, and to my new editor and friend, Ryan Fischer-Harbage, for believing in this far-fetched project from the beginning and for nurturing it (and me) every step along the way. Thanks also to everyone at Simon Spotlight Entertainment for taking a chance on a first novel and for making me feel so welcome within the company.

My parents, Anne and Michael Greenwald, acted as my best friends and fans during the writing of this book, and I truly couldn't accomplish anything without them. Loving thanks to my grandmother, Sylvia Greenwald, for being a constant believer and my de facto publicist for Northeastern Pennsylvania.

More love, gratitude, and cocktails need to be showered on: Matt Jolly, Chris Ryan, Lara Cohen, Sean Howe, Allan Heinberg, Chris Baty, Marc Spitz, and Chuck Klosterman.

Thanks and a big shout-out to all of the kids who have reached out to me since the publication of *Nothing Feels Good* and especially to all of those who keep me company (and keep me honest) on the andygreenwald.com message board.

I'm extremely grateful to the Brooklyn Writers Space for providing me with a quiet place to type away at this beast—as well as for keeping me away from my Ethernet connection long enough to actually finish the damn thing.

And finally, the biggest thank-you goes to Rachel Bien, for everything you have put up with and everything you have pushed me to do. This book isn't about you, but in every way it exists because of you. I love you.

Thank you, New York City. Good night!